Hot to Trot

Also by Lou Wakefield

Tuscan Soup
Rural Bliss
Sleeping Partners

LOU WAKEFIELD

Hot to Trot

HODDER &
STOUGHTON

First published in Great Britain in 2006 by Hodder and Stoughton
A division of Hodder Headline

The right of Lou Wakefield to be identified as the Author
of the Work has been asserted by her in accordance
with the Copyright, Designs and Patents Act 1988.

A Hodder & Stoughton Book

1

A CIP catalogue record for this title is available from the British Library

ISBN 978 340 735147 (hb)
978 340 735 15 5 (pb B)
978 340 89942 5 (pb A)

Typeset in Sabon by Hewer Text UK Ltd, Edinburgh
Printed and bound by Clays Ltd, St Ives plc

Hodder Headline's policy is to use papers that are natural, renewable
and recyclable products and made from wood grown in sustainable forests.
The logging and manufacturing processes are expected to conform
to the environmental regulations of the country of origin.

Hodder and Stoughton Ltd
A division of Hodder Headline
338 Euston Road
London NW1 3BH

To Avril, and to my mother, Joyce Wakefield

My thanks to Buffy Davis, Peter Davies,
Monica Murambwa, Natasha Sherry and Georgia Gerstein

I

So quick and so impulsive had been her decision to fly to the aid of the Canadian cowboy that Kate Thornton was three-quarters of a mile in the air and halfway to British Columbia before it even crossed her mind she might not have both feet on the ground. Even then it wasn't her own mind it crossed, but Minnie McAlpine's.

Both of them travelling alone, Kate had helped the seventy year old to settle into the adjacent seat at the start of their journey from Heathrow, and what had begun as a polite neighbourliness between two strangers, was developing now into a more intimate swapping of confidences.

'Wait,' said Minnie. She held up her hand to stop Kate's flow, eyes bright with interest. 'You're saying you've never actually met this man you're flying out to see?' She had felt that *she* was being intrepid, a septuagenarian who'd rarely been out of her native Yorkshire, flying unescorted to the other side of the hemisphere to see her first new baby great-grandchild, but what she was hearing from this young woman made her own big adventure seem very small beer by comparison.

'Not met him as such,' Kate admitted, brushing away this minor detail as one might wave away a midge. 'But over the last few weeks I really feel as if I've got to know him very well. He's lovely, Minnie. You'd really like him.'

Minnie was rather less sure, but she was prepared to reserve judgement till she'd got it all taped down. 'And you're going to his ranch,' she said slowly, trying to get a grip on this story, 'to help out with the calving?'

'Because of his broken arm, yes,' Kate confirmed. 'And, you know, because of the death threats.'

'The death threats,' said Minnie. She shook her head as if to clear it. 'No, I must have missed something. You're going to visit a man who somebody's trying to kill?'

'No, me,' Kate corrected her patiently.

Now Minnie was totally lost. '*You're* threatening to kill him?' she offered.

Kate laughed. 'How wonderful,' she said happily, and even more puzzlingly added in a low voice, 'you don't recognise me at all do you?'

Minnie pulled away from her to survey her anew through narrowed eyes. Was she sitting next to a notorious female felon? Her mind raced to recall recent front pages of the *Daily Mail*, to scan them for photos of a red-headed murderess lately let out on parole, but all she came up with was a vague impression of . . . 'Are you on the telly?' she asked doubtfully.

'Shhh!' said Kate, and glancing round furtively, disconcertingly peeled back her hairline. Underneath what now proved to be a wig, she was blonde. 'I'm Sally Black,' she whispered anxiously. 'The home-wrecking, child-abducting banshee from hell.'

'Right, that does it,' said Minnie McAlpine decisively, and grabbed the arm of a passing flight attendant. 'I'd like a big Bloody Mary please, dear – and the same for my friend?'

Kate nodded her assent.

'I've got a feeling we're going to need a bit of liquid libation,' Minnie continued gaily, settling herself more comfortably in anticipation of dirt about to be dished. 'Now then, love, start again right from the beginning. And this time, remember – the devil's in the details. Don't leave any bugger out.'

★   ★   ★

The story which emerged, this time with all the i's dotted and t's crossed to Minnie's satisfaction, began with Kate's glittering career as a theatre actress, which lately had lost its shine. Having achieved the great age of thirty-mumble, she had discovered to her horror what the majority of actresses had to face after they left their twenties behind: she had lived long enough to become all but unemployable.

' "Resting" they call it with you actors, don't they?' offered Minnie.

Kate laughed hollowly. 'You wouldn't call it that if you were me. This last year I've been a cleaner, a barmaid, a cook, a decorator, a masseuse, a salesperson; I've stood on street corners giving out flyers, pretended to have fatal diseases for doctors' exams—'

Her recitation was interrupted by the flight attendant plonking four miniature bottles of vodka, four tins of tomato juice and two plastic glasses in front of them. 'I brought you two each,' she said crisply, pinning them with a practised eye. 'Save your time and my legs.'

'You're a jewel,' Minnie told her, not stinting on the praise. 'And I say – if you wanted to make it three each we wouldn't have to bother you again at all.'

A pursing of the lips, a sigh suppressed, a rapid return to the drinks trolley, and all was ready for the rest of the tale.

It transpired that Kate was not the only one to fear for her future prospects, which should have been cheering. After all, as Minnie said, a trouble shared was a trouble halved. But the sharers in this instance were the DSS, who had suggested that Kate might like to retrain for a more useful career than the dramatic arts, and her parents, who had bought her a computer, pre-loaded with a learn-to-type program and learn-to-build-websites software, and which had come with a card bearing the legend, 'Merry Christmas, Kate, and a Prosperous

New Year! – It never hurts to have a second string to your bow. All love, M & D xx'

'They meant well,' said Minnie, a mother herself.

'Oh, they meant well,' Kate agreed sadly. 'It's just that, at the time, it felt as if nobody believed in me any more.'

'So have you been learning to type and build web pages?'

'No,' Kate admitted. 'It would have been like giving up on myself. Anyway I was too depressed to do anything constructive. I played online backgammon instead. But then, if I hadn't, I wouldn't be sitting here next to you now!'

Minnie's brow furrowed for a moment, trying to work this one out. 'You never met this cowboy chap on the internet!' she exclaimed, after the penny had dropped.

Kate grinned. 'I did, you know.'

'You're going out to the Canadian wilderness to stay with a man you don't know? Are you mad?'

'He's in trouble. He needs help. He's got what's called a guest ranch, which means it's a working ranch, but people can stay there for holidays. It's not been doing so well so he can only afford a skeleton crew, and since he fell off his horse recently and broke his arm, and what with it being calving season . . .'

'And what with you being a vet in your spare time, and an expert, no doubt, with the lasso,' said Minnie, who was no stranger to irony.

Kate conceded the point with a wry smile, then rallying said, 'I am an actress though, and a very quick study. I've had to learn all sorts of skills for parts. Tap dancing, roller blading—'

'That'll be a help,' said Minnie.

'And I used to have riding lessons when I was a kid. For a couple of years.' Kate faltered. She knew her case sounded thin even without Minnie's raised eyebrow flagging it up. 'At the very least,' she continued, lifting her chin in a gesture of defiance, 'I can help out in the kitchen. Free up Old Pete, who's been retired indoors. He'll probably jump at the chance of getting out on the range with Andy again, while I do the cooking.'

Having seen off her first Bloody Mary, Minnie popped the tab of her second tomato juice and drowned it in vodka. 'You've got a thing for him, this Andy, haven't you?' she challenged. 'You wouldn't be going to all this trouble if not.'

Kate's expression softened, a dreaminess afflicting her eyes which belied her swift denial. 'Not at all,' she said. 'I just believe in people helping each other out when times are hard. I'd do this for anybody. You know, "Love thy neighbour, do unto others, et cetera." I'm not religious, but I do think that some of the tenets are sound.'

'That's nice,' said Minnie drily. 'I left a mound of ironing behind me in Skipton. I'll save it for when you get back. You shouldn't find going up to Yorkshire too much of a trial, given you think of Canada as being just next door.'

'All right. He is rather special,' Kate admitted. 'He's been bringing up his daughter, Robyn, single-handed, ever since she was a baby. How rare is that? And he was so sympathetic to me banging on about being out of work. Really supportive. Especially lately, since I've become Britain's most hated woman. You should see some of the letters I've been getting, Minnie. Horrible.' She lowered her voice again, although everybody else was sensibly sleeping around them. 'Do you know how to use the internet?'

'I'm not half as green as I'm cabbage looking,' Minnie said elliptically. 'I do keep up with the modern world, yes.'

'Then try doing a Google on That Bitch Sally,' said Kate. 'There are whole web sites devoted to wanting me dead.'

It transpired that Minnie was more au fait with computers than with soap operas, so she had to be told what twenty million British viewers already knew: that a serpent had crawled into *Paradise Street*, and that serpent was called Sally Black.

'What did she do that was so terrible?' asked Minnie. 'And how come you got to play her if you're so old and unemployable?'

Kate sighed. 'I took what turned out to be bad advice from my agent, God help me,' she said. 'Although to be fair, it did seem to make sense at the time. I told you that I work in theatre. I much prefer it to telly. I've never been into celebrity, or been after fame and fortune. I just love acting on the stage. It's all I've ever wanted to do since the day I was taken to see my first pantomime at the age of six. But these days, just being a good actress isn't enough. You have to be able to put bums on seats, which means bringing your audience with you, which means being a household name. Which means doing a bloody soap.'

'Speaking of bloody, drink up,' said Minnie. 'You've fallen behind me by one, and you need the tomato juice to replace the vitamin C that's lost through flying. I read it in a magazine.'

'I think the vodka does away with vitamin C too,' said Kate.

'Oh well, never mind. Now it's neutralised,' said Minnie pragmatically, handing back her replenished glass. 'So – you were saying about your agent.'

'Richard, yes. Well, he pointed out to me what I'd already started to see myself – that all the theatre parts I would have expected to come my way were going to soap stars. People who get famous simply by being in the corner of the room while the nation eats its TV dinners. They even *mike* them on stage because they can't project, can you imagine?'

Obligingly, Minnie could not.

'So Richard said, "if you can't beat them, join them" kind of thing. He said he'd look out for a small flashy part for me in one of the soaps. A character part, since I'm too old to play juves now, apparently. Not a long-running regular, but some-body who comes in for a few episodes and stirs things up, gets noticed.' She laughed ruefully. 'Did that all right.'

Minnie was keen to cut the cackle and get to the point. 'So what did she do, this Sally?'

'You really don't know?' Kate marvelled. 'I didn't think there was anyone left in the whole of England who hadn't heard my name and cursed it.'

'Life's too short to spend it round the goggle box,' said Minnie disparagingly. 'I come from a generation that was used to making our own entertainment. And cooking our own dinners from scratch. Namby pamby folk are now. Spoon fed on pap. But don't get me started. Go on.'

'There's a couple in *Paradise Street*,' Kate informed her, 'Steve and Sara Haywood, who the nation has taken to its heart. They've watched them grow up, survive bad relation-ships, trumped-up shop-lifting charges, Sara's family wiped out by fire, Steve having his foot run over by a hit-and-run dust cart, teenage pregnancy and miscarriage of same—'

'I get the picture,' said Minnie archly. 'An everyday story of ordinary folk. And?'

'Last year they finally got together in the wedding of the century. Almost as many people tuned in as watched Charles and Di, they are that popular, Minnie. Anyway, I arrive in the street – or Sally Black does – and in the space of fifteen episodes I seduce Steve Haywood, abduct their child, get Sara sacked from the part-time job she was so pleased with, and basically wreck their marriage for ever. England hates me like the plague. A woman spat at me in the frozen-food section of Tesco's after the first ep was broadcast, and chased me nearly all the way home. I had to stop going out.'

'And start wearing disguises,' said Minnie, understanding the red wig at last.

'Exactly. And then the so-called fan mail started to arrive.

Terrifying. The worst ones are always in green ink, I don't know why. And no back-up from the telly company, because I was out of the show by then.' She rummaged in her handbag and pulled out a crumpled sheet of lined paper. 'Here – take a look at this!'

Minnie surveyed the childish lettering which was written, as Sally had said, in a virulent verdant. ' "I no were you live. Youd better lok your dors bitch. You are ded meet." Shocking!' she exclaimed. 'The state of grammar now. Wouldn't have tolerated this when I was a teacher! But what on earth have you kept it for?'

'I'm trying to come to terms with it,' Kate told her. 'I can't get it out of my mind. I keep looking at it and trying to make sense of it.'

'You're wallowing, that's what you're doing,' said Minnie crisply, tearing the page into tiny bite-sized pieces. 'There, that's what you do with unwanted junk mail. You shred it and bin it. The poor soul's just a bit soft in the head, that's all.'

'She's not the only one,' said Kate. 'It got so I couldn't go out of my own front door what with the journalists camping out on the step and the stalker who seemed to have an endless supply of rotten eggs.'

'So you stayed indoors and played backgammon with strangers,' Minnie concluded.

'And made friends with a policewoman in Idaho who was on nights, a housewife in Barnsley who should have been doing her ironing—' Kate began, stressing the upside as was her habit.

'How come *she* didn't want to kill you, then, this slacker from Barnsley?' Minnie challenged her. 'I thought you said the whole nation hated you? Last I heard Barnsley was in England, albeit in the ignored bit called The North.'

'Well,' said Kate, 'that was the beauty of it really. Because when you play games and chat on *Yoohoo*, which is the web site I mostly use, you have to have a playing name, so nobody knows who you really are.' She grinned. 'I picked Mata Hari after the exotic spy, because it all felt so cloak-and-dagger at first. Then you realise it's just ordinary people you're chatting to – they just happen to be in Krakow or New Jersey or Beijing. It's great. It's like having a big window on the world.'

'Instant friends at the click of a mouse,' Minnie suggested.

'Exactly!' Kate enthused. 'Of course, there are a few pervs out there too – mostly adolescent boys, I suspect. They're either telling you where to shove it, if you're winning, or telling you where they'd *like* to shove it given half the chance. But you can spot them straight off once you learn the lingo. The first thing they type is "ASL?" and then you pretty much know that all they want is to talk dirty.'

'ASL meaning?'

'Age, Sex and Location.'

'And they say that romance is dead,' Minnie sniffed.

'So you can see why I was so taken with Andy,' Kate continued. 'I mean some of the stuff the kids type when they're losing is just so rude. "Suck my ass. You are a zero." And if they're after cheap thrills it gets even ruder. But Andy's a gentleman and a really good sport. Compliments you when you make a good move, congratulates you when you're having a run of good luck. And he's got a great sense of humour.'

'What's he call himself when he's playing?' asked Minnie. 'The Saint?'

'Andy The Cowboy,' Kate said. Her face had gone to mush, a silly grin bisecting her features in a direct line from east to west.

'Eee, lass, you've got it bad,' said Minnie. She had lived long enough to know the difference between being in love and being insane: not an atom.

'I haven't, honestly!' Kate protested. 'You know, I mean

he's a nice man, obviously, otherwise I wouldn't be bothering to go and help him out, but it's more for the adventure, really, as far as I'm concerned. Ask anybody who knows me, they'll tell you, I'm always off doing something or other that everybody thinks is madcap at the time, but it always turns out all right in the end. I just love new experiences, that's all, and meeting new people. I suppose it's a kind of occupational hazard. No, not hazard, habit,' she corrected herself quickly. 'An occupational habit of mine. Of all actors. The more experiences you have, the more people you get to know, the greater the catalogue you've got stored away in your character bank.'

'So I'm stored away in there now am I?' asked Minnie.

'That's right,' Kate laughed, tapping her temple. 'You're tucked away up here now, there's no escape.'

'Well, I look forward to seeing myself played by you on stage then, at some time in the future.'

'I'll make sure I credit you in the programme,' Kate joshed.

'Very nice,' said Minnie, having played the younger woman like a fish on a line. She was so guileless and unsuspecting it was a wonder she'd made it to thirty-whatever-it-was still in one piece. 'And I can't wait to see you playing a single-parent Canadian cowboy, since researching him's apparently the sole reason for your trip. Although, thinking about it, wouldn't they be more likely to get a man to play the part?'

'Oh Minnie,' Kate sighed. 'Okay, you don't believe me, but I assure you it's true. I'm not looking for a man at the moment, there's no room in my life for that sort of thing just now. I'm looking for a job. That's the only thing that's important to me at this point in my life – my work.'

'As a ranch hand.'

'No! I mean generally, that's where I'm putting all my energy!'

'Right,' said Minnie. 'And is there a lot of acting work to be had in rural British Columbia?'

'I told you, I'm taking time out to get away from unwanted attention from murderous soap fans. I'm hoping that by the time I get back to London Sally Black will be forgotten and I'll be able to stop wearing this dreaded itchy wig,' said Kate, raking underneath the elasticated edge with her cocktail twizzler by way of illustrating her point. 'As for relationships, they're way down my agenda. Impossible to have one really anyway, when you're constantly having to go away to some theatre or other, miles away from home. Especially when the only men you meet are actors and directors. You spend so much time apart it's hardly worth the bother or the grief. And then they always end up going off and having affairs.'

'Speaking from experience?' asked Minnie, more kindly.

'Scads,' Kate acknowledged. 'And I'm barely over the last one as a matter of fact. I walked in on him having it away with the publicity woman in his dressing room after the show. I'd thought I'd surprise him, go up to Bolton for the weekend unannounced. I'd spent hours getting there on the damn coach, and then I turned right around and got straight back on it. Silly me, eh?'

'Silly him,' said Minnie. 'Losing a lovely girl like you.'

Kate smiled a tired acknowledgement of the compliment. 'So you see, I am just after a bit of a break in a country where they don't want to kill me, to escape all the hoo-ha, and to get out into some wholesome fresh country air.'

'And think about somebody else's problems other than your own.'

'That's right.'

'If I was your mum, then, I wouldn't have bothered with trying to get you to retrain for IT. I'd have recommended a career as an agony aunt. You'd be in seventh heaven, and get paid for it.'

Kate laughed. 'I feel as if I do that already, on the side. I'm not the only one who's been suffering from faithless lovers – nearly all my friends have been in the same boat lately.'

'The good old *SS Betrayed*,' Minnie offered. 'Yes, I had a voyage on that myself once upon a time.'

'Your husband had an affair?'

'You can call him that if you like,' said Minnie. 'I call him the Toothless Old Git.'

'I'm sorry, Minnie.'

'No need to feel sorry for me. Best thing to have happened as it turned out. He's developed Alzheimer's since, and she's having to look after him. Has to introduce herself afresh to him every day and pin a label on his coat: "If found, please return this man to such and such an address." Been me I'd have put a false one down by now, be shot of the old bugger. But enough about me. Back to you. If your Andy's so wonderful what happened to the mother of his child? Didn't like backgammon, so she walked?'

Kate's eyes lit up. This was her favourite part of the story. 'This is the amazing thing about him. Apparently she was a bit of a free spirit who he met one night at a rodeo, and it would have been a one-night stand for both of them except that a few weeks later she pops up at the ranch to tell him she's pregnant. By him. Imagine!'

'If she was that much of a free spirit how come he believed her?' said Minnie.

'Hmm, don't know, didn't think to ask him that,' Kate mused. 'But, you know, it would be just typical of him to take responsibility for the child anyway, regardless of the paternity issues, because this woman said she didn't believe in abortion, but neither did she believe it was her destiny to be a mother, so once the baby was weaned she took off to "find herself", leaving Robyn with Andy.'

Only the no-smoking rule on aeroplanes prevented Minnie

from spontaneously self combusting on the spot. 'Didn't believe it was her destiny to be a mother?' she fumed. 'What's belief got to do with it when you've already got a child in your belly, for crying out loud?!'

'I know,' said Kate. 'But she was a bit of a dippy hippy as far as I understand. Called herself Rainbow. Reckoned she had an Indian spirit guide telling her what to do, which was to go off and live in a teepee and make bead necklaces apparently.'

'Doesn't say much for your Andy if that's the type of woman he takes up with,' said Minnie censoriously.

'No, well, I don't think it's something he brags about exactly,' Kate said, rising to his defence. 'He admits he was a bit worse for wear the night that Robyn was conceived, what with the carnival atmosphere of the rodeo and everything, and him having just won the roping contest, he might have had a couple of beers too many . . . And he was young, you know, twenty-one or twenty-two. Anyway, whatever you think of his behaviour back then, Minnie, you have to admit that he's more than made up for it since, bringing Robyn up on his own while running a ranch. Not many lads would have done that in his position.'

'Mmm,' was as much as Minnie would concede. 'Well, all I can say is it's a marvel he hasn't found another woman to settle down with since, if he's that wonderful. Maybe he's got two heads. Have you seen a photo?'

'I'm not sure,' said Kate. 'I mean, they've got a web site which I looked up and there's several pictures of men on there, but I'm not sure if Andy was one of them. They could all have been guests.'

'Didn't you ask him?'

'Well no, actually. I only looked it up a couple of days ago, to see if they gave directions as to how to get there. Luckily they did. The Blue Yonder Guest Ranch it's called. Isn't that lovely?'

'What, you're flying nearly five thousand miles at your own expense and he expects you to make your own way from the airport!' Minnie expostulated. 'I thought you said he was a gent?'

'He is,' Kate averred. 'So much so that if I'd told him I was going out to help him he'd have said that he could manage fine, despite his broken arm. He reckoned he was only going to rest up for a couple of days before getting back on his horse, but I think that's dangerous. What if he fell off again, somewhere remote?'

'What do you mean *if* you'd told him you were on your way?' Minnie spluttered. 'Do you mean to say you didn't?'

Kate shook her head and grinned. 'I can't wait to see his face when I show up,' she said happily. 'He's going to get such a surprise!'

2

Nothing Minnie could say in the two hours remaining of the flight had any impact at all on Kate's optimism and enthusiasm for her big adventure with the unknown, and it was with great misgivings that she took her leave of her at Vancouver airport. All she could do under the circumstances was to press her granddaughter's telephone number into Kate's hand and make her swear she would call them immediately if 'anything untoward were to happen'.

Kate hugged her goodbye and duly promised that they would be her first port of call in an emergency, but the giddy look on her face didn't inspire Minnie with much confidence.

'I'm afraid that young woman is riding for a fall,' she told her granddaughter Ruth and her husband as they watched Kate stride over to the car hire desk without a care in the world.

'Looks to me like she's already had it,' said Ruth damningly. 'Somebody ought to tell her that she's gone a tint too far.'

The colour of Kate's wig was the least of her problems, as we know, but taking the damn thing off to ler her scalp breathe was all that she could think of. The only thing that stopped her tearing it off right there and then in front of the Avis rep (astonishment be damned), was her uncertainty about being recognised. Although she had jumped at the chance of getting away from the stalkers back home, she was also mindful of Uncle Remus's wisdom that you can't run away from trouble as there's no place that far. Particularly in this day and age of satellite and cable deals. She was sure that the *Paradise Street* sales executives wouldn't have missed the trick of selling it to Canada, but what she didn't know was how far behind they were in the storylines here.

'Have you guys had all the stuff about Sally Black yet?' she asked the rep after she'd signed on the dotted line.

'Pardon me?' he queried, looking up from the forms. 'Did you want Miss Black to be a second named driver?'

Kate giggled. 'No, no sorry, just me. Sally Black's a character in a British soap – *Paradise Street*? I was wondering if you get it over here. It was hard to come away from England just at the moment, what with the plot having hotted up lately.' She watched him carefully for signs of recognition, but saw instead only censure.

'It would be an awful pity for you to drive all the way out to the beautiful ranch lands of the South Cariboo,' he told her, having elicited this information while guiding her towards the right choice of vehicle, 'only to stay indoors and watch soaps.'

'You're right,' she said happily. 'I shall be too busy roping steers and birthing calves, won't I?'

A flick of a glance at her Titian ringlets said he doubted it, but he wasn't about to waste time giving beauty tips for country living with such a long queue of customers behind her. 'If you'll follow me?' he asked with a polite smile, and led the way outside to the huge four-wheel drive which he'd persuaded her she would need out on those ranch roads.

It was typical of Kate that she didn't let the fact that she hadn't driven for more than two years diminish her elation when she saw the monster Sports Utility Vehicle she'd hired, nor that the last car she'd been in charge of had been a Micra. The prospect of driving this giant through mountainous terrain for six hours on the wrong side of the road just added to the excitement as far as she was concerned, and after a bit of a rehearsal in the car park and a study of the map, she was burning rubber towards Hope, a hundred miles distant, where she would pick up Highway 1, the Trans-Canada route.

The idea that she was travelling towards Hope pleased her hugely. How cool was that after these past weeks of being a prisoner in her own home! In fact it had been a pretty rough year, or year and a bit, she mused – oh God, make that two years. Two years of watching her career slow down to a horrifying full-stop and her boyfriends proving themselves less than worthy of her trust. She shuddered at the thought and then shrugged, as if to release the load she'd been carrying on her shoulders. She did feel lighter already actually. On the road and free, and in such an impressive getaway truck! She could see now why all those mothers in Barnes and Islington favoured the 4x4 for their school runs. You were up so high you felt inviolate and, surrounded by so much metal, unassailable. You just had to be able to afford to buy it a gallon of petrol every twenty-five miles and, like George Bush, not buy into the myth about global warming. But unlike those school-running city women, she would really need this four-wheel drive apparently. Where she was headed, two wheels on her wagon just wouldn't be enough.

As she left Vancouver behind her she began to feel more confident at the wheel, and watched in awe as the countryside unfolded on either side of her on the wide, empty highway. The land stretched away from her in every direction on a huge and grand scale such as she had never seen before, from the towering trees nearby to the snow-capped mountains in the remote distance. And everywhere there was sky, vast acres of blue, which to a Londoner seemed nothing short of a miracle.

She started to hum, optimism filling her glass way past the half-full mark, and she found herself improvising a ditty about driving towards Hope which, by the chorus, had become 'I'm going to Hope.' She smiled. What a wonderful word hope was, and how brilliant it must be to live there. Everything you did would sound like an act of faith. I'm going shopping in Hope. I'm walking in Hope. I'm going to lunch in Hope.

Not a bad idea, she decided with a grin, and in Hope I shall also ditch this damn wig and leave Sally Black's curse far behind me.

The town offered everything she had anticipated and more, and by the time she left it she was replete, having consumed a huge plate of waffles topped with maple-cured bacon and covered in maple syrup (when in Rome, had been her thought), and had turned herself into a blonde cowgirl, right down to the Wrangler jeans, the hat, the distressed suede jacket, and the utterly fabulous and to-die-for cowboy boots with the turquoise snakeskin trim. A serendipitous stop in a tourist shop had produced not only the postcards she'd gone in for but also a T-shirt which proclaimed she was 'Living in Hope', and thus transformed and uplifted, she was back on the road again, motoring up the Trans-Canada Highway.

If she had thought that the scenery had been awe-inspiring before, the further she drove, the more astonishment she felt at the grandeur of nature's bounty. Following the massive Fraser River which made the Thames look like a stream, she crossed canyons, climbed hills, went through mountains via long winding tunnels, and still the land went on and on in huge swooping, sweeping green vistas.

Everything was perfect: she had a fun new costume, it was a glorious day, the sun was shining, the view through her windscreen was quite simply astonishing, and Celine Dion was busting a gut on the radio every fifth song. (Well – almost everything was perfect anyway.) With nothing to do but cruise along for another few hours enjoying the scenery and trying to out-yodel Canada's national treasure, her thoughts turned inevitably to Andy, and how much she was looking forward to meeting him in the flesh.

She'd been honest with Minnie. She wasn't in this for romance, and it didn't matter at all what he looked like. For all she cared he could be a potato head with bow legs and stem-to-stern skin tags – although naturally if he did turn out to be drop-dead gorgeous you wouldn't hear her complain. He was just so different from anyone she had ever encountered before, with his homespun wisdom, his dry sense of humour, his dependably empathic and insightful response to her problems, and his terrific sense of responsibility where his daughter Robyn was concerned. He was an all-round regular guy. A true friend. A grown-up. Somebody you could turn to in troubled times, and know with certainty that he'd be there for you, that he'd go that extra mile.

Which was why she was going out to his aid. Quid pro quo. He'd scratched her back, and now she would scratch his. Metaphorically speaking, of course.

At Cache Creek she left Highway 1 for Highway 97 and Minnie's voice came into her head, pointing out in her phlegmatic Yorkshire accent that if she didn't watch out she'd find herself up Cache Creek without a paddle. Kate grinned. What a character. But Minnie didn't need to worry. Whatever happened on this adventure, however dangerous it may prove to life and limb (witness Andy's broken arm, and him an experienced rider) it would be infinitely more exciting and rewarding than hiding behind her computer, going nowhere, holed up in her flat alone.

She just couldn't wait to get started, to roll up her sleeves and pitch in at her first birth. Or to flip her first waffle. Whichever would be the most help. If Old Pete was still limber enough to get mounted, then perhaps he, with his vast cowboy experience, would be more useful out on the range than she could ever be, in which case she would happily take over his cooking duties. According to Andy, the old timer still hankered after the good old days before his advanced age drove him out of the saddle and into the kitchen.

And then there was probably stuff she could do to help out with thirteen-year-old Robyn, giving her a hand with her homework perhaps, and driving her to school – at least she had the right vehicle for it! She'd just be adaptable and slot in wherever she was needed. She certainly wasn't afraid of hard work, and she was definitely no wimp. Until the recent Sally Black débâcle, she'd been a four-times-a-weeker down at the gym.

Despite the fact that she'd had an almost sleepless nine-hour flight followed by a six-hour drive, she felt energised and enthusiastic and ready for anything – especially meeting these three people who she already felt so fond of – so it was with great excitement that she saw the sign to Green Lake where, according to the excellent directions on Andy's web site, she would finally leave the highway. Ms Dion now having been silenced, Ms Thornton broke into a spirited rendition of 'Home, Home on the Range', and before you could say 'head 'em up and move 'em out', she was bouncing down the Blue Yonder Ranch road with all four wheels driving, and feeling on top of the world.

The only trouble with being on top of the world, as Minnie McAlpine might have pointed out to her if she'd been riding shotgun in the SUV, is that it can be an awfully long nose-dive to the ground.

3

Here at last, two miles down the unmade road, in a picturesque pastoral idyll, was the ranch house, looking reassuringly familiar to Kate from the photos she'd seen on the web.
Built from logs and stone, it had been in Andy's family for
generations apparently, his great-grandfather having staked
his claim here as a young man. With its steep pitched roof and
wooden verandahs, its curl of wood smoke spiralling from the
chimney, it was everything she had hoped for. Driving into
the deserted yard, she parked and turned off the engine, and
for a moment did nothing more than sit and listen to the
stillness. Bliss. Getting out, she stretched luxuriously and
filled her lungs with fresh clean air, looking around her for
signs of life. Of that, there was plenty. A tabby cat walked by,
eyeing her warily, carrying a kitten in its jaws; a gaggle of
chickens streaked across the yard towards her, hoping no
doubt to be fed; a young colt kicked its heels in the nearby
corral.

Humans beings, however, were in shorter supply, she being
the lone representative. Well, that was soon solved. No doubt
Robyn was at school, Old Pete must have taken the guests out
riding, and Andy was probably in the kitchen, trying out his
one good arm at cooking the supper. Or maybe – wouldn't this
be a hoot – maybe he was at the computer even now, trying to
find her in cyberspace for a game of backgammon and a chat.
There was only one way to find out.

Opening up the back of the SUV, she was dragging her case

out when a 'Yee-haaa!' broke the silence and a small posse of cowboys rode into the yard. She raised her hand in welcome. 'Hello there!' she called, and was rewarded by an answering, 'Howdy, pardner!' from an ebullient man in his mid-forties. Surely this couldn't be Old Pete – wasn't he at least twenty years too young? Shielding her eyes against the sun she walked towards them, making out as she did so that three of them were women, and that the only other man in the party was tall, dark and totally toothsome. Yee-ha indeed!

'Is Andy around?' she asked as she approached them.

The tall dark stranger gave a brief nod in reply. 'Be with you in a minute, ma'am,' he said, swinging one long lean leg over his saddle to dismount. 'Okay, you folks know the drill,' he told the rest of the posse. 'Tack off, brush down, horses in the corral.' Not a man to waste words then, but with his looks, who needed a solilquy?

The groans as they got off their horses, and the way they all staggered about stiff-limbed once they'd hit the ground told Kate that those he'd addressed must be holiday guests, so who the devil was he? For one wild moment of breathless excitement she studied his arms for signs of a plaster cast, and was disappointed to note that he appeared to be using both hands to groom his horse without any trouble at all. Must be a hired hand then. Although Andy had told her he didn't have the money to employ extra staff, only an occasional student during the peak summer weeks, and this man must surely have left his student days behind him at least ten years ago. Well, whoever he was, he was gorgeous!

'Hi,' she said, edging her way through the horses to his side.

'Hi,' he answered, not pausing from his labours. 'Weren't we expecting you tomorrow?'

Kate smiled, trying to engage him in eye contact, which was pretty tricky as he was bending down to clean out his horse's hoofs at the time. 'I wasn't expected at all,' she told him. 'This is something of a surprise visit.'

The speed with which he stood up to look her over properly almost sent her flying, but as far as eye contact went she couldn't have asked for more – he was practically boring holes through her head. What she could have done without, however, was the look of fear and loathing that filled his gaze as he examined her, his jaw muscles tensing, as if to prevent words of bile pouring out. 'You don't say,' he said finally.

Thoroughly wrong-footed, Kate tried to maintain her friendly smile. 'Oh yes I do,' she said flippantly. The effect on him was immediate and explosive.

'Do you call this fair?' he demanded. 'Do you call it right to hound us like this, when I'm clearly doing the best job I know how?'

She blinked at the force of his fury. 'I—' she began.

'You know, you'd have thought that maybe I'd've gotten some help from you people,' he continued. 'Instead of being threatened like this, and sneaked up on, like I was some kind of criminal.'

'I'm sorry,' said Kate, flapping her hands weakly in a placatory fashion and backing away. 'I think there must be some kind of misunderstanding—'

'Damn right there is, and it's all over on your side of the fence,' he spat venomously, abandoning his horse to pursue her, his finger jabbing the air in the direction of her chest. 'So just so we set the record all nice and neat, read my lips: Robyn has been in school every damn day since you sent that last letter, and if you're telling me different, then you're calling her a liar, and you're calling me a liar. Is that what you want to do?'

'Absolutely not,' Kate averred nervously. 'No way at all. Heavens forfend. Not a chance.'

Surprised by this retreat, the heat went out of him. 'Okay then,' he said. 'So, don't let me keep you. I'm sure you've got other people to harrass.' And with that he turned his back on her to return to his horse.

'You know,' Kate called after him, trying to muster a non-threatening smile, 'I think we just might have a case of mistaken identity here.'

He turned slowly then to look at her, suspicion in his eyes, but still he remained silent. Surely this couldn't be . . . could it? 'Andy?' she chanced. For who else but Robyn's father would jump to the conclusion she was here about her poor school attendance? 'Are you Andy Barrett?'

'And if I was?'

'Andy the Cowboy?' she asked incredulously.

By way of an answer he glanced down at his boots, tipped back his hat with one finger, and leaned against his horse. 'No, I'm Andy the Astronaut,' he said, without a hint of a smile. 'I just dress this way and live out here to avoid the publicity. But damn, you found me, Miss . . .?'

How funny. Here, in the flesh, was the dry sense of humour which had been tickling her funny bone for the last few weeks at her computer. Well, two could play at that game. 'Hari,' she said, eyes twinkling. 'Mata Hari, at your service.'

A look of puzzled wariness met her mischievous smile which she barely registered, her interest focusing instead on his uninjured limbs. Now the puzzlement was all hers. 'But, Andy, what happened to your arm?' she said.

Slowly his eyes slid downwards, examining first one arm then the other. 'Nothing?' he replied.

'But you broke one,' she protested. 'That's why I'm here.'

A sudden flash of comprehension crossed his face. 'God dammit,' he said. 'Is that what she told you, that I'd busted my arm?'

'Who?' she asked, completely at sea.

'Robyn of course, who in hell are we talking about?' he replied crossly.

'You, we're talking about you! *You* told me,' she said with a strained laugh, feeling rather tetchy now herself.

'*I* told you,' he repeated, turning this over in his mind. 'What, on the phone?'

'No, on the computer!' Why was he denying it; what was wrong with the man? 'Oh, for heavens sake, Andy, come off it! You wrote and told me that a bird had flown up from the brush and spooked your horse, and that you'd ended up somersaulting backwards over its tail and landing badly.'

At last the penny appeared to have dropped. 'So, with a busted arm I needed some help around the place?' he checked.

'Exactly!'

He shook his head in angry disbelief. 'Jeez,' he said finally. 'Just wait till I—'

But there was no need to wait, apparently, since he broke off immediately, glaring over Kate's right shoulder to bellow, 'Robyn Barrett, get over here, right now!'

Turning to follow his gaze, Kate saw a pint-sized cowgirl rein in her palomino pony as she arrived in the yard. 'Seems to be the trouble?' she asked warily, holding her ground.

'I said get over here,' Andy growled, pointing at a spot in front of him.

Reluctantly the child obeyed, pressing her pony into a slow amble towards them. 'Howdy, Mr and Mrs Matheson. Nancy. Louise,' she said to the guests, who had been spinning out the grooming of their horses for some time in order to catch the interesting developments between Andy and Kate. 'Ain't it just fine to hear that old Blue Yonder welcome when a person gets home?'

But before any of them could think of a noncommittal reply – indeed, before the words were out of Robyn's mouth – Andy had hauled her down to ground level, gripping her shoulders and looking her fiercely in the eye. 'Have you been in school like we agreed?' he demanded. 'Have you?'

'Yes, I've been in goddamn school, for all the goddamn good it's doing me, learning stuff I'll never have no goddamn use for!' she countered, matching his fury.

'Language!' said Andy.

'Shiiiit,' returned Robyn.

'Young lady, you are grounded!'

'You mean I can't ever leave the ranch, not even for school? Oh no, Brer Fox! Anything, anything but the briar patch!' she cried, in mock alarm.

'That's right, go ahead, make it worse,' Andy told her, gesturing towards Kate. 'Let your teacher hear how you twist things around.'

Kate found herself being examined by yet another pair of scowling puzzled eyes. 'Who, her?' Robyn challenged him. 'Ain't no teacher of mine.'

Now Andy's baleful glare swivelled Kate's way too. 'She's right,' she shrugged. 'I've been trying to tell you but you haven't been listening.'

'Well hey, here's something new,' said Robyn drily. 'Now will you let go of my goddamn arm?'

'What have I told you about swearing?' said Andy, determined to have the last word.

'What have I told you about child abuse?' Robyn parried back. 'And now I got witnesses. Ow. Ow. *Ow.*'

'Did you or did you not tell the folks at school that I'd busted my arm so you had to stay off school to help out around here?' Andy demanded, trying to keep a grip on the proceedings, if not on his child.

'No way!' Robyn protested. 'And if that's what she told you, she's a goddamn liar!'

'I didn't!' said Kate. 'I said—'

'You said that I'd written to you, but I know that I didn't,' Andy said hotly. 'Which leaves only one person it could've been.'

Kate suddenly felt exhausted, which was hardly surprising since she'd been awake now for twenty-two hours. 'Look, let's all calm down and start again,' she said wearily. 'It's all very simple if you just get the idea out of your head that I'm here about Robyn. I'm not.'

'See?' said Robyn.

'Andy, I'm Mata Hari,' Kate enunciated carefully. No joyous cry of recognition came her way.

'Mata Hari,' she insisted, but still his look remained blank. 'Doesn't that ring any bells at all?'

'Sure it does,' he replied eventually, having clearly decided she was delusional. 'And it's good to see you looking so well. I guess reports of your death by firing squad back in nineteen-seventeen have been a mite exaggerated? Now if you'll excuse me . . .'

'Backgammon!' Kate prompted him, beside herself with exasperation. 'Andy the Cowboy and Mata Hari!'

He fixed her with a pitying look. 'Mind if I take a rain check, Mata? See, I'm a little bit busy right now.'

'No, not now, then! Like, two days ago? And every day before that for weeks! We play backgammon on the internet practically every day, sometimes two sessions, depending on your work, and we chat – we've become friends!'

'Not me,' said Andy firmly. 'I haven't played backgammon in years.'

'Oh my God,' Kate said slowly, after an uncomfortable silence in which every drop of her blood drained from the rest of her body and found its way to her face. 'I'm so sorry. I think I've been the victim of a rather sick joke.'

4

There had been times in her life when Kate Thornton would have given anything for an audience as attentive as this. There were no ringing cell phones, no coughing, fidgeting, no flicking through programmes, no banging of seats for someone to visit the loo, not even the surreptitious rustle of sweet papers sullied the silence. Even the distant lowing of cattle had eerily faded, as if, in their far-off pasture, they were standing alert, ears twitching, to catch the next improbable part of her tale. Does it need to be said? She had come to the bit about the soap star and the death threats.

'So I thought, you know, what the hell?' she floundered self consciously, longing for some welcome interruption to her monologue. 'I needed to get out of the country for a while, and Andy needed help on the ranch. Or at least, I thought he did. Wrongly, obviously. So I just jumped on a plane, hired that whacking great SUV thingy, and here I am.'

'Weren't that wrong,' Robyn offered generously, the only one of the assembled company, apparently, who was prepared to give Kate the benefit of the doubt in the credibility department. 'Can always use help around here.'

Andy quashed Robyn with a dark glance. 'Well, sorry your trip was wasted, Miss . . .?'

'Thornton. Kate Thornton. Call me Kate,' she invited him with a hopeful smile.

'But as you can see I'm all in one piece and we've got

everything covered here,' he replied, eschewing her offer of first-name terms. 'And speaking of which, better get on.'

'Seems to me,' said the unquashed Robyn to his retreating back as he attempted to cross the yard to the ranch house, 'that if Kate here had've been your internet friend, she couldn't have been more faithful and true. Shows some spirit, spending all that money on flying out all this way to help you birth them calves. Wouldn't you say so, Mr Matheson?'

'Well,' said Bill uncomfortably, with an eye on his irascible host.

'Would you do that, Nancy?' the child pursued. 'Cross the Atlantic to go help out somebody you ain't never even met?'

'Got me there. Can't say I would,' Nancy allowed, scuffing the dirt with her toe.

'Would you do that, Andy?' Robyn challenged him.

'Can't see where this conversation's heading,' he replied tersely over his shoulder, 'except putting off getting down to your chores.'

'It's heading to offering this lady a room while she catches her breath and tries to figure out what to do next,' she declared, raising her voice to reach him. 'Not as if we're exactly over-booked right now, is it, Andy? Think we could squeeze her in someplace.'

For a man who was hopping mad he managed to execute an almost militarily perfect, albeit eerily slow, about-face. 'Okay,' he said finally, acknowledging defeat. 'Lot on my mind. Wasn't thinking. You're welcome to stay the night, ma'am, no charge. Supper's at seven thirty. Robyn'll take you to your room.'

'Really? Thank you so much, that's really kind of you,' said Kate, relieved and grateful beyond measure. 'I'm absolutely cream-crackered, actually,' she told the assembled company. Their raised eyebrows told her that this was not in doubt. 'Tired,' she explained hastily. 'And, you know, I wouldn't dream of not paying. At least Sally Black has improved my finances,' she joked. 'Under a death sentence I may be, but solvent.'

'As you please,' Andy said curtly. 'Robyn, I'll see you in the office after you've shown her to her room.'

'Gotta do my chores first,' was her cheery reply.

'After your chores then,' he said, in a voice that was not wanting in intensity, and he disappeared into the ranch house yelling vituperatively, 'Old Pete? We got one extra for supper.'

The show being over, and their horses having been groomed to within an inch of their lives, there was nothing further to detain the city slickers from Vancouver, and they too retired inside. Grabbing Kate's suitcase, Robyn led the way to her room.

'Thanks for getting him to let me stay,' said Kate.

'Welcome.'

'So you're Robyn,' she said, examining the tomboy at her side with affection. 'It's good to meet you at last. At least you're how I'd imagined.'

'And you're the Dutch belly dancer turned spy. Not how I imagined you at all, Mata Hari.'

Kate laughed. 'I'm impressed,' she said. 'The two of you seem to be very well informed about my namesake.'

Robyn heaved a damning sigh and rolled her eyes. 'Yeah, well, that's on account of us having gotten on to H just this last week. Andy's idea of fun is him and me reading the encyclopaedia together of an evening. Swear to God you could test me on any useless thing from A through G right now, and I bet I'd have the answer.'

'How about A for Andy?' Kate enquired.

'Not much to tell there that you don't already know,' Robyn snorted. 'You just seen him at his best.'

'Seems like he's under a lot of pressure?'

'Yeah, and he don't mind sharing it around.' She kicked

open a door with her boot. 'Here's your room. It ain't much, but it's the best one we got left. Bathroom's down the hall. Settle in, and I'll see you at supper. Like he said, it's at seven thirty, and Old Pete gets pretty ornery about latecomers. Been known to turn 'em down flat.'

'Righty-ho,' said Kate bravely, surveying her room with a sinking heart. This was the 'no frills' end of the guest ranch industry then. There was a bed, a wardrobe, a dresser, a chair, a bare bulb hanging from the ceiling, a telephone. 'A telephone,' she said, brightening.

'No international calls, no room service,' said Robyn. 'Catch you later,' and with that she was gone.

Kate collapsed on to the bed in total shock. Which way was up? It was no use asking her. Her head was vibrating like a struck gong.

'Gordon Bennet,' she said to the silence.

To have been so taken in. And by whom? Was Andy lying, for reason unknown, and if so, what might that reason be? She gave this her full attention for a while, but her brain felt too foggy with tiredness to come up with a credible explanation. She was tempted just to give in to her exhaustion and let herself drift to sleep where she lay, but then, she reminded herself sharply, sitting up to put herself out of temptation's way, she would miss supper, and with it any chance she might have of solving this puzzle. One night, that's all he'd given her. One night to try to make sense of all this.

No. It was absurd. Ridiculous to come all this way only to turn tail immediately and go back home, where Sally Black's assassins still lay in wait for her. She'd geared herself up for a big adventure in a far-off land, and she'd certainly found it. She couldn't just walk away from this mystery now, return to her small life in her small flat, weld herself back to the computer screen after a mere two days of freedom. And why should she? she thought, warming to her theme. She was paying to stay here after all, and as Robyn had said, they weren't exactly chocker. She could stay on for as long as she liked. Certainly till she'd got to the bottom of all this. She couldn't be the subject of a bizarre enigma and just walk away from it, could she? No way.

Thus emboldened, she became more energised, and she got up from where she lay to unpack. A nice hot shower next, and then she'd be ready to stroll down to dinner and start trying to unravel this riddle: to whit – was Andy lying, or was he an innocent pawn, just as she was, in somebody else's weird game? She would have to quiz him and Robyn, and talk to Old Pete. It must be one of them, surely? Certainly it was some-body who knew the set-up here, knew their names and what they were like.

Except, of course, they weren't at all what she'd expected. Okay, Robyn was the feisty tomboy 'Andy the Cowboy' had described, but she'd been led to believe they had a warm and loving relationship, not the clash of personalities she'd just witnessed. And Andy just couldn't be more different from the man she'd felt she'd got to know. Where was the sensitivity, the empathy, the humour of the good listener she'd been chatting to for weeks?

The bathroom, which she found after a couple of false turns, was as cheerless and utilitarian as her bedroom, but at least the water was hot and plentiful, and taking a shower did much to restore her energy and spirits. No wonder business was bad, with so few creature comforts to attract new guests, or tempt old guests to return. And there was so much they could do here to improve the look of things, she mused as she dried herself, gazing at the bare walls as if at a blank canvas. It could be done really cheaply and so easily, just by using a little imagination. She always got loads of compliments about her own flat, and everybody was always astonished to hear how almost everything in it had come out of skips. Not that skips would be as plentiful in the South Cariboo as they were in Kentish Town, she reminded herself, but even so there must be *objets* that could be *trouvé*-ed even here, which would brighten up the drabness, add a little excitement to the Spartan bareness of it all.

A rattling of the doorknob, a muttered apology from the other side of the door – or was it a muttered oath? – and the sound of footsteps retreating down the corridor reminded her that this bathroom was shared, and she'd been hogging it. Bad start to her potential good relations with the other guests, she rebuked herself. She'd been meaning to go down to supper early and chat with them in the lounge in the hope that she might glean any clues about the set-up here. Like where the computer was kept, for instance, and who sat behind it most often. She could do without annoying them at this early stage if she wanted their cooperation.

However, a piece of advice from an older actress at the beginning of Kate's stage career still held her in good stead. After a particularly trying first day of rehearsals, she had arrived at the dinner table of their grungy digs with a bottle of vodka. 'Darling, never travel anywhere without strong drink,' she had counselled Kate then. 'It helps after the hell of a day such as this, and it means you will always make friends wherever you go.' So after a change of clothes, which included forsaking the gorgeous but crippling new cowboy boots for a more forgiving pair of shoes, she was soon ensconced in the guest lounge with a bottle of single malt scotch, enjoying a nice visit with Joyce and Bill Matheson.

'I'm going to get the girls. They shouldn't miss this,' said Joyce, setting down her drink and struggling out of her chair to stagger across the room on aching muscles. 'It's the most fun we've had since we got here. Okay with you, Kate?'

'Absolutely. The more the merrier,' she declared.

'Yeah, that's what we figured when we booked,' said Bill

ruefully. 'Come in a bunch and have a few laughs. Got it wrong there.'

'Why? Are you not getting on with Nancy and Louise?' Kate asked.

'Oh! No, we go way back, we're like that,' said Bill, crossing his fingers to show the closeness of their friendship. 'It's this place. Atmosphere here kind of sucks the fun right out of you. End up going round on tippy-toe, trying to avoid contact with the evil eye.'

'That would be Andy's, would it?'

'Andy's, Old Pete's. Andy's the worst though. At least you know where you are with Old Pete – he just hollers when he gets stressed. Like at meal times.'

'But he's the cook isn't he?'

'Yup. Picked the wrong job, huh?'

'Well, if what I was told on the internet is true,' said Kate, leaning across to freshen Bill's glass, 'Old Pete used to be a cowboy, but he's been retired to the kitchen, for safety's sake.'

'Can't think of a single place Old Pete would be safe,' Bill chuckled. 'Certainly not the kitchen.'

'The food's not great?'

'Depends. Do you like beans?'

'What kind?'

'The burnt kind.'

'Ah,' said Kate. 'That'll explain the smell then. I thought maybe he'd accidentally left something on the stove.'

'No accident about it. That's the house style.'

A chorus of agonised groans presaged the rest of the party's limping arrival to the lounge, followed by grateful collapsing into positions of abandoned recumbence. 'Hear you got a good anaesthetic in that bottle there,' said Nancy, licking her lips as she watched Kate pour the amber nectar into glasses.

'I can vouch for that,' said Bill. 'Goes straight to the spot. I don't even know if I *have* an ass any more, let alone if it's sore or not.'

'Honey,' said his wife. 'Take it from me, you have an ass.'

'Ice?' Kate asked of the newcomers.

'Ice?' said Louise in an awestruck tone. 'Where did you get ice?'

'Chipped it from our host's heart most likely,' said Nancy darkly.

'She went through that door,' said Joyce, nodding over towards the kitchen.

'And came out alive?' Louise marvelled.

'Alive and with ice,' Joyce confirmed. 'What did I tell you? This woman knows no fear.'

'There wasn't anyone in there, so I just helped myself,' Kate demurred modestly.

'Don't tell me Old Pete's passed out already,' Bill chuckled. 'Wondered why he hadn't sniffed this scotch out by now.'

'Your very good health,' said Nancy. 'And thanks.'

'Cheers,' said Louise. 'Boy that's good.'

'Here's to the cavalry,' said Bill, tipping his glass towards Kate.

'Only two more days,' Joyce comforted them.

'You know what? I'd pay for the privilege of making that one,' Nancy replied. 'Can you believe that we've been looking forward to this trip for weeks?'

'Mary Beth's going to have a lot of explaining to do when she gets here,' said Louise.

'Mary Beth?'

'The missing gang member,' Bill explained. 'Gets here tomorrow. All her fault, 'cos she booked us in.'

'Ah,' said Kate. 'So that's who Andy thought I was at first. He said I wasn't expected till tomorrow.'

'Not all he said as I recall,' said Nancy. 'Had a fancy we

were going to be in for a fist fight when he thought you were here checking up on Robyn.'

'Well now, you can understand that,' said Joyce. 'Must be hard, bringing up a kid on your own while you're trying to run a business.'

'Can think of a few dozen women who do that without turning nasty,' Louise said in a superior tone.

'Ah, women, yes,' Joyce conceded.

'Here we go,' said Bill amiably.

'It's okay, you're here as an honorary, you're in our camp,' Louise reminded him.

'You're right,' said Bill. 'Which must be why I've suddenly become so good at multi-tasking. Look at me. I can sit *and* drink at the same time.'

'Never had any problem there,' said Joyce. 'Why, I've even seen you do both of those things while simultaneously watching TV.'

'I don't see why he makes it so hard on himself – and no, Bill, I am not referring to you or your campaign to get Joyce to buy you a Lay-Z-Boy chair for Christmas,' Louise said, dashing Bill's hopes of an ally in this regard. 'I'm talking about Andy and the way he runs this place. He could have us helping him around the place instead of taking us out for rides, using up his time. I'd like to learn more about ranching, as a matter of fact. And didn't I read somewhere once that's how guest ranches got started? City folk going out into the country for a working holiday and paying for the privilege? I tell you, I'd have much preferred to have been mending fences today, or cleaning out the barn, or even picking up horse do-do, than being taken along on a ride by somebody who clearly wished we weren't here taking up his valuable time.'

'We offered,' said Joyce.

'Face it, we begged,' said Nancy.

'Well, maybe we could suggest that at supper?' Kate said.

'Who to? Robyn? She's the only one we see at this time, when she brings the food in, and she doesn't have any say around here. Least, that's what she's always complaining about.'

'Andy won't be here? He doesn't eat with the guests?'

Nancy drained her glass and shook her head. 'I suspect he doesn't eat at all. Just climbs back into his coffin till the moon comes up.'

'Another, Nancy?' Kate asked.

'Ooh, I don't know if I could. Could I?'

Louise rolled her eyes. 'It's been known.'

'Where is supper?' asked Bill, checking his watch. 'It's a quarter to eight already. Way past Old Pete's time to down tools.'

'I'll go and find out,' said Kate recklessly. 'We need more ice anyway. And while I'm there I'll ask them all if they'd like to join us.'

'Listen, hon, you got death threats back home – you really want to start that up here?' Nancy warned.

Kate laughed as she scooped up the empty ice bowl and walked over to the kitchen. 'I think I'll be safe. He can hardly go killing off his paying guests now, can he?'

'Try telling that to Janet Leigh,' said Bill, as they all watched the kitchen door close behind her.

Robyn had managed to spin out her chores longer than usual by deciding to clean her saddle, which was already spotless, and to tackle a loose hinge on one of the stable doors which she'd been meaning to get round to for ages, so this was Andy's first opportunity to give her the dressing-down which had been building up inside him for an hour and a half. He was yelling accusations at Robyn, Robyn was yelling her denials at him, and Old Pete was shouting to anybody who'd listen that the beans would go cold if'n somebody didn't stop their bellyaching and take them the heck in, so for a moment or two Kate's entry into hell's kitchen was unobserved. However, since Old Pete and Robyn were both roughly facing the direction of the door, they soon saw her and fell silent, leaving Andy shouting solo at the top of his voice, 'Don't *lie* to me, Robyn – it had to be you! You're the only one who's always messing on that damn computer! And now you've gone too damn far, getting some wacko internet weirdo who thinks she's a soap star to fly out here from England!'

Clearly Robyn was enjoying this, judging by the poor effort she was making not to grin. 'You think *she's* lying too?' she asked him with faux innocence.

'Of course she's goddamn lying!' he spat. 'Maybe she can't help it, maybe she's just plain off her head, but either way we don't want her here. And what if she'd been some kind of pervert? Huh? Did you ever think about that? One of these men you read about who prey on young kids in chat rooms?'

'Oh,' said Robyn, wide-eyed with wonder. 'Do you think that she's really a man?'

Andy sighed loudly in frustration. 'No, I don't think she's a man, Robyn, I think she's some sad person who's got nothing better to do with her life than fantasise about being more important than she is.'

'Why don't we ask her?' she said, looking past his shoulder at Kate. 'Hi there, Mata.'

'Yeah, right,' Andy said wearily. 'Like I'm going to fall for that one. You don't think you're in enough trouble already, young lady, without playing the fool?'

'Actually,' said Kate, mortified, as she watched Andy's back stiffen at the sound of her voice. 'I, er—' She waved the ice bowl. 'Just popped in for some ice if it isn't too much trouble.'

'No trouble at all, ma'am, I'll bring it out directly,' said Robyn jauntily, walking past Andy, who was unable to bring himself to turn round, to take the empty bowl. 'But while you're here, could you clear up a few points for us, like are you a man, an internet weirdo or just plain off your head?'

Kate took a moment to think about this. 'Just plain off my head obviously,' she said stiffly, before retreating with wounded dignity to the other side of the door.

'So, there's your answer, Andy,' Robyn said smugly. 'And for your information she is a soap star and they do want to kill her. I looked her up on the web. No question about it. She is That Bitch Sally Black.'

'So, are they coming to eat with us?' asked Bill as Kate rejoined them, swiftly followed by Robyn bearing ice.

'No,' she said quietly. 'I thought better of it.'

'Yee-hah!' said Nancy. '*Now* we can party.'

Naturally enough Kate didn't feel much of a party animal for the rest of the evening, despite her new friends' best attempts. Nor did she feel at all hungry when Robyn arrived with the food.

'Always wondered why they call it a mess of beans in the movies,' said Bill, looking at the grey goo on his plate.

'And now you know,' said his wife. 'Bon appétit, one and all.'

'Don't need a good appetite to eat this,' said Louise. 'You need to be two calories short of starving.'

'Or in so much agony with the rest of your body you don't notice fresh pain,' said Nancy, tucking in with gusto. 'Not going to eat that belly pork, Kate?'

'It's all yours,' she said, rising. 'As is the scotch. I've suddenly come over completely exhausted. Sorry to be a party pooper, but I just have to go to bed. I feel as if I've been up for days.'

'And now you're down, at Blue Yonder,' said Bill. 'We know the feeling. Sleep well.'

'See you tomorrow?' asked Joyce.

Kate faltered. 'I'm not sure. Probably not. I expect I'll go home.'

'Well, don't miss breakfast,' said Nancy. 'Unless you want to miss seeing these beans again. What we don't eat gets refried. That's why I'm doing my bit now.'

'Amongst other reasons,' said Louise. 'Like being a human hoover.'

Nancy grinned. 'Survival of the fattest,' she said good-naturedly.

'Good night then,' said Kate.

'Good night,' they chorused and, waving the bottle of scotch in the air, Bill called, 'And thank you for raising our spirits!'

Kate smiled with a brightness close to mania. Now all she had to do was to raise her own.

5

Sleep took Kate hostage and threw away the key. She was too tired even to dream, and when she finally managed to struggle awake and look at her clock, it took her some minutes of utter confusion before she realised it was telling her what the time was in Kentish Town. Never having been an absolute whizz at maths, she had no idea at all what time of day it might be here, but when she pulled open the curtains, she knew from the height of the sun that she'd slept most of the morning away. And it was so beautiful out there, it was such a waste. She would go and explore, clear her head, and decide what to do.

One thing she knew she would not be doing today, despite what she'd said to Joyce, was to go home. Her last waking thought the night before had been that her air ticket had been cut-price on the understanding that she would stay at least one Saturday night. Today being Tuesday, that meant she would be spending a good while longer in Canada come what may, or face punitive extra charges. What she hadn't yet decided though was whether to bottle it out with Andy here at Blue Yonder, or just get back in her car and drive until she found a warmer welcome elsewhere.

It hadn't been pleasant hearing herself described as a wacko internet weirdo. The thought hadn't struck her till then how her turning up might look to somebody who didn't know her from Eve, but viewed from Andy's angle, she could see now that dashing across the Atlantic, unannounced, to visit somebody she'd never even laid eyes on, might be interpreted as the actions of a person who had a few unresolved issues regarding mental stability. Maybe if she were to seek him out for a good old one-to-one, she could disabuse him of this notion. And at least he now knew from Robyn that she wasn't the delusional person he'd first thought, making up stories about being an actress for purposes of self-aggrandisement.

Outside, she was struck by the rugged beauty of the place, and became more determined not to leave it. She should at least get on a horse and explore the countryside before she headed home, for heaven's sake, or what was the point of coming out here at all? Maybe if she could help him out in some way she might endear herself to him a little more. Like brightening up the decor inside with flowers, say, or with cowboy-type things she might find lying about in a barn. Give him a nice surprise when he got back at the end of the day. Or help out Old Pete. Take over the cooking for tonight's meal. That would make her popular. She'd never yet failed to win praise for her culinary skills. And she could advise Andy on how to make Blue Yonder more welcoming, like teaching the guests about ranch work as Louise had suggested, making them feel useful and wanted.

Wandering back inside, she viewed the bareness of the lounge with a critical eye. It should be like a stage set, with harnesses hanging on the walls, and cartwheels, maybe even some bales of straw dotted about, she thought, not this austere uncared-for functionality. And the dining room could be jollier, just by moving all the tables to make one big one, so people could eat all together like a family. She felt sure that Robyn would like that. She must miss having a mother, living in this very male atmosphere. If she ate with the guests then she would often have women's company.

Kate wondered now if Andy had been right in his accusations. Had it been Robyn who she'd been playing backgammon with and getting to know all these weeks, Robyn who had

tricked her into coming here? It seemed an obvious explanation. Unless Andy was an accomplished actor or a poker-faced
liar. And if so, what would have been his motive? Then again,
'Andy the Cowboy' had shown a maturity and sensitivity
which she had yet to witness in Robyn's conversation.

A crashing of falling pans and a cascade of oaths told her
that Old Pete was in the kitchen, and bracing herself for a
barrage of insults she pushed through the door, where she was
not disappointed.

'Don't you go expecting any breakfast at this hour!' he
yelled as soon as she saw her. 'You're too damn late and I've
got enough on my hands as it is what with another damn
visitor arriving today! Anyways you should be gone by now.
It's check-out by twelve, don't you read the damn notices?'

'I've decided to stay a while longer,' she said, bending to
pick up the fallen pans. 'And don't worry about breakfast. I'm
fine, really. I was wondering more if there was anything I could
do to help you? I've worked in kitchens professionally. I've got
my food hygiene certificate. Not with me, obviously, but I've
got one at home. I did the course.'

Old Pete regarded her with eyes narrowed by cunning.
'Hygiene,' he said, rubbing his bristly chin. 'Now don't that
got something to do with cleaning?'

'That's right,' she agreed.

His eyes now swept from her to the sink, which was heaving
with dirty dishes from breakfast and last night's supper.

'Would you like me to do the washing up?' she suggested.

'Well, since you got a susstiffikit,' he said, taking a seat at the
table and putting his feet up, 'I reckon I could allow it.'

Willingly she rolled up her sleeves and bent to the task.
'Have you worked here long?' she asked conversationally.

'Twelve year near enough.'

'Always in the kitchen?'

'Nope. Came here as a ranch hand.'

'Which do you prefer?'

'No contest,' he said. 'I'm an outdoors man, born and bred.'

Well, she thought, at least that was consistent with what she'd been told about him on the internet. 'So how come you swapped?'

'Took a fall, busted my shoulder. If I wanted to get paid and have a roof over my head I had to do something, so I came inside.'

'You fell off your horse and broke your arm?' she queried. 'How strange. That's what I was told had happened recently to Andy.'

Old Pete shrugged, giving nothing away. 'You could refill that and put it on the range,' he said instead, speaking of the coffee pot now in her hands. 'Seems a shame for me to be setting here taking a break without refreshment.'

'Good idea,' she agreed. She was gasping for a cup. 'So how come you stayed in the kitchen after your shoulder healed, if you prefer working outdoors?'

'Woman who was looking after Robyn left and Andy never got around to finding another one. I ended up stuck with cooking the food and minding the kid.'

'But you still ride?'

'Rarely find the time around the house chores.'

'You could go out riding today, if you wanted to,' she offered. 'I could do your work here for you.'

'What's the catch?' he asked her suspiciously.

'No catch. I'd just like to be helpful. It's why I came,' she said.

'Wouldn't mind riding out to the lake, do a spot of fishing,' he conceded.

'That would be wonderful!' said Kate, putting two clean mugs on the table. 'And I could cook your catch for tonight's supper.'

'You after my job?' he demanded.

'Absolutely not,' she averred. 'Not long term anyway. Just while I'm here. Give you a chance to get out and do what you enjoy best. I should think Andy could do with the help too, couldn't he?'

Old Pete gave a dry humourless laugh. 'You don't help Andy. Andy don't need no help. Andy knows best about everything.'

'Is that right?'

'Nope. But it's what he thinks.'

'That must be very frustrating for you,' Kate suggested, pouring out coffee and settling down at the table with him. 'With all your years of experience you'd think he'd jump at the chance of a bit of advice.'

'Well he don't,' said Old Pete. 'Only jumping he does is down my throat if I do try to tell him how to go about things. Robyn's as bad. Stubborn as mules, the pair of them.'

Kate suspected that went for all three. 'Why do they call you Old Pete?' she asked him. 'Why not just Pete?'

Old Pete's eyes widened in surprise. 'In all the years I been here nobody ever thought to ask me that,' he said. 'Guess they just figure I'm old and I'm called Pete, so Old Pete it is.'

'But you're not old,' said Kate. 'You're what – fifty-five?'

'City folk and their flattery,' he sniffed. 'I'm sixty-three, if it's any of your business.'

'Never!' Kate exclaimed, genuinely surprised. She'd had him pegged for seventy. 'But still, that's young. So what's the story?'

'Got called it way back when I was seventeen, on my first job as a ranch hand. There was two of us called Pete. Young Pete was sixteen, so they called us that way so's they could tell the difference. Just kinda stuck till I grew into it.'

'Goodness! Seventeen to sixty-three! That's—' The sum defeated her. 'A lot of years ranching. You must have so many great stories.'

'I guess,' he conceded.

'So tell all,' she encouraged him, putting her elbows on the table and propping her chin on her hands. 'I love a good yarn.'

And so it was that by the time the coffee pot was drained and Old Pete had saddled up and ridden off with his fishing rod to bag supper, Kate had formulated the definitive master plan which would convince Andy of her sincere desire to be helpful, and make everything jollier for everybody at the Blue Yonder Guest Ranch that evening.

6

Robyn's nose told her that something strange had been going on while she'd been at school as soon as she walked through the back door. The smell that hit her made her mouth water, and she could honestly say that that had never happened to her before in their kitchen. There were pots and pans all over the place, a sponge cake spilling jam out round its edges which was just begging to be neatened up with a swiped finger, and bits of food all neatly chopped in dishes near the stove looking as if they'd been put there by somebody with a gift for forward planning, so she knew it wasn't Old Pete.

The next new thing she noticed came via her ears, and it was a sound that was as foreign to her in her own home as the smell of good food. It was the sound of laughter, which she followed.

Going through into the dining room she was stopped in her tracks by the layout. Instead of the tables standing in corners keeping their distance from each other, they'd all been pushed together in a line and covered with a white sheet, with nine chairs surrounding them. Nine, she thought? She knew there was a new guest arriving today but that still only made six including Mata Hari, if she was still here. But in front of those nine chairs were nine place settings, so it looked as if somebody knew something that she didn't. And there was still the mystery of that laughter to be solved that was coming from next door.

Going through into the lounge room she found Bill Matheson standing over Nancy, who was lying beneath a bale of straw, which accounted for the laughter from the two of them, and from Joyce Matheson and Louise who were creased up over another bale they must have been carrying in before Nancy decided to take up clown work. A new woman, who she correctly assumed was the Mathesons' friend Mary Beth Walkuski, was hanging onto a step ladder where she was laughing so hard she couldn't finish the job she'd begun, which was to hang up an old harness on the wall. Robyn was astonished. 'Have you all gone *insane*?' she demanded, but since that just made them laugh all the harder she backed out of the room to try to find Old Pete, and instead ran into Kate, who was carrying a pitcher of wild flowers through from outside.

'What in hell is going on here?' she demanded. 'Who gave them permission to move the barn in here? Andy'll go ape!'

Kate grinned. 'Oh no he won't. We're planning a surprise! We're having a bit of a do tonight – do you fancy helping?'

'What kind of a do?' she asked suspiciously. 'And what would a person have to do to help?'

'We're having a Banquet and Evening of Entertainment. A person would have to dress up in her cowboy finest and turn up to eat the food I've cooked.'

A smile slowly lifted a corner of Robyn's lips. 'Uh oh,' she said, eyes twinkling. 'Not that old briar patch again, Brer Fox.'

Andy had had an exhausting and testing day. He'd been hugely relieved earlier when the guests had announced that their 'sit-upons were too sore' to go riding and they'd elected to entertain themselves. Without them he'd have a chance to get up to Two Mile Creek and mend the broken fence he'd been trying to see to for a week, and also have time to ride around and check on the stock. But before he'd reached the creek he passed the river which it fed, and found that a calf had wandered in and somehow stranded itself on a small rock in the middle of the rushing water, with its mother beside herself, floundering up and down the muddy bank, soaked to the skin from her many abortive rescue attempts. The normally waist-deep waters had swollen from the recent heavy rains, but he'd hoped nevertheless that his horse would be able to pick his way across to the rock so he could rope the calf and pull it ashore. One wrong step later, he and his mount both found themselves swimming and fighting the unexpectedly strong current, and being swept further away from their goal. Parted from his horse, they had both managed to scramble out safely, but to opposite banks of the river, and no amount of whistling or cajoling would make Rusty join him on the other side. Now he was stranded too, which meant hiking on foot for an hour before finding a calmer place where he could swim back, then hiking for another hour on the other side of the river till he was back where he'd started, by which time – how, he didn't know – the calf was with its mother and grazing placidly next to his horse. Long and the short of it was that by the time he came home, covered in mud and with boots still heavy with water, it was late, he was tired and tetchy and hoping that Robyn and Old Pete were well on the way to having the guests fed and finished with, and that all he had to do was to slump down in the kitchen with a glass of bourbon and a plate of chow.

Sliding in the back door he was arrested, just as Robyn had been, by the shock of smelling good food, and he was lifting lids off pans and eyeing the sponge cake as if it was something from outer space, when Kate walked in on him from the dining room.

Hi!' she said, holding out a glass of bourbon as if she were a psychic. 'I thought I heard you come in! Robyn tells me this is what you like to drink after a hard day's work. Look at the time! I bet you're ready for your dinner.'

In fact all Andy was ready for was to say, 'What in hell are you still doing here?' but before the words could find their way out of his mouth, Kate turned in the doorway and, lifting her voice over the merriment in the next room called, 'Ladies and gentlemen, the moment you've all been waiting for, I give you – Our Host!' to which there was a rousing reply of, 'Yippee!' and 'Yee-haaa!' and a great banging of cutlery on the table.

'They're hungry,' Kate explained with a grin, 'and they've had rather a lot to drink while they've been waiting.'

Standing there open-jawed and feeling as if he'd come home to the wrong ranch house, he was the more surprised when a chant went up of, 'Andy! Andy! Andy!' But with Kate standing there with the door open wide for him, there was nothing left for him to do but to go through it, where he was cheered and applauded and shown to his chair at the head of the table like some movie star. The only difference being that a movie star would no doubt have craved the attention, and Andy totally did not.

Catching sight of Robyn sitting there in her best cowboy dudes he glared a questioning frown at her, but all he received in return was a cheerful grin and a 'Howdy!' He could hardly believe his eyes at the sight of Pete out-duding everybody at the opposite end of the table, having swapped his habitual uniform of greasy dungarees and frayed tartan shirt for a silver-tipped bootlace tie, silver-toed boots, and a short black jacket embroidered in silver thread. Completely lost for words, his vocal abilities were not aided one bit by the platter of tiny pastries which Kate brought through from the kitchen, except for a small groan of pleasure escaping his lips when he bit into one.

'It's just a little *amuse bouche*,' she explained, returning at once whence she'd come and calling back over her shoulder, 'I'll bring the first course through in just a moment.'

'What's she call it?' asked Robyn, swallowing one whole and helping herself to another.

'*Amuse bouche*? It's French for getting your mouth interested in what's coming next,' Louise explained.

'Done deal,' said Robyn, spraying crumbs.

'Would you like some wine, Andy, or are you going to stick with your bourbon?' Bill asked. 'We laid in supplies today when we were in town. We're celebrating Joyce's birthday and—'

'My divorce,' said Mary Beth pointedly, leaning forward to show Andy a little more cleavage.

'Stick to the bourbon thanks,' he said stiffly. 'And no wine for Robyn either.'

'Don't want none,' she countered. 'Mata's made me a whole jug of real lemonade.'

'I'll keep you company, Bill,' said Old Pete, holding out his empty wine glass for refilling.

'Old Pete,' said Andy, with a frost in his voice which made Alaska seem cosy by comparison, 'would you mind telling me what in hell you're doing sitting at the table and letting one of the guests do your kitchen work?'

'Why surely,' said Old Pete, draining his glass in one great gulp and wiping his mouth on his sleeve. 'I'm letting everybody enjoy an evening of good food for a change.'

'Amen to that,' Nancy muttered.

' 'Sides,' said Old Pete as, with eyes widened by desire, they all watched grilled marinated salmon garnished with deep-fried scallions, sour cream and lemon wedges approach them, 'took me all afternoon to catch that damn fish. Least she could do was cook it.'

Robyn's portion had no time to linger on its plate, but was down her throat before most people had lifted their forks. 'No offence, Mata,' she said. 'Slipped down real easy, but generally speaking we're used to bigger servings round here.'

'That's good,' Kate smiled. 'Then you'll be able to do justice to the main course.'

'Would that be a red main course?' asked Bill, pouring the

last of the Pouilly Fumé into everyone's glasses with some regret.

'It would indeed,' said Kate, rising yet again to go back into the kitchen. 'I hope everybody likes roast beef?'

'Oh my goodness!' exclaimed Nancy. 'Have I died and gone to heaven?'

'Roast beef?' Bill checked anxiously with Joyce. 'She did say roast *beef* and not roast beans?'

But this was no longer in doubt when Kate returned, staggering under the weight of a huge sirloin on the bone, and set it down in front of Andy. 'Will you carve?' she said, handing him a sharpened knife.

'Wow!' said Louise, and then added guiltily, 'I hope it's no one we know.'

'It's very pink in the middle,' Kate told them. 'So if anyone wants it well done—'

'The rarer the better for me,' Nancy said gaily, rubbing her hands together in anticipation. 'Although, of course, I draw the line if it's actually still moving.'

Slicing through the tender meat, Andy was glad to have something to do, but he could have done without everybody's greedy eyes on him as he carved. He preferred to keep a professional distance between himself and his paying guests, and he was feeling very uncomfortable being seated here with them, where they could make all kinds of unreasonable demands and ask all kinds of dumb questions. And what in hell was the cyber-nut still doing here, and how had she managed to take control of his business in the few hours he'd been away? Now here she was back again, getting 'oohs' and 'aahs' for her presentational skills. Well hell, who couldn't arrange vegetables in wedges of colours in a dish for gosh sake? Typical actress, trying to get everybody's attention all the time, he thought derisively. Well, not his. No siree. The meat was cut, and they could damn well help themselves, he wasn't going to wait on them. Forking a great slab on to his own plate, he drove a spoon into the vegetables and mussed them up as much as he could as he served himself.

'Gravy?' Kate offered, already at his side, poised to pour.

'I'll take it when I want it,' he said, refusing to look at her, and shovelled a forkful of food into his mouth.

'I'll take some right now, please, Kate,' said Robyn with uncharacteristic and pointed politeness. 'And I'd like to thank you very much for sparing time from your holiday to cook for us and organise this evening of entertainment.'

'Hear hear,' said Joyce Matheson.

Andy was too busy eating to join in the spontaneous round of applause this earned the cook. *What* evening of entertainment was what he wanted to know, but he'd sooner have cut his tongue out than ask her. He supposed she'd be doing an excerpt from her damn fool soap opera later on, or maybe – God help them – she was going to do a song. Well, soon as he'd chowed this lot down, he was out of here. Tired as he already was, there was still plenty of work to be done in the office. Taking a sneaked glance at everyone, he saw that they were now fully occupied with eating, and he judged it safe to go for the gravy and the waffle-like creation that everybody was groaning over.

'What on God's good earth is this marvellous fluffy, puffy, gravy-soaking-up device called?' asked Nancy. 'And will you please give the recipe to Louise?'

'It's an English delicacy called Yorkshire pudding,' said Kate.

'Listen up, group,' said Bill to his party. 'Our next holiday will be taken in Yorkshire, no argument. Better get back on the internet, Mary Beth, and start booking now.'

'Why is it always me who has to do the research on the trips?' Mary Beth grumbled.

'We each have our role,' Bill answered equably. 'You work

in IT, you do the web work. I know about good wine, so I do the hootch.'

'Yeah, and what about you others?' asked Mary Beth.

'We just come along and look beautiful,' said Nancy. 'And test drive the new foreign food. I give this Yorkshire pudding a five-star rating. I'm in with Bill.'

'Pardon me,' said Robyn, taking her first pause from eating. 'Would that mean you folks found us on the web?'

'No,' said Mary Beth. 'Not those folks. This folk.'

'You picked the Blue Yonder off of the internet?' Robyn checked.

'Yes I did.'

'Well well,' said Robyn. 'Did you hear that, Andy? Did you hear her say she found us on the web?'

'No I didn't,' said Andy. 'I'm too busy eating, and that's what you should be doing, young lady. I'm sure you've got schoolwork to do after supper.'

'Already done it,' said Robyn. 'Kate sat me down at the kitchen table soon as I come in, so's I'd be free for the rest of the night. But, you know, getting back to the Blue Yonder web page now, the web page I built myself for the very purpose of people finding us. Looks like it worked then, don't it?'

'*You* built the web page?' Mary Beth asked. 'That's good, Robyn, I'm very impressed.'

Robyn grinned with satisfaction. 'Hear that, Andy? I've impressed her with my computer skills. So would you say that was time and money well spent then, Mary Beth?'

'Absolutely. Did you hear that, Bill? A *child* can build web pages. You'd think then that the average adult should at least be able to access them.'

'If only I was average I'd be able to do it easily then, but . . .' Bill shrugged genially. 'More of this excellent wine, anyone?'

'See, when I was constructing our page, Andy got mad. Said that me slaving away at the computer was a waste of my time and his money,' Robyn continued mercilessly. 'But I guess you just proved him wrong.'

Andy eyed her critically. 'You know why I got mad, Robyn,' he said. 'Now get on with your food.'

'Oh yeah, me borrowing your credit card to order the software online. Sorry about that,' she said, sounding more gleeful than apologetic. 'Gee, fifty-nine dollars ninety-nine cents down the drain. And let's see, that only brought us in one, two, three, four, *five* paying guests, not including Mata, who, according to her, you got here all by yourself, Andy, by playing backgammon on the web. Good ploy. One to you, five to me. Let's see, five guests at three hundred bucks a night each for three nights, that's a profit of – oh dear – only seventeen hundred forty-four dollars and one cent. Tell you what, if you take the seventeen hundred forty-four dollars, could I keep the one cent, call it even? For inconveniencing you about the card and all?'

An uncomfortable silence had fallen round the table, which Kate assessed could only be filled by another culinary distraction. 'Excuse me,' she said quietly, 'I just need to sort something out in the kitchen.'

'There's more?' Nancy asked jovially, who was never too uncomfortable to think about food.

'Yes, but it's going to take about ten or fifteen minutes,' Kate said over her shoulder, and quickly took cover behind the kitchen door.

'Well, team, that sets us an interesting challenge,' said Bill. 'Can we empty these plates before she brings another full one through?'

'If you don't you're damn fools,' said Old Pete, reaching over to stab another piece of beef on to his fork. 'With me back in charge tomorrow, you'd better eat your fill today.'

The assiduous scraping of cutlery on plates was all that filled the silence until Kate's return, when she arrived carrying the sponge cake she'd just decorated, complete with lighted candle.

' "Happy Birthday, Joyce!" ' said Robyn reading the iced message on the top. 'And what's it say around the sides?'

' "Mary Beth – Life Begins!" ' said Joyce.

'Let's hope!' said Mary Beth, smiling round the table, and ending with a lingering look at Andy. Together, she and Joyce blew out the candle.

'Made your wish?' asked Bill of his wife.

She nodded. 'You'll know more about that later, after we retire.'

'What was your wish, Mary Beth?' asked Robyn, who had witnessed the eyelash-fluttering that had been going Andy's way.

'If I tell you it won't come true,' said Mary Beth coyly, biting into the cake. 'But, oh, my goodness, maybe it's happening already. Kate, this is delicious! What a great start to my new life! Thank you.'

'A toast. To the chef,' Bill remembered to propose, as they put paid to second helpings.

'To the chef,' they all echoed, all except Andy, whose mouth was still too full of cake to risk opening it.

'And to Old Pete,' said Kate generously, 'for catching the salmon. And to all of you for helping set the stage for tonight's entertainment. Shall we take our drinks through now, and get started?'

'On what?' asked Andy suspiciously, over the scraping of chairs which ensued.

' "Tales from the Range – An Evening of Cowboy Yarns," ' Kate supplied.

'Well, enjoy it,' he said stiffly, throwing down his napkin and making off in the opposite direction to the rest of the herd. 'I got some office work to finish up.'

'Oh no you don't,' Kate said firmly, and taking him by the

arm she steered him towards the guest lounge. There was nothing he could do but follow his captured limb, short of wrestling her to the ground. 'By the way,' she continued, 'if you're wondering why I'm still here, I've decided to stay on for a while. I hope that's all right – as a paying guest, of course. I gave Robyn my credit card details this afternoon.'

As if this last piece of information wasn't enough cause for anxiety, Andy stopped dead in his tracks when he took in the lounge, which now looked like the set of *Oklahoma!*

'What in hell—' he spluttered, on seeing the bales of straw, but Kate had taken her position in the centre of the room and was addressing the seated audience.

'Fellow guests,' she began. 'An extraordinary thing. Yesterday evening, Louise said that she wished she knew more about the actual business of ranching, with which you all agreed, and today I stumbled on a local historian, right here at the Blue Yonder Guest Ranch.' She paused for dramatic effect, and Andy, colouring uncomfortably, hoped to God she didn't mean him.

'Now, this historian hasn't learned his stuff from text books,' she continued. 'No, he's been a lifelong student at the University of Life on the Range. So without further ado, may I introduce Old Pete, and his wonderful tales of true adventure!'

As Old Pete stepped forward to enthusiastic applause, Mary Beth patted the bale of straw she was using as a seat and said to Andy, 'Plenty of room here. Won't you join me?'

'No, that's all right,' said Robyn, grabbing his arm and pulling him down. 'I saved him a seat here, between me and Mata.' As far as she was concerned, if Andy was going to get interested in either of these women, she'd far sooner it was the one who'd already proved herself as a cook.

'Well now,' said Old Pete, as Andy was shunted uncomfortably into his captive position. 'Now you're all sat there looking at me I've clean forgot what I was going to say.' But with Kate's encouragement he soon remembered, and during the next couple of hours they were taught the history of guest ranching (it was, as Louise had suspected, that they were meant to pay for the privilege of helping), and Andy and Robyn learned more about their fellow rancher than they had ever discovered in the twelve years he'd been with them.

'Boy,' said Robyn at the end of the evening, when she'd helped to put things away. 'How do you do that, Mata? How do you get at somebody's stories like that? I never even knew Old Pete had been married.'

'Least of all to a nimble-fingered Mexican woman who loved him enough to ruin her eyesight embroidering that jacket,' Nancy remarked in a low voice as she passed by. 'Must've been more of a looker in his youth.'

'So how come he spilled the beans for you, Mata?' Robyn pursued. 'When he's never told us half of what he said tonight.'

Aware that Andy was busy nearby trying not to look as if he were listening, Kate said, 'It's easy, I'm just nosy. I ask the questions most people are too polite to ask. My advice is, if you want to get to know people, encourage them to talk about themselves.'

'I'll bear that in mind,' said Robyn darkly, throwing a glance at Andy's back, 'if I ever do want to know about somebody. Good night, Mata, and thanks for a great evening. Specially the cake.'

'You're welcome. Good night.' Turning now to extend her nocturnal salutations to Andy, and in the hope that she might draw him into conversation, Kate was disappointed to see that he had disappeared from the room like a silent shadow. 'Good night, everybody,' she said to the remaining guests, who were putting paid to the last of Bill's wine. 'I'm turning in. Mind if I have first go in the bathroom?'

'Have whatever go in the bathroom you like,' said Nancy. 'We're all en suite.'

'Really?' said Kate. 'Oh.' But due to her tiredness, she made no connection between this statement and what she had experienced the day before, save to feel aggrieved at having drawn the short straw with her room allocation, and thus she set herself up beautifully for yet another blow to her ego and another rebuff from her host.

Having taken refuge in his office, Andy was having a fruitless few minutes shuffling papers from one side of his desk to the other. He was unable to concentrate, due to Kate's words to Robyn preying on his mind, damn her. He was left with an uncomfortable feeling of shame that it had taken the arrival of this meddling, inquisitive stranger to elicit information from Old Pete which he should have asked about himself, shouldn't he, sometime during the last twelve years?

Which led to another uncomfortable feeling involving his poor record of communication with Robyn of late. Sitting in his office, unable to kid himself any longer that he was doing anything remotely productive with the accounts, therefore, and after sighing deeply, he went to Robyn's bedroom and knocked on her door.

'How are things going at school?' he asked awkwardly, as he let himself in and sat on her bed to gaze at his hands.

'Same old same old,' she said cautiously, wondering what was coming next. As she knew to her cost, Andy wasn't given much to polite conversation, so when he asked her a question like this, it meant it was more than likely leading somewhere she didn't want to go.

He sighed and pursed his lips and scratched his eyebrow. 'Sorry I grabbed you so hard yesterday,' he said eventually. 'Never done it before, have I?'

'Nope,' she said suspiciously.

'No excuse for it, and it won't happen again.'

'Okay,' she said. 'Good night then.'

'So,' he said uncomfortably, 'you're getting on all right at school now, even though you don't much like going?'

Robyn's eyes narrowed to give him The Look which Old Pete had often remarked could curdle milk at a thousand paces. 'I am going to school every day,' she spat. 'Surprised you ain't rung them to check, being as you never believe a word of what I tell you.'

But for once Andy didn't rise to the bait and shout back. 'Reason it's important, is your future life,' he said in a controlled and reasonable voice. 'You need to pass exams to be able to make something of yourself.'

Robyn grunted and slid down in her bed. 'Since when do you need a college degree to work here? Because that is what I am going to be doing with my future life, and no arguments from you, nor not even a nice reasonable discussion is ever going to change that. Soon as it's legal to leave school, I'm gonna be coming out of them gates with a big smile on my face,' she said. 'So get used to it and good night.' From under the covers, she heard him get up and cross the room.

'Owe you an apology too about that website you put up,' he said from the doorway. 'Sounds from what the guests said that you were right about it,' which shocked Robyn enough to make her sit up.

'Thanks,' she said.

'So, looks like the teachers at your school are good for some things, then,' he smiled.

Robyn scowled. 'First time you give me some praise, you can't resist turning it around and saying it was all down to somebody else,' she complained bitterly.

'Not how I meant it,' he said stiffly, welded to the doorframe. He felt unable to leave it like this, but equally unable to bring himself to go without pursuing another subject about which he was anxious. 'By the way,' he said eventually, 'I hear somebody gave you their credit card today.'

Robyn pursed her lips and folded her arms. 'And?'

'What did you do with it?'

'I fed it into the machine and verified her details and gave it back to her,' she said. 'After I'd bought a few items for myself, of course, like a plasma screen TV, a new computer, and that hand-tooled saddle I've been hankering after. What in hell are you getting at?'

'Just making sure that we're all square here,' he said. 'And if we are, that's good. Good night.'

'What were you worried about? That I'd steal money from a *guest*?' she yelled angrily.

'Ssh! Calm down, they'll hear you,' he urged her in a whispered voice. 'I just have to be sure that proper procedure was followed. You can understand that.'

'No,' she replied coldly. 'I don't understand you at all.'

'Did she – er,' he began, knowing he had lost significant ground. 'Did she say how long she was figuring on staying when she gave you her card?'

'Why?' Robyn demanded provocatively. 'You missing playing backgammon with her on the computer?'

It was in the tense silence which followed this taunt that Kate, padding back from the bathroom in bare feet, saw Andy a few feet further down the corridor, framed in the light from Robyn's room and heard him say angrily, 'Robyn, this would not be the first time you tried to set me up with a woman, and I have told you on those occasions that I am not the marrying kind. Now you brought that interfering meddlesome woman here, and I am holding *you* responsible for sending her back where she came from. Good night.'

Closing the door angrily and turning on his heel to march off to his room he found himself almost tripping over the subject of his rant, which embarrassment was compounded by

Robyn having the last shouted word, 'Yeah, you stick to your story, Andy! Go ahead, blame me for what you done your own goddam self! But if you want rid of her, *you* tell her! Me, I like her cooking. I'm happy for her to stay!'

'Well,' Kate laughed bravely, while shrinking into the wall and wishing she were dressed in more than her bathrobe. 'If you've got something to say to me, now might be a good time.'

Andy swallowed hard. 'Good night,' he said finally, striding past her. 'And thanks for the meal.'

Back in her bleak room, Kate put herself wearily to bed. Did this solve the mystery? she wondered, trying to dismiss from her thoughts the hurtful fact that Andy still wanted her gone after all her hard work. Was it Robyn, wanting a mum and happy-ever-after, who'd brought her here?

Well, if it was, young Robyn was bound for disappointment. Personally, she'd sooner be stoned to death with frozen peas by crazed soap fans than have anything further to do with anyone so churlish and rude.

7

Having fallen asleep when her head hit the pillow, Kate woke early the next morning when the pillow hit her head.

'Hi there,' said Robyn. 'I hollered and hollered but you wouldn't wake up. Thought maybe you was dead.'

For a moment Kate considered this as a possibility. She tried and failed to focus her eyes in the gloom. 'What time is it?' she asked.

'Five thirty, near enough.'

'In the morning?' Kate demanded, disbelief colouring her tone.

Robyn laughed. 'Course in the morning. Do you often wake up at five thirty in the afternoon?'

'No,' Kate lied. In fact, since the Sally Black débâcle she had more often than not stayed awake the whole night and slept most of the day. 'But why have you woken me now?'

'You said last night you wanted to learn about ranching. So I thought I'd start teaching you.' Mercilessly, Robyn pulled open the curtains. 'Making some coffee for you,' she said enticingly, already on her way out of the room. 'Come and get it . . .'

Great though the temptation was just to flop back down and snuggle under the covers, Kate dragged herself out of bed, into her clothes, and down the corridor to the kitchen, where the lukewarm brown water she was offered completely failed to deliver the caffeine kick she craved.

'Okay,' said Robyn, as Kate put down her mug with a

suppressed shudder of distaste. 'Know anything about horses?'

'A bit,' said Kate. 'I used to go for riding lessons when I was about your age.'

'All righty,' Robyn returned enthusiastically. 'Let's go and catch us some then.'

Following her young teacher outside to the corral, Kate remembered Minnie's ironic observations about her non-existent skills with the lasso, but though she was game to cultivate them – even at this early hour of the morning with sleep still fogging her brain – it transpired that Robyn had a much easier method of persuading the animals to come to her: she just called them by name.

'Know how to put on a halter?' she asked Kate, slipping one over the head of the nearest horse with consummate ease and leading it back to the yard.

'I did once,' said Kate uncertainly, struggling to recall her riding-school days. 'The thing is,' she added, 'I gave up riding lessons for tap classes after only a year.' She felt rather vulnerable alone in the corral with these huge quadrupeds milling around her, with only the memory of how to do a soft shoe shuffle for her defence. Even more so when one of them nudged her arm with its muzzle. 'Nice horsey,' she told it in a quavering voice. 'Be nice to Kate and put your head in here please.'

'Trying the polite approach are you?' Robyn said with a grin, having returned with another halter and already leading another mount away. 'His name's Rusty by the way, in case you want to get better acquainted. Don't forget to ask him if he's having a nice day.'

'Very funny,' Kate sniffed. Her frustration getting the better of her fear, she made a lunge for the animal's neck with the rope halter, and fell her full length in the dirt when Rusty dodged away. 'Bloody hell!' she complained, scrambling to her feet, but not quickly enough not to be noticed by Robyn, who gave a shout of delighted laughter. 'I'm glad you find this so amusing,' she said frigidly, having lost her sense of humour somewhere on the ground. 'Obviously I'm not being any help here, so if you'll excuse me I think I'll go back to my bed.'

'Hey, no, Mata, I'm sorry,' Robyn said earnestly, grabbing her arm as she tried to walk away. 'Don't go.'

'That was actually quite scary,' Kate said severely, torn between her own embarrassment and the girl's obvious sincerity. 'Humiliating somebody is no way to teach.'

'No, ma'am.'

'What if I'd been kicked?'

'Kick me if you like, make you feel any better.'

'No thank you,' said Kate.

Robyn scowled at her feet. 'I can be a bit childish at times,' she admitted.

'Oh me too,' said Kate, and swiftly executing a judo throw she'd learnt once for a play, she threw the thirteen year old to the ground.

'Shi-it,' Robyn giggled, getting up to dust herself down. 'You are a woman full of surprises, Mata Hari.'

'That's me. International woman of mystery. Now, do you want to show me how to catch that damned horse?'

'Sure,' said Robyn graciously, leading the way back towards Rusty. 'Hell, that was one neat move. You wanna teach me that?'

'What? And give away my advantage? Do I look that stupid?' said Kate.

Robyn grinned. 'Do I look stupid enough to answer that?' she said.

Annoyingly enough Rusty ducked his head obligingly for Robyn to pass the halter over his nose, as she gave Kate her first lesson in horse management. 'See you just have to show 'em who's boss,' she told her. 'You got to win their respect, then they're good as gold.'

'Why are we catching them all anyway?' Kate asked, after she had successfully ensnared a bay mare under Robyn's watchful eye.

'We're not catching them all, just them who's going out today. They got a big ride ahead of them, so we want to make sure they're all fed and watered ahead of time. Andy's taking everybody up to Green Lake, which is a full day there and back. You going with 'em?'

'No, I don't think so,' said Kate. A whole day in the company of someone who thought of her as interfering and meddlesome? No thank you. 'So,' she continued in a critical voice, 'if Andy is taking everybody out, why isn't he the one catching the horses? Is he having a lie in?'

'That'd be the day,' said Robyn, hauling a hay bale over to the tethered horses. 'No, he's in the office, catching up with the paperwork. Okay, we'll let them have their feed and come back and brush 'em, check their hooves, after we've gone and got our breakfast milk.'

'Is it far? Do you want me to drive?' Kate asked.

'Where to?'

'To the shops. To get the milk.'

Robyn laughed. 'No, we can walk right there. Come on. Let me introduce you to the store keepers.'

Naturally, they were of the four-legged variety and were found in the barn. 'This here is Mata Hari,' Robyn told the two cows. 'She likes to talk to four-legged people like yourselves. Mata, this is Milker One and Milker Two.'

'Hello, girls,' said Kate. 'Those are no names for beauties like you, are they?' Tentatively she leaned over the stall to scratch Milker One's neck.

'Nice start,' said Robyn drily, 'but wrong end.'

'My, aren't you the one for the witticisms this morning?' Kate smiled dangerously. 'Anyone would think you actually like being thrown to the ground.'

'I'll go get the pails,' said Robyn, backing off in mock fear, 'while you get more acquainted with the head end of operations.'

'Well yes, I think it's only right that I introduce myself properly before we get intimate,' Kate told Milker One. 'I wouldn't be too impressed if somebody grabbed my boobies before even saying hello.'

Robyn laughed. She wasn't used to grown-ups talking dirty. Come to that, she wasn't used to grown-ups being anything like Kate at all. She was fun. 'So how come you ain't going out riding with the others today?' she asked, while her student grappled with the mysteries of coaxing milk out of teats. 'You scared you'll fall off?'

'No, not really,' said Kate. 'I'd like to go one of these days, just not today. Maybe you could take me out at the weekend?'

'Be happy to,' Robyn assured her. Speaking of happiness, she thought, she couldn't remember having seen anyone wear such a contented smile on their face while milking a cow. It kind of made her want to wear one too. 'Enjoying that, are ya?' she asked.

Kate looked up, eyes sparkling, her head leaning against the animal's flank, the milk now spurting in a satisfyingly regular rhythm against the sides of the metal bucket. 'You have no idea,' she grinned. 'This is just *so* grounding! If you could bottle this, you could make a fortune from stressed-out city people.'

'News fresh in,' said Robyn, in a voice loaded with irony. 'City people already buy it in bottles.'

'Not the milk, smart arse,' Kate batted back. 'This sense of being connected, this sort of earthed feeling. In touch with reality kind of thing, you know?'

'Can't say I do,' said Robyn, tickled pink with the way her new friend pronounced 'ass'. She couldn't wait to get to school to try it out on Kenny McIntosh. 'So – why do you want me to take you out riding, not Andy?' she asked after a while. 'Don't you like him?'

Kate paused from her labours to give this her whole attention. 'I think it's rather the other way round, isn't it?' she asked candidly. 'I don't think I'm his favourite person exactly.'

'Shouldn't take it personal,' Robyn said encouragingly. 'He's like that about everybody.'

'Is he? Why?'

Robyn shrugged. 'He's just a grouch I guess.'

Mellowed by the milking, Kate strove for her usual generosity concerning human nature. 'Nobody's a grouch for no reason. Is he particularly stressed at the moment?'

Robyn considered this. 'Money's tight. Too much going out, not enough coming in. Never known that to be no different though.'

It was odd, Kate mused, that most of what she had learnt about the Blue Yonder Guest Ranch during her games of backgammon was proving to be true, when the real Andy was so at odds with the person she thought she'd got to know. 'I have definitely got a knack for this,' she said proudly, having emptied Milker One. 'Shall I do Milker Two now?'

'Be my guest.'

When she was settled by the other animal's rump, she said, 'Do you mind if I ask you something, Robyn?'

'Go right ahead.'

'Was it you who got me here? Was it you on the computer, pretending to be Andy?'

'No, ma'am,' said Robyn, looking her directly in the eye. 'It was not me.'

Kate couldn't make up her mind if she was being as truthful as she sounded, or whether she was just very good at fibbing with a straight face. 'I overheard Andy and you rowing last night,' she pressed. '*He* seems to think it was you, doesn't he?'

'He can think all he likes, but he'll still be wrong,' said Robyn stiffly. 'Same as you'll be if you believe him over me.'

'So you weren't trying to set him up with me as he accused you, like he said you'd done in the past?'

'Oh, I was just a kid when that happened!' Robyn exclaimed crossly. 'I had a thing for my fourth-grade teacher, Miss Harris, and I was stupid enough back then to think that it'd be real neat if she came here and lived with us. So yeah, I tried to push 'em together a little bit. But now I'm grown up enough to know that no woman in her right mind would ever want to marry Andy, and to believe him when he says he is not the marrying kind. End of story.'

'I see,' said Kate. 'No offence taken by my checking, I hope?'

From the grim set of her mouth it looked as if there had been, but after a moment's reflection, Robyn sighed and said, 'No. I guess you had to ask after you heard Andy saying it. He never believes a single thing I ever say, so why should you?'

'If you say you're telling the truth then I believe you,' said Kate diplomatically. 'So, do you believe Andy when he says it wasn't him?'

Robyn screwed up her eyes the better to contemplate this. 'What kind of stuff did you used to chat about when you was playing with – whoever it was?'

'Andy the Cowboy,' Kate supplied, her face softening with the memory. 'Oh, everything and nothing. My work. My lack of work. My worries about money. He was just so lovely. Very funny, and kind, and sympathetic. Particularly when the public turned nasty over Sally Black.'

'Funny, kind and sympathetic, huh?' said Robyn. 'Then yeah, I guess I do believe Andy when he says it wasn't him. You seen him being any of them things since you been here?'

'Not really,' Kate agreed, her expression souring. 'Which leaves me with a bit of a conundrum.'

'Gee, that sounds bad,' said Robyn. 'What is one of those?'

'A puzzle,' Kate supplied. 'A mystery. Because if it wasn't you, and it wasn't Andy, who else has access to your computer, and knows so much about things here at Blue Yonder that they could have got so many of the facts right? Whoever "Andy The Cowboy" is, he or she knew all about you, and Old Pete, and about how bad business is just now . . .'

'So it kinda sounds like an inside job?'

'Kinda,' Kate concurred.

'So what we need to do is to write down a list of suspects,' Robyn offered. 'Like in a cop show. Then we eliminate them from our enquiries one by one.'

'But who's on it if not you and Andy? Old Pete?' Kate asked doubtfully.

'All three of us I guess. We'll all have to be guilty until proven innocent.'

'Anybody else locally who could have done it for a bit of mischief?'

Robyn cocked her head on one side while she pondered this. 'Not that I can think of right off. I'll keep thinking about it though while I'm at school, bring you some names later.' She glanced at her watch. 'Speaking of school, I still got a pile of chores to get through before I go. You okay to finish off here while I go get started on the horses?'

'Absolutely. I think she's nearly finished anyway, aren't you, girl? Do you want me to come and help you when we're done?'

'You could collect the eggs from over there,' said Robyn pointing towards the hen coop. 'And then, if you really really wanted to help . . .?'

'Yes?'

'You could fix breakfast. 'Stead of Old Pete?'

Kate laughed. 'Not a problem.'

'And packed lunches for everybody, including me?'

'Can do.'

'Yee-haa!' said Robyn, punching the air, and skipping her way out of the barn.

When Kate made her way back to the kitchen with the fresh milk and eggs, she found Robyn's elation matched by Old Pete's.

'Me, I'll have two eggs, easy over, and a mountain of bacon,' he told her, as he ceded space to sit and watch her work. 'And if you're doing the lunches, you can pack me up one as well. Thought I'd take a gun out and catch a few conies for you to cook up tonight.'

Kate turned to look at him. 'You don't mind me taking over the cooking?' she checked.

'Hell no,' he said happily. 'I like eating good grub as much as the next man. I'm just hoping and praying you decide to stick around for a goodly long while.'

'That's nice to hear,' she said, flashing the kind of smile at him that his young bride had used to tenderise his heart so many years before.

'Y'ain't telling me that a pretty young woman like you, with cooking skills to match, don't get told that all the time,' he said gruffly, which was the closest he'd come to flirting in thirty years.

'Oh! Thanks for the "young"!' said Kate. 'Can I quote you on that to casting directors? But in answer to your question, no, you might be surprised to hear that quite a few people are resistant to my charms.'

'Damn fools should ought to go hungry then,' said Old Pete darkly, casting a withering glance in the direction of the office. He stood up to stretch. 'Ain't going to spoil things by trying to make coffee the way you do, but I will go next door and see what the folks want for their breakfast. Sounds like they come down at last.'

'Offer them eggs fried, poached, scrambled or boiled,

mountain of bacon optional,' she called after him, and once this news had spread around the dining room, together with the information that Kate was again in charge of the kitchen, all these options were taken up with alacrity by one and – almost – all.

8

After the kind of night's sleep that could be described in any number of ways except 'untroubled', Andy had woken tired and tetchy and with a war going on inside his head. With the ranch's finances being in such a mess he was quite used to anxiety, dread and doom slugging it out for possession of his first waking thought, but now something else had joined in the fray, some new feeling nagging at his brain, and he couldn't say he liked it one bit.

If guilt hadn't been his constant companion he might have mistaken it for that. Or shame, maybe. But few knew better than he that both of these emotions made a man feel icy cold in the pit of his stomach, and this was something way warmer. So warm, in fact, that almost immediately on waking it made his cheeks tingle, which helped him pin it down at least. It was red-faced embarrassment, plain and simple, and it was no kind of feeling for a full-grown man. Particularly not on an empty stomach.

For here he was now, skulking in his office, instead of obeying his nose and following the smell of frying bacon. He'd tried. God knows he'd tried. Made it as far as the kitchen, full of pleasant expectations of getting his belly filled. But then he'd seen That Woman standing at the range (fortunately her back had been turned at the time) and he'd ducked back into the hallway rather than face her out, had high-tailed it back to his desk and the insoluble problem of unbalanced books. This was what they meant, then, when they talked of being between a rock and a hard place. Damn.

The more he skulked, the more resentful he felt. Trapped in his own home, too scared to move about freely, to wander where he wanted, when he wanted. And all because of Her. The interfering do-gooder. The meddlesome madam. The cyber-nut. The freak. (Had he shouted that last night too?)

He couldn't remember now exactly what he'd said to Robyn about her, nor knew what she might have overheard. Mata Hari. Good name for her. Lurking in the shadows, spying. Sooner she was gone the better. Good riddance. She was like a tick, clinging on – and about as welcome. He was well within his rights to speak his mind about her anyhow. Her fault if what she heard about herself when she was spying was unflattering. He hadn't asked her to come out here, and he definitely hadn't asked her to stay. So sure, okay, she'd done a nice dinner, but the price of it was way too high. Who wanted three courses and a home-made cake? All a man needed to keep body and soul together was just a little bit of bacon. And some bread. Maybe a dollop of that creamy yellow scrambled egg he'd seen her spooning out the pan. And a cup of strong coffee.

God, the smell of that alone was enough to drive him mad out here, with not even a glass of water to wet his whistle. How did she do it? How did she make a simple thing like a pot of coffee dance around in a man's nostrils like that, teasing his saliva buds into over-activation, tormenting his gastric juices into a senseless, useless, unnecessary flood?

Damn, he'd be glad when she was gone. She made him feel off-centre. Awkward. Like a colt who needed to grow into his legs. All clumsy angles and big bony knees. Nervy. Skittish.

Starving.

His stomach groaned loudly, and he knew exactly how it felt. God, if he could take back that moment in the hallway last night he'd do it like a shot. It didn't sit well with him being rude like that. Made him feel like an idiot. Graceless. Foolish.

Famished.

And wouldn't you know it. At the exact same moment that he decides he cannot stand it another second longer, makes up his mind to face it out and go get his damned breakfast, he opens the office door to find her standing the other side of it, about a foot away from his face.

'Spying again?' was what he almost said to her as they both recovered from the shock of it, but what he said in fact was 'Oh.' She gave a little squeal, of course, and clutched her chest. Typical actress. Over-dramatic shenanigans at every turn. Then she laughed.

'We have to stop meeting like this,' she said, and then it's her turn to be embarrassed, lowering her lids, biting her lip, looking back up at him with those annoyingly big blue eyes – transparent almost, like you could see right through them, right down to the bottom of the pool, and what you saw actually, when she took you by surprise like that, was an open friendliness, a sense of humour, a wanting to be liked. 'Sorry,' she said. 'Inappropriate. Typical of me! I've come to take your breakfast order. Everybody else has been fed. You're going to be late if you don't stop doing your office work, and you can't go out on an empty stomach.'

'I can do anything I damn well please in my own home,' was the riposte that was battering at his lips and tongue for the freedom to be aired, but, 'I'm busy,' was what he allowed to pass beyond his teeth, followed by a turning away and a heavy sitting back down at his desk to frown at papers and shuffle 'em.

'Doing your accounts?' she said, drifting into the room after him, refusing to take the hint. Damn tick.

No need to look back up at her. Only encourage her. No need even to reply when the answer was self evident. A grunt'd do it, just as a matter of principle, to stay this side of polite.

'I hate having to do mine,' she said. 'Gets me in a dreadful mood every year. I put it off and put it off, but actually, when you do eventually get down to it, it's quite satisfying, isn't it, the feeling that you've achieved something? And it's never quite as bad as you thought it would be once you get into it. But oh! Figures. Sums. Sifting through receipts. Boring boring boring. Anything but that!'

Something had to be done. Decisive action had to be taken. Because if he bit his cheek any harder he'd put a hole right through it to the air. 'Don't mean to be rude, but the longer you stand there talking, the longer it'll take me to finish up here,' he said, aiming for a firm but friendly smile. A scowl was what he managed, with a look of flint around the edges of his mouth. Didn't need a mirror to know that. Just had to see it reflected in her eyes. Hell, in her whole being. Like watching the air go out of a party balloon. Another thing to make him feel proud. If there had been a little old lady wandering by he could have knocked her walking stick away, made a hat trick out of being mean.

'Sorry,' she said. And blushed. As if his cheeks weren't red enough for both of them already. But then, there goes that goddamn laugh again. 'Typical, typical! Insensitive as a sledge hammer, that's me! I'll bring you some coffee and a sandwich, tell the others you'll be a few minutes more.'

'Don't bother,' he said, rising lumpenly from behind the desk and sending papers flying 'I'll come back to it later. Better get on.'

Passing her in the doorway was kind of awkward, having to squeeze between her and the filing cabinet and out to safety, where a man could breathe. Except he could feel her behind him, trotting along in his wake like a pet dog, wagging her tail, still eager to please.

'Is there anything I could do to help you while you're gone?' she asked, as she followed him through the dining room, but his attention was now all with Robyn, who was sitting alone at the big table getting herself outside a plate of pancakes and maple syrup with bacon and eggs. He swallowed hard and practically choked on his own drool.

'Mind me asking where the guests are?' he asked archly through a fit of barely suppressed coughing.

Robyn waved her knife towards the window, shovelling a forkful of food inside her with the other hand. 'Outside saddling up,' she said, and he was driven almost mad as a bear as the syrup oozed down her chin.

'Those damn fool city folk wouldn't know how to fit a bridle if you gave them an instruction book and a year to do it!' he said angrily. 'Do you want them to have an accident while we're out there today? Or hurt one of the horses' mouths with their stupidness?'

'Old Pete's showing them how,' she said, shrugging off his attack with hardly a hiatus between one mouthful of food and the next, pausing only, in fact, to swill it down with a big mug of steaming hot coffee. Sheer grit alone was all that stopped him from ripping it right out of her hand and draining it.

'Got it all nicely taped down then, haven't you,' he said acidly. 'Got everybody running around doing your work while you sit here like the Queen of England, taking your breakfast at your leisure.'

'That's not fair,' said the English cyber-nut, from somewhere behind him, 'Robyn was up bright and early to feed and water and groom the horses. And she taught me how to milk a cow! And Joyce and Bill and the others wanted to help tack up. We all took on board what Old Pete told us last night at the Cowboy Evening, about the history of guest ranches and what they were for originally. We're supposed to be here to help you, not to waste your valuable time.' He felt her at his elbow. 'Here you are,' she said in a softer tone. The damn woman was holding out a cup of coffee and smiling. 'You might as well be drinking this while you're standing there being told off. Honestly, what am I like?' He could have answered that.

'No time,' he said abruptly instead, and swept from the room with an accusatory, 'And don't be late for school, young lady!' flung over his shoulder.

'So now you know what I have to put up with,' said Robyn into the silence which he'd left behind. 'Sound anything like your kind and sensitive Andy the Cowboy?'

'No,' Kate allowed, sipping the coffee he'd refused to take. 'He does sound like a person under an awful lot of pressure though.'

'Ain't we all,' said Robyn tartly. She pushed her empty plate away at last and got up to go. 'Well, like the man said, mustn't be late for school. Did you do the packed lunches yet?'

Seeing the girl retreating from the dirty dishes, Kate said, 'Yes, Your Majesty,' and bobbed a curtsey, which provoked a guilty scowl and a graceless return to help carry.

'Suppose you want me to wash up now?' Robyn grunted resentfully, an anxious eye on the kitchen clock. It was easy to see where she'd learnt her manners.

'No, no, I can manage, thanks,' said Kate, hoping to teach a gentler form of discourse by example. 'And thank you very much for waking me up this morning, Robyn, to give me my ranching lesson. I really enjoyed it. Can we do it again tomorrow?'

'Sure thing!' Her whole face had been transformed with such a little bit of encouragement. It almost made up for having to withstand all Andy's rudeness.

'Fabtastic,' said Kate, and beamed back.

'Thanks for breakfast then, Mata,' said Robyn. 'Gotta go. Got my lunch?'

'Aren't you going to change into your school clothes?' Kate asked, looking at the dirty boots and frayed jeans the girl had worn to do her chores.

'I change when I get to Mrs Ford's, which is where I keep my pony till classes are over,' Robyn informed her. 'Can't ride there in my school clothes. They'd think I'm even weirder than they already do.'

'Well, whoever "they" are, they must be weird if they think you're weird,' said Kate. 'I think you're lovely. Then again, I also like weird. Here's your lunch.'

She was rewarded with a burst of sunshine in the form of a grin. 'Been called a lot of things in my time, Mata, but never lovely. What we got in here?'

'Wait and see. Something to look forward to.'

'Something else that's new,' said Robyn, and she whistled cheerfully out of the door to be replaced by Old Pete singing his way back in.

'So much musical talent here at the Blue Yonder,' said Kate. 'What's put you in such a good mood?'

Old Pete's face cracked open wickedly to reveal more gaps than teeth. 'Rebellion's been mounted,' he sniggered. 'Some of 'em wanted me to take 'em out 'stead of Andy. Say I taught 'em a lot last night and they want to know more. He weren't having that. No way no day. Now they're trying to change his plans. Can't do that. Not allowed. He's got to be in control. Sky might fall in else.' He wheezed a phlegmy laugh. 'Nice to see 'em trying though. Specially that woman with the chest that's fighting to get out of her shirt.'

'Rebelling against what?' asked Kate, craning to see out of the window. Mary Beth had got Andy covered all right. Every way he turned, it seemed, her cleavage got there first. 'I'll just pop out with their lunches,' she said, in a poor simulation of off-handedness. 'And take Andy his breakfast roll.'

'Looks like he's being offered that already,' said Old Pete gleefully. 'Mind you don't get caught in the crossfire!'

Walking towards them outside, Kate could hear Bill making a last-ditch attempt to change his host's mind. '. . . in the spirit of the guest ranch,' he was saying. 'Any kind of activity is a novelty for us, we really don't need to—'

'You've paid for a full day's ride out to Green Lake as part of your package,' Andy said tersely, trying but failing to find a mammary-free vista on which to rest his eyes, 'and that's where we're going. So let's everybody mount up now, please.'

'Oh well, I can see we're not going to win this battle,' Mary Beth smiled, parking herself under his nose. 'Could you give me a hand to get on then, kind sir?'

'Just put your foot in the stirrup and pull yourself up on the horn, ma'am,' he said stiffly.

'Sounds like fun,' she said provocatively, not a woman to take rejection at face value, it seemed.

'Hi there, Kate,' said Nancy, greedily eyeing her basket of goods. 'What have you got there for us in those dinky foil packets?'

'Lunch,' said Kate.

Nancy licked her lips as she selected the largest. 'You make it, or Old Pete?'

'Me.'

'That's my girl,' Nancy grinned, squeezing her chummily with an ample arm around her waist.

'Mind you don't break her in two,' said Louise drily. 'Then who'd feed you?'

'We've been trying to persuade Andy to let us help him today,' said Joyce, in an attempt to enlist Kate's help. 'Instead of being a millstone around his neck, taking up his time.'

'Sounds like a good idea, no?' Kate offered supportively. 'How about it, Andy? What would you be doing today if you weren't having to take them out on a ride?'

'A million things probably, but none of them worth mentioning,' he said, as he swung one long lean muscular leg over Rusty's back, making Mary Beth pop-eyed with admiration.

'He makes it look so easy,' she said breathlessly, after her own third attempt to mount Trigger. 'And so-o-o damned attractive.'

'On account,' Andy concluded, turning a deaf ear to her aside, 'of us going out to Green Lake. Now if you folks are ready, let's go. We got a long way to ride.' Neck-reining Rusty who, unlike his owner, could turn on a sixpence, he trotted briskly out of the yard, followed obediently by all the other horses, despite the protestations of their riders.

'Your lunch!' Kate called after him.

'I'll take it, if I ever get up on this damned horse. Or if I can ever *keep* up with it,' said Mary Beth, straining ineffectually to stop her mount from taking her off for a walk. 'Whoa there, you great prehistoric idiot, whoa!'

Catching hold of the reins, Kate held it steady and, at last remembering some of her riding-school lessons, she offered a hand to give Mary Beth a leg-up into the saddle.

'Okay,' said Mary Beth, all arms and legs and yards of loose rein, with no control at all of Trigger, who was already attempting to catch up with his lost herd in a hurry. 'Gimme the packet, Kate, quick!'

Running along beside her, Kate held up the packed lunch, which was grabbed and somehow pocketed. 'I made him a breakfast sandwich too,' she said breathlessly, striving to keep up, her arm held aloft, but Trigger was easily out-pacing her.

'Throw it!' Mary Beth shouted, half turning in her saddle as she was bounced energetically out of Kate's reach.

'Here goes nothing,' said Kate to the parcel, and lobbed it as far as she could.

'Yee-haa!' said Mary Beth, after she had niftily caught it with the outstretched fingers of one hand. 'May not be much of a rider, but I'm a demon in the outfield!' and she, and Andy's breakfast, were gone.

Returning to the ranch house, Kate found Old Pete cleaning a shotgun at the kitchen table.

'Can make you feel a damn fool without even trying can't he?' he chuckled. 'Want me to ride after him and shoot him down?'

'No thanks,' said Kate. 'I don't think he'd taste very nice, and I'm sure he'd be too tough even if I casseroled him for a week. Honestly. How inflexible can you get? He's got to be a Taurus. Or a Capricorn.'

'That a fact,' said Old Pete, peering down the open barrel of his gun with satisfaction. He snapped it shut. 'Clean as a whistle. That's me on my way, girlie. Leave you to get on with my old job unhindered. Bring you back some nice conies for that stew you no doubt got in mind to make for dinner. Take me one of them packed-up parcels for my lunch too, if you got one ready.'

'Not so fast, partner,' Kate told him, blocking his way to the door. 'What is the full extent of your job exactly?'

'Well now, you'll want to clean and tidy the guest rooms and make their beds that they're too plumb lazy to do their own damn selves, wash and dry that hill of pots over there, feed the chickens if you ain't already done it, catch up with the laundry, sweep and dust, and if you've got time over, I got a couple pairs of socks need darning on the chair over there. See you later.' He tried and failed to dodge past her, and took a step back. 'Wouldn't want to have to shoot my way out of here, so if you'll just step over to one side, nice and gentle—'

'Here's the deal,' said Kate, standing defiantly arms akimbo in his path. 'I'm very happy to take over the cooking, milk cows, groom horses, collect eggs, and *help* with the washing up, but that's as far as I'm prepared to go, spirit of guest ranching or no. I'll even help you do the cleaning and tidying if you ask me nicely. And when we've finished everything to your satisfaction, I'll allow you to go, unhindered, with a nice fried-chicken lunch.'

'Goddamn it,' Old Pete grumbled, but nevertheless leaned his gun against the wall. 'Well, let's do it then if we're going to do it. Ain't got time to stand around here all day, facing off a contrary woman who's got no respect for an armed and dangerous man.'

Since neither Kate nor Old Pete trusted the other to get on with the housework if they were out of each other's sight, they worked together, first tackling the guest bedrooms, which gave Kate an opportunity at least to see the rest of the house.

'What this needs is a bit of TLC, starting with a coat of paint,' she said, surveying the stained walls and ceiling of Joyce and Bill Matheson's upstairs room. 'I mean, I know money's supposed to be tight at the moment, but that wouldn't break the bank would it? And if it's a question of nobody having the time, I could do this whole room in an afternoon.'

'That'd be an afternoon wasted then,' Old Pete said sourly. 'You want to help, get up out on the roof and replace it. Water'll come back in else, all over your nice new decorations. Place is full of holes. Should see us in a rainstorm. Better'n one of them fancy power showers up here then.'

'Does it really need to be completely replaced? Can't it be mended?' asked Kate, for whom a little knowledge often went a long way. 'I had a terrible leak in my flat last year, and it turned out to be just one cracked slate.'

'What do I know – do I look like a roofing expert to you? I ain't been up there on it, and even if I had've, I'd be none the wiser. But that's what Andy reckons, and he practically lives up there on occasion. And have you seen the size of it? It'd cost thousands of dollars. Tens of thousands maybe, and we got plenty ways to spend that kind of dough, if we had it. Vet's bill for a start. Been fobbing him off for months. He don't want to take Andy to court to get it, but he don't want to come out here and do no more work for free either.'

'Ouch,' said Kate. 'That must be a worry, with so much livestock here. I suppose some of them are bound to need medical attention from time to time.'

Old Pete gave the town dweller a pitying look. 'You could say. What we need is more money coming in and less money going out, but that never seems to happen.'

'How are the bookings? Haven't you got a busy season ahead?'

He shook his head. 'When these folk go back home, we got nobody coming for weeks. Animals still got to eat though.'

'But why not?' Kate asked incredulously. 'Surely it's almost the height of the season, and it's beautiful here. It should be an absolute tourist magnet.'

'So's a whole heap of places in the area. But they don't have rain coming through the ceiling, nor an ornery boss like Andy, nor not even a bad cook like me. People go to them places, they go home, they tell all their friends, then their friends go visit. People come to us, they tell their friends, "Stay away! You want a nice dry bed, good home cooking, and a warm, friendly welcome? Go someplace else! Hell'd be better than the old Blue Yonder." '

'Well, I can't mend the roof, but I could teach you to cook better, Old Pete,' Kate offered. 'We could make dinner together tonight, if you like.'

'You gonna teach Andy to be friendly too?' he asked drily. 'Book me in for them lessons. That's something I'd sure want to see.'

'Mm,' said Kate. 'Probably be quicker and easier to teach you how to boil an egg.'

'Damn right. Then when you done that you can teach me how to suck 'em.'

Kate smiled back blithely. 'It's a good job you're talking to somebody who knows the difference between sarcasm and irony,' she said, 'otherwise your witty form of badinage might be quite hurtful.'

'Good job you swallowed that dictionary earlier,' Old Pete batted back, 'otherwise you wouldn't have a single thing to say.'

It was a good two hours later before they found that they had cleaned their way back into the kitchen, where they both gratefully collapsed for a coffee break.

'So how come this place doesn't make a profit?' Kate asked. 'Is Andy bad at business would you say?'

Unexpectedly, Old Pete rose to his defence. 'He tries his damnedest. Most other men would've walked away from it long ago, but he keeps plugging on. Way he sees it, he's caretaking Robyn's inheritance till she's old enough to take over. Only thing is, that inheritance keeps getting smaller. Sold off some land couple of years back to get us out of a hole, and looks like he's going to have to do the same thing again, which is why him and Robyn are at each other's throats right now. This old house eats up money. Barn'll fall down next, just take one good storm – or wait till winter and watch it collapse under the weight of the snow.'

Since he'd got himself on such an unexpectedly good conversational roll, Kate kept quiet, leaning forward to pour more coffee into his mug by way of encouragement.

'Ranching's a risky business, like gambling,' he continued, stirring in three spoons of sugar. 'You buy in steer at a certain price, but you don't know for sure that the market won't have gone down by the time you come to sell 'em. Got caught like that last year, and that's what's put us in this mess. That and the tractor finally giving up the ghost and needing to be replaced, may she rust in peace. Which is what she is doing, in the far pasture. Damn thing's so old we couldn't get the spares no more.' He wheezed a rueful laugh and rubbed his injured arm. 'Ain't the only one.'

'Was that a bad break?' Kate asked.

'No, it was a real good one,' said Old Pete drily. 'This shoulder's better'n a barometer now at forecasting rain.' He heaved himself to his feet and grabbed his gun. 'And what it's telling me now is it's going to be a fine day for hunting conies. Good day to you, girlie.'

'Just one thing before you're on your way – well, two if you count this,' said Kate, handing him his lunch. 'What is a coney exactly, and how do you cook them?'

Old Pete feigned a heart attack. 'What's this we got now? The teacher asking the student what to do?'

'In all humility,' Kate told him, grinning back.

'Well now, a coney's a rabbit, and me, I'd roast 'em on a stick over a campfire till they're black. The advantage of that is that nobody'd want to eat 'em after, 'cept me.' He pocketed a box of cartridges and made for the door. 'But you'll probably want to put 'em in a pot and cook 'em real nice and slow with some vegetables, end up calling it something French.'

'Yes, well, speaking of vegetables,' she said, following him, 'I couldn't help noticing that the larder is bare. Are you going to shoot some onions and carrots too while you're out?'

'Not me,' said Old Pete. 'That'd be my old job that you've took over. You'll want to get yourself over to see Peggy Davies, lives just outside the edge of town on Fraser Road. She shoots the onions and carrots around here.' He heaved himself up on his horse and gave her a salute, eyes twinkling. 'Might shoot you too if she don't like the look of you. Give her my kind regards.'

It wasn't until she had waved him out of sight that Kate realised she had organised everybody's day beautifully except her own, and that now she was quite alone. She looked haplessly round the kitchen, which seemed bigger and emptier than a moment ago, and her eyes alighted on Old Pete's socks. To stay in and darn holes, or to go out and risk being shot by Peggy Davies? Well, no debate there then. Adventure called.

9

Though the decision to visit Peggy was made in an instant, getting there took rather longer. But after several wrong turns and fruitless miles driven, Kate finally found the right edge of the town, and a sign outside a house saying 'We sell veg' told her, if the profusion of plants and polytunnels didn't, that she had at last hit her mark. She was looking forward to chatting to another woman, hoping to make friends and to gather more clues, possibly, about who had played the trick on her to get her over here. So far, though Robyn had denied any involvement, she was still her chief suspect. Maybe Peggy could shed some light on it.

It was a small house with a huge garden – perhaps a couple of acres – and when her knock at the front door went unanswered, Kate obeyed a further notice which instructed the applicant: 'If no answer, come find me'. Weaving her way through neat rows of vegetation, she aimed for the large greenhouse in the distance, hoping to find Peggy there, but instead found her at her feet, and literally tripped over her as she turned a particularly floriferous corner between beds.

'Ooph! Sorry! Are you okay?' Kate asked her, as they untangled their limbs and stood up to survey each other. A fierce-looking fiery woman in her late fifties glared back.

'I was better before I got the bruises,' she declared crossly, frowning at the scattered trays and squashed plants. 'And so were these seedlings.'

'I'm so sorry,' said Kate again. 'Can I help you retrieve them? I'll pay for any damage, of course.'

'English,' said Peggy damningly, of Kate's accent.

'That's right,' Kate smiled, offering her hand. 'Kate Thornton. Come all the way from London to kick you in the dust. Sorry, Peggy. You are Peggy, aren't you? Old Pete sends his regards, from the Blue Yonder. I'm staying there at the moment, and he's sent me to stock up.'

'So you'll be the soap star,' Peggy told her, hands on hips as she looked her over. 'Heard you was trouble, but I didn't think you'd stoop so low as to knock a woman down.'

Kate laughed. 'My fame runs before me, I see. You must have been talking to Andy.'

'Small place like this, everybody knows everything about everybody. You just wait till this story hits the bush telegraph and it gets polished up along the way. Way folks'll tell it is you came over here to steal my plants and hit me over the head with my own shovel. Should hear the fantabulations I heard about you.'

'Oh do tell,' said Kate. 'I love a bit of gossip.'

'That's where you and I differ then,' said Peggy trenchantly, stooping to pick up the fallen seedlings. 'Can't abide gossip and don't go nowhere near it. So what else can I do you for today?'

'Right,' said Kate, her hopes of befriending Peggy fading. 'Well, vegetables, obviously. What does Old Pete usually buy?'

'Potatoes, onions and beans.'

'That's all?'

'That's it.'

'Well I'll take potatoes and onions, of course, but I'd also like some carrots, garlic, shallots if you've got some, courgettes – or zucchini, whatever you call them here. Any chance of celery? And what greens do you have at the moment?'

'Whoa, whoa, this isn't a shop where you just point at any old stuff and I put it in a bag. This here you get fresh out the ground, we got to go pick them. We'll start with the carrots.' Shoving the seedling trays into Kate's hands she stalked off purposefully, adding, 'You can carry those along since you say you're paying for them. Some of them might grow, despite you trying to squash them flat. Hope you like lettuce. You've got seventy-two of them there.'

'I do actually,' said Kate, trotting behind her and trying to keep up with her remarkable energy. 'I've only got a tiny roof terrace with my London flat – more of a balcony really – but I managed to more or less keep myself in salad last summer. And I even grew some potatoes in an old tin drum I salvaged from a skip.'

'Got a green thumb, huh?' said Peggy. 'So you can help me pull your carrots then.'

'Great,' said Kate, and together they worked in companionable silence.

'Is it true what they say about your cooking?' Peggy asked presently.

'I'm not sure,' said Kate, with a smile that anticipated compliments. 'What do they say, and who's been saying it?'

'Robyn rode through this morning, told me it's good enough to eat.'

'Damned with faint praise,' Kate laughed. 'Then yes, it is. Or at least I hope so. I eat it anyway.'

'So you're in charge of the kitchen there now?'

'Not in charge exactly,' Kate demurred. 'Just trying to help out where I can, while I can.'

Peggy regarded her shrewdly. 'And why are you trying to do that?'

Kate shrugged. 'Why not? I've got nothing better to do.'

After considering this, Peggy nodded. 'Got enough carrots here?'

'Heavens, yes,' said Kate, looking at a couple of kilos of the harvested crop. 'I was getting quite carried away.'

'Time to get carried away with the potatoes then,' said Peggy, and strode off to another bed. 'Bring that barrow along with you.'

'Did Robyn tell you how I came to be here?' Kate asked, when she had found Peggy again and had been furnished with a fork.

'Something about being chased out of town back home for stealing a baby,' said Peggy, 'but I don't believe half of what I hear.'

'I'm glad about that,' Kate laughed. 'That's my soap character, not me. No, I met Andy, or rather, somebody pretending to be Andy, on the internet. Whoever it was knew enough about Blue Yonder to be fairly accurate on quite a number of things.'

'That a fact?' said Peggy noncommitally, not pausing in her labours long enough even to look up.

'Yes,' said Kate. 'I'm wondering if maybe it could have been Robyn.'

'And if it was?' said Peggy, a slight edge to her tone.

'Then the mystery would be solved and I'd know what was what.'

'And what would that be?' Peggy asked, standing up at last to pin Kate with her sharp green-eyed gaze.

'That Robyn was trying to match-make, I suppose, however ill advisedly. That she'd like to have a mum.'

'Robyn's a good kid,' said Peggy with a note of warning.

'Oh, she is,' Kate agreed.

'She has a hard enough time of it as it is, what with being different from other girls her age at school. Kids can be awful cruel.'

'Well, I'm sorry to hear that,' said Kate. 'I like her a lot, what I know of her. Even if she did get me up at the crack of dawn today to milk cows and collect eggs.'

Peggy's features relaxed into a fond smile. 'You'll find that Robyn has quite a few moms around here. We all watch out for her. Got a lot of time for that young girl. For all of them over there. Haven't had it easy.'

'No,' said Kate. 'That's what I've been hearing from Old Pete this morning. Big money worries. The roof, the vet, the lack of customers, Robyn's shrinking inheritance.'

'You got that much conversation out of Old Pete?' Peggy asked in surprise.

Kate grinned. 'Oh, yes, he loves me now I've taken over his work in the kitchen and left him free to get outdoors. He's shooting rabbits today for our supper. Hence the carrots and potatoes et cetera for the stew. I'm surprised actually that they don't have their own vegetable garden at Blue Yonder. Not that I'm trying to do you out of business,' she added hastily.

Peggy looked reflective. 'Used to be one there,' she said finally, with what seemed to Kate to be nostalgia or regret. 'Might still find the remains if you look hard enough. Over to the right of the back door, between the house and the barn. Robyn's mother made it, raised beds and all.'

'Isn't that weird?' said Kate, remembering the story of flaky Rainbow, the mother who ran away to join the Indians, abandoning her child. 'I mean, that shows some commitment, doesn't it?'

'What's weird about that?' asked Peggy crossly. 'You got something against commitment?'

'Absolutely not. But Robyn's mother had some issues there, didn't she?'

'Not to my knowledge,' Peggy said, returning to the task in hand.

'But to leave your own baby like that,' said Kate. 'I don't know how she could.'

Peggy put down her fork to eyeball Kate fiercely. 'You think she planned it that way?' she demanded.

'Didn't she?' Kate faltered. 'Why, was it a spur of the moment thing then?'

Peggy shook her head, but in dismissal rather than disagreement. 'Got enough potatoes here?' she said.

'Yes, yes, thank you,' Kate said contritely.

'Garlic next then,' said Peggy stiffly, and stalked away. Obviously, thought Kate, she'd just put her foot right in it, but she had no idea why. Perhaps Peggy had been very fond of Rainbow? Maybe she was even related to her in some way. Could she be her mother? That would certainly explain her rising to the woman's defence.

'I know you don't like gossip, Peggy,' she said, when they were reunited and pulling up garlic bulbs. 'And I wouldn't want you to think I'm being nosy, but—'

'—but what else could I think if you were?' said Peggy, again pinning her uncomfortably with the directness of her gaze.

'Right,' said Kate. 'Point taken. I'll shut up now shall I?'

Peggy shrugged. 'Your choice. I'm happy to talk about gardening.' Which is exactly what they did until they were loading stuff into Kate's car and it was time for her to go.

'You going to plant these lettuce seedlings when you get back to Blue Yonder?' Peggy asked her.

'Why not?' said Kate. 'It'll save them a few pennies. And speaking of which, how much do I owe you for all this?'

'You ever heard of the barter system? It's how things run out here mostly. I'll come over tomorrow and get enough milk and eggs to cover this.' She paused, regarding Kate thoughtfully as if sizing her up. 'I could let you have some other stuff to plant too, in exchange for a nice piece of beef. If you've a mind to reclaim that old vegetable patch that is. You say you want to help them.'

'What a great idea,' said Kate with enthusiasm. 'Self sufficiency. And the guests would love it, eating vegetables that they've just seen pulled from the ground.' In her mind's eye she pictured a host of perfect plants growing dutifully in neat rows, could see herself, in a few short months, harvesting them into a picturesque rustic basket and . . . 'Oh!' she said suddenly, the bubble bursting. 'But what about after I've gone – who'll tend it then? I can't see Old Pete doing it, and I don't want to leave Robyn with even more chores than she already has.'

'Thinking of going somewhere? You only just got here,' said Peggy, and with a dryness akin to aridity, added, 'You got commitment issues?'

Stopped in her tracks, Kate grinned. 'Touché.'

Peggy nodded acknowledgement of a point well made, but just in case Kate hadn't learned her lesson said, 'You see what I mean now about gossip and idle chatter? If you don't watch out, it's got a habit of creeping back behind you and nipping you in the ass.'

'I hope you're right,' Kate laughed. 'There's a few English tabloid journalists I can think of who I'd like to see that happen to, after the grief they've been giving me lately. But anyway, no, I don't have commitment issues, it's just that at some point I'll have to—'

'Better get back and start digging then,' said Peggy. 'I'll be over in the morning with the plants,' and so saying, she disappeared from view behind a row of sweetcorn, signalling unequivocally that their present business was at an end.

10

Seeing the bush moving when she rode into the yard from
school, Robyn thought at first that her English teacher had
beaten her to it. For hadn't she been reading them this exact
same thing in class today, as foretold to Macbeth by the
witches? But on closer examination she found that it was
nothing as dramatic as Birnam Wood taking a walk, just Kate
– although a different kind of Kate from the one she'd said
goodbye to at breakfast. This one had weeds in her hair, mud
on her cheeks, and was staggering on her ruined snakeskin
cowboy boots under the weight of a shrub she'd just yanked
out of the earth.

'Mind if I ask you why you're rearranging our yard?' she
said, as she got down from her pony and walked over for a
closer look.

'I'm making a vegetable garden,' Kate told her, huffing and
puffing and dumping the bush on a pile of previously dumped
stuff. 'Or rather, reclaiming the old one that —' She stopped
herself. It would be tactless to bring up the subject of Robyn's
missing mother, and possibly hurtful. '— that had got all
overgrown,' she amended. 'Peggy Davies is going to give us
some plants in exchange for some of our meat, and then we'll
be almost completely self sufficient for food, except for a few
groceries, like flour and sugar.'

Robyn suppressed a smile of pleasure. 'We.' Kate had said
'we', and 'us'. That was good. That meant she was reckoning
on staying put, and not running off back to London. 'Give you

a hand with that after I've done my chores, if you like,' she said, leading her pony over to the corral. 'And then I'll tell you what I've been thinking about how to solve your mystery.'

'You've worked out a way?' Kate called after her, impressed. 'What is it?'

'Wait and see,' Robyn called back, and echoing Kate's earlier words that morning, shouted, 'something to look forward to!'

Watching her go, Kate felt a warm glow of affection. She hadn't spent this amount of time with a thirteen year old since she was thirteen herself, and she'd forgotten how much fun it could be. And of all the locals she'd met here, Robyn was the only one who was easy to get on with and who seemed actively to enjoy her company. She'd been glad to learn from Peggy that there were women in the area who were keeping an eye out for her. With only Old Pete and Andy as role models, she wouldn't have rated her chances of growing up into a well-rounded human being otherwise.

Of course Kate had always wanted kids of her own, and ever since she'd hit thirty – between one and seven years ago, depending on whether you believed her agent's website or her own birth certificate – this desire had grown both stronger and more thwarted. She'd just never seemed to have the knack of attracting (or, if she was honest, being attracted to) a man who was good father material. For some reason or another she always ended up choosing the tricky ones. Which was why, despite what she'd said to Minnie McAlpine to the contrary, she had been so excited at meeting Andy the Cowboy online. Not only was he funny and empathetic and a good talker and listener, he also had proven parenting skills. She should have known it had been too good to be true.

She stretched her aching back. She'd done some serious hard physical graft today, and looking at the ground she'd cleared, she felt much more satisfied and virtuous than she did after she'd been to the gym. In fact, thinking about it, working her muscles on gym machines now seemed rather decadent by comparison, paying to exercise and producing nothing, as opposed to working for free and gaining food. There was definitely something to be said for this living-in-the-country lark.

By the time Robyn rejoined her, she was cleaning her tools and packing up for the day, the raised beds now revealed in all their bare and dug-over glory.

'What do you think?' she asked Robyn, wanting praise.

'I think something's wrong with Milker One and Milker Two,' Robyn replied, looking worried. 'They're both empty.'

'But the fridge is full,' Kate smiled, taking a bow.

'You milked them? Thanks a lot, Mata.'

'Well, you were so late coming home, I thought you'd never get through all your chores and your homework before it was time for bed.'

'Had softball practice,' Robyn lied, who had in fact been detained at Mr Briggs' pleasure for fighting in the schoolyard the week before.

'So tell me your devilish plan for finding the imposter,' Kate said, as Robyn helped her put the gardening tools away. 'Did you add anybody to our list of suspects?'

'Well now, that's the thing. I've been thinking about that list and who should be on it, and at first I thought it had to be somebody who could get to our computer, then I realised it didn't. They could have used any computer at all, just said they lived here and used Andy's name.'

Kate thought about this. 'You're right, you know,' she agreed. 'I'd been assuming that it had to have been done from here too, which would have narrowed down the field somewhat, but if it could have been done from anywhere, heavens, where do we start?'

'With this,' said Robyn, fishing a tattered and graffittied

exercise book from her school bag. 'This here's a list I made. See, I put me and Andy and Old Pete at the top, guilty until proven innocent like we said this morning, and after us, everybody who knows us.'

Kate took it. 'Who are Bobby and Timmy?' she asked, reading the first entry of many.

'Friends of mine from school who visit here sometimes.'

'Likewise Steve and Mike?'

'They were a couple of students who worked here for a few weeks.'

'And who are "Guests"?'

'Anybody who's stayed here. I need to check the register.'

'But that could be hundreds of people!'

Robyn laughed hollowly. 'If we'd had hundreds staying here, we'd be able to pay the vet's bill and Andy wouldn't be threatening to sell off more land. Anyway, we only have to count in people who've stayed here before you started playing with Andy the Cowboy. How long ago is that?'

'Maybe about six weeks, I can't quite remember exactly when I met him,' Kate said, then seeing the next name on the list she exclaimed, 'Peggy Davies!'

'I put her down when I was still thinking it had to have been done from here, from our office. All these people,' Robyn told her, indicating the bulk of the page, 'have been inside the ranch house and could've used our computer.'

'So this last entry,' said Kate, reading, 'Everybody in town' with lowering spirits, 'was after you realised it could have been done from anywhere?'

Robyn nodded. 'Could have done it from anywhere, and who knows us.'

'*Everybody* in town knows you?' Kate queried.

'It's a small town,' Robyn shrugged.

'Right,' said Kate. 'But not that small. How on earth do we narrow it down?'

Robyn tapped the side of her nose, looking smug. 'Haha!' she said. 'That's where my devilish plan comes in.'

Kate smiled expectantly. 'Which is?'

'We find out who on this list knows how to play back-gammon. Not everybody does. Timmy and Bobby said they'd never even heard of it.'

'They could have lied,' Kate suggested. 'Not that I suspect Timmy and Bobby of having done that, of course,' she added hastily, seeing Robyn's brows darken at the thought. 'But – surely anybody could say they don't know how to play, and how would we ever prove otherwise?'

Robyn frowned in concentration, chewing the inside of her cheek. 'We say you'll teach them!' she exclaimed suddenly. 'Then we'll know, depending on how quick they pick it up. Think about it, Mata! Nobody likes losing, and they wouldn't be able to help themselves from making good moves if they knew how.'

'Interesting psychological insight,' Kate said, trying to sound upbeat and impressed. This was almost certainly true of the thirteen-year-old tomboy standing before her, but she couldn't see it working as a universal rule. Then again, since the tomboy in question was still her number one suspect . . . 'Well,' she concluded as they were walking back towards the ranch house, 'that's an interesting plan, let's give it a go. Do you have a backgammon set? It'd be a bit tricky having to play everybody on the computer.'

'There's one in the guest lounge, in the games cupboard,' Robyn said, skipping ahead. 'I'll go get it.'

'And since you're at the top of the list,' Kate called after her, 'do you want to be the first to road-test your plan?'

'You betcha!' she cried.

Once again on entering the kitchen Robyn's tastes buds were awakened by the delicious smells of cooking, which added to her mounting sense of excitement. There was no getting away from it, she thought, life had improved a hundredfold since Mata Hari had come to stay. Even Old Pete looked as if he was sober as she flashed past him, which by this time of day was nothing short of a miracle. And hadn't she seen that at last he'd been mending the socks that had been shifted from the dresser to the chair to the shelf to the dresser for almost a year? Unheard of. Dashing through to the guest lounge she flung herself at the games cupboard and riffled through boxes until she found what she was after. How great was this? To be happy to come home to an uncritical adult who valued her ideas, to know she was going to have a tasty dinner, *and* to play a game instead of reading the damned encyclopaedia with Andy . . . Could things get any more perfect?

Yes, she answered herself, her face falling at the thought, the spring going out of her step. Andy could have a personality transplant and decide to like Mata too.

Yeah.

Right.

Like that was going to happen this side of hell freezing over.

II

If Robyn's gloomy prediction was true then it is distinctly possible that a chill breeze could be felt in the underworld that day, for, having enjoyed his breakfast sandwich like a starving man, and relished his fried-chicken lunch, Andy was feeling much more kindly disposed towards Kate on his way home than he had been on his way out. All in all, he thought, as he led his weary party back towards Blue Yonder, it had not been as bad a day as he'd been fearing. To his surprise, Old Pete's tuition had paid off, and the guests had all managed to take their horses' tack off by themselves when they'd stopped for lunch, leaving him with some time to relax for a change – or at least, to relax as much as he could with the woman with the threatening bazoomas getting in his face every which way he looked.

It wasn't that he was made of stone. Over the years he'd had several 'understandings' with women like Mary Beth Walk-uski. Women who, whether recently divorced like her, or even settled in their marriages, didn't want the usual hearts and flowers that a lot of females insisted on, weren't hankering after a relationship and commitment. They just wanted a no-strings affair, which suited him real fine. But he had one rule that was unbreakable: he never ever conducted these affairs where Robyn could see them. Which meant never fouling his own nest, which meant never rolling in the clover with the paying guests, however much they might make it plain they'd like him to.

But some time during the lunch break two of the women – Joyce and Louise, he thought they were called – had managed to calm down the behaviour of the rampant one, taking her aside and speaking to her in low murmurs, so that by the afternoon she had given up on getting his attention, and left him free to enjoy the ride. It wasn't all they'd talked about while they were eating either. They'd been full of praise for the cyber-nut's cooking skills, and quite rightly in his grudging estimation. The chicken was so crunchy on the outside and so moist on the inside, with a slight kick of chilli and a fragrance of lemons and something none of them could quite put their finger on, that he could almost have eaten the bones when he'd finished tearing off the meat.

But what was more interesting to him was their generous assessment of her. They seemed to take her motives at face value, seemed to believe that she was just a genuinely nice person who liked to help out, and that's why she'd flown to his aid.

This was a way of looking at things that hadn't even occurred to him, and he kept turning it over in his mind on the long trek home. It challenged his perceptions of the world as he thought he knew it. In his experience, women like that, women who were eager to please him, women who brought him gifts, unasked – like last year, the fruit pies that Eileen Townsend had taken to leaving on the porch daily, until he'd been cold enough and rude enough for her to get a grip on herself – those women were after one thing and one thing alone, and that involved wedding bells and apron strings and expectations that he just could not, would not, ever in this lifetime, meet. He was a loner, and that was the long and the short of it. Self reliant. People came and people went, but he was his one true constant.

But this cyber-nut . . . He should call her Mata really, or what was her real name – Kate? What if they were right? What if she was an honest-to-goodness girl-scout type, not after anything but her reward in heaven, motivated by nothing other than neighbourliness? There were women like that out there – God knows, Robyn and he wouldn't have survived as well as they had all these years without them. It's just that the ones who'd genuinely helped out before were older, like Peggy Davies and Carolina Ford, or happily married with six kids like Jane Judge the preacher's wife – sensible, capable women with no hidden agenda to rope him and break him and control him.

His mind came back to that moment in his office when he'd met her eyes and been astonished to find himself falling right in. Most people had a veil there somehow, a barrier just beneath the surface of the cornea. They reserved judgement, and didn't let you in until you'd proved yourself. He knew he did. It was self protection, and for a good cause. You didn't go into a pack of coyotes with your arms held out and a friendly smile, and if you did, you were no better than a fool and got what you deserved. You got torn to pieces.

When he'd seen how undefended she was, how eager to please, despite his rebuffs, he had become one of those coyotes though, hadn't he? He'd felt only contempt for a person who would lower herself so much to try to please him, when he'd made it plain that there *was* no pleasing him other than by disappearing off the face of the planet toot sweet. That type of person brought out the worst in him: the slavish type, the Eileen Townsend pie-maker type, the cheek-turning hit-me-again type, which was how he'd automatically seen Kate.

But what if these guests here were right about her, and Kate was not a masochistic martyr but a latter-day saint? It was an uncomfortable thought and, when mixed with his embarrassment about her overhearing his less than flattering words about her last night, it made him shift in his saddle uneasily, to concede that maybe he should scratch out his earlier judgement of her and start again afresh. For couldn't it be that she was like one of those original guest ranchers Old Pete had been telling them about last night, people who wanted to help, just for the fun and the outdoor exercise and the good feeling it gave them?

Like these people here, he forced himself grimly to acknowledge, Joyce and Louise and Bill and the rest, who'd tried so hard to persuade him this morning that they didn't need to ride for the day to get that cowboy feeling, would have been just as happy – happier, if you believed them – to nail shingles, chop wood, hell, to jump through any hoop he pointed to, at double-quick time and gladly. The suggestion made him feel mean and foolish, trapped in his own thick hide like a crab, peering out sullenly from underneath his armoured carapace, ready to claw friend or foe alike if they came too close.

He became self conscious, felt their eyes on his back as he led them into the Blue Yonder yard, judging him as harshly as he'd judged them . . . Damn, he was doing it again, getting into that introspective, navel-gazing black pit of bad feeling about himself, the place he'd had to learn so painfully to climb out of, back when . . . back when . . . back . . .

What in hell?

He pulled Rusty up short to gaze in amazement at the vegetable garden come back to life. Or at least, not to burgeoning life, but to its original virgin state when She-who-still-could-not-be-thought-of-by-name without him wanting to howl in anguish and rend his clothes and tear at his own skin, had first created it.

Who had done this thing? Who had plunged him back to a time of innocent beginnings, of laughter and good humour and great plans for a great future?

It had to be the . . . He stopped himself before he automatically said 'cyber-nut' in his mind. It had to be Kate. Helping out again where she hadn't been asked.

A seething mess of hot anger against her and gut-twisting, unbidden, unwanted memories made him clench his teeth lest bile spew right up and out of his mouth, and turning Rusty roughly again, he turned his back on that nightmare vision of hope thwarted, of innocence defiled.

'Tack off, horses brushed down and watered,' he growled at his party as he got down to do the same thing himself, but even as he worked he kept feeling his eyes sliding in quick glances to the neat patches of dug-over earth between back door and barn. Why had she done this? Why would she, literally, rake over old ground that was dead and that he had wanted buried so deep it got choked in weeds?

A pale, quiet answer struggled against the darkness of his thoughts, trying to be seen. *Because she wanted to help out?* it suggested. *Like you were thinking just now about her only wanting to be helpful, not playing any kind of game?* He let the thought float around in his mind to calm himself as he let Rusty and the other horses into the corral, barely acknowledging the guests as they thanked him for the day and started to make their way back inside.

Hadn't he just been criticising himself for a judgement made too harshly and too soon? Sure, he could go in there, guns blazing, shoot her down for her meddlesome ways, but wouldn't he look three hundred kinds of idiot again when she turned her hurt gaze his way and said – what? What could she say to save herself from this fury he felt towards her at this moment, this murderous rage that made him want to crush the breath right out of her, to grind her underfoot?

'I hope you don't mind, but Peggy Davies offered to give us some vegetable seedlings so we could get Blue Yonder being a bit more self sufficient,' was what she said nervously the second his foot was through the back door. She was sitting at the kitchen table with Robyn and Old Pete. 'So I dug over the old vegetable plot she told me I'd find. I know, I know,' she continued hastily, holding up a hand against whatever he might say, 'who'll look after it when I've gone? I've asked myself that too. I don't want to add to anybody's work here, you've all got more than enough to do already, I can see that. But then I thought, well, if you can't manage to keep it up afterwards, then don't. At least you'll have the vegetables I'm planting tomorrow, and that's better than nothing, isn't it, getting some food for free? And, you know – guilty secret, shock horror! – I've really enjoyed myself today, getting mucky and in a sweat. So satisfying to bring order to chaos, barren to fertile! So I hope you'll forgive me.' She got up and went to the dresser, pouring out a glass of bourbon and handing it to him with a quick hopeful look before taking refuge again at the table.

The smell of something stewing on the stove was having an oddly calming effect on him, passing straight through his defences and entering a place far beneath his skin, wrapping itself around a part of him like a thick wool comforter, giving him a feeling like when he was a boy in his mother's kitchen, a feeling he'd forgotten and hadn't even noticed that he'd missed. Everything orderly, everything cosy, everything safe and secure. Cared for, is how he felt. He wrestled with his earlier murderous thoughts as he tipped his head back to drink, and coming back down out of the glass, managed to twist his lips into a thin semblance of a smile while he gazed steadfastly past her shoulder.

'Good thought,' he forced himself to say, and turning from the three pairs of eyes which shamed him with their nervous look at how he was going to take this, he spent a long time washing his hands at the sink to give himself a piece of breathing space. He could almost hear them let their breath out in a collective sigh of relief, could feel almost palpably the lightening and brightening of the air behind him. What a bunch of fun he was, who could terrify and threaten three good people just by coming home. He plunged his head under the tap, drowning out the possibility of having any more of his senses uncomfortably awakened, and scrubbed at his face, hoping that they would seal up the vacuum he'd created, carry on where they'd left off before he'd arrived to spoil things, start talking amongst themselves again, so he felt safe enough to turn back around.

When he came back up for air and was towelling himself dry he was gratified to hear that was exactly what they'd done. 'Three-one, you are dead meat, Mata!' Robyn was crowing, followed by the sound of counters being thumped down on a board, and a rattling of dice in a cup. Did this mean what he thought it did? Slowly he turned round, the towel held to his face so he could peek over the top of it. He let the towel drop.

'Playing backgammon,' he said in a loaded voice.

'Yeah, and I'm mashing her to a pulp,' said Robyn, her attention riveted to the board.

Here then was proof positive that it had been Robyn messing about on the computer, getting this woman here. Andy didn't know whether to laugh or cry or bellow with rage. It hurt him that she wanted a mother so badly that she would come up with this inventive, dangerous ploy to get him fixed up against his will. Hadn't he made it more than plain over the years that this was the one and only thing that she just couldn't ask of him? But he also found it disturbing that she had so strenuously denied it. Robyn wasn't an easy kid, but she had never bare-faced lied before, that much he'd been able to teach her at least. And now she had, on several occasions.

He took another slug of bourbon to give himself some time. Hell, he was still feeling too frayed around the edges with the vegetable-patch thing to deal with this. He knew he'd handle it badly if he tried now, go off into a rant, say mean things in anger he'd later regret maybe. And he could do without the audience of Old Pete, not to mention Robyn's conspiring accomplice who was sitting there like butter wouldn't melt in her goddam mouth. He'd deal with this later, when he had Robyn on his own.

'Going to the office,' he said, swiftly leaving the room.

'Dinner will only be ten minutes,' Kate called after him, 'It's the Mathesons' last evening, so we thought we'd all—' but she was speaking to a closed door. 'Eat together,' she finished lamely.

'Double six! Mata, you are so dead and you are so buried,' Robyn crooned beside her, oblivious to everything but winning the game.

It came as no great surprise – at least not to Kate – that Andy elected not to eat in the guest dining room that night, and that furthermore, having ascertained that Robyn had not yet done her homework, that he didn't allow her to either. Old Pete joined them for a while, regaling them with more stories of his cowboy heyday, but having been out hunting for the best part of the day, he stretched and yawned and announced his early retirement as soon as he had eaten.

In the kitchen, where she was making coffee, Kate heard raised voices from the office, and slammed doors, indicating yet another explosion between father and daughter. Don't get involved, she counselled herself, but the thought of Robyn sulking alone in her bedroom, when she could have been enjoying some company, took the shine off the rest of the evening for her. Not that it was without entertainment, for Mary Beth had a new theory she was eager to share.

'He's got to be gay,' she said, as Bill doled out digestifs.

'Because I chose Armagnac over brandy?' Bill protested.

'Not you, idiot,' said Mary Beth, clearing up that point succinctly. She jerked her head towards the staff quarters.

'Him. Andy. I've never known a man be less interested in breasts.'

Looks were exchanged amongst the women of her party, Louise's eyes rolling practically right into the back of her head, and small talk was taken up with great enthusiasm amongst them. But Mary Beth was unwilling to let this conversation die.

'Don't you think so, Kate?' she asked. 'Don't you think he's got to be a shirt-lifter? Wouldn't that explain a few things?'

Nancy huffed and puffed beside her in disapprobation. 'Enough with the homophobic terminology,' she warned. 'Some of your best friends are blouse-lifters if you've forgotten.'

'Yeah, yeah, you know what I mean,' said Mary Beth, who was no slave to political correctness. She turned back to Kate. 'You should have seen him with me today, Kate. Didn't know where to put his eyes. Well, he did. Anywhere but near what I was offering him on a plate, frankly.'

'You fancy him then, do you?' Kate asked lightly. She didn't know quite how she felt about that.

'Hell, I fancy anything in trousers at the moment – no, Nancy, not you, you can relax,' she said. 'I'm a freshly divorced woman! I need to celebrate that as soon as possible! I was hoping I might do it tonight, but—'

'But he wasn't having any,' said Louise with an air of finality. 'So that's that.'

'Are they expecting more guests tomorrow, after we've gone?' Joyce asked Kate, trying to introduce another topic into the conversation.

'Apparently not.'

'Wow!' said Mary Beth. 'So you'll be left here all alone with him?'

'With Robyn and Old Pete too,' Kate smiled. 'Yes. It'll feel rather strange without you all to keep me company.'

'The best of luck,' said Louise.

'Last you told me, you were leaving,' Joyce reminded her. 'Changed your mind now and going to stay?'

'I think I'll stay on for a while longer,' said Kate, who was looking forward to planting the vegetables the next day. 'There's nothing to rush back home for at the moment, except more abuse from *Paradise Street* fans, and my agent knows where to find me, when – I'm hoping not "if" – things change for the better, work-wise.'

'In that case we'll tell all our foodie friends to come visit,' said Bill. 'Drum up a bit of custom for your cooking.'

'And come stay with us in Vancouver before you do fly off again to England,' Nancy offered with enthusiasm. 'Our kitchen is your kitchen, isn't that right, Louise?'

'It so is,' said Louise. 'We could both cook together, Kate. That way, maybe we could keep up with Nancy's appetite.'

Mary Beth, whose appetite was more for sex than food, was bored with where this conversation had gone and, refilling her glass, sat down beside Kate and said, 'Tell me more about what these guys told me, about how you came to meet him on the net.'

'I met "Andy the Cowboy", whoever that was,' Kate corrected her. 'Not the Andy that you've met.'

'So, dish,' Mary Beth commanded salaciously, settling back for a bit of dirty talk. 'What did the two of you used to chat about online?'

Kate smiled an apology. 'Nothing to get excited about, I'm afraid. Just ordinary stuff. My life, his life, everyday ups and downs. He was very supportive and understanding. I came to feel close to him, as if he was a really true and special friend. A trusted confidant.' Her eyes took on a wistful look. 'Actually, I miss him,' she confessed.

Since everybody had put in several hours of hard physical labour one way or another (and because Mary Beth finally acknowledged that she was going to get no revelations at all of an intimate nature) the party soon broke up in a rash of weary yawns and rueful stretches.

It seemed to Kate that barely had she snuggled down under the covers of her bed and closed her eyes than she heard Robyn announce bitterly at close quarters, 'Well, that master plan sure backfired. Now he thinks you and me are in a plot together!'

It was five thirty a.m. Another day had dawned in Blue Yonder.

12

Bristling with righteous indignation as she was after speaking to Robyn, Kate found it hard to muster the smiles and the small talk required during breakfast by the departing guests. All she could think about, as she fried bacon and scrambled eggs, was what she would say to Andy when she finally managed to get him on his own for the dressing-down he so richly deserved.

How dare he accuse her of plotting with his daughter on the internet to engineer all this? And for heavens' sake, why would she – what was in it for her? Did he really think that he was so devastatingly attractive – or that she was so desperate? – that she would cross the Atlantic just for the privilege of working in his kitchen while he (surprise surprise) hid in his office, twiddling his thumbs, no doubt, while he waited to be fed?

Well, he could forget that, she thought viciously, as she banged pans down with unnecessary vigour. If he was too much of a coward to come and talk to her directly, then he could starve as far as she was concerned. Who the hell did he think he was? Good grief, she knew famous leading actors with egos smaller than his!

By the time she had served and cleared breakfast, seen Robyn off to school with her packed lunch, helped ferry luggage to cars, checked rooms for things forgotten and dashed back outside with books and toothbrushes, had Nancy's card pressed into her hand with a reminder to visit, and waved her new friends out of sight, she had wound herself up for a battle royal, but still Andy hadn't dared to show his face. Well, if Mohammed wouldn't come to the mountain, then the mountain would jolly well thunder over to Mohammed and drop itself on his worthless head, she decided, and she stormed back to the ranch house in high dudgeon. But just as she opened the back door to enter, Andy came barrelling out. Even with her dander up and reeling, she couldn't help noticing that he was dressed in rather smarter clothes than he habitually wore for work around the ranch, and looked none the worse for it.

'Beg pardon,' he said perfunctorily, without bothering to check his stride.

'I'd like a word with you actually,' Kate called after him through gritted teeth.

That made him stop. He turned round slowly, crinkling his eyes against the morning sun, and gave a curt nod. 'I'd like one with you too,' he said.

'Right,' said Kate. 'Well to begin with, I'd just like you to know—'

'Be back with you directly,' he said, disappearing off into the barn.

Having wrought herself up to fever pitch, Kate gave an impatient huff. If he expected her to wait there obediently for him he had another think coming. He could come and find *her* this time.

Going into the kitchen, she found Old Pete struggling through with a pile of sheets and towels for washing.

'This here's for you. I've done my share,' he said, dumping his load on the floor to grab his fishing rod for a quick exit.

Kate moved to block his egress, hands on hips. 'I shall be too busy with the garden today, and I'm just about to have a talk with Andy when he deigns to come in from the barn, so I'm afraid the pleasure of doing the laundry is all yours,' she said firmly, but the effect was ruined by Andy entering behind her, knocking her out of the way with the door.

'Beg pardon,' he said, for the second time in minutes.

'For heavens' sake!' Kate exclaimed crossly, rubbing her bruised arm, as Old Pete took advantage of the hiatus to slip outside with a cheery wave.

'Hurt yourself?' asked Andy brusquely.

'No, I didn't hurt myself, you hurt me,' she complained, without a shred of her customary graciousness.

'Stand in front of doors, that's going to happen,' he shrugged.

Kate pursed her lips, turning away from him to the stove. 'Silly me for expecting sympathy,' she said acidly. 'Coffee?'

'No thanks, let's get this over with, I've got work to do. What was it you wanted to say to me?'

Kate was so angry she felt her nostrils flare (one of the down-sides of being an actor was always watching yourself from the outside, making notes for future reference, even in tense moments such as this). 'We can hardly have a civilised chat with you standing there tapping your foot impatiently,' she said. 'Can't we at least sit down?'

He nodded over towards the chairs. 'Don't let me stop you.'

Clearly he wasn't going to join her if she did sit, and already being at a height disadvantage, she decided against lowering herself further. She stood her ground and folded her arms, glaring at him pugnaciously. 'Well if you're so keen to get it over with why don't you start,' she challenged him.

'Okay.' Now that she'd invited him to have his say, Andy didn't know quite how to begin. He had done a lot of thinking since he had confronted Robyn the night before, and reluctantly had been forced to change his position where Kate was concerned. If Robyn had gone to the bad, which she gave every indication of having done recently what with the truanting, using his credit card without permission, and now all these lying denials about what she'd been up to on the computer, then it was nobody's fault but his own. It had been tempting to blame an outsider instead but, thinking it over in the cool light of day, he was now fairly certain it was unlikely that Kate had conspired with the kid to come here. That theory had stood pretty well when he'd written her off as a cyber-nut, but having listened to the other guests talking about her he was inclined to agree that she had been motivated by nothing more than a desire to help, and the need to leave England for a while. He had followed Robyn's example and looked Kate up on the internet, and everything she had told him – however unlikely – appeared to be true. According to the web she had what appeared to him to be a successful career as an actress over in London, which she would hardly want to abandon to come out here to mess with him. Somehow he had to convey an acceptance of this without making himself sound as if he'd been behaving like an hysterical fool.

'I had been thinking, particularly since I saw the two of you playing backgammon together last night,' he began, wishing now that he had accepted her offer of coffee, if only to give himself something to hide behind, 'that you'd had something to do with this internet trickery yourself, but on further consideration I realise I owe you an apology in that regard. I'd also like to thank you for all your help around the place, particularly in the kitchen. I think maybe I haven't sounded too grateful about that, so I'd like to set it right. You've worked hard and served us up some good food, and I appreciate your time and trouble.'

Having been more than ready for verbal fisticuffs, Kate was astonished and completely disarmed, and her frown melted at once into a warm smile, the aggressive posture of her fighting stance slipping into something much more girly, one leg relaxing enough to curl around the other. 'You're more than welcome,' she assured him. 'I can't tell you what a relief that is to hear. I was worried that you just thought I was an interfering old bat.'

'I apologise if I gave you that impression.'

'That's quite all right,' she conceded generously. 'I know you've got a lot on your mind at the moment, what with the vet's bill and the roof et cetera, and not having enough cash. It must be a terrible worry.'

She could see at once that she had put a foot wrong by the darkening of his eyes and the clenching of his cheek muscles, but she had no idea what in her words had upset him. Damaged pride perhaps? Did he think she was being critical of his competence? 'I know what it's like running a business,' she continued, hoping to regain lost ground. 'Being freelance, as I am, is much the same thing. Always seems to be feast or famine doesn't it, and by the time you actually get some money coming in, it's already been spent.'

He nodded curtly, anxious, it appeared, to let this subject go. 'What was it you wanted to talk to me about?' he asked, casting an anxious glance at the wall clock.

'Perhaps it isn't relevant now,' she said. 'Robyn told me this morning that you suspected us of concocting this whole "Andy the Cowboy" thing together, and I wanted you to know that wasn't the case. But evidently you've since worked that out for yourself.'

'I have. Well, if that's all,' he said, donning his hat and edging towards the door.

'How?' she asked. 'Just as a matter of interest.'

He stopped in his tracks and did one of his slow turns to give himself a little more thinking time, and boy did he need it. How to tell her in a tactful way that he'd decided she wasn't an internet weirdo after all? 'Realised it's all down to Robyn,' he said finally. 'She's been running wild lately. Not going into school – as you know.' Their eyes met and they both gave an embarrassed laugh, acknowledging the misunderstandings of their first meeting. 'And now lying about all this web stuff. It's not like her. Probably her age, I guess.'

'Actually, Andy, I really don't believe she is lying about the internet,' Kate said.

'Good of you to say so, but the evidence all points her way.'

'That's what I thought originally, but playing backgammon with her yesterday persuaded me otherwise.'

Andy frowned quizzically. 'How so?'

'Because the person I played on the net who called themselves by your name was much more sporting than Robyn's competitive spirit would ever allow her to be. You heard her yesterday, yelling in triumph when she had a good throw, crowing with delight when I had a bad one. My internet opponent was always much more modest and more encouraging,' she told him. 'The style of play was completely different too. Robyn takes pieces whenever she can as soon as she can. He – if it was a he – played more strategically.'

'Maybe she's got more strategy than you give her credit for,' he suggested. 'Couldn't she have changed her playing style last night to throw you off her scent?' But even as he was saying it, Kate could see he had difficulty believing it.

'Do you really think she's capable of being that sophisticated and devious? Robyn's reactions seem to me to be so knee-jerk and heartfelt. What you see is what you get with her, isn't it?'

'Used to be,' Andy said regretfully. 'These days, I don't know. She's changing. Growing up fast.'

Kate shook her head. 'Not that fast and not that grown up. This "Andy" had a much more mature feel to him, as if he'd lived a life and had a wealth of experience to draw on. His advice was always dependably wise and considered, and he had a very laid-back, dry sense of humour. No, I've been thinking about it a lot. It was tempting to suspect Robyn because, frankly, who else could it be?'

Andy stared hard at her. 'It wasn't me, if that's what you're coming around to,' he said.

'No,' she acknowledged, marvelling that he could have thought for one moment that she had just described any qualities that he had ever displayed. 'And neither was it Old Pete.'

'So where does that leave you?' he asked.

'Nowhere,' she said, throwing her hands up in frustration. 'Up the Swanee. Completely clueless. It could have been anybody who knows all of you and the Blue Yonder.' She smiled. 'Robyn's suggestion is that I play the whole town at backgammon to discover the culprit through a process of elimination. But as for motive, why would anybody want to pretend to be you? That's what I can't work out.'

Neither could Andy. 'Beats me,' he said finally.

'Me too,' said Kate, and couldn't resist adding jokingly, 'At last, some common ground between us!' which Andy acknowledged with a rueful grin. Well, thought Kate, this was an improvement in their relations.

'Will you have that cup of coffee now?' she invited him, taking up the pot.

'No, I'd better get on,' he said, glancing again at the clock. 'Looks like you're going to be tied up too,' he added tersely as he opened the door and looked out. 'Here's Peggy Davies with your damn plants.'

A small and temporary improvement, she amended, as she watched him stride across to his beaten-up utility truck. What a strange and difficult man he was. But gorgeous, in a young Clint Eastwood kind of a way. If only he had Andy the Cowboy's personality, she sighed.

Out in the yard Peggy greeted him as she got out of her truck and Andy got into his.

'Planting up your garden,' she told him.

He switched on the engine and rammed it into first gear. 'So I hear.'

'It's high time, Andy,' she ventured carefully. 'Life goes on.'

A grunt, and he was gone in a cloud of dust.

13

Having previously bought small bags of compost from her local Homebase, Kate felt as if she was the real farming McCoy at the Blue Yonder as she forked freely available manure into a wheelbarrow and took it across to her newly made vegetable beds. It was a shame about the pretty turquoise cowboy boots already looking way past their best and not yet even a week old, but then again the distressed condition just made her look more the part.

She had hoped that Peggy Davies might stay for a while to help and advise her, but as soon as they'd loaded her share of the deal onto the truck she had left Kate to it, which gave her plenty of time, between digging and planting and sowing and mulching, to think about the new side of his personality which Andy had shown her. Just like his daughter, when he did actually drop his guard long enough to let a smile through, his whole face was transformed for the better. Not that she hadn't fallen for a whole lot of men with sullen looks in the past, having had the idiotic notion that maybe, just maybe, she could be the one to love them better. It had been her last boyfriend, Jon, who had put her straight about that. 'Nobody can love me better except me,' he had yelled at her percipiently during the closing moments of their final row, 'and I think I'm fine as I am.'

Well, it was no use dwelling on the past, she reminded herself: it was the present and the future she should be focusing on now, and how to continue to be able to make her living. And it was no use dwelling on Andy either. However cute his bum was, or finely chiselled his features, he was a crotchety and graceless lump most of the time, with dark unresolved issues so hidden she couldn't begin to guess at what they might be. Which didn't, of course, stop her trying, until all the plants were in the ground and mulched with muck, the tools cleaned and neatly stacked away, and it was time to retire indoors for a well-earned cup of tea.

Even then her busy mind wouldn't let him go. It was definitely the smile that had done it; that, and the little laugh he'd given in embarrassment. Inside that grouchy exterior a much more sunny disposition lurked, she just knew it. After all, who wouldn't look grim-faced with his financial worries and family responsibilities? Clearly he was at the end of his tether with it all, and wondering how much longer he could hold on. And it must be even worse if it was as Old Pete had told her, that Andy felt he was merely in the role of caretaker of the Blue Yonder, until Robyn was old enough to take it over. What a sense of failure he must be feeling as he watched things spiral out of his control.

She wondered how desperately in debt he actually was, how much the bills came to altogether, and if there wasn't any chance of a temporary bank loan, say, or a second mortgage, to tide him over until he could get back on course. The more she thought about this, the more curious she became. Maybe, if she just took a look at the mess of papers he was always so busy shuffling on his desk, she might be able to figure something out. Not that figures were her thing, exactly, but surely it was worth a try? Maybe her fresh eye might come up with something that Andy had missed, being so close to it for so long.

Feeling like a proper sleuth, she went to the office to sit at Andy's desk, and tried to feel more like an accountant. So much paper, so many columns of figures! Well, at least he was organised, which supported Old Pete's assertion that this financial crisis had happened as a result of bad luck rather than bad management.

The first book she opened turned out to be a record of the steer: when each one had been bought and for how much, when sold and for how little. Old Pete had been right about that too then. How utterly depressing it must be to realise that you've just worked your fingers to the bone for months and months and months and achieved literally less than nothing, she thought. She turned her attention to a pile of bills. The old tractor giving up the ghost must have been the final straw, according to the date that the new one had been bought, which had been immediately after the disastrous sale of the beef. And all the while the relentless drip drip of other monies going out, on fuel, on feed, on fencing, and to the dreaded vet.

An idea suddenly occurred to her, and she sorted through all the bills she could find, pulling out the ones headed 'John Connor, Veterinary Surgeon,' of which there were an even dozen. Only two of them bore the legend, 'Paid in Full', which meant that if Kate was to get the whole picture of the debt to the vet, she would need to add together ten separate total sums. Eek. If only she had a calculator. She was sure she'd seen one lying around the desk when she'd been in this room before, but there was no evidence of it now. Perhaps it had been tidied away into a drawer.

Feeling more like a burglar than a detective now, she guiltily opened the middle drawer of the desk and started to riffle through the assortment of staplers and Sellotape and handbooks and computer disks and more papers and . . . what appeared to be a photograph, shoved away right at the back, trapped in the small crack between the side and bottom of the drawer. Now this, she admonished herself, was downright snooping and not to be even contemplated. How would she feel if a guest of hers started going through her personal stuff? Nevertheless, it was intriguing. She shot an anxious glance at the door and sat very quietly for a few moments, straining her ears to catch any sound of anybody having come home since she'd been here. Nothing. She was safe.

Carefully teasing the photograph out of its tight trap so as not to tear it, she finally pulled it free and brought it out to stare at it in astonishment. There, grinning happily back at her was Andy in his early twenties, one arm around a man who looked so like him it could have been his brother, and the other around a pretty, smiling young woman holding a baby. Could this be the dippy hippy ex-lover Rainbow, holding Robyn? She wasn't dressed as Kate had imagined her, in flowing ethnic prints with loads of bangles and beads and feathers in her hair, but perhaps she was dressed more sensibly for working on her vegetable garden, judging by the state of her muddy dungarees.

But what really captured Kate's attention was how different Andy looked – not just in age, but in his outlook, his whole personality. Here was the sunny disposition she had been convinced earlier must be lurking somewhere deep inside him, but it was right out in the open for all to see, as if he hadn't a care in the world. It was the picture of somebody who was almost bursting with happiness, bonded to these two other people, and the baby, with what seemed unmistakably to be pure shining love. So what had happened to him that had been so catastrophic that it had driven that happiness away? Was it just the daily grind of ranching, or had he been more cut up when Rainbow had left than she had been led to believe by her chats on the web?

In fact, the photograph reminded her of something she'd seen once before, she realised, but she couldn't for the life of her think what it was, nor where she might have come across it. It had something to do with cowboys, and with two men and a woman, was all she could remember. Was the other man in the picture his brother, or just a friend who was of a similar height and colouring? It was hard to tell, even when she held it under the desk light and brought it close to her eyes to peer at it and squint. It had been taken as a full-length shot, so their faces were too small for a truly accurate comparison. Maybe she could bring the supper conversation round to siblings, mention that she had a sister and a brother, and casually ask Andy and Old Pete if they had any themselves. Well, that was for later, she told herself briskly, putting the photograph back just as carefully as she had removed it, taking pains to trap it again at the back of the drawer, and replace all the things she had taken out in her fruitless search for the calculator.

But then, she realised, she was sitting right in front of one. The computer. How soon would it be before anybody came back? she wondered. In Robyn's case it would be at least another hour before she rode home from school, but there was no way of knowing about Andy or Old Pete. In the latter's case it would depend if the fish had been biting, and in Andy's, she didn't even know where he'd gone off to in his truck, dressed, as he had been, not for ranch work, but in a suede jacket and clean jeans and polished boots. Still, if either of them did come in and disturb her, she could just apologise and say she'd been checking her e-mail. Which wasn't a bad idea, come to think of it. She could see if there was anything from Richard, her agent. She knew she hadn't been away long, but maybe, now the paparazzi hadn't had her within shooting range for a few days, things might already have died down, Sally Black-wise.

Turning Andy's computer on brought back the familiar feelings of excitement and anticipation she had so recently experienced on a daily basis back home, when she had been passing her time on the internet. The opening jingle, courtesy of Bill Gates' boffins, was the usual cheery welcome, and she was more than half tempted to go straight online and immerse herself in the soothing avoidance tactic of playing backgammon and chatting things over with her internet friends. Except this time there would be no Andy the Cowboy from whom to seek counsel.

Or wouldn't there? she wondered, suddenly excited. If her theory was right, and it had nothing to do with the three people she currently found herself living with, then why shouldn't this person, whoever it was, still be playing and pretending to be Andy?

A further thought occurred to her as she turned on the modem and prepared to visit the *Yoohoo* site. Since she'd had to sign up with them in order to have the chat facility while playing, she remembered that there was always a line at the top of the opening page which said 'Welcome *Mata Hari*. Please log in', and then she would have to enter her password. If the culprit was somebody who did have access to this computer, then this same invitation would be extended to *Andy the Cowboy*. Of course! Why on earth hadn't she thought of that before?

But if she had thought that the mystery could be solved so simply, she was doomed to disappointment. Nobody was welcomed to the page by name, just the generic *Guest*, which meant that nobody here had been using the site as Andy, or as anybody else come to that. Then again, she sighed, was it possible to delete that information, to cover their tracks? Could somebody have done that after she had turned up here, and they had known that the game was up? Without more knowledge of computers than was within Kate's gift, it was impossible to know. Maybe Robyn could tell her. Unless she *was* the culprit, after all.

This was getting her nowhere fast, and neither would giving

into the temptation to lose herself in play. She must be businesslike and professional: send her e-mail to Richard, and add up these wretched figures from the vet's bills so she knew precisely what the damage was.

14

As far as bad days went, this one had shaped up to rank amongst one of the darkest of Andy's life. God knew he was no stranger to misfortune, but what made this day stand out for special mention was that he had been foolish enough to face it with the optimistic notion that he might yet buy himself enough time to turn things around.

It hadn't started out so bleak. The talk with Kate hadn't gone quite as badly as he'd feared, and although it had thrown up the question of who it was, if not Robyn, that had stolen his identity, in the current big picture, this figured kind of small. He hadn't been too pleased with Peggy Davies sticking her snout into his affairs, but neither was he going to die of seeing carrots growing in his back yard.

But the big event of the day, the meeting with Jim Russell at the bank on which he had pinned all his stupid hopes, had been like running again and again into a solid-built brick wall. It signalled the end of a hard and rocky road, and there had been no way through it, no way over or under it, nor even the slightest possibility of sneaking in around the side. Regret had been expressed, of course, and coffee served, formalities observed. Jim had had the courtesy at least to hear him out, had looked carefully through the portfolio Andy had sweated over in his office this last three days to support his application for a loan, but both of them had known all along, really, that the odds were stacked high against the bank taking on such a risky bet as him. Nevertheless, in a small town such as this there was still a certain neighbourliness in most business relationships which had provoked Jim to make a call to his head office to see if there weren't a couple of boxes which could go by unticked this one time, a special case made for a relaxing of the rules on this single occasion. Naturally the corporate answer was no.

Even then Jim hadn't been willing to abandon him to his fate. Computer programs had been summoned up to see if remortgaging might be an available option to a man with more money outgoing than incoming, but it was not. Which left only one way to go, the one-way ticket they'd avoided talking about until now, the reason that, after they had done so, Andy found himself ordering a single shot of Dutch courage in McCready's Bar at ten forty-five in the morning. A magic formula only four words long, but bitter to the ears and tongue, and death to his soul.

Sell.

Off.

More.

Land.

He gazed into the anaesthetic depths of the glass. This was no time for sorrows to be drowned, nor to dwell in the land of 'If Only'. For a man to keep hold of a single shred of his self respect, this was the time for the bullet to be bitten, the monster to be faced. By eleven-oh-five he had drained that bitter cup and was back in his truck, driving out to the place where he must finally acknowledge an end to his struggle: to Jed Gray's ranch, where all hope was to be buried.

As the fortunes of the Blue Yonder had foundered over the past few years, so had the Wild Cayuse grown from strength to strength. It was the way of nature that there was always a winner and a loser, the eater and the eaten, the big fish growing at the expense of the small. Andy could acknowledge that. He had no right to feel resentment or animosity towards his neighbour. How could he, when it had been Jed who'd saved his bacon last time, by buying up the other parcel of land that had once been part of Robyn's inheritance. It was no use complaining that he had never had the kind of money Jed had at his disposal to protect him from the bad times. Sour grapes to point out now that the Blue Yonder had always been underfinanced. The fact of the matter was that Jed had prospered while he had failed, and now he must swallow any false notion of pride and go begging for crumbs from the wealthier man's table. Jed Gray wasn't a bad man, but he was hard-headed at business. Wasn't him who needed this to happen any time soon. He could bide his time, get those acres at the price he wanted later, when Andy was even more desperate than he was now, if such a thing could be imagined.

Driving through the gates under the sign of the Wild Cayuse, Andy marvelled, as he always did, at the size of the spread in front of him, which constantly grew bigger. Indeed, even now it looked as if new construction work was going on to extend one of the stable blocks, and weren't there twice as many guest cabins fanning out from the main ranch house than there had been when he'd been here the last time?

Following the arrows which directed guests to the reception building, he parked in the immaculate yard and sat for a moment to compose himself and get things straight in his head. He had been toying with figures ever since he had phoned from Jim Russell's office to ask for this meeting, trying to strike the balance between the sum he needed to achieve for the land and what he might get Jed to agree to. He needed to present a realistic starting offer and let himself be bargained down, but how high exactly should he go in?

In the event it had proved immaterial, and half an hour later he was driving out of the Wild Cayuse gates again with nothing but a promise from Jed that he would think it over.

He was regretful to hear Andy was in trouble, but he didn't really need those few acres, he told him. Even if he did, when it came to talking price, well now, there was no lake frontage on it, no highway access to it, nothing to commend it but a small creek, some awkward hilly ground, and a few trees that taken all together couldn't really claim to be a wood. But to help Andy out he would mull things over and call him with his decision maybe tonight, possibly tomorrow, anyhow, some time soon. He understood, he said kindly as he shook him by the hand, that time was of the essence.

Andy went away with his phrase stuck in his head, repeating itself over and over. Time was of the essence. Yes, Jed had got that right as far as money coming in was concerned. But without it? Time was immaterial. What did it matter how it got filled? To chase back to the Blue Yonder now and mend that fence, clear that path of the fallen tree, patch up the barn, do any one of the thousand jobs that were crying out for his attention, why he'd be like the emperor Nero, playing his fiddle while Rome burned to the ground all around him. For there was no Plan B. This had been his trump card, his ace in the hole, the only contingency manoeuvre he'd been able to come up with. To think how long he'd been agonising over the making of this last-ditch stand, and now to find that there was likely none to be had . . . A man could almost laugh at the irony, if he wasn't too busy howling with despair.

Stupidly, it had stuck in his craw to hear Jed running those acres down like that too, and he'd found himself driving there, and abandoning the truck to walk around them. Admitted, it had no lake frontage, but that creek Jed had written off as 'small' was particularly pretty here, as it wound back almost on to itself, creating the illusion, if you stood in the right spot, that you were surrounded by water as on a small and peaceful island, enclosed and shaded by those old and graceful trees which Jed didn't think merited the dignity of being called a wood. As for the hilly ground he'd complained of as being 'difficult' – difficult how exactly, and to whom? It didn't tax Andy's muscles overmuch to climb it, and when he reached the small summit he was rewarded, as always, by the double image of the creek as it lay coiled like a silver snake below him, and the prospect of a gentle downhill stroll to join it at its shore.

Memories came back of course. Snapshots of a happier past. It had been their favourite picnic spot in those brief old days of yore. They'd taken Robyn there first as a baby, tied on to her mother's back in a shawl, squaw-style, and later – afterwards – as she'd got bigger, grown taller, she and he had continued to visit it regularly on their own, just the two of them, to swim and paddle in the cool waters at the bend in the creek, or for her to poke about with a stick, exploring the small sandy bank which had been created by its meandering flow, while he lay down, head propped on one hand, and watched this miracle that was her, this independent, growing creature who had fallen from the heavens into his lap, and who'd become his sole responsibility.

He sat down heavily, and could almost see her as she'd been then, those few short years ago, paddling about in the shallow water, calling to him to, 'Come quick! Andy! Here's a shark!' when she'd seen a minnow flash between her tanned little legs. Robyn, oh Robyn. How in hell was he going to break this to her when she got home from school? He groaned aloud. How to tell her that he had mismanaged their affairs so completely that she might have to give up *all* the land that she so loved, not just this little piece here that Jed looked as if he was going to pass up on, but the whole estate, lock, stock and barrel, all of the horses, even her own adored pony that she'd bred and schooled herself? Because that was all that was left to them to dig their way out of this hole. To sell up everything that she held dear, that he had been supposed to mind and protect until she was of an age to take it over.

He could still feel the transit of the cry which had ripped itself from his lungs all those years ago, when he'd sworn to the heavens on that dark and chilly winter's day that this would be his life's work from here on in, that he would willingly give up his liberty and his own desires to bring her up safely, single-handed. Well, he'd failed spectacularly. Like as not he had only succeeded in bringing his young charge to her ruin.

Quietly and slowly, the day unfolded around him, unseen by his eyes, as he sat in abject misery and called up ghosts. Clouds crossed over the sun, the sun arced over the sky, the wind rustled through the leaves, the light dappled ever-changing patterns on the waters of the creek, where the birds skimmed over the surface hunting flies, and the big fish ate the small fry down below.

15

Having entered the amounts of the ten unpaid vet's bills into the computer's calculator, Kate had been appalled to discover that Andy owed a staggering $41,674.98. She had been entertaining the notion of offering to lend him the money to get him out of his current crisis, but as profitable as *Paradise Street* had been for her, her bank account held nowhere near this giddy figure. Just to be sure, she entered the figures again, only to find that the placement of the decimal point was apparently crucial to the outcome of the final sum, since it now totalled $4,167.49. Employing that old acid test the best-out-of-three rule, it came out as $13,606 dead on, at which point she decided that a small break might be in order, after which she would try again, but next time paying real attention to entering each figure correctly, and making absolutely sure that she pressed the + key rather than the ×.

What was uppermost in her mind anyway, and probably the reason she was making even more of a pig's ear of adding up than normal, was trying to access the buried memory of whatever it was that the photograph of Andy, possibly Rainbow, and maybe Andy's brother, reminded her of. She'd been thinking and thinking but nothing had come, so while she waited for it to surface she e-mailed her agent to ask him if there had been any change in her popularity rating with the British public since she'd been out of the tabloids, and if there was any sign yet of her ever being employed again. No mail of any importance came into her Inbox when she sent it, so she idly did a Google on Sally Black to fill in time, and was shattered to learn that there was now a dartboard with her face on it which was selling like hot cakes through all leading games retailers, and which was even available second-hand on e-Bay. She didn't know which hurt more – that people hated her so much that they wanted to throw sharp objects at her, or that a couple of darts players were already so bored by doing so that they were trading her in.

Utterly dejected, she couldn't think why her mind had chosen this moment to play the irritatingly cheerful 'Raindrops Keep Fallin' On My Head' until, in a marvellous moment of synchronically firing synapses, she had captured the elusive image which had resonance with the discovered snapshot. Of course. It was the sound-track behind the bicycle scene in *Butch Cassidy and the Sundance Kid*, which she had always found so sexy: the idea of Paul Newman and Robert Redford competing for a woman's favours was one of her all-time favourite fantasies.

So was that what was in Andy's previously happy past, she wondered? Had his brother, or the man that looked as if he could be his brother, stolen Rainbow away from him, and left Andy literally holding the baby? That would more than account for him being so permanently glum, with or without his present pecuniary disadvantage. She was about to prise the photograph from its hidden mooring place again to see what she could divine, when a slam of the back door and the sound of Robyn's voice alerted her to the fact that she was no longer alone. Quickly reshuffling the contents of the drawer she shoved it closed, turned off the computer, and rearranging her features from guilty to innocent went in search of her in the kitchen. To her horror, she found that not only was school out, but that Old Pete was standing at the sink cleaning the fish he'd caught, and judging from the amount of bloody entrails already on display, he had been there for some time. Was it Kate's imagination, or did he cast her an accusatory look?

'Hi!' she said. 'I hope nobody minds. I've just been checking my e-mail in the office. Wow, Old Pete, what a fantastic catch!' she continued at a feverish pace, and joined him at his side to count them. 'Eight, nine, ten rainbow trout! What a talent!'

'Them or me?' he answered, with a gleeful chuckle which let her know that she at least was off the hook. 'Well, I guess they had a talent to be caught, but no talent at all for spotting that the fly they all thought they was going to swallow up was just a bit of twine and feather hiding my hook. Tell you, they kept rising to my lure like kids to candy. Only reason I stopped is my damn shoulder couldn't pull no more out.' He paused in his labours to roll it around, and grunted with pain. 'There'll be rain tonight all right,' he predicted darkly.

'I'll give it a rub for you later if you like,' Kate told him. 'I did a course once in holistic massage.'

'Got a susstiffikit for that too?'

'Hanging up on my wall at home. You'll have to take it on trust. Hi, Robyn. How was your day?'

'Not bad,' the girl answered, emptying her school bag of the backgammon board and her notebook. 'Bobby and Timmy weren't lying when they said they'd never even heard of this game. I beat the crap out of both of them. So, that's two off our list, Mata.'

Kate smiled. 'Leaving just the rest of the total local population still on it, I suppose?'

'Nope. I beat the crap out of Sandy Miller, Robbie Greenblatt and Pokie Simmons too, so we got rid of five names in total,' Robyn said proudly, setting out the counters. 'And I started a new craze in the schoolyard with it. Now they all want to get a set so they can practise and win. Want to see if you can succeed where they failed?'

'After chores and homework,' Kate said firmly, knowing to her own cost how addictive backgammon could be. 'Come on, let's go and tackle Milkers One and Two, and you can admire my new vegetable patch on the way.'

Sitting by the creek for several hours had eventually mellowed Andy's mood, despite his self-accusatory frame of mind, and he had decided that, since there was nothing he could do until he had Jed's decision, he might just as well lighten up a little and hope for the best as beat up on himself. Worrying about the future was no excuse for neglecting the present, he reasoned, and allowing himself to lie down and roll over was a self indulgence that he simply couldn't afford right now.

He couldn't remember the last time he had spent a whole afternoon doing nothing other than sitting on his ass watching the world go by – or at least, this small piece of the world where there were at least as many happy memories as guilt-inducing feelings of failure. It had given him time to reflect on things in an unhurried way, and the main thing he'd been reflecting on was the recent deterioration in his relationship with Robyn.

Letting his mind wander over the subject, he had been surprised to discover that he felt jealous about her new friendship with Kate. It was only natural for the kid to want female company, particularly at this tricky early adolescent stage of her life, and small wonder that she responded positively to it now she'd got it. And, if he was really honest, he guessed he could see what she saw in Kate's company compared to his. The English actress was all laughs and nice food, and he was all tension and barked orders. Perhaps he had been hard on Robyn, automatically assuming that she'd been lying about the internet. If Kate, who had been the main victim of the prank, didn't think it had been her, who was he to say she was wrong? He should try to mend fences, lighten up a little, praise her occasionally like he'd heard Kate doing, instead of always being critical and on her case. After all, he needed her onside if things didn't work out the way he hoped with Jed. They'd have to face the fall-out together, decide what to do if the ranch couldn't be saved.

It was in this spirit of amnesty, then, that he climbed back into his truck and started the drive home, and on a sudden impulse swung the wrong way onto the main road and headed towards the gas station to buy ice cream as a peace offering. He had a brief, but nevertheless powerful, moment of rebellion against this new resolution however, as soon he was parting with his cash: not just because of the extravagance of spending money at such a tight time, but also because he suddenly questioned his own motives, wondering if what he was really doing was trying to buy her favour rather than to win it. But being in the process of handing over his twenty-dollar bill to Grant Bentley he could hardly snatch it back again without looking a complete fool, particularly since he'd just agreed with him that yessir, Robyn would be happy to see him coming home with this and, ahuh, strawberry was her favourite flavour.

Clearly, he thought, as he drove towards the Blue Yonder, this turning against the tide of his own nature was going to be something of an ongoing challenge, and never more so than when he first set foot in the kitchen. He knew now from experience that however happy they all were before he arrived, they'd clam up as soon as he got there and look apprehensive, expecting his usual catalogue of complaints and commands.

He tried to visualise how he would overcome this. At all costs he must resist the temptation of bolting straight off into his office, must quell any feelings of envy or resentment against Kate, and whatever Robyn might or might not have done, whatever provocative jibe or hurtful thing she might say, he must ride over that, just give her a smile and the ice cream and sit himself down with them, try to appear casual and relaxed and willing to join in.

Quite how he was going to introduce the subject of having offered the land to Jed Gray in this same casual and relaxed manner, however, was a whole other matter, and one which occupied his thoughts right up to the very moment that his hand reached out to grasp the handle of the back door. Say nothing about it at all till you know his response, he counselled himself, no point getting her all heated up while things are still up in the air and, fixing a smile on his face, he entered his own kitchen.

He was glad he'd practised this meeting in his mind because it was almost exactly as he'd visualised it, with the three of them sitting around the table in a cosy picture of a happy and harmonious family, heads bent over what appeared to be Robyn's schoolwork: a picture which, if he hadn't prepared himself, would have made him feel rejected and resentful, an outsider.

'Howdy,' he said with forced cheeriness, as three sets of eyes raised themselves warily to meet his. He held out the ice cream and tried to hold on to his smile. 'Passed by the gas station so I brought this for dessert.'

'Kate's made an apple pie,' Robyn told him dismissively, and buried her head back in her book.

'You're a life-saver. It means I won't have to go through all the palaver of making custard,' Kate told him, shooting a reproving look at Robyn, and she got up to take it from his hand. 'Yummy – strawberry, my favourite.'

'Strawberry?' Robyn scoffed. 'You can't have strawberry ice cream with apple pie. You should have brought vanilla.'

'And where is it writ, on what tablet of stone is it carved, that this is an immutable law?' Kate cried. 'Live dangerously, Robyn, try something new! Who knows? This might be the culinary discovery of the century! Sit down, Andy, I was just about to make a cup of tea. Or would you prefer a glass of bourbon?'

'Tea would be fine,' he said, grateful for her social graces, and he slid into a seat at Robyn's side. 'What's this, English, History?' he asked in an attempt to meld into the group, referring to the exercise book which had all her attention.

'No, this here is my defence document against people what accuse me unfairly of doing stuff I never did,' she sniffed disparagingly, throwing a dagger of a look his way.

'People who,' Kate corrected her lightly. She was painfully aware that Andy was trying hard to be conciliatory, assuming it was as a result of her having successfully persuaded him that morning that Robyn had not been in any way to blame for her arrival here. Her eyes twinkled a smile at him, inviting him to share the joke. 'This is what I was telling you about earlier, Andy. It's the list of suspects for the bogus Andy the Cowboy. The plan is to play them all at backgammon to see if they reveal themselves. Robyn's already made a good start today during break time at school. Eliminated five, haven't you?'

'Six now, including him,' said Robyn, pointing her pencil at Old Pete, and grinning despite her peevishness with Andy. 'He couldn't remember which way the men moved around the board, not even after he'd watched three whole games between me and Kate.'

'Fishing's my game,' Old Pete defended himself. 'You win at that, you've got something to eat at the end. You'll thank me over supper.'

'Guess I'm on that list?' Andy offered.

Robyn's grin turned nasty as she pinned his eyes with hers. 'Numero Uno, right there at the top. You are my prime suspect, Andy the Cowboy. Play me if you dare.'

'Well now, let's see if I can do any better than Old Pete at remembering which way round they go,' he said, tipping the pieces out onto the board. 'Might have to help me set this up, though. Been a long time since I played.'

'Sez you,' said Robyn, positioning the men with a practised

hand. 'But be warned. We already know that the real culprit will try to pretend he don't know how to play, and we have our tried and tested methods of seeing plain through that.'

Of all the things that were troubling him right now, this was pretty low on his list. 'Ooh, sounds scary,' he said with a smile. How long was it since he'd played a game with Robyn? Years maybe. At least he had the power to do something about that. He gazed at the board and rubbed his hands together. 'So, just remind me of this one last thing and I'll try not to bother you again. Am I white coming this way round and you're black going that way round, or is it the other way about?'

'Right first time,' Robyn said cynically. 'But you know that really, cowboy, don't you?'

By way of an answer he just gave a tease of a grin. 'And now we roll one dice each to see who starts?'

'You betcha. Go.'

A one to him and a six for Robyn meant that she was off to a flying start, crowing in triumph as usual. From her vantage point at the stove where she was dragging out the making of tea, Kate watched father and daughter exhibit the same traits, whooping when they were ahead, glowering darkly when they were behind, goading each other during runs of bad luck, slamming pieces on the bar vindictively when they had the good fortune to take the other off the board. The only difference between them was that for Andy it was clearly all play, but for Robyn, winning was a matter of life and death.

'Beat. Your. Ass.' she declared, as she thumped the last three of her men off. 'Try again?'

'If you don't mind losing,' said he.

'Looks to me like you cornered that market,' she batted back, intent on setting up the board.

Old Pete stretched and rolled his shoulder again, wincing a little with the effort. 'Well, I've watched it another time and it still don't make no sense to me,' he announced. 'So if I'm in the clear, I guess I'll take myself off and go soak myself in a hot tub before supper.'

A flash of concern crossed Andy's face as he raised his eyes from the game to his employee. 'Don't tell me your shoulder's acting up?' he asked.

Old Pete shrugged. 'Probably don't mean nothing.' He was as happy as anybody else to witness the accord that currently reigned here, and he didn't want to spoil things by setting Andy off worrying about the roof and the possibility of rain. 'Overdid it at the river is all. Them damn rainbows wouldn't stay off of my line all day.'

Hearing him use Robyn's mother's name, Andy's ex-lover's, to describe the fish, Kate shot a look at both of them to see their reaction, but Robyn's attention hadn't left the board, and Andy's was now on the patch of clear sky that was visible to him through the window.

'Don't look like it's going to rain,' he suggested doubtfully. 'But your shoulder's seldom wrong.'

'First time for everything,' Old Pete said, heaving himself to his feet. 'How long before I get my revenge on them trout there, girlie?' he asked Kate.

'Depends how you want them done,' she said. 'You caught them, you get to choose. Baked, fried or grilled?'

Old Pete grinned. 'Shared the secrets of my cooking with you already. Spike it with a stick and burn it in a fire.'

'Fried in batter!' Robyn cried. 'With french fries on the side!'

'Right. And shall I fry the apple pie and ice cream too?' Kate asked.

Robyn's eyes widened at the possibility. 'Can you?'

'Duh, no,' said Kate. 'Andy, do you have a preference?'

'Seems to me,' he said, forcing himself to abandon his worry about the weather since he could no sooner influence that than any of the others things which were troubling him, 'that we should ask the one who's best at cooking here.' He looked around him in a mock quest. 'Anybody know who that might be?'

Robyn lifted a disappointed eyebrow as they all gazed back at Kate. 'Guess you're going to grill 'em then,' she said flatly.

Kate thought that she might burst with pleasure. At last, some nice acknowledgement from Andy about her contribution. 'I might just surprise you on that. I've got a feeling that I'm about to come over all inventive,' she told her, and started immediately to forage in cupboards.

'Is that a long invention or a short one?' asked Old Pete impatiently from the doorway, ''Cos I've got a powerful feeling about taking that soak.'

'You're safe for half an hour at least,' Kate told him. 'More than that if I can't find the bloody peppercorns.'

'Then I ain't going to tell you where I hid 'em,' said Old Pete wickedly. 'See y'all later.'

Remarkably for the Blue Yonder, the harmonious, jokey atmosphere persisted for the whole forty-five minutes that Old Pete took to soak his aching bones, and while Kate cooked, Andy and Robyn continued to rattle their way round the backgammon board, goading each other, good-naturedly in Andy's case, and with red-clawed competitiveness in Robyn's. By the time Kate had brought spice-encrusted trout fillets to the table with sweet-potato fries, tomato salsa, and salad, it might have been that there had never been any bad feeling in this family, for father and daughter had found some common ground, and Robyn had got what she'd been craving for so long – Andy's affectionate company, with no grousing and no complaints.

'So did I put myself in the clear? Am I off the suspect list?' Andy asked her over the apple pie and ice cream.

'You so are,' said Robyn, striking his name out of her

exercise book. 'With fifteen games to me and a pathetic two to you, I guess we can say you have no talent for this game at all.'

'Don't that put *you* fair and square in the frame then?' Old Pete queried. 'If you're the best one around here at this damn game, who else we got to point the finger at?'

Robyn held out the long list in her book for his inspection. 'Where'd you want to start?' she said. 'With all the locals – barring Bobby, Timmy, Robbie, Sandy, Pokie and us three – or with all the guests that've passed through here?'

Curious at last about this, Andy took the book and frowned at the names. 'But what would be their motive?' he asked. 'Why would anybody want to pretend to be me?'

Everybody frowned in concentration at this one, but none of them could come up with an answer. 'Must've been somebody with friendly feelings towards us though,' Old Pete offered cheerfully, ' 'cos look what we got out of it. A pretty girl come all the way over from London, England to look after us.'

Kate flushed with pleasure. 'Just call me Mary Poppins,' she said.

'How many names you want there, Mata?' Robyn challenged her.

'The more the merrier,' Kate replied. 'I'm a woman of many parts.'

'Hate to introduce this subject when we're getting on so well,' Andy said gently, 'but have you done your schoolwork yet?'

Robyn glowered immediately. 'Yes I have. Ask them if you don't believe me.'

'No need,' he said. 'If you say you have, then you have.'

'And I don't want to read no encyclopaedia now, as my so-called reward for having done it without you getting on my back,' Robyn told him ungraciously.

'That's great,' said Andy. 'Me neither. Tonight's for having fun.' And nobody in this room knew better than he that this might be the last evening they might have any fun, or anything close, he thought, with a pang of apprehension. 'No, all this detective work you've been doing has put me in mind of another game we used to play.'

'*Clue!*' Robyn shouted, banging the table in her hurry to fetch it from the guest lounge cupboard. She had no idea what had occasioned this sea change in Andy's attitude towards her, but suddenly it felt like Christmas.

Even the rumbling sound of distant thunder buoyed the festive mood rather than threatened it, as Colonel Mustard battled it out in the conservatory with Miss Scarlett, Mr Green and Professor Plum. 'There's your answer,' Old Pete told Andy, looking out at the pale distant sheet lightning. 'Rain's back over where I was fishing, that's how come my shoulder was acting up. Won't touch us here.' He kept to himself the fact that his joint ached no less now though, despite his long soak in the hot bath and a couple of pain killers. Why spoil the party? This state of peace was fragile enough, he guessed, without him breaking the mood, and in that supposition, sadly, he was absolutely right.

They were taking a break from the game while Kate made hot chocolate all round, with added strawberry ice cream for those adventurous enough to try it, when the trill of the phone made Andy's voice and body stiffen in alarm.

'Expecting an important call,' he said hurriedly, getting up to head off anybody else from talking to Jed Gray. 'I'll take it in the office.'

'What important call?' Robyn demanded of his departing back, but he was gone. Her eyes pinned Old Pete. 'Who's he been talking to today?'

'Don't ask me, I been out fishing all day. Ask him.'

'Don't think I won't,' she said pugnaciously, all trace of her previous good humour threatening to leave the room forthwith.

Andy returned surprisingly swiftly, and was swiftly surprising. 'It's for you,' he told Kate.

'For me?' she echoed. 'But nobody knows I'm here, except my agent. My agent! Is it him?'

Andy looked doubtful. 'Only if he's called Minnie McAlpine and has a female-sounding voice.'

'Not that female sounding,' Kate laughed, on her way out to the office, 'although at times of great excitement he can come close. Sorry about this. It's a lovely lady I met on the plane. I'll tell her I'll call her back tomorrow, if that's all right, as you're waiting for a call.'

Behind her as she left she heard Robyn challenge him, 'What important call?' and heard his noncommital reply, 'Oh, you know, just some business stuff, nothing much.'

Calling from her granddaughter's house, Minnie wanted reassurance that all was well. 'Was that him?' she asked. 'Was that The Saint who answered the phone?'

Kate laughed. 'It was Andy, yes, and everything's fine, Minnie. A little bit different from what I was expecting, touch of a tricky start, but now—' Her voice faltered at the yelling in the background.

'What's all that noise?' Minnie asked. 'Who's doing all the shouting?'

'Robyn,' said Kate, mystified. 'I don't know why. We were all getting on so well a moment ago.' They could both plainly hear her yell, '*So why are you all dressed up, where in hell have you been?*'

'Where has he been?' asked Minnie.

'I don't know,' said Kate, putting one finger in her ear to block out Robyn's '*I knew you were up to something, pretending to be so goddamn nice to me all night! I knew that couldn't be right!*' A slammed door. A thumping of feet past the office and up the stairs. Another door slammed. More thumping feet, more shouting. 'Minnie,' she said, 'can I call you back tomorrow?

To be honest I can't really hear you very well at the moment, and Andy's expecting a call.'

'Are you going to be all right?' Minnie asked doubtfully.

'Yes, yes, of course. I'll call you in the morning.'

She found Old Pete alone in the kitchen pouring himself a bourbon. 'What was that all about?' she asked.

He drained his glass before he replied. 'Andy's offered that land up for sale like I told you he was going to. That's the call he's waiting on, and Robyn ain't happy about it.'

From upstairs they heard her shout, '*You carry on like this and there'll be nothing left for me to inherit!*'

Old Pete shrugged, and winced in pain as he did so. 'Peace was nice while it lasted, but now it's back to business as usual: all-out war.'

'Is your shoulder still playing up?'

'Could say.'

Kate regarded him critically. 'Well, I'm hardly surprised. Look how you're holding yourself, you're all hunched up with tension! Slow breath in, slow breath out. Relax!'

'How in hell am I going to do that when likely I won't have a roof over my head before long?' Old Pete demanded tetchily. 'Andy's been to the bank today and they won't lend him no more money, and he ain't holding out any hope that Jed's going to buy the land, nor offer much for it if he do.'

'Oh my goodness!' said Kate, matching his distress. 'No wonder Robyn's upset.'

'She ain't the only one,' said Old Pete. 'How many other ranch owners do you think there are in these parts who'd be dumb enough to employ an old guy with a busted shoulder who can't cook?'

'Andy's not thinking of selling up the business, surely?'

'What else can he do if the money's only going one way?'

'Make a concerted effort to drum up more trade,' Kate suggested. 'Advertise.'

'Using what to pay for it? Beans? 'Cos that's all we got, and we won't even have any of them left soon, after I've burned 'em and served 'em.'

'Well, there's nothing we can do about any of that tonight,' said Kate pragmatically, moving behind him purposefully. 'But at least there's something I can do about this. Get your shirt off.'

'Don't you get fresh with me just 'cos we got left alone!' he protested, as she undid his buttons and slid his shirt down, but as soon as he felt her touch he was putty in her hands. 'Ooh, that's—Aah,' he groaned.

'Gosh, yes, this is knotted,' she said, gently pressing the bunched muscles around his shoulder blade. 'And it's been like this for an age from the feel of it. This calls for desperate measures. Don't go anywhere. Wait here.'

'Don't know where she thinks I'm going to go this time of night, half naked,' he complained, as he gathered his shirt back around him, and his dignity. 'Taking advantage of an old crippled fella like that.' But on her return, he realised that this had only been foreplay, and that things were about to get even racier now.

'Have we got any candles?' she asked, after he'd watched her lay out a duvet and pillow on the kitchen table and cover them with towels.

'Depends what you got in mind to do with them,' he said suspiciously.

'Create a warm and relaxed atmosphere of course, what else?'

'That case, they're in that cupboard over there.'

When she'd finished dotting them about the place in jam jars, even he couldn't argue that the place didn't look cosy and soft, same as the bed she'd made out of the duvet and towels.

'Rightyho,' she announced cheerfully, having washed her

hands and heated up some fragrantly scented oil, the very smell of which was already making him feel dozy. 'Get your kit off and hop on the table then.'

His eyes widened in alarm, the tension in his shoulders increasing tenfold.

'Trust me, I'm an actress,' she said firmly, bearing down on him to relieve him of his boots. 'There is absolutely nothing you have got in your trousers that I haven't shared a dressing room with on tour.'

Having been ejected from Robyn's room after he'd been treated to every nasty thing she could think of to say to him, Andy stood out on the landing and cursed himself. Could he have handled things any worse? He didn't think so. He should have been more casual when the phone had rung – particularly as it had proved to be a damn false alarm – then he could have taken more care to prepare the ground with her. As things stood, he'd been forced into telling her about the danger they faced, that they might lose the Blue Yonder, not just the little bit of land she'd kicked up such a fuss about, off his back foot and cack-handed. Well, it had taken the heat out of her anger all right, but it had been replaced with cold loathing, and when she'd told him that she hated him, he had no reason to disbelieve her.

Now he didn't know what to do, but one thing was clear – he couldn't lurk about on the landing for the rest of his life. It was no use trying to appeal to Robyn to let him back in, judging from the muffled sobs that were coming from her room: she hated for anyone to see her cry. He didn't relish going back in to the kitchen to face Old Pete either, now that he, too, knew that his days at the ranch might be numbered. But that was where the bourbon was, and that was all Andy could think of, getting some of that inside him to calm himself down. The best he could hope was that he'd been so long with Robyn that both

Pete and Mary Poppins had taken themselves off to their beds. He could certainly do without her brand of cheeriness and hot chocolate at a time like this.

What a night, with the thunder continuing to rumble apocalyptically in the distance, and even the air feeling oppressive, too thick to breathe, almost. But that, likely, was just his fancy, a mental projection of how he was feeling inside. Like that he had no right to any more breath, given that he hadn't done anything constructive with the air he'd already used up in his miserable existence. On the contrary, he'd only ever caused damage of the most heinous kind, particularly where Robyn was concerned. And the worst of it was that, while she was feeling at her most wretched with the threat of losing the ranch hanging over her, he actually felt something akin to relief. The thought of not being just allowed, but being forced to lay down this heavy burden was, for him, like facing the prospect of a long holiday. The only difference being that with this holiday, there would be no end ever. And what would he do to earn their keep, where would they stay if the worst did come to the worst? These days, even though he clearly had no talent for it, ranching was all he knew how to do. He smiled humour-lessly to himself as he walked down the stairs. Be some kind of cosmic irony if he had to end up working for Jed Gray. He only hoped that if that happened Jed would agree to take on Old Pete too, as part of a package. He couldn't bear to think that by his ineptitude he had caused two more people's downfall beside his own. God, how he needed that drink.

He didn't know what shook him most when he stepped inside the kitchen: whether it was finding it looking like some kind of hippy festival of light in there; seeing Old Pete lying half naked on the table with Mary Poppins leaning over him and up to no good; the huge clap of thunder, the vicious fork of lightning, or the tumult of rain which suddenly fell out of the sky by the bath-load. But there was no time to figure any of this out right now. There was only time enough to fill his lungs with as much air as he could grab and use it to scream, 'Man the buckets!' before fleeing back upstairs.

16

'They talk of it coming down in sheets, but honestly, Minnie, it came down more in a massive chunk, as if the bottom had just suddenly fallen out of the sky, and every drop of water that had been collecting there since time began fell out of it. I've never seen anything like it. And it just went on and on and on for three solid hours while we raced about with buckets and bowls as if we were in some awful crazy game show. Almost as soon as we'd emptied one and put it back under a leak, it was full again. It was unbelievable! And then when it was over and we'd wrung everything out and mopped up, I found that we'd missed one – right over my bed. I had to bunk up with Robyn in the end, but by then it was about three in the morning. I'm absolutely exhausted. We all are.'

On the other end of the line in her granddaughter's house, Minnie clamped the phone under her chin while she made a cup of tea. 'What's the forecast like for today where you are?'

'It's gorgeous. You wouldn't believe it could ever have happened. Except for the water damage inside, of course. But thank goodness, the sun's shining and it's really hot, so I'm drying rugs and chairs and duvets outside in the yard, and I've got all the doors and windows open to air the place.'

'And what are the rest of them doing? Watching you? Sounds as if you've become the unpaid skivvy.'

'Not at all,' Kate protested. 'Andy's up on the roof replacing tiles, and Robyn and Old Pete have gone off to check on the livestock, to see how they fared through all of it. For once

Andy was only too glad for Robyn to bunk off school for the day. The worry is that some of the calves or the foals might have become bogged down in mud if they were on low ground, or even been swept away if they were too close to the banks of the river. And if any of them have been injured, I don't know what will happen. Andy's exhausted his credit with the vet, apparently.'

Taking her tea into the conservatory at the back of the house, Minnie sat down and made herself comfortable. 'Bad payer is he?' she asked.

'Not on purpose,' Kate said loyally. 'He's just had a terrible run of bad luck. He's offered to sell some land to a neighbour and he thought your call last night was him ringing back to tell him yea or nay. Robyn's very upset about it, that's what all the shouting was about that you heard on the phone. They have a fairly volatile relationship, to put it mildly.'

'Really? That wasn't the impression he gave you when you were chatting on the internet was it?'

'Ah. Right,' said Kate. 'Of course, you don't know.' And she proceeded to fill Minnie in on everything that had happened since they'd parted.

'What did I tell you?' Minnie exclaimed. 'What did I say?'

'As far as I can remember you told me that Andy was probably luring me out to remote parts where he would have his evil way with me,' Kate reminded her. 'And I'm unhappy to report that's not been happening. We've got mystery here, and mistaken identity, but no sex of any kind I'm afraid.'

'Thank heaven for small mercies,' said Minnie. 'Anyhow, is he like you imagined him to be?'

'Not in any way at all.'

'And do you believe him when he says it wasn't him?'

'Without a shadow of a doubt. It wasn't any of the inmates here, I'd bet my life on it.'

'So who was it?'

'You tell me.'

Minnie's tone changed to one of envy. 'Sounds as if you're having the adventurous time you were after, at any rate,' she said.

'And what about you?' Kate asked. 'Is it lovely seeing your granddaughter and her new baby?'

Minnie gazed about her at the empty house. 'It's quite nice when I do see them,' she said. 'But that's only after seven at night and before seven in the morning.'

'She's gone back to work already?'

'That's right.'

'But can't you help her by looking after the baby? At least that would be some company for you, wouldn't it?'

'Just got her settled into a nursery, apparently, so Ruth doesn't want to break the routine.'

'Oh, Minnie, I am sorry. So what are you doing to pass the time? Are you getting out and about?'

'It's a bit of a one-horse town,' Minnie told her. 'And I'm not even in it. I'm stuck out on an "executive" housing estate, with no bus service because all these executives have got two bloody cars each. I'm trying to make up my mind whether to go back home early, or go walkabout. Maybe take a coach trip somewhere to one of the big cities. In the meantime all I'm doing to exercise my brain cells is educating the folk here about how food can taste if you cook it from scratch. Left to herself, all my granddaughter can do is take stuff out of packaging and bung it in the microwave.'

'Yes, I'm doing quite a bit of that too. So why not come here?' Kate suggested. 'We could do educative cooking together.'

'And get rained on in bed? No thank you. I value my health too much for that.'

'Minnie McAlpine, you've been too long on the housing

estate!' Kate admonished her. 'You've gone all suburban on me and lost your spirit of adventure!'

'Sticks and stones,' said Minnie. 'Besides, if you had my knees you'd think you'd got adventure enough.'

'I did wonders for Old Pete's aches and pains last night before the rain came down,' Kate boasted, 'so maybe I could work a miracle on your knees.' But nothing she could say would persuade the Yorkshirewoman to join her. 'So what are you going to do for the rest of the day?' she asked at last.

'Oooh, now, I'm torn between rubbing out the crossword and redoing it, or going out and graffiti-ing this cul-de-sac with a snappy line about the correlation between global warming and obesity,' said Minnie. 'That's how suburban I am.'

'The correlation being . . .?'

' "Fat cats: save fuel and save the world! Get out of your cars and walk, you chubby buggers!" '

'Might need a little refining before it can go to T-shirt,' Kate mused. 'Anyway, I'd better get on. I've yet to check on what all that rain did to my new fledgling plants.'

'I say, before you go,' said Minnie, ever the terrier at getting information taped down, 'did the neighbour ever ring back to say whether he was buying the land?'

'Not so far. Not that I know of,' Kate said. 'Even more reason to get off the phone I suppose. But keep in touch, Minnie, and if you do go walkabout, let me know where you are.'

'I'll do that.'

Outside in the yard, Kate found that most of the plants were none the worse for their drenching, indeed if anything they were looking surprisingly perky beneath their thick mulch of muck. She just hoped that Andy and Robyn and Old Pete would still be there to reap the benefit when all this free food was fully grown and ready for harvest. If only one could barter cream and eggs and beef for vet's fees and roofers, she thought, then all their troubles would be over.

But why not? she asked herself suddenly. It was worth a try wasn't it? Glancing up at the roof she saw that Andy was still fully occupied with replacing broken tiles, and looked as if he'd be at it for some time. 'Want some coffee?' she called, just to be sure.

'Not now, thanks. When I'm finished,' he called back. 'Maybe half an hour.'

Half an hour. Long enough even for Kate to add ten numbers together and to get the vet's address, surely?

17

Sonia Driesen was a very busy woman, as she had been telling Pritti Patel for the last twenty minutes. Pritti wouldn't believe, for instance, how hard it had been to get the four maids of honour to agree on the material for their dresses, and having finally reached consensus on that, how many more meetings it had taken to turn Frances Blatt around on the sleeve-length issue. Just when you thought you'd got that particular horse to water, she'd bolt off again without taking so much as a sip. Even now it was touch and go, apparently, and all dependent on the efficacy of Frances' new diet and exercise regime, which was designed to target upper arm flabbiness specifically. All this, *and* the printers getting the wrong date on the invitations, so Pritti just shouldn't even get her started on the caterer, who hadn't been answering her calls all week. Fortunately Sonia was an adept multi-tasker, so she was able to consult a nail art catalogue and keep re-dialling said errant caterer as she talked. She was not a woman, however, who could take a hint, not from Kate, who was shifting her weight from one foot to the other while she waited in line for her attention, nor from Pritti's Alsatian, Bonnie, who had now resigned herself, after her series of huge yawns had failed to make her point, to lying down dramatically with all four paws in the air and playing dead.

During Sonia's oration, John Connor himself had come out of his surgery three times with clients to provide them with their pet's medication, grab more notes, and call the next one in, and given that some of these jobs, surely, must have been within the remit of his receptionist, Kate marvelled at his forbearance. It augured well, she thought, for the negotiations she hoped to have with him when at last it came to be her turn.

Pritti, who was beginning to show every sign that she was seriously considering taking Bonnie's lead and might join her dog on the floor at any moment, was visibly relieved when her mobile went off in her handbag and, though in reality it was only her mother reminding her to buy lentils on the way home, she used the call as an excuse to force Sonia to take her money, and bustled out of the door as if on a life and death mission. Which meant that Sonia's attention now belonged fully to the pretty blonde stranger next in line. The eyes narrowed, the nail art catalogue was swiftly swept aside, and the telephone receiver summarily discarded.

'Help you?' she said, in a steely voice, which carried with it the unspoken rider, ''Cos I'd sooner die than do that.'

Kate gave a non-threatening smile which didn't have Sonia fooled for a minute. 'Yes,' she said. 'I'd just like a quick word with Mr Connor when he has time.'

Sonia regarded her with pursed lips for what seemed like an age, before slowly and dangerously enunciating, 'And that would be concerning . . .?'

'Private business,' Kate said firmly, which had the effect of lobbing an incendiary device behind the reception desk, and ensuring that the only remaining clients in the waiting area, Clarrie Harris and her cat, Mog, now delayed their tussle over whether Mog would like to get back into her box to go home, to regard Kate with a fascinated and unblinking gaze, ears pricked for whatever might come next.

Sonia folded her arms like a roadblock. 'If you're a drugs rep you should have paid more attention to the sign on the door,' she said. ' "No reps without appointment. No exceptions." Mr Connor's a very busy man.'

'I'm sure he is,' Kate replied, 'and no, I'm not.'

'So where's your pet then?' Sonia challenged her.

Kate tried the smile again. 'Actually, it's a rather delicate matter. If I could just make an appointment to see Mr Connor – I don't mind waiting. Or I could come back later if it's not convenient now.'

Seeing she was getting nowhere with her current line of questioning, Sonia changed tack. 'Name?' she asked, while riffling through the appointments book to find a blank space several weeks ahead.

'Kate Thornton.'

There was something about that name, and about the accent in which it was delivered, which rang a far-off alarm bell in Sonia's mind. If only her head hadn't been so full of wedding plans for so many weeks, she was sure she would have efficiently filed away the piece of gossip she'd been told about this woman, and been able to retrieve it now in a trice. But judging from the way that Clarrie Harris and Mog were straining forward to listen, she knew she'd better access it and fast. She chewed her cheek while she regarded Kate anew. 'Address,' she said finally, hoping that might help her pin it down.

'Currently, care of the Blue Yonder Guest Ranch,' Kate told her innocently, and was met with a sharp intake of breath and an accusing finger pointing her way.

'The husband-snatching child-murderer from England!' Sonia's memory supplied, so forcefully that it came out in a hiss.

Kate took a deep calming breath and exhaled on a count of five before saying, 'The *actress* who *played* the husband-snatching child-*abductor*, actually.'

Sonia was less than impressed. 'And what "private business" would a petless English actress have with my fiancé?' she demanded to know. As did John Connor, who was on his way out of his surgery with what he'd hoped had been his last patient of the morning.

'Oh, it's Mr Connor you're marrying! Congratulations, both of you!' said Kate, understanding at last the receptionist's unwelcoming attitude. The penny having dropped, she added reassuringly, 'In real life I'm a great respector of marriage. A huge fan.'

Sonia, however, was unconvinced, and now turned her icy glare on her husband-to-be. 'Why's she here?' she demanded. 'What private business do you have with her and why don't I know about it?'

For answer he laid a calming hand on the small of her back and gave a light kiss to her cheek. Over the last few weeks he had grown used to these anxiety attacks from his betrothed. 'I don't know, Sonia,' he said in a soothing voice, 'but if you'd like to take thirty-eight dollars fifty from Miss Armstrong here and give her a tube of Fluffy's usual ointment, I'll go find out.' He turned to Kate with an arm outstretched towards his surgery door. 'If you'd like to come this way, Miss . . .?'

'Thornton,' Kate supplied gratefully, and with a quick apologetic smile in Sonia's direction, she followed John's lead.

'Now then,' he said, when they were both safely on the other side of his door. 'What can I do for you?'

'Actually I was wondering what I could do for you,' Kate said, 'with regard to Andy Barrett's outstanding bill.'

Of all the things John might have been expecting her to say, this clearly took him by surprise. 'What would be your interest in the matter?' he asked. 'Because if you're offering your services as a debt collector, that isn't how I like to run my business at all.'

'On the contrary,' Kate reassured him. 'I'm offering different services altogether. I was hoping that you and I might be able to come up with some amicable arrangement to suit both parties, where the bill might be settled in kind.'

A puzzled frown crossed John's brow and he glanced anxiously at the closed door, wondering if Sonia's ear might even now be pressed against it. 'What kind of "in kind" did you have in mind?' he asked, his mouth turning dry at the thought.

'Well, that's what I'm not sure of,' said Kate. 'I'd offer to pay it with money as a temporary loan to Andy, but I don't think he'd be able to bring himself to accept that as a matter of pride. It's about three thousand dollars, isn't it?'

'Thereabouts,' said John shiftily. 'In that region, yes.'

'You see, I got the idea from Peggy Davies. She explained to me how things work out here with quid pro quo.'

'Mrs Davies suggested you come here with this offer?' John asked, running a nervous finger round the inside of his collar, his eyes wide with disbelief. What on earth could he ever have said to Peggy that might have given her the impression he was that kind of a man?

'Not exactly, no. She gave me some plants and vegetables the other day in exchange for eggs, milk and beef,' Kate explained. 'Now I appreciate that three thousand dollars' worth of Blue Yonder produce would take an awful lot of eating, so I was wondering if there wasn't something else I could provide that you might prefer?'

'Nothing at all that I can think of,' John said stiffly. 'Now if you'll excuse me—'

A strangled scream from the reception area presaged Sonia's sudden wild appearance in the doorway, hyperventilating and beyond coherent speech.

'I don't know what you heard, but I didn't accept her offer, and she's just on her way out,' John told her hastily, but Sonia waved her arms about and shook her head dismissively like a determinedly drowning woman refusing the offer of a life-buoy.

It seemed to Kate, who had seen plenty of histrionics in her time, that if Sonia inhaled any more air without breathing any of it out, then at the rate she was going she would soon be floating up towards the ceiling. 'Shouldn't we be putting a paper bag over her mouth?' she suggested helpfully to John. 'To de-oxygenate her,' she added hastily, as he looked at her appalled.

'Oh,' he said, and turning to his fiancée he raised his voice over her impassioned squeaks. 'Well, Sonia, which is it to be – do you want Miss Thornton here to put a bag over your head, or for me to get the tranquilliser gun? Whichever way, you have got to calm down somehow before I can understand you.'

The mere prospect of either of these remedies had something of a steadying effect, and sinking back against the wall to clutch her chest, Sonia managed to pronounce in a strangled and halting voice, 'The wedding's off! It's all in bits! I can't hold it together any more!' before sinking slowly to the floor in a tide of tears.

'Satisfied?' John Connor said to Kate coldly. 'Now I think you'd better leave.'

But Kate was busy digging through her handbag for a cure. 'Here it is,' she said at last with some relief, and produced a small brown bottle marked 'Rescue Remedy'. 'Open wide, Sonia,' she instructed her patient, and addressed John's look of mistrust with, 'It's just extracts of certain flowers, a homeo-pathic remedy. Very effective for shock and all kinds of nervy-type situations. Part of the standard kit of most actors.' She measured out four drops on to the afflicted woman's tongue. 'That should just take a few minutes. Do you have tea-making facilities anywhere?'

'I really don't think that this is the time—' John began crossly, but Sonia, who was enjoying being nursed, waved towards the reception area and sniffed, 'Room behind my desk.'

When Kate returned with three steaming mugs, she found

Sonia being cuddled on John's lap on his office chair. 'Very British, I know, but it is a magnificent cure-all for shock,' she said, as she administered hot sweet tea all round. 'Did she manage to say anything yet?'

John nodded grimly. ' "Caterer." That's all so far.'

Sonia wailed.

Kneeling down to her height, Kate said gently, 'They've not been taking your calls, have they?'

Sonia shook her head and gulped a sob.

'But have you just heard from them now?'

The head nodded, the face crumpled.

'And there's some problem,' Kate suggested, taking her hand. 'Don't rush. Drink your tea. It'll make you feel better.'

Having been quick to judge her harshly on first meeting, Sonia was now warming to Kate's soothing presence and was happy to sip her medicine obediently. Minutes later, when she was ready to lift her face from the mug, she suffered it to be mopped of tears with a tissue, and even agreed to 'blow' when instructed.

'Now I want you to concentrate on breathing from your tummy and not from your throat,' Kate told her, putting her own hand on Sonia's stomach. 'From here, okay? Nice and slowly. Very good. And while you're doing that, I know it sounds funny, but I want you to imagine that you have roots growing out of the soles of your feet, which push right down through the floorboards and anchor themselves in the cool brown earth. Excellent, Sonia, excellent. So now please, in your own time, tell us all about it.'

It emerged, through the odd hiccup and sniffle, that Sonia had finally found out why her calls to Solveig Hansen had not been returned. Tasty Bites (Catering) had gone belly-up. Or rather, Solveig had. 'Her husband's finally gotten around to checking her mobile and called me back,' Sonia explained. 'Neither of them had a clue that Solly even could get pregnant, let alone that she is. They've been trying for years and nothing. Then suddenly last week she had a "showing", and they rushed her to hospital and told her she's got to lie down nice and quiet for the next six weeks or maybe she'll lose it. So that's it. It's a one-woman outfit. No Solveig, no wedding. We'll have to postpone.'

Kate sat back on her heels and gazed up at the betrothed couple with a happy smile. 'Well now, Sonia, if that's all the problem is, it can be solved just like that!' She snapped her fingers to illustrate her point. '*I* am a caterer. And if I say so myself, a jolly good one! Ask at the Blue Yonder, and they'll tell you. Better still, if you're free tomorrow evening I can bring you some sample tasters over and you can choose the menu. Is it a sit-down do, or a buffet?'

'Buffet,' Sonia said eagerly, clutching Kate's hands in her own.

'Lovely,' Kate said approvingly. 'My favourite.'

'For a hundred people,' Sonia added.

Kate smiled bravely. 'Excellent,' she said.

'In eight days' time,' said John.

Imagining that she had roots growing from the soles of her feet, pushing themselves down into the cool brown earth, Kate breathed deeply from the bottom of her diaphragm. 'Not a problem,' she exhaled slowly, on a count of five beats. 'Venue? I'd like to check out the kitchens ahead of time.'

A series of strangled sobs from Sonia about printers and invitations was translated into English by her betrothed. 'Was to have been at Solveig and Arnie's. Now, who knows?'

'Me,' said Kate. 'We'll do it at the Blue Yonder. I can take care of all the decorations, and you can phone or e-mail most of your guests to let them know.' Standing up to her full height to get some leverage in the negotiations she said firmly, 'I'll do it for the price of Andy Barrett's bill.'

'Done,' Sonia said quickly.

Clearly she'd just undercut Solveig Hansen dramatically, Kate now realised, and with her fingers crossed behind her back she decided to up the ante. 'Plus one thousand dollars' credit for future treatments of Blue Yonder stock.'

'We'll take it!' Sonia enthused.

John Connor, however, was a tougher nut to crack. 'Let's see how the tasting goes tomorrow evening,' he said, scribbling on a Post-it note. 'Here's Sonia's address. We'll see you there at four thirty, and if we like your cooking, we'll accept.'

'Oh, you'll like it all right,' Kate said confidently. 'In fact, once you've tasted it you'll want to get married every week!'

Outside on the street, Kate was elated, and it was all she could do to stop herself punching the air or doing a little jig on the sidewalk. However, since she was a stranger in a very small town she decided she was already conspicuous enough to the few curious passers-by, so instead she decided to see what the shops had to offer. This wedding would have to be planned within an inch of its life if she was to stand any chance at all of bringing it off single-handed, and she needed to know what range of foodstuffs she might have to work with to complement the free food which was available at the Blue Yonder. The beef and chicken could be roasted of course, and the milk and eggs could become quiches or tarts, but if this was to be a buffet for a hundred people she needed to think up a lot more quick and easy finger foods for variety. Hard-boiled eggs stuffed with anchovies and mayonnaise, for instance, if she could source the anchovies.

Walking along the short main street in a northerly direction she passed a funeral parlour, a saddler, a fishing tackle shop and a bar before the stores gave way to houses. Turning round and retracing her steps she walked back past the vet's surgery and found an outdoor-wear shop, a hardware store, and finally, much to her relief, a shop called 'Charlie McGarry

– General Provisions'. It worried her slightly that the window display featured cans of creamed corn as this week's must-have, but in her current mood of optimism she decided that Mr McGarry just had a nice line in irony. Once inside his store, however, it took a cursory sweep of his shelves to disabuse herself of this.

'Find what you're looking for?' he asked her sourly.

'Not exactly,' Kate admitted.

'Didn't think so,' he said with an air of satisfaction. 'You city people never do. You want bottled water with bubbles in it, you should have brought it out here with you. Folk around here don't need expensive gimmicks with their weekly supplies.'

'Quite right,' said Kate. 'It makes no economic or ecological sense to fly designer water all around the world, does it? Personally I always drink whatever comes out of the tap wherever I am. And I must say, the local water here is delicious.'

Charlie McGarry frowned at her in dismay. This wasn't how he usually insulted the tourists. In the normal run of things they sniffed and blushed and stammered their way out of his store while he gave them the uneconomic, spoilt town-dweller, decadent argument. 'So what can't you see here that you can't do without?' he challenged her, rallying quickly. 'French wine, Italian cheese?'

'Actually it was anchovies,' Kate said.

Charlie's disapproving face now cracked into a smile. 'Well now, I can help you there, you're in luck.'

'Fantastic,' Kate enthused.

'Didn't take you for a fisherwoman,' said Charlie, reassessing the blonde stranger in the turquoise Cuban-heeled boots. 'Can get them down the road at the rod shop.'

'The rod shop,' Kate mused. 'You mean where they sell the fishing tackle?'

Charlie nodded. 'Where else? Round here we don't waste our time eating those tiny little things. We use them to catch bigger fish. Best bait around for hooking salmon.'

'Right,' said Kate, and nodded sagely. 'Terrific, I'll go and get some then.' About to leave, she tried a punt at a longshot. 'I don't suppose you have any olive oil, do you,' she asked him doubtfully.

'Of course I've got olive oil,' he told her, taking an un-expectedly sympathetic tone as he crossed behind his counter to the pharmacy section and produced a small bottle. 'Got the earache?'

She suppressed a giggle. 'Really badly,' she said. 'I think I'd better take four of those.'

There would be no salvation from Mr McGarry in the way of other cooking ingredients, she acknowledged, as she made her way back to her SUV by way of the rod shop – unless she wanted tins of corned beef or packets of pre-made macaroni cheese ('Just add boiling water!'). She would just have to use the produce from the ranch and whatever she could get from Peggy Davies in the way of vegetables. As for the anchovies, she would buy some for Old Pete, and if he'd returned from checking on the livestock, she would send him straight back out again to catch some salmon. In the meantime, while she waited for the food to arrive, she would check out the barn. No way was the dining room at the Blue Yonder going to be big enough for a hundred hungry people.

18

The good news back at the ranch was that all the animals were safe and unharmed by the torrential downpour of the night before. The bad news was that the cease-fire between Andy and Robyn had lasted only as long as the storm, according to Old Pete, and now it seemed that the whole of British Columbia wasn't space enough to have between them. Having dispatched her pet angler to his favourite fishing spot, happy beyond measure to receive his present of the bait, Kate found Robyn gazing morosely at the horses in the corral.

'Hello,' she said, leaning her arms on the top of the fence rail to follow Robyn's gaze. 'Good to hear that all was well with the animals.'

'Huh,' said Robyn. 'What does it matter if we can't get to keep them?'

Bursting with her news, Kate would have loved nothing more than to share her secret about the vet's bill, but struggled to keep her own counsel. It would be cruel to get Robyn's hopes up in case she failed tomorrow's cooking audition and it all came to nought. 'Any news from Jed about the land?' she asked.

'What do I know?' Robyn said viciously. 'You think Andy'd let me in on a little thing like that? No, ma'am, he'll just sell the ranch off under my nose, and the first I'll know of it will be when I see the horses being led away by strangers.'

'I know this is a very hard time for you, Robyn,' Kate dared to say, 'but don't you think you're being a bit hard on him?'

Robyn rounded on her, her eyes full of betrayal. 'Since when did you join his side?' she demanded.

'I haven't. I'm not on any side. I feel sorry for both of you that things have been going so badly.'

'Well don't look at me,' Robyn said bitterly. 'That's his fault.'

'I'm sure be blames himself enough already without you helping to make him feel worse.'

'Good,' said Robyn. 'And so he should.'

Kate settled her chin on her hands to watch a young foal who, blissfully unaware that it might have to go under the hammer before too long, was gadding about kicking its heels in the air and having all manner of frolicsome fun. 'So if you were in charge of the ranch, what would you do differently?' she challenged the girl.

'Sell off the beef and concentrate on breeding horses and ponies,' Robyn said immediately, her depressed air lifting. 'Everybody round here knows I got an eye for it. Bred and trained my own pony. Picked out the sire and dam real careful, and I just knew their foal would be a winner. All the foals you see here have been bred by me.'

'Wow. And what does Andy say about that idea?'

'Oh, like he'd listen to me,' Robyn scoffed.

'Have you suggested it to him?'

'Few hundred times.'

'And?'

'I can do what I like when it comes my turn, but in the meantime the Blue Yonder has to be run like he says, like it was always going to be run when it was first set up. Nothing can be changed. That's his attitude.'

'That does sound a bit inflexible,' Kate conceded. 'Why do you think that is?'

' 'Cos he's a damn fool.'

Kate bit her lip against what she knew would sound to

Robyn like nagging, and instead said, 'You love him really. And I know he loves you.'

'Says who?'

'It's written all over his face whenever he looks at you, Robyn. Surely you can see that?'

Despite her bad mood, Robyn regarded her with curiosity. 'No? All I see is that I never measure up.'

Kate sighed and let her arm fall around Robyn's shoulders. 'He is critical, I'll give you that. But sometimes, people who are in the habit of judging themselves very harshly can't seem to help themselves from judging others harshly too. I don't think it makes them very happy. Do you?'

Robyn reflected on this for a moment, her eyes crinkling into a shrewd look beyond her years. 'Guess you're talking about me there too, ain't you?' she said after a while.

'Do you think you're critical of other people?' Kate asked.

'Of him, I guess. That's a two-way street. Maybe of some of the kids at school too. But you should hear what they say about me.'

'What do they say about you?'

Robyn looked down and kicked at the fence post. 'Nothing,' she said.

'Kids can be very harsh at your age,' Kate said carefully. 'They're growing up fast, getting bombarded by hormones they're not used to handling, and worrying all the time that they're not "normal", whatever that is. There's a great desire to conform and be like everybody else, and just as strongly, there's a huge feeling of wanting to rebel and be different. Difficult time. But it doesn't last for ever. The older you get, the more confident you feel to just say "Sod it", and be who you are.'

'Do you feel that confident now?' asked Robyn.

'Getting there,' Kate smiled. 'Work in progress.'

'Bet you was popular in school though.'

'Then you'd lose your bet. I was far too busy wanting to be liked, which marked me out as a victim. It was easy to hurt my feelings, and easy to make me cry. I'm still a bit like that. I don't take rejection very well, which for an actress, I'm afraid, is a fatal flaw.'

'Anyone who'd want to reject you is just stupid,' Robyn said stolidly.

'Ditto,' said Kate.

They stood then in companionable silence, Kate's arm still given leave to be round Robyn's shoulders, and Robyn's arm snaked round Kate's waist. She really was an affectionate and engaging little creature, Kate reflected – all she needed was the tiniest bit of encouragement and all her angry defences just melted away.

'Getting back to you and Andy now,' Kate mused after a while.

'Which I kinda knew we would,' said Robyn testily.

Kate smiled an apology. 'I'm a great believer in clearing things up as one goes,' she said. 'It can save centuries of conflict. You mentioned earlier about it being a two-way street between you, in relation to criticising each other.'

'You've heard him,' Robyn protested. 'I just give back what he gives me.'

'So in an ideal world, how would you prefer him to treat you?'

Robyn scowled. 'Nice.'

'Like how?'

'Not be on my damn case all the time. Cut me some damn slack.'

'Be less quick to criticise you?' Kate suggested.

'You got it.'

'That sounds reasonable enough. What else?'

Being offered the floor to air her grievances, Robyn accepted with alacrity. 'Give credit where credit's damn due. He never tells me when I'm doing something right, never says, "Yay, great, Robyn, you've done all the chores I set you, and then some!" Just cusses me out when he spots something I done wrong or haven't gotten around to doing yet.'

Kate nodded understandingly and squeezed the girl's shoulders. 'Yes, it's always nice to get praise, isn't it? And to be shown some affection? Like we're doing now.'

'Yeah, well, I wouldn't want him to get too all-out soppy,' said Robyn with a break in her voice. 'But, you know, he could give me the odd hug, maybe a pat on the head now and then. I wouldn't exactly kick him away.'

'So, just to sum up, you'd like him to be less critical, to praise you when you've done something right, and to be a bit more touchy-feely, within reason. Is that about it?'

'Guess that about covers it right enough.'

Kate nodded again reflectively. 'And then, I suppose, it being a two-way street, if he was more like that with you, you'd be more like that with him.'

'Stands to reason,' Robyn agreed. 'It's like training a horse. If you're mean to them, you can be sure as hell that they'll be mean right back at you, but if you're gentle – well now, then you got 'em eating right out of your hand and nuzzlin' you for more.'

'So if we wanted things to change between you and Andy, we'd just have to persuade him to behave differently towards you, and then you could behave differently towards him. Cut him some slack maybe.'

'Why not?' said Robyn, rolling her eyes. 'But, like that's going to happen.'

'Yes, you're right,' Kate admitted. 'Even if we could persuade him of the wisdom of being nicer to you, it might feel strange to him at first. Might be hard for him to make the first affectionate move.'

'Why should it be?' Robyn protested hotly. 'It ain't so hard.

You can do it easy enough, and so can I.' She squeezed herself more snugly under Kate's arm. 'I mean, how hard is this?'

'Well, maybe that could be the answer,' Kate said, as if this thought had just occurred to her and she hadn't been shamelessly leading the girl by the nose. 'Given that you find it easy to be kind and affectionate and nonjudgemental, it might be up to you to lead the way.'

'But he's the grown-up, he should be setting me an example,' Robyn protested.

'Then maybe you could think of him as a naughty horse,' Kate suggested, 'and yourself as the gentle trainer.'

That image amused Robyn enough to say that at least she'd give it a shot. 'I like the way we can talk things over like this, Mata. I'm gonna miss you when you're gone. Wish you could stay here for ever,' she said, a question mark hovering at the end of the sentence.

'Me too,' said Kate. 'It's much nicer being here than in London, buried alive in my flat, waiting for jobs that never come. All this space, that huge sky, the mountains, the trees, the animals—' She gazed around her with regret, knowing that it was only hers for a short time. 'It's like having a lovely holiday from my life.'

'So why not make it permanent?' Robyn insisted.

'I'll stay as long as I can, Robyn, and as long as I'm welcome, but eventually I'm going to have to go back and try to earn my living.'

'Well, if I ever do get to inherit this place, there'll always be a job for you here. You and me together, Kate, what a team that'd be, huh?' Robyn said, eyes shining. 'Me breeding horses and teaching people how to ride, and you coming over all creative in the kitchen. Folk'd come from miles around. We'd clean up, make a fortune.'

'We might at that,' Kate grinned. 'And thank you so much for calling me Kate at last.'

'Welcome, Mata.'

With a deft flick of Kate's ankle, Robyn found herself on the ground. 'Damn,' she said, and shook her head. 'You ever going to teach me that trick?'

'Last thing before I leave,' Kate promised. 'I wouldn't dare do it before then.'

Robyn bounced back up and slapped the dust off her behind. 'In that case, though it hurts to say it in more ways than one, I hope I never learn. Now, if you want to come inside and get mashed at backgammon. .?'

'Done the milking?' Kate asked, who was eager to take a look at the barn with a wedding planner's eye.

Robyn scowled. 'Chores chores chores,' she complained.

'So let's make a game of it,' Kate suggested. 'Race you to the barn. Only,' she added, as Robyn made to get off to a head start, 'we have to hop all the way, ten paces on each leg, while making silly faces.'

As they hopped and grimaced and giggled their way to the milking, Robyn said, 'Are you ever going to grow up?'

'Hope not,' said Kate. 'Doesn't look much fun.'

The race was a photo finish, but as neither of them had thought to bring a camera, they agreed to share the prize, which Kate announced was to milk the cows. She gazed round the lofty space while Robyn went in search of the pails, trying to work out how to decorate it beautifully but inexpensively, since she'd already decided that she would personally meet any extra costs which might arise. It would certainly be big enough to hold everybody, but it would need an awful lot of titivating to make it look festive. For the first time since leaving John Connor's surgery, she started to feel nervous that she was biting off more than she could chew.

'What are you doing?' Robyn asked on her return, watching Kate pace out the length and breadth of the barn while muttering to herself, but Kate was spared having to dissemble an answer by a great triumphant hallooing outside in the yard. Charlie McGarry was good for something apparently. The anchovies had gone down a treat, and Old Pete had returned home victorious from his battle with the salmon.

19

Had there ever been such a day for weather? Andy didn't think so. From the torrents of last night, to the warm blue skies of this morning, through to the chill wind that he and Rusty had to push against, eyes stinging, as they made their way back home: it was as if the other three seasons were so impatient for their turn that they were doing all in their power to make summer nothing but a brief memory.

After such a day he felt alone as could be, and how could it be otherwise? For it was all down to him, make or break. Everything rested on his shoulders, from mending the damn sieve of a roof, to figuring out how to settle the outstanding bills, to what the hell would happen now he'd been and done what he'd done. He was the dot on the map where the buck stopped, and he knew himself to be unequal to the task.

He'd had plenty of thinking time up on the roof after he'd dispatched Old Pete and Robyn to go check on the herd, crawling about on his hands and knees with the word 'hypocrite' ringing in his ears. He couldn't blame her for saying it. Hell, he'd have been thinking it himself even if Robyn hadn't flung it at him when he'd told her she was excused from school for the day. On her back all the time to go get herself an education, then as soon as it rains he's telling her not to because she's needed here at home. So he could bear the criticism; it only reflected his own way of thinking. No, it wasn't the words that came out of her mouth when he'd sent the kid off to do a man's job (his job, as should have been, for what else justified his existence except to be there as her protector?). It was the look of ice-cold hatred in her eyes that had chilled him to the marrow and left him feeling so alone and so bereft. And such a fraud.

So there he'd been, fraudulently working all morning as a roofer, when any damn fool who'd witnessed the times he'd been up there and come back down thinking that he'd fixed the damn thing over the years could have pointed out the lie in that, playing and replaying the image of her eyes in his mind, feeling her contempt wash over him and through him and leaving nothing but a shell. Hollowed out. That was how he was left feeling. A useless, empty, hollow shell of a man, who would do everybody a big favour if he left off telling them what to do and how to do it and admitted that he didn't know, he had no idea how to fix things now, it was all too bust up, all too much, all too late in the day for anything to work. But work he did, like an automaton, replacing one tile for another in a useless, endless quest to make a roof out of a colander; then on to the barn to hammer nails into flapping boards, as if it made any difference what he did, as if it wouldn't all come loose again as soon as he'd walked away. And all the time thinking, thinking, thinking, which way to turn? What to do next? Is there something else I could have tried? Did I leave a stone unturned?

Zero followed zero, until finally he had to admit that there was nothing that he could come up with that would make any of it any better, except maybe just one thing. Wouldn't save the ranch. Wouldn't mend the roof. Certainly wouldn't pay the bills. But would it take the hatred out of those eyes which he treasured above all others? Saddling up Rusty and cantering out of the yard, he had to believe that it might. At least it would prove that he loved her, at least it would show that he cared.

For better or worse, it was done. His frantic gallop out had turned into a dispirited walk home. Arriving back at the ranch and seeing Robyn's pony in the corral, he took his time grooming Rusty until even his horse couldn't wait to be free of him, and he squared his shoulders and set his jaw to enter the kitchen and meet that pair of eyes. What he didn't expect to see in them was affection, even after he'd told her, but that's what he saw and it nearly undid him.

As always, Kate was cooking. She'd become a fixture of the kitchen now, just as much as the range itself. The air was fragrant and steamy, and it seemed as if she had every single pot and pan out of the cupboards and put to use. Old Pete was holding forth about how he'd caught a four-foot salmon, and that same salmon was lying in two dozen pieces, some of it cooked and being eaten, some of it being fussed over by Kate even now, as she looked over towards him with a welcoming smile, and sent a quick questioning glance over to Robyn, which was answered by a tumult of emotion in the kid's expression, but which settled, as she got up to approach him, into something so gentle that his breath caught in his throat.

'Been thinking about how I left things with you,' she told him, taking his hat out of his hands and hanging it on its peg, 'and I'd like to apologise. I was way out of line.'

Andy swallowed hard, and his kerchief was pressed into service on account of the dust being blown up by the wind on his way home.

'Had the same trouble myself,' Robyn sniffed, occasioning her shirt sleeve to be wiped across her face and a rather wet and sticky paw to be offered. 'No hard feelings? Shake?'

He shook.

Another raised-eyebrow glance of encouragement from Kate to Robyn was frowned right back at, boots were narrowly examined, reclaimed hand was wiped on the seat of her pants and then, about to turn away, Robyn's body changed its mind and her arms were around his waist, her face pressed against his chest, then just as quickly withdrawn. A grin was fighting to claim her mouth and if he hadn't known her better, Andy would have said that she looked shy.

'We're putting Mata through her paces,' she told him, as she returned to her seat and the morsel of salmon which awaited her attention, without further comment about the hug. 'Come try this. It's a competition. We have to decide which way we like it best.'

'Sounds good,' said Andy, settling down beside her to eat. 'Mm, is good. You catch this, Old Pete?'

'Nope,' said the old timer. 'Just waved them anchovies about that Katie brought me, and the damn fish near jumped out of the water and onto the bank their own selves. Got so many I thought my horse's legs were going to give out on the way home carrying them back. Tell you, freezer's stocked to the gills with them. Going to be eating these damn fish till Kingdom come.'

'That why you're trying out all these recipes, Kate?' Andy asked her, as she clattered about at the stove and swiped her hair out of her eyes with her forearm. 'So's we don't get bored?'

'Sort of,' she said, her attention all given to the cooking. 'Sorry, I'm just at a crucial stage at the moment. I'll just get this lot done and then I'll . . .' Her voice trailed off in a flurry of activity.

'She came over all creative again,' Robyn explained. 'Can't seem to help herself when there's food about.'

'Oh, this one is it!' said Andy, having chosen another titbit off a plate. 'This is the downright winner in my book so far. What's in it?'

'We have to guess that too,' said Robyn. 'But so far, me and Old Pete ain't scored much in that department. All we can guess right is the salmon part of the recipe.'

'If I had more choice of ingredients,' Kate lamented, bringing another platter to the table. 'More spices to play with. But Charlie McGarry doesn't go a bundle on exotica, does he? Beyond creamed corn, that is, which I have to say I've never encountered before.'

'Went into town, then?' Andy asked conversationally.

Kate coloured slightly, although her complexion already being rosy from the cooking, nobody noticed but herself. 'Just thought I'd see what the bright lights had to offer,' she joked.

'Surprised you're back so early then,' Andy bantered back. 'So much to see and do down there you might have got caught up for days.'

Robyn grinned. She hadn't heard Andy being so light-hearted in an age. 'Hey,' she said to Kate, who had gone back to work at the counter, 'come sit with us and eat.'

'I will in a minute. I just want to try this next thing out,' Kate said. But the minutes passed and then an hour, and still she cooked and still they ate, chatting amongst themselves, swapping stories of their day. The two big stories, though, remained untold. Kate's, because she didn't want to get everybody excited about the wedding and John Connor's bill in case it didn't happen, and Andy's because the atmosphere was so friendly, he didn't want to spoil things by reminding them of the knife edge on which the fortunes of the Blue Yonder currently rested. They were playing a spirited and good-humoured game of backgammon and begging Kate not to feed them any more when the phone rang and Andy answered it, and suddenly everybody stopped breathing, the atmosphere changed, and fun was put on hold.

'Don't sell, don't sell,' Robyn breathed, her hands clenched into tight fists, as Andy went 'Uh-huh,' and 'Okay', and finally, 'Hang on', into the receiver, after which he replaced it in its cradle and left the room with a backward, 'Just need to take this in the office.'

'Don't sell!' Robyn yelled after him, but he was gone. 'Damn it to hell!' she shouted, banging her fists on the table. 'He's going to sell my damn land!'

Kate's mind raced. Should she follow him and tell him that she might have won him a reprieve or should she leave it? Surely, even if he accepted Jed's offer, if indeed it was Jed on the phone, then he wouldn't be bound by a verbal agreement. He'd still be able to change his mind if the news was good after tomorrow night's visit to John and Sonia, wouldn't he? But it was hard to think with Robyn yelling and banging like this, and it was such a shame, because the girl had been doing so well all evening with her new mode of conduct, and Andy had shown his softer side, and everything had been lovely. 'Robyn,' she begged, 'do calm down, you could be getting all excited about nothing. It could be anybody calling.'

'Then why'd he take it in the damn office?' Robyn flung back. 'So's I couldn't hear him and stop him, that's why. See? What did I tell you? He don't ask me nothing. It's all him. And here's me being nice to him all night, and here's him—'

And here he was indeed, arriving back in the kitchen with a blandly genial smile.

'What did he say?' she demanded.

The smile crinkled around his eyes. 'He said there'd be two of them.'

Robyn blinked. 'Two what?' she asked suspiciously.

'Guests,' said Andy, taking his place back at the table. 'Friends of Nancy's, he said, that woman who was staying here before? Wanted to know if the English gourmet cook was still with us, and when I said she was, he got all excited and made the booking. You've brought us luck, Kate, with your creative talents. Hope there'll still be some of this salmon to go around.'

'Terrific!' Kate said, her expression overbright with anxiety. 'When?'

'Damn,' said Robyn at the same moment, shaking her head both in relief and embarrassment. 'I thought it was that damn Jed Gray.'

'Oh,' said Andy, for once not telling her off about her language. 'Guess I didn't get around to telling you about that, did I?' He picked up the dice and shook them. 'Was it my go or yours?' he asked.

'Didn't get around to telling me about what?' Robyn said, grabbing his hand to get his attention and shoving her face aggressively in his.

'Damn Jed Gray,' he said, and to everybody's surprise, including, it seemed, his own, he suddenly dived forward and kissed her on the nose. 'I do believe it was my turn you know.'

'Yyyyek! Andy Barrett, if you don't stop horsing around,' Robyn threatened, ostentatiously wiping her face.

'What will happen?'

'I'll kill you.'

'In front of all these witnesses?'

'Just spit it out, for Pete's sake!'

'No need to spit on my account,' Old Pete contributed drily.

'Tell me!'

'Rode out there this afternoon and told him the land isn't for sale,' he said. 'Nothing to get het up about. Doesn't solve our problems.'

Robyn was perfectly still, regarding him in wonder. 'Why?' she asked eventually in a small voice.

' 'Cos my partner didn't go along with the idea,' Andy said gruffly. 'And it seemed to me it wasn't worth losing her for the few dollars it might've fetched.' Again he rattled the dice. 'Now can we finish this damn game?'

But apparently they couldn't, since Robyn was too busy jumping on him and punching him and burying him in a hug.

'Now ain't this like old times,' Old Pete murmured, with a grin from ear to ear. He looked at Kate to share his enjoyment, and saw in her expression a person who was waiting for the other shoe to drop. 'All right there, girlie?' he enquired.

Kate struggled to show unqualified approval of the change in relations between Andy and Robyn. 'Fantastic!' she asserted, nodding vigorously. 'Really great! I was just wondering when the new guests have booked to come?'

'Weekend,' Andy provided softly, for with all the food inside her and the little sleep she'd had the night before, the fight had gone out of Robyn and she had nestled in his lap with droopy eyes.

'This coming weekend?' Kate asked shrilly.

Andy looked up at her. 'Is that going to be a problem?' he asked.

'Problem?' said Kate. 'Problem?' She laughed in a strangely febrile manner. 'Why on earth would that be a problem?'

20

Having been bounced awake by Robyn, as always, at an un-
reasonably early hour, Kate was not her usual ebullient self.
There was no hopping, face-pulling race to the barn to milk the
cows, no high jinks ju-jitsu throw to have Robyn sent sprawling
to the ground and giggling her way back up again, and little in
the way of conversation. She looked very small, hunched up
under Milker One's hindquarters, as if, thought Robyn, she was
frightened that something dreadful was about to happen.

'You okay there, Mata?' she asked, as she watched Kate's
eyes flick nervously about the barn.

'Fine,' said Kate.

But Robyn was unconvinced. 'You worried about something?' she suggested.

Kate forced an inspirited smile. 'Absolutely not!'

'That's good,' Robyn smiled back. ''Cos it's Saturday. No
school. I can take you out on that ride if you like. Pack up a
lunch and go all the way out to Green Lake.'

'That would have been lovely,' Kate said regretfully. 'But
I'm afraid I can't go today. I'll be far too busy.'

'What you got planned?' Robyn asked with interest.

'Oh, you know, cooking,' said Kate.

Robyn looked at her as if she feared for her sanity. '*More*
cooking? You didn't cook enough last night?'

'I'm . . . on a sort of a cooking roll,' Kate explained with
difficulty. 'I've had a few new ideas, and I just feel the need to
try them out.'

'You don't seem all that happy about it,' said Robyn, examining the anxious face before her.

'Well I am,' Kate asserted in a doom-laden voice. 'I'm raring to go in actual fact. Dying to get back behind that cooker. Can't wait!'

Robyn just couldn't see it and knew something was wrong. 'Is it because you're nervous about the gourmet guests coming next weekend?' she suggested.

'Yes! That's it!' Kate said gratefully. 'I need to practise for the gourmet guests.' She stood up suddenly, almost knocking over the pail of milk in her haste. 'Better get started,' she said brightly.

'Need to practise making pancakes?' Robyn called after her hopefully. ''Cos I could sure use the practice at eating them.'

Kate turned in the doorway, but instead of looking at Robyn, again her eyes swept the barn anxiously. 'Absolutely,' she answered distractedly.

'And fried chicken for lunch?' said Robyn, pushing her luck, since clearly Kate's mind was elsewhere.

'Fried chicken,' Kate repeated and, as if waking from a daydream, said, 'fried chicken, of course! What a brilliant idea! Excellent!' before scurrying out.

'Welcome,' said Robyn. She didn't know what strange ailment was afflicting her friend, but if the main symptom was cooking to order, she hoped she didn't recover too soon.

Rarely, if ever, did Andy allow himself to be bossed about and organised into doing something he hadn't already made up his mind to do himself, but that morning, where he had planned on doing more work around the ranch house, he found himself saddling up Rusty and going out for a 'nice long bonding ride', as prescribed by Kate, with both Robyn and Old Pete.

'It must be ages since the three of you went out for a ride together,' she said, as she watched them stow the food she'd cooked into their saddle bags. 'So just enjoy yourselves and take your time. Don't worry about me! I'll be very happy here, making nice things to eat for supper. Stay out all day! Good-bye!'

Being waved out of his own yard felt kind of strange, but she was right, it had been a long, long time since the three of them had enjoyed a whole day in each other's company on horse-back, and as they trotted out on the trail, Andy felt his spirits lift and his feelings of foreboding evaporate – at least for the day.

'Shoulder holding up okay?' he asked Old Pete as he drew abreast with him.

'Ain't give me no trouble since girlie gave me that rub down,' Old Pete told him, demonstrating his newfound mo-bility. 'Don't ask me how, but it's fixed. Got a susstiffikit in miracles for all I know.'

'Mata can fix anything,' Robyn contributed happily. 'Spe-cially pancakes.'

'Amen to that,' said Andy, his stomach comfortably full. He was aware that the feelings of jealousy he'd harboured towards Kate were now unnecessary and irrelevant. Like Old Pete, he didn't know how she worked her magic, but the change she'd wrought in Robyn's behaviour was something miraculous to behold. 'Race you to the bluff!' he cried impulsively, suddenly feeling as if he were thirteen years old again himself, and they all galloped like the wind, hallooing like idiotic city slickers on a weekend break.

After slaving over a hot stove all day, Kate was as prepared as she possibly could be for her audition. She had rehearsed her patter, dressed the part – as well as she could with her limited holiday wardrobe – and baked, grilled, roasted and fried any amount of dainty dishes for John and Sonia to sample. Never-theless she was more nervous than she'd ever been as she

ferried the food from her SUV to Sonia's front porch, for
never before had she had the added pressure of trying to
succeed on somebody else's behalf rather than her own. She
had, of course, taken her four drops of Mimulus, the homeo-
pathic tincture for 'fear of the known', which was her habitual
remedy for stage fright and without which she never left home;
she had grounded herself so thoroughly that she feared she
might be immobilised completely by the roots she'd visualised
growing out of her feet, and which had found a home deep
down under Sonia's decking; and her old drama school voice
coach would have been proud indeed of the control she was
currently exercising over her breathing.

For a vet's receptionist, Sonia had an unexpectedly large
house, and everything that could have been done to it in the
way of decoration had been done, but in terms of home
improvement, Kate felt that it might have been better left
unimproved. The curtains at the front were what her mother
always called 'tart's knickers', swags of coffee-hued net
bunched up into pouches, featuring lace trimmings in cerise,
and peeking out from under them on the interior sills were any
amount of china figures, jammed in, cheek by jowl, three deep.
Clearly, Sonia was no slave to minimalism. There was so
much furniture out here on the porch, including false dec-
orative shutters on every window, a three-seater canopied
swinging chair, wagon wheels either side of the front door,
planters and pots of all shapes and sizes, a huge enamelled
foot-scraper in the shape of two brightly coloured elves
carrying something which looked disconcertingly like a ma-
chete, that Kate wondered if there would be room enough
inside for her and all her samples. She rang the front-door bell
and tried to persuade herself that there was nothing whatever
to be worried about: not the fact that she had just proved to
herself that there was no way she could cater such a large event
single-handed, nor that to convert the barn into a suitable

venue for a wedding reception would take more money and ingenuity than she could currently muster (particularly now that she had seen Sonia's cluttered, over-blown taste in decor), nor that she was expected to provide gourmet meals for two new guests at the same time as catering for a hundred. Appearing confident and selling herself was all that mattered at the moment, she reminded herself, and as she waited for the door to be opened, she arranged her smile as if she were about to step out of the wings and onto the stage for the biggest, most important performance of her life.

As the door swung open, the interior more than lived up to the promise of the porch, with its comprehensive collection of framed prints covering almost every inch of every wall, its highly polished pieces of occasional furniture which fought to be seen under their burden of knick knacks, and Sonia Driesen swathed in a profusion of pinks. Standing by her side, John Connor looked rather out of place in his comfortable taupe corduroys and beige sweater.

'Hi there!' said Kate, as she carried in her baskets and boxes with no help at all from her hostess, but with a great deal of gentlemanly assistance from her host. 'What a lovely house!'

Sonia nodded graciously, accepting this as no more than her due. In contrast to her heightened mood of hysteria the day before, she appeared beadily businesslike as Kate assembled her wares in her dining room, but having tapped into the local jungle tomtoms of her gossip circle since their last meeting, the business she wanted to get right down to straight away was, 'Is it true you hit on Andy through the internet?'

Kate choked on a short laugh of surprise. 'Not exactly hit on!' she protested.

'No?' said Sonia, in a disbelieving tone.

'No,' Kate confirmed firmly. Having taken the cling film off a plate of bite-sized savoury tarts, she offered it for Sonia and

John's inspection with a professional air. 'Now what we've got here is—'

But this lady was not for turning. 'So what would you call it then?' she asked, settling into a seat, the better to enjoy Kate's performance.

'Now, Sonia,' said John, who wasn't used to being party to women's gossip, and felt sympathy with Kate's evident embarrassment. And besides, he was hungry. 'Shouldn't we get on with the tasting?'

'Sure, taste away,' Sonia told him dismissively. 'I can't eat those things now, not with my wedding-dress diet. You want to go down the aisle with me busting out of my zip?'

'Well, no,' John conceded.

'So eat, eat for two,' Sonia told him. She turned her beady gaze back on Kate. 'You were saying.'

'Yes,' said Kate, attempting to wrest back control of the proceedings. 'What you've got there, John, is the mushroom and onion.'

John nodded and swallowed, pastry crumbs clinging to his lips. 'Very good. Very light, and tasty, and—'

'And next to it,' said Kate, keeping up her momentum, 'going clockwise, is spinach with—'

'Just keep eating clockwise while we girls talk,' Sonia advised him severely. She turned a bright smile of inquisition Kate's way. 'Have you dated quite a few guys on the internet?'

'No,' said Kate. 'Absolutely not. Never.'

'They can be quite racy, I understand, these chat rooms,' said Sonia, flicking a quick glance John's way. 'Or so some of my girlfriends say.'

'Probably,' said Kate. 'I wouldn't know, I never use them. I play backgammon on the net – for amusement, I hasten to add, not to gamble. And, you know, players get chatting, you make friends.'

'So you "made friends" with Andy Barrett,' Sonia marvelled, demonstrating the quotation marks with her crooked fingers. 'Quite a feat. He's very resistant to "making friends" with the ladies.' Again the flicked glance towards her betrothed. 'Several girls of my acquaintance have grown into old maids trying.'

'And mine,' John offered, through a spray of pastry crumbs, having already eaten his way round to four o'clock.

Sonia turned on him swiftly. 'Are you calling me an old maid?' she demanded.

'No,' John smiled. 'I'm just saying that one man's resistance was this man's good fortune.'

'He's talking through his ass as usual,' Sonia confided to Kate, with a withering look at her fiancé. 'No, with Andy it's just that I used to feel sorry for the poor guy, bringing up Robyn all on his lonesome.'

'He's doing a very good job of it,' Kate said, searching through boxes for another prop to distract her hostess, and finding the mini Yorkshire puddings stuffed with roast beef. 'Ah, now, these little beauties would be served hot on the day. Do you have a microwave I could use?'

'Well, he has if you think bringing up a little girl to be a little boy is a good idea,' Sonia said damningly. 'Personally I think she's suffered from not having some feminine influence around her.'

'Can't really see Robyn going for frou-frou,' Kate said with a smile, eyeing Sonia's costume.

'Not now, that's my point,' said the woman in ribbons and frills. 'She'd have turned out very different if she'd just been given a little bit of encouragement about what she wears and how she presents herself. Could have been quite the young lady.'

'I like her the way she is,' Kate said shortly. 'The microwave?'

'He'll eat them cold,' said Sonia, with a dismissive wave

towards her beloved. 'So, you're playing backgammon and "making friends" with Andy, and what – he invites you over to Canada?'

Kate sighed. Clearly there was going to be no selling her culinary skills to this woman until she'd been given the full story. 'Not exactly, Sonia. He said he'd broken his arm after a fall from his horse, and with him being short-staffed, and with me being – at a loose end, shall we say – I thought I'd come over and help out on the ranch in any way I could.'

'What kind of a loose end?' Sonia asked, being unwilling to leave anything of that nature herself in her desire to get down and dirty.

'I was – in a bit of a pickle,' said Kate elliptically. Goodness knows she didn't want to get into the whole Sally Black débâcle now. 'Sort of housebound, for one reason and another, and with a lot of time on my hands.'

Sonia's eyes widened. 'This was after you murdered the baby?' she suggested, sitting forward with interest. 'Tell me, how come they didn't arrest you?'

'I'm an actress, for heavens sake!' said Kate wearily.

'So that gives you the right to kill and get away with it?'

'No, it means that sometimes I play unpopular parts. My character, in a soap opera, abducted a baby and had an affair with its father. It became difficult for me to go out, because of exactly this kind of misunderstanding.'

'An actress,' Sonia mused salaciously. 'So what's it like? Is it true what they say about the casting couch?'

'Not that I've ever encountered,' said Kate.

'But what's it like to have to kiss somebody, or get in bed with them, that you hardly even know?'

'It's just a job, like any other. We're all professionals.'

'I'll bet you are,' Sonia drawled, admiration and envy vying for ascendency in her tone. 'So go on, you've got Andy going on the internet, he tells you some lie about busting his arm to get you over here, and then what? How was it when the two of you laid eyes on each other? You must have been happy to see how good looking he is. What if he'd been pug ugly? Would you still have gone after him then?'

'I haven't gone after him, Sonia,' Kate protested.

Sonia regarded her with a smug smile. 'So why are you doing all this then, trying to pay off his debts? Hey – that must have been a disappointment, finding out he was broke. Bet he didn't tell you that while he was busy "making friends" with you.'

'He did actually. But as it turned out, the person who'd been calling himself "Andy the Cowboy" wasn't Andy at all. And don't ask me who it was, because I have absolutely no idea.'

'Explain yourself,' Sonia commanded, forgetting for the moment her wedding-dress diet, and sinking her neat white teeth into a piece of fried chicken. 'Mm! You know, this isn't bad! For an actress.'

'I do have catering qualifications too,' Kate said stiffly, inflating by omission of detail her Certificate in Basic Food Hygiene.

'Aren't you the prodigy?' said Sonia. 'So anyway, go on. What are you saying? That he pretended he didn't know anything about asking you over when you got to his ranch? That would be so like him. Leading a girl on and then coming over all innocent when she makes a move.'

'There was no pretence about it,' Kate protested. 'He was quite genuinely surprised.'

'I'll bet. Didn't expect you take him up on it is why. I've often wondered what he does for sex, but I guess it figures, these days, that he'd find it on the web,' Sonia said reflectively. 'Must be a godsend to him, having a computer, all those long lonely nights up there, with only the kid and the old man for company.'

'We didn't talk about sex!' Kate said hotly. 'We played

perfectly respectable games of backgammon and talked about everyday things – my work, his work, London, the Blue Yonder. But that's beside the point. It was *not* Andy I'd been chatting to, there's no question in my mind, I'm absolutely certain about that.'

'What makes you so sure?' Sonia asked.

'Because this person, whoever they were, had an air of experience about them that I just don't see in the real Andy Barrett.'

'"Experience," eh?' Sonia echoed, this time her arched eyebrow demonstrating the inverted commas. 'What kind of "experience" are we talking here?'

Really, thought Kate, this was like talking to her Uncle George with the relentless double entendres, or like being in an old-fashioned West End farce entitled "Plenty of Sex Please, I'm Canadian". However, she reminded herself, this was no time to fall out with her potential employer. She mustered a friendly smile. '*Life* experience, Sonia,' she said. 'Talking to Andy the Cowboy on the net was almost like talking to a girlfriend.'

'Where's the fun in that?' Sonia asked, mystified. 'Or what – you talked about clothes?'

'No, we talked over problems. My problems mostly,' Kate recalled guiltily. 'And he was always so – attentive, and receptive. I don't know about you, but I don't know many men – except my gay friends, of course – who are really good listeners.'

Sonia was indignant. 'John,' she said, indicating her intended, who was currently chewing ruminatively. He became aware that he was the focus of both women's attention.

'Sorry?' he said, swallowing rapidly. 'Sorry, I didn't catch what you—*That*,' he continued, his attention entirely absorbed by the plate he was pointing at, 'is the most remarkable thing I have ever eaten! What on earth is it?'

Kate was stricken with anxiety. 'It's something I made up. Salmon profiteroles. Andy and the others voted it in last night. But if you don't like it . . . I mean, that's what today's all about, you choosing the ones you prefer.'

'Sensational,' said John enthusiastically, helping himself to another, and offering one to Sonia. Her baleful glare stopped him in his tracks. 'Sorry, sorry, you were about to say something?'

Sonia swivelled her gaze to Kate. 'Yeah, okay, you've proved your point. But normally, when he's not distracted by food . . .' She paused to reflect. 'Or work . . .' And again. 'Or his damned hockey team . . .'

'Absolutely,' Kate agreed eagerly, who was now completely won over by John. 'I'm sure he's really empathetic and kind. But is that how you'd describe Andy?'

'I can think of other words,' said Sonia. 'Like cold, rude, and son of a bitch.'

'I'm sure he doesn't mean to be,' Kate said loyally, hoping this had now put an end to any further probing from her hostess. 'Anyway, Sonia, to get back to your wedding reception—'

'You're hired,' said John decisively.

'Really? That's fantastic!'

'How come?' said Sonia, pursuing her last line of enquiry.

'Because this is the best food I've had since—' John diplomatically halted his eulogy. 'Since the last time you cooked for me, my love.'

'Yeah, yeah, I'm taking that as a given,' said Sonia. 'Given that your snout hasn't been out of the trough since she got here. And as far as I'm concerned, she was hired before she arrived. I mean, at this notice, who else is there?'

Kate could have hoped for more fulsome praise, but nevertheless she was elated at having succeeded in her bid. 'So shall we go through which are your favourites?' she asked John,

taking up her pen and notepad, which Sonia promptly re-
quisitioned and handed to him.

'Make a list,' she instructed him. 'Mark them out of ten.'
She turned back to Kate. 'What do you mean when you say
you're sure Andy doesn't mean to be such a son of a bitch? If
he doesn't mean to be, why does he behave that way?'

'I'm not sure,' said Kate, who had of course been pondering
this question since she'd first met him. 'You're probably better
qualified than me to guess at that, given that you've known
him for much longer than I have. But he seems a bit of a
troubled soul to me. I get the sense that he's very lonely. I don't
mean for company,' she hastily amended, 'but that he has a
deep sense of aloneness for some reason.' It occurred to her
that being in the company of one of the town's most assiduous
gossips, she might expand her knowledge of him now, if she
asked the right questions. 'I've been wondering if he misses
Rainbow,' she mused. 'Do you think he has any regrets in that
direction?'

Sonia looked confused. 'If he misses rainbows? What do
you mean by that? Is it English slang?'

Kate laughed. 'No, no, Rainbow, Robyn's mother.'

'Rainbow? He calls her Rainbow?'

Now it was Kate's turn to be bewildered. 'Isn't that her
name?'

Sonia shrugged. 'The rest of us called her Laura,' she said.
'First I've ever heard of Rainbow. Why would he call her that?'

'Because she's a hippy?' Kate suggested.

'A hippy! Laura, a hippy?' Sonia laughed. 'Do you hear this,
John?'

John looked up from his list wearing a perplexed frown.
'Mm,' he said, and addressing Kate, confessed, 'to be honest
I'd be happier if you picked the dishes. It's all good to me. I'd
be sorry to leave any of it out. I keep giving everything ten out
of ten.'

Kate thanked him with genuine pleasure, as she struggled to make sense of Sonia's amusement. 'Actually,' she said finally, 'it wasn't Andy who told me she was a hippy called Rainbow. It was the person who was pretending to be "Andy the Cowboy".'

'Got that wrong then, didn't they?' said Sonia.

Kate nodded thoughtfully. 'Which is strange, since an awful lot of other stuff he told me turned out to be pretty accurate. The plot thickens, as they say.'

'Who *is* this person?' Sonia wanted to know.

'Your guess is as good as mine,' said Kate. 'Somebody who knows him quite well, but not as well as I'd first thought.'

'What are you doing with that?' Sonia said sharply, as she watched Kate start to pack up the food.

'I thought we'd finished?' said Kate.

'Finished? We've hardly even started,' said Sonia emphatically. 'We need to discuss all the finer details. And you can leave that food right there. It'll do for our supper. After all, we've paid for it.'

It was a moot point which Kate was happy to let pass, but when it came to other factors for which Sonia felt they had already paid by cancelling Andy's debt, including the matter of six cases of imported champagne and enough wine and beer to ruin the livers of the entire wedding party, she had to draw the line.

'It's just the food and the venue we're providing for the negotiated sum,' she protested.

' 'T'isn't,' Sonia countered, in the adversarial manner favoured in most schoolyards.

Kate grew quite flustered and wished her agent was there to help her with his expertise in clauses and subclauses and heretofores and thereins. 'Honestly,' she admitted, appealing to a better nature that Sonia had given no indication of possessing, 'I'm sorry if you misunderstood, but there's no way I can do that and come out anything like even. Any extras are coming out of my own pocket.'

'Not my problem,' Sonia informed her. 'A deal's a deal.'

'Actually that wasn't the deal, Sonia,' said John, unexpectedly coming to Kate's defence. 'It wasn't the deal with Solveig, and it isn't the deal with Kate and Andy. I've already ordered the booze, which I'll arrange to have delivered to the ranch on the day. Sonia likes to negotiate hard, Kate,' he explained equably. 'It's nothing personal. You could call it a kind of a hobby of hers.'

'My hobby, your loss,' Sonia sniffed. 'And you know what they say about a fool and his money.'

'Well, at least we're parting on friendly terms,' John smiled.

'What about the cake?' Kate asked. 'Is that to be delivered to the Blue Yonder too, or will I need to pick it up from somewhere?' But it transpired that the cake *had* been part of the deal with Solveig, since her main talent was as a patissière.

'A traditional three-tiered fruit cake with marzipan and perfectly smooth icing?' Kate queried anxiously, since she had never before attempted such a feat.

'No!' said Sonia in disgust. 'I want to be able to eat the thing! A four-tiered chocolate-frosted fudge cake with coffee-cream filling and whipped cream and chocolate sauce served on the side.'

'Not a problem,' said Kate with some relief.

'I'm getting the glasses loaned with the wine,' said John, 'so you won't have to worry about that—'

'Unless any get broken, in which case, you bear the cost,' said Sonia, busy with her hobby again.

John bit his lip, and managed to convey to Kate with a wink over his fiancée's head that this was not a thing to worry hers over. '—but will you have enough plates for a hundred people?'

'I'm afraid not. If you know anywhere I can hire some at a

reasonable cost, I'd be most grateful for your local knowledge,' she said.

John made a jotting on his notepad. 'Give Chris Pope a call. He can help you with that, and if you tell him it's for Sonia, he'll automatically do it at a loss,' he joked. 'How about tables and chairs?'

'And how in hell are you going to fit them all into that poky dining room?' Sonia wanted to know. 'I don't like being cramped.'

'I've thought about that,' Kate told her, as one who was about to deliver a marvellous gift. 'And I've decided to do it in the big barn. It's a wonderful, huge space, almost cathedral-like in height—'

'The *barn*?' Sonia expostulated. 'Do you think that I'm a cow?'

Choking back the obvious answer, Kate extolled the virtues of her chosen venue instead. 'I promise you won't be disappointed,' she concluded. 'It's one of my talents, transforming spaces for next to nothing with a little ingenuity and improvisation.'

'Of that I have no doubt,' said John tactfully, 'but are you going to have time to do all that as well as the catering?'

Kate was worried about this herself. 'The others will help,' she said doubtfully. 'I'm sure that we can manage.'

'Gary Strange,' said John, adding to his notes. 'He directs and designs all the Drama Society shows here. If you feel the need for a fellow artistic eye, or help in locating furnishings, he's your man.'

Sonia's eyebrow lifted to vie with her hairline. 'Strange Gary – not in name only, I am here to tell you – is nobody's *man*, exactly,' she opined. 'But you being an actress, I guess he'll be nothing new to you.'

'This is so kind of you, John,' Kate told him gratefully, taking the contact details as he showed her to the door.

'Well now, there's something we have in common then,' he replied. 'It's very kind of you to be helping out the folks at the Blue Yonder. I've been feeling bad about being unable to go on providing unpaid visits, and I've got a lot of respect for Andy Barrett. He's been having it tough lately, and it's a relief to know that at last he's got a good woman at his side.'

'Well you know, not in *that* way,' Kate qualified, a becoming blush rising to her cheeks.

'In any way,' said John. 'I think I heard you mention his sense of aloneness earlier when you were talking with Sonia? Very astute of you. I'm glad for him that he's got some company now.'

'Don't know why she came over all coy about it,' Sonia remarked after Kate had been waved off. 'I'll lay you twenty to one that the two of them are at it night and day up there, like rabbits on Viagra.'

21

The trio of cowboys who sat, at first patiently, round the table in the Blue Yonder kitchen were tired, hungry, puzzled to find no sign of Kate, and frankly astonished to find none of the food she'd promised would be waiting for them on their return.

'Maybe she's took it to give out to the deserving poor,' Old Pete remarked drily, in the early stages of their wait. 'She'll be walking on water next, or turning it into wine, you mark my words.'

'But that's us,' protested Robyn. 'We're the deserving poor.'

Again she checked out the larder, the cupboards, the icebox, and lifted every lid off every pan in case she'd missed something, but there was no evidence at all of Kate having been on a cooking roll that day, save for the faint tantalising aroma of roasted meat and baking which lingered in the air enough to torment their taste buds something terrible.

'Think she's packed up and gone?' Old Pete suggested, which had Robyn making a frantic dash to Kate's room and a breathless but relieved return.

'Nope,' she announced. 'Her stuff's still there.'

Still they sat at the table like Skinner's rats, slaves to learned behaviour, and to fill their time, if not their stomachs, Old Pete rested his head on it, Robyn kicked her heels under it, and Andy drummed his fingers on it. After their happy hours together in the saddle they were now inclined to be of a more sombre frame of mind. Not that they hadn't had the best day ever, on that they were all agreed. They'd felt light as air, turning their backs on chores at the ranch house, turning their thoughts away from their troubles, just doing what came naturally to a cowboy, riding across country checking on the stock, noting the condition of the pasture and the new calves, telling each other stories which they all knew by heart but which were in no way diminished by repetition.

Being in each other's company and removed from the daily grind, there was no need for Robyn to sulkily rebel and therefore no need for Andy to censure her, and no reason for Old Pete to grumble about being housebound, so old wounds had been given a chance to heal and chasms of misunderstanding had been bridged. It had, in short, been the kind of bonding experience that Kate Thornton had prescribed. They'd had time to share their worries rather than to fight about them, and when they passed through the land which had been saved from joining Jed Gray's ever-expanding spread, Robyn at last began to appreciate that this had been a mixed blessing, for beautiful as it was, and full of happy memories, it didn't line their pockets: after such a day of enjoyment the piper still had to be paid – along with their other creditors – and hence the sobriety of their mood now, made worse by hunger, and from a strange, gut-deep, ancient feeling which, if they had given vent to it, would have had them all red-faced and bawling, 'Momma!'

Andy's drumming ceased abruptly, occasioned by a sudden thought. 'You don't think she could have come out after us?' he asked. 'Can she ride?'

Robyn sniggered. 'She says yes, but from the look of her landing on her butt when she tried to get a halter on Rusty, I'd say no.'

A meeting of three pairs of eyes, now made round and large with alarm, preceded three pairs of legs rapidly conveying their owners outside to count the horses and check the tack room, but all was in place, and nothing was missing except Kate's SUV.

'If this don't beat all,' Old Pete grumbled, echoing his empty belly, as they made their way back indoors to sit again round the table. 'First we can't wait to see the back of her, and now she ain't here we don't know what to do with ourselves.'

The truth of this struck Andy as absurd. 'We managed okay without her well enough before she showed up,' he said, getting up again to rummage in the larder. 'There must be something here we could eat. Bread and jam? Cereal?'

'Grilled salmon in that pastry confabulation,' moaned Old Pete.

'Roast beef with them Yorkshire gravy suckers,' whined Robyn.

'Beans,' said Andy firmly, bringing out the sack.

Old Pete shook his head. 'Since girlie shunted me out the kitchen I got out the habit of keeping some soaked. Can have them tomorrow if I do it now, but we can't eat 'em like that.'

Heads were scratched, brows were creased, lips were pursed.

'Granny and Gramps!' Robyn announced of a sudden. 'Still got the birthday money they sent me! Let's go to the diner, dinner's on me!'

The flames of hope flared up in all their hearts as they scrambled for their coats, but was as quickly extinguished by Andy's glance at the clock and his utterance of the dreadful word, 'Shut', prefixed and suffixed by another word of an alliterative nature, the repetition of which was taken up with vigour by one and all. It was during this scatological out-pouring that the sound of tyres swishing on pea shingle allowed them swiftly to reflect, as one, that their behaviour was reminiscent of very small people suffering from the syndrome known as 'full nappy', and without another word spoken amongst them, they simultaneously took up sedentary positions of hastily assumed nonchalance, accompanied by a tuneless air whistled by Old Pete. Thus came the effervescent, conquering heroine into an arena with no triumphal atmosphere to greet her victorious return, but a studied indifference, and a muted, ragged ripple of offhand greetings which put Kate in mind of a matinee audience who had come to the theatre to snooze.

'Is everybody okay?' she enquired anxiously, her good news put on hold.

'Sure, sure,' came the reply, while fingernails were studied, shirt cuffs examined, hat brims brushed.

'Good day yourself?' Andy enquired politely.

'You are not going to believe how good!' Kate bubbled, unable to keep her secret to herself any longer. Like a magician, she produced a bottle of champagne from under her jacket. 'Ta-daa!' she carolled. 'It's celebration time!'

The three famine victims exchanged puzzled looks. 'Okay, you got my interest going,' said Old Pete. 'What happened? You get your sainthood susstiffikit while you were out there feeding the poor?'

'The poor?' Kate queried. 'I wouldn't call them that exactly. But what makes you think I was out feeding anyone?'

'There's no food and you said you were on a cooking roll!' Robyn exclaimed, giving way to her frustration at last. 'And we know you have been 'cos we can smell it, but if you hid it you hid it real good, and what I want to know is why would you do a thing like that to hungry people who've been out all day long and ain't had nothing in their bellies since that fried chicken you sent us off with, what we all ate after about half an hour out, 'cos we couldn't stand knowing it was in our saddle bags all warm and crispy, and now it's a whole day later and the horses have had more to eat than what we have, and we've been waiting and waiting and we almost thought you'd gone back to England, you've been so damn long, and then we thought you'd had a riding accident, and worrying folk who are already dying from starvation is about as low as a person can get!'

Kate laughed. 'Wow, Robyn, I'm impressed. That was almost all on one breath. So you're hungry, I take it?'

An alimentary growl of rage leapt from Old Pete's mid-section, where the wild beast who measured these things resided. 'I'm okay,' he told her, patting his tummy, 'but the fella I keep in here's telling us he could do with some chow.'

'Then we should give him our full attention and do every-thing to put him at his ease,' Kate said happily, arming herself with ingredients which the others had passed by during their hapless forage, and putting them together in a fashion which none of them could have guessed at, but which everybody admired. Already they felt their anxiety melting away as they watched her chop and blend and grill. Momma was back home. All was well with the world.

'Bruschetta,' she said, minutes later, when she plonked down a plate heaving with fresh tomatoes on toast with torn basil and garlic, dressed with the recently acquired olive oil. 'Get yourselves outside that, as they say where I come from, while I knock up the next course.' She hummed to herself as she flapped an apron and fixed it round her waist and went to the larder and came back out and started breaking eggs into a large bowl and putting water on to boil, and watching her, three people noted privately that if they felt any more affection for her at that moment, their hearts might explode with the strain.

'Spaghetti carbonara, hungry people,' she said by way of introduction as she delivered a huge bowl to the table and sat down. 'Hungry people, spaghetti carbonara. And if this doesn't entirely pacify your growling friend, Old Pete, I can knock up a steak when you've finished.'

Andy swiped at a dribble of olive oil on his chin with his

thumb and got up to fetch glasses. 'Forgot about this wine and you having something to celebrate,' he told her, popping the cork and pouring. 'But now you've given us all something to celebrate too, I guess we're ready to join you. Half a glass for you, Robyn Barrett, and mind you make it last.'

It was gone in one quaff and two burps. 'If that's champeen, I'll take homemade lemonade any day,' was the verdict that followed.

'Well, so long as we're broadening your education,' Andy said wryly. 'The other thing to know is that normally we wait for the toast before we drink.'

'I thought we'd had the toast before we got this carbon spaghetti,' Robyn quipped.

'Aren't we the wordsmith. You'll pardon those of us who are late coming to polite society, I hope, Kate. But from the rest of us, here's to you, for cooking us another great meal, and for whatever good fortune has come your way since we last met,' Andy proposed.

'Thank you,' said Kate after they'd all drank. 'And I'd like to propose a toast to all of you and the good fortune that's come your way since we last met.'

'That would be this dinner,' said Old Pete, helping himself to more pasta.

'Well, that's kind of you to say so, but there's something else too,' she said with a grin.

'You've found out who Andy the Cowboy is!' Robyn offered excitedly. 'How?'

'No, I'm afraid not, that mystery remains unsolved,' Kate admitted. 'This news has more to do with the fortunes of the Blue Yonder.'

Andy stopped chewing, a proprietorial prickle starting to crawl up the back of his neck. 'Now what could that be?' he wondered aloud.

'Okay,' said Kate, rubbing her hands together with glee now

that the floor was all hers and she could at last share her secret. 'As you probably all know, John Connor is getting married to Sonia Driesen next week.'

'God help him,' Robyn muttered. 'Last time she came over here she brung me a dress and tried to put me in lipstick. Damn near broke her arm. Did break one of her false finger-nails though,' she concluded with evident satisfaction. 'Ain't been seen near here since then.'

'What's John and Sonia getting married got to do with us?' Andy asked. He had his own set of feelings about that impending union, and chief among them was gratitude to John Connor for drawing Sonia's fire. Few women of his acquaintance had such difficulty as she in understanding the significance of a cold shoulder.

'It's got everything to do with us,' said Kate, 'since Solveig Hansen fell unexpectedly pregnant!'

'Sol's expecting?' Old Pete checked. 'Good for her. Arnie must have took my advice. Kept telling him all he needed to do was to keep on practising and he couldn't help but get it right one day.'

Andy was struggling to compute the information that he'd just received. 'So Sollie's doing the catering for John and Sonia's wedding and what – she's asked you to help her?'

'No, Sollie can't do the catering because she's having a difficult pregnancy and she's got to take it easy for a while,' Kate informed him. 'So we are stepping into the breach.'

'*We* are doing the catering for Sonia Driesen's wedding?' said Robyn.

Kate nodded happily.

'Can I poison the cake?'

'No,' said the head chef, 'but you can certainly help make it if you want to.'

'Just let me try to get this straight,' said Andy, although he doubted such a thing was possible. 'John Connor, the man we owe so much money to that he's stopped calling, *that* John Connor has asked that we do the food at his wedding?'

'That John Connor,' Kate agreed. 'We do the catering, and in exchange, he's cancelling the debt completely, and extending you a thousand dollars' worth of credit towards future visits.'

There was an astonished silence round the table, which was broken at length by a low whistle from Old Pete. 'You son of a gun,' he said.

Robyn said nothing at first, but slid under the table to emerge at Kate's side and hug the breath out of her. 'Mata Hari, you are the best secret agent I ever did know,' she said. 'How long you been planning this?'

'Just since yesterday,' Kate admitted. 'I didn't want to say anything in case I didn't pass the test. That's why I was force feeding you all last night. I was trying to work out which dishes to do. Your salmon went down a treat, Old Pete. You're going to have to go out and catch some more.'

'Aw shucks,' he grinned. 'Me go out fishing? Well, if I have to, I guess I could.'

Kate shot a glance at Andy who was the only one who had not yet given his seal of approval, and meeting her eyes, he forced a tight smile and a brief nod. 'Very good of you to organise that,' he said. 'Thank you.'

Conscious that he might be feeling she was treading on his toes, she checked anxiously, 'Is it okay, Andy? Did I do the right thing?'

He strove for generosity to warm his voice. 'Clever move,' he attested. 'Wouldn't have thought of that myself in a thousand years.' That was the trouble, he thought darkly. He'd got them into this mess over the unpaid vet's bill, but it had taken a total stranger to get them out of it. And even if he had managed to figure it out over the course of a millennium, he couldn't have done anything about it. He wasn't exactly known for his skill at the stove.

'I'd never have thought of it either,' Kate assured him, 'if it hadn't been for Peggy Davies showing me how the local bartering system works.'

Old Pete slapped his knee in delight and wheezed his way into his characteristic laugh to voice Andy's thoughts. 'Dammit, here's the answer been sitting under our noses the whole time, and girlie goes and spots it right off! Suppose if I asked you to marry me you'd turn me down flat?' he joked.

Robyn, who had not yet let go of Kate, now slid onto the bench next to her, her arms possessively round her waist and neck. 'She's mine,' she said, snuggling up to her. 'You'll pick me over him, won't you, Mata?'

'So many offers in one night,' Kate said solemnly. 'I'll have to give it a lot of thought.'

'Well, I guess we're in your hands to pull this off,' said Andy. 'I'm no cook, but if you tell me what to do I'll try to do it.' The irony of the situation suddenly occurred to him, and despite his feelings of failure, he gave a dry chuckle. 'When I heard that John was going to marry Sonia I thought I'd dance at their wedding, but I never thought I'd be making the sandwiches.'

'Sandwiches are the least of it,' Kate told him. 'We'll have such a lot to do to make the barn into the venue of Sonia's dreams.'

'The barn!' Old Pete exclaimed. 'You persuaded Sonia Driesen to have her wedding breakfast in our old barn?'

'It's the only space big enough for a hundred people,' Kate explained. 'But we'll do a make-over on it and it'll look great. John kindly gave me some numbers of people who'll be able to help us source things. Chris Somebody-or-other, and a chap called Gary Strange, who's big in the local amateur dramatic society?'

'There's nothing amateur about Gary's dramatics. He's a true pro at 'em,' Old Pete chuckled, rising. 'Well, I'm for my bed. Long day in the saddle, and plenty of sweet dreams for me tonight. Sonia Driesen dancing around our manure heap for one. Looks like the little Robyn bird's already beat me to it,' he noted, indicating the somnolent child wrapped around Kate.

'She's out cold,' said Andy softly, affection crinkling his eyes in a smile as he gazed at her sleep-softened face.

'Not,' she mumbled, tightening her grip on her heroine.

'That a fact,' said Andy, coming round the table to lift her in his arms and carry her to bed. 'Looks to me like somebody can't hold their champeen.' He turned in the doorway to address Kate. 'I'll be back directly to help you finish up that bottle, and to clear away these dishes. You've done more than enough for one day. Don't lift a finger till I'm back except to pour, okay?'

'Aw shucks,' said Kate in a fair impression of Old Pete. 'Well, I guess I can if I have to.'

Helping Robyn off with her boots as she sat on her bed, Andy said, 'Good day today, wasn't it? We should do that more often, instead of getting out of sorts with each other all the time.'

'I will if you will,' she said sleepily, and ruffled his hair. 'If you promise to be a good little boy, I'll promise to be a good little girl.'

'Hm,' said Andy. 'Now wouldn't that involve you wearing that nice dress Sonia brought over? Pity you put it out in the trash. Told you you'd regret it later.'

Robyn grinned at the memory. 'Didn't put it in the trash, that would've been a waste of good material. Check out the cloth you're using next time you wash the pick-up.'

He shook his head and laughed at her incorrigibility. 'I'll do that. Don't forget to brush your teeth before you go to sleep,' he instructed her from the doorway. 'No sliding into bed still wearing your clothes.'

'Okay. Hey, dude!'

He stopped, and turned back towards her.

'Bet you're happy now that somebody got on a computer and got Mata over here, ain't you?'

Andy lifted an eyebrow. 'Sure. But you tell that somebody when you see her that it's strictly a business arrangement between us, and that's how it will stay.'

'Tell him yourself,' Robyn countered. 'Next time you look in the mirror.'

They regarded each other in a competitive standoff.

'You never going to admit it was you?' he asked her at length with a smile.

'Can't,' she yawned. 'I was brung up not to tell lies.'

'You was brung up to use better grammar than that too, but I guess some things just don't stick. Night, partner.'

'Night, partner,' she returned, and as soon as he was out of the room, she snuggled under the covers fully clothed, her heart warming her from the inside out, and dreamt the sweetest dreams she'd dreamt in a long while.

Returning to the kitchen, Andy was happy to discover that Kate had evidently been brung up not to tell lies neither, since the only finger she had lifted by way of doing chores, as agreed, had been employed solely to recharge their glasses. She had, however, taken off her boots and lifted her legs onto the bench in the pursuit of further taking her ease, and it unsettled him a little to see a grown person of the female species looking so relaxed and at home under his roof. He felt oddly self conscious to be in a room with her alone. Not that it hadn't happened before, but never at night time, with the lights low like now, which cast soft pools of illumination and even softer shadows, some of them commingling across her features to a most attractive and flattering effect.

He was glad of the displacement activity afforded him by the dirty dishes needing to be cleared and washed and put away, an employment to which he gave himself fully while he tried to think up something to say in the order of a relaxed conversational opening gambit. No matter. She'd already beaten him to it. So no surprise there.

'Was it nice, the three of you going out riding together today?' she asked, being a dab hand at asking the kind of questions which elicited stories.

'Yes. It was good,' he replied succinctly, crashing some pots in the sink to demonstrate that he was too occupied with chores to add anything further at the present time. He felt churlish and awkward, features of his personality which this woman seemed so adept at bringing out, and he snatched a breath and let it out in a sigh to try to unwind his over-wound muscles.

This, Kate interpreted as a sign that he was cross with her, and already feeling guilty that she might have done a good deed too many, she nervously gulped down the champagne she'd just sipped in anticipation of listening to his interesting reply, and guiltily asked, 'I hope you don't think I've been too interfering, organising you into hosting a wedding.'

'No, no,' he asserted, being conscious as he said it that he did feel exactly that way, as well as being grateful to her for getting them out of a hole, embarrassed that it hadn't been him, resentful that she'd been able to bring it off, annoyed that he'd started to find her attractive, challenged that she had tipped the scales of power away from him, envious of her easy intimacy with Robyn, admiring of her gall, angry at her invasion of his space . . .

'Truly?' she checked.

His shake of the head couldn't begin to encompass all that he was feeling, but Kate was happy to interpret it as a sign of agreement, and now it was her turn to let out a sigh. 'That's a relief,' she said. 'I do like to be helpful, but I know I can come over a bit bossy at times, and give more help than is wanted. You just have to say.'

'No need in this instance,' he contributed tersely, at war with himself over his uncomfortable mixture of emotions, few of which he felt did him credit. Standing at the sink with his back towards her, he wished she'd made more washing up for him when she'd cooked their supper. Only one pan now stood between him and having to sit back down to face her, and if he scrubbed at it any more he'd scour clean through the metal. He felt claustrophobic, pressed in on all sides by her attention, making him feel that every movement of his was keenly observed and might betray him.

This hadn't been at all how he'd meant it to be when he'd recklessly extended the polite invitation to help her finish the bottle, but back then he hadn't thought out how differently things would feel when he was left on his own with her. He felt an unwelcome return of his customary closed-in gruffness – another reason to feel envious of her, with her unselfconscious natural friendliness that extended from her like a warm blanket, and another reason for his resentment of her to be reawakened, what with her making him feel all awkward again by it, a stranger in his own skin.

She was chattering again, in her easy way, telling him about her interview with Sonia and John, and he was glad that this afforded him the luxury of silence on his part, since each time he'd opened his mouth since he'd been back in the kitchen, he'd been shamed by his grouchiness and lack of social ease.

She'd asked him a question, of that much he was aware, but with his own inner voice so loud in his ear, and his concentration all being turned inside, he hadn't caught it. 'Pardon me?' he said, as he took up the tea towel to dry the dishes with slow and thorough precision.

'I said, John Connor is a nice chap, isn't he?' she repeated, sticking out her tentacles to snare him into a conversation.

'Oh yes, yes he is,' he said, and felt anew his mortification at owing the man money.

'He spoke very highly of you,' she told him, which gave him pause to stop rubbing the glaze off the plate he was drying, and to comment, 'That's good of him, under the circumstances.'

'Circumstances which he fully understands,' she told him. 'He seems to admire you a great deal. Got a lot of time for you, is what he said.'

Andy felt the muscles around his ears relax somewhat, and realised he'd been clenching his jaw. 'He's a good man. Good vet, too.'

'So what,' said Kate, sensing that she now had a more attentive audience, 'has he done to deserve dear Sonia?'

Andy let out a short laugh. 'He must be blind to the faults that the rest of us see. Then again,' he reflected, 'she's not the only one who has cause to be thankful of his selective myopia in that respect. I owe the man more than just money. He's been a good friend to us.'

Kate was struck, not for the first time, that this cowboy had a larger vocabulary than she'd been led to expect from the Westerns she'd watched. Had it been acquired during his encyclopaedia evenings with Robyn, she wondered, or had he gone off to college after school? 'Did you always want to work here on the ranch, or were there family expectations of you to stay?' she asked.

The effect of this seemingly innocuous query was immediate and electric, and he whipped round to face her, his eyes glowering darkly, his face a defensive mask. From his angry posture it wouldn't have surprised her if he'd whipped out a gun. 'I – I'm sorry,' she said immediately, her hands making tumbling gestures as if in a vain attempt to reel the enquiry back in. 'I didn't mean to pry. I always ask people questions about themselves. I just love hearing stories. I didn't mean to – you know, invade your privacy or anything.'

Had somebody told her, he wondered, or had she just been making conversation? 'What *did* you mean by it?' he asked, uncomfortably aware that he might have overreacted.

Kate licked her lips nervously, put on the spot. She'd been surprised and glad when he'd told her he'd be returning to drink the champagne with her after putting Robyn to bed, and she'd been looking forward to having her first proper conversation with him, finding out a bit more about what made him tick. What she hadn't expected was that by doing so, he would tick quite so loudly, and so like a time-bomb. 'It's just that you told me, when we were chatting on the web that—' She stopped to correct herself, realising her mistake. 'Ah, no, sorry. *Somebody* told me when we were chatting on the web that your great-grandfather built the Blue Yonder, and I was wondering if therefore it was expected of you to take over from your father, as he must have taken over from his, and so on.'

'Then somebody doesn't know the facts,' said Andy, turning away again to calm himself down and to hide his embarrassment. Damn. That was the trouble with knee-jerk reactions, as he'd tried to teach Robyn on more than one occasion. The knee jerked before the brain had time to engage, most times causing more trouble than was being offered in the first place.

'Do you mind me asking nosy questions?' Kate asked anxiously.

'No,' he lied, and followed it swiftly by one of his own to throw her off his scent. 'What about you? Were you following in the family tradition by becoming an actress?'

'God no!' she replied. 'My parents have both got proper jobs, they were appalled when I told them that's what I wanted to be. Still keep trying to get me to see the light and settle down to be a secretary or something. In fact,' she expanded, turning the conversation back round to him, 'they are partly responsible for me being here now. In their attempt to get me to retrain for a sensible job, they bought me a computer for Christmas, but instead of practising my typing as I was meant to, I started playing backgammon on it and met – whoever it was who was pretending to be you.'

'Fool of a person to want to do that,' he said drily.

'Who, me or them?' she asked.

'Both of you, I guess,' he replied, attempting to mimic her jocular tone and get them back on track. 'Look where it landed you. Saddled with feeding us and Sonia Driesen's hundred best friends.'

'You have no idea how much nicer that is than what I left behind,' she assured him. 'Believe me, it's no fun at all being a prisoner in your own home, nor being hated by twenty million people.'

'I can't imagine that it is,' he said with an empathetic smile, adding perceptively, 'especially not for a person like you.'

'Why especially me?' she asked, surprised and flattered that he'd spent any time at all thinking about her, let alone enough to come up with a character assessment.

Damn, he thought, why had he said that? He'd unwittingly slipped right into her conversational snare, and now she'd be thinking he was interested enough to notice things about her, which he was not. 'Some people don't care what other people think of them, but you're not one of them. You care too much about being liked,' he said, and just in case she took that as a compliment, he followed it up with, 'isn't that why you like to be so helpful?'

Well, he didn't get that insight out of an encyclopaedia, Kate thought, embarrassed and indignant for her motives to be thought so suspect. 'You think that, do you?' she asked. 'Minnie McAlpine, a woman I met on the plane, thought it was to do with me preferring to sort out other people's problems rather than my own.'

Now he felt badly. He of all people knew how it felt to be constantly aware of being judged by others. And oneself, of course. 'And you?' he asked more gently, hoping to inspirit her. 'What do you think?'

She was about to rise to a stringently argued case for the purity of her intentions and the philanthropic nature of her aid, when honesty got the better of her and her face fell. 'It's both things probably,' she said, the wind taken out of her sails. 'Bit pathetic, really, isn't it?'

'Not at all,' he said gallantly, having won himself around from the position that he had argued. 'World might be a better place if more people were motivated to do things that would get them liked.'

She smiled gratefully and brightened visibly. 'That's really very nice of you to say so,' she said. 'Look, Andy, I'm sorry we got off on the wrong foot just now, but won't you sit down and drink your champagne? It's rather odd having a conversation with your back, and I really don't think you're going to get those dishes any drier.'

Made aware that he had been swiping the same three plates over and over with the cloth, he set them down ruefully and wished that he hadn't backed himself into this corner. Not only had he trapped himself in a room with her alone, confused her, maybe, about his intentions, but worst of all he had painted a big red arrow in the direction of something he didn't want to talk about ever. This is what came from talking to strangers, he thought bitterly. With locals, he didn't have to wonder what they knew: they knew everything. And part of what they knew was never to talk about it – leastways not to him. Hell, it haunted him enough every night and every day, he didn't need to relive it in conversation.

Without turning round to face her he said, 'You have the

champagne if you like it. Wouldn't want to waste it on me. I'll
take a bourbon,' which gave him a little longer to compose
himself while he fetched a fresh glass and the bottle from the
dresser and, as there seemed to be no other course of action
open to him without looking a complete fool, he reluctantly
joined her at the table.

'I hope you cut yourself a nice deal with John and Sonia
when you negotiated the price,' he said, bringing the conversation back firmly to the present and the tangible.

'I told you the deal,' she answered, puzzled. 'He clears the
debt and gives you a grand in credit. Do you think I should
have asked for more?' she checked, suddenly suspicious that
she might have been taken for a ride. 'I'm afraid I had no idea
what a wedding reception should cost in Canadian dollars, so I
just picked a figure out of the air and hoped they'd go for it.'

'You didn't add on your fee?' he asked.

'No,' she said. 'Anyway, wouldn't that be illegal? I'm on a
tourist visa, I'm not here to work.'

'You've done nothing else since you arrived,' he reminded
her.

'In the spirit of guest ranching, yes,' she said. 'Which, as Old
Pete explained it at the Cowboy Evening, is to give your
services for free.'

'No, no, no,' he said, clearly shocked. 'I can't accept that
from you. I thought when you told us about catering the
wedding that you stood to make a profit too. You can't do all
that work for nothing. And it will be you doing the work, Kate,
make no mistake about it.' Again he gave the short dry laugh
which she was beginning to find so attractive. 'You've sampled
Old Pete's cooking, and you should be thankful you haven't
sampled mine. As for Robyn – hell, I can't even get her to
make her own sandwiches to take in to school.'

'Then she can practise on Sonia,' said Kate. 'It's always
good to have a new skill.'

'Even when that skill is poisoning?' Andy quipped.

Kate laughed, delighted that he seemed to have forgiven her faux pas (whatever it was) sufficiently to joke again. 'Anyway, seriously, I don't mind the work at all, I relish it in fact. I've been so unproductive these last few weeks, I've been going stir crazy at home with nothing to do. It's as I told you when I first arrived. *Paradise Street* was a double-edged sword. It made me the target of some people who seriously need to get a grip on reality, but it also made me enough money not to have to start panicking, for a few months at least.'

'Well, least I can do is to put that panic off a bit longer,' he said firmly. 'There'll be no charge for staying here at the Blue Yonder, however long you plan on staying.'

This was said with a slight lift at the end of the sentence, denoting a question, she realised, which she didn't know how to answer.

'Anything that we have already billed you for,' he continued over the silence, 'I'll credit back to your card account.'

'You still don't get how a guest ranch works!' she laughed. 'I'm supposed to do the work, and pay my own way!'

'Maybe you don't get how pride works,' Andy suggested, the laughter lines round his eyes hardening slightly. 'Or reciprocity.'

Put that way, Kate knew when to back down. 'Well, that's very kind of you then,' she conceded. 'Thank you very much.'

'Thank you,' he said, and they smiled at each other briefly and sipped their drinks.

'So, how do these things work in your business?' Andy asked, before she could come up with one of her own dangerous questions. 'Doesn't your notoriety make you more sought after by employers, rather than less?'

'Apparently not,' Kate said glumly. 'I haven't had a sniff at another job since I took that wretched part, and the irony is that I only took it in order to get seen and get more work. I've become totally unemployable – at least until all the excitement dies down, and it's anybody's guess how long that will take. I keep hoping that another plot line will take the heat off me, but even since I've been out of *Paradise Street*, they've been milking my character. Hardly an episode goes by without bloody Sally Black being mentioned by somebody, having been seen doing something terrible. According to my agent he can't even *give* my services away while her curse is still hanging over me. And I mean that literally. He doesn't normally do PAs, but—'

'Doesn't normally do PAs?' Andy queried. 'Sorry, I don't quite follow?'

'Personal Appearances,' Kate explained. 'Soap stars opening supermarkets, that sort of do. Anyway, my agent doesn't normally get himself involved in that kind of thing, but in my case he made an exception on the premise that if you can't beat them. You know, if he couldn't get me any proper work, then we might as well capitalise on my "notoriety", as you call it. Anyway, he was turned down flat by every big chain. Not only were they worried that I might cause a riot by being seen in their bloody shops in the flesh, but they were also convinced that I'd damage their bloody sales. Imagine!'

Andy couldn't. Rarely watching television himself, the whole thing baffled him. 'Won't last for ever though, surely?' he said, trying to lift her spirits.

'That's the theory. Actually, I e-mailed him the other day to see if things had changed at all, but it's probably too soon – I hope you don't mind me using your computer?' she asked guiltily.

'Be my guest,' he said. 'And had they changed?'

'Haven't checked for his reply. Completely forgot about it.' She grinned. 'You see what a tonic it is for me to be over here and occupied!'

He nodded in acknowledgement of the two-way street they

found themselves in, the tell-tale lines around his eyes now employed once again to denote warmth and amusement. 'Here's to that tonic,' he proposed, tipping his glass in her direction. 'I only hope you still think it's doing you a power of good this time next week.'

'Oh no worries there,' said Kate, clinking her glass against his, 'this time next week, I'll be completely hysterical!'

'That'll make you and Sonia then,' Andy said, with a comic air of doom about him.

'Yes. We could make a contest of it,' Kate laughed. 'Hissy fits at fifty paces.'

Andy shook his head. 'From what I've seen of the two of you, you'd lose by a mile.'

After what she'd learned earlier, Kate almost made a joke about Sonia evidently having made an unsuccessful play for him, but thought better of it in case he treated it as a further invasion of his privacy, or worse, that he mistakenly thought she was interested in him herself, which was of course ridiculous. Even if she were, she mused, which she absolutely and utterly was not, nothing could come of it. As she'd told Robyn, she had to go home some time to face the music, and try to pick up what was left of her career. She couldn't stay here for ever.

'I guess you must be missing acting,' Andy offered. 'It's one of those professions which is a vocation, isn't it? A part of your make-up.'

'It is and it isn't,' Kate said reflectively. 'The stage is my first and only love. I've never been interested in telly – even less so now. It's like working in a factory these days, although older actors tell me it wasn't always so. No time for rehearsal any more in TV. Everything's done as cheaply as possible. In theatre you get at least three weeks, sometimes four, or if you're very lucky, six. Rehearsal is my favourite bit. It's the most creative time.'

'So why didn't you stick with the theatre?' he asked, reasonably enough.

She raised her eyebrows and pursed her lips in sad resignation. 'I'd love to, but apparently I'm too old, or not old enough. There's loads of work for actresses in their twenties – well, their early twenties, anyway. But when you get to my age parts start to get pretty thin on the ground, so there's more of us, proportionally, chasing the same few jobs, and everybody can name the ones who get them. They're called Money. Bankable. Bums on seats. That's the reality. Not a household name? Sorry, love, not employable. No, I have a horrible suspicion that my best hope now is to stay in the game long enough to get the granny parts.'

Andy frowned. What a dreadful conclusion to come to. It dismissed hope entirely. 'That's a hell of a lot of waiting time,' he said, in the careful way he had when he was trying to lead Robyn to a more mature way of thinking. 'So what'll you do in the meantime?'

She smiled ruefully. 'That's what I can't figure out. But I can tell you this: secretarial work definitely isn't it.' She made an effort to pull her thoughts away from the gloomy track they seemed bent on going, and added, 'Maybe after I've practised on Sonia and John, I could start a second-string career in catering. I've worked in cafés and restaurants in my time, but I'd sooner be my own boss, have more of a creative input.'

Andy slugged back his drink and poured out another. 'Being your own boss has its pitfalls. No one to blame but yourself if things go wrong.'

Her own glass being empty, Kate indicated the bottle of bourbon. 'Can I try that?' she asked.

He got up to get her a fresh glass. 'Sure. Didn't mean to hog it. Never tried this before?'

'No.' She sipped at it gingerly, and grimaced as it burnt her throat. 'Nice,' she said, 'once the anaesthetic properties kick in.'

'Now you can call yourself a proper cowgirl,' Andy told her, with a twinkle in his eye. 'Except for the small matter of getting on a horse.'

'Yes, well,' she said. It was a fair cop, but how could she put this? She just didn't want to. 'All in due course. I'm still smarting from when your great hulking beast, Rusty, got the better of me, and I wasn't even on his back at the time.'

'No, you were on yours, I believe,' he said. 'Or so your ranch trainer advised me.'

'Your bloody daughter, what a snitch!' Kate exclaimed. 'Can't a person have any secrets around here?'

From the immediate darkening of his expression, she knew she'd just put her foot thigh-deep in it again, but she was quite at a loss to know why. 'I'm sorry,' she said, taking a guess at what it might have been. 'I meant "bloody" in an affectionate way? We're a bit of a foul-mouthed mob in the theatre.'

His jaw muscles were working frantically, and so was his mind. Out of habit, the usual two options presented themselves to him: to leave the room quickly, or to bite her head off. But since she had just been so candid and open with him about her own worries, neither of these courses of action felt right: in fact, they made him feel that he'd be behaving like a damn hypocrite if he tried either one of them. 'The bloody bit's fine,' he said after a supreme effort to come clean. 'It's the daughter part that you got wrong.'

Kate couldn't understand what he meant. 'You mean it wasn't Robyn who told you?' she asked. 'So who was it – Rusty? Don't tell me – you got it straight from the horse's mouth!'

Wishing he'd never opened this can of worms, he forced himself to finish what he'd started. 'No, it was Robyn all right,' he told her. 'But she isn't my daughter.'

Kate was momentarily stunned into silence, not daring to ask the obvious question, as in whose the hell was she then, in case he got all offended and defensive again. Only hours ago she had learned that she'd got Robyn's mother's name wrong, but now she found she'd also got the wrong man down as the father? It was too much information in too short a time – or not enough information by half. Could it be as Minnie had suspected on the plane, she wondered, that Rainbow/Laura could have lied to Andy about the baby being his? In which case, how did he know that now? Had he taken a paternity test since then and discovered he wasn't the father, and if so, what had motivated him to do so, given that he clearly loved the child? But before she could unscramble her wits enough to say anything to elicit further illumination on the subject, he had stood up and stretched and said, 'Well, like Old Pete said before me, it's been a long day in the saddle, so I'm for my bed. G'night.'

As she sat, open-mouthed, and watched the door close behind him, it as quickly reopened and his head popped back in. 'Don't let me hurry you off, though,' he said politely. 'Feel free to use the computer to check if your agent's mailed back yet, if you want to.'

'Thanks,' she said, as she watched him disappear all over again. But she was far too busy trying to puzzle out the deepening mystery of this cowboy called Andy to want to look at her e-mail just then, so she sat and finished her bourbon and went over all the conflicting facts until her head spun and, alas, none the wiser, she eventually went to bed.

Thus she put off making a discovery of something far more shocking, and far closer to home, than any of the astonishing revelations she had heard that day.

22

Being bounced awake by Robyn the next morning was even more of a surprise than usual, since Kate had been dreaming about her being born in a teepee, delivered by a witch doctor with no face.

'Coming out riding with me today after we've done the chores?' Robyn asked, but Kate had the perfect excuse of needing to start planning John and Sonia's reception immediately, so was glad to be able to demur.

'You think you came out to the right place?' Robyn complained as they did the milking together. 'Seems to me you'd have been happier if you'd had to go out to rescue Andy the Restaurant Owner, rather than Andy the Cowboy.'

The cowboy of that name, having remembered on first waking that he had said more than he had meant to on a certain subject the night before, was happy to cede his office space to Kate while he went out riding with the person who was not his daughter, leaving only Old Pete for her to pump for information.

'Tell me about Robyn's mother,' she said, when she plonked down a plate of fried bacon before him.

'Can't,' he said, stuffing the bacon between two hunks of bread and leaving the table immediately. 'Never knew her. Gone before my time. See you later, and thanks for the chow.'

Left alone, Kate wandered into Andy's office and scrutinised the hidden photograph again, but to little effect other than to give herself eyestrain. Defeated, she forced herself to

start making a definitive menu for the wedding, followed by a
list of food she'd need to get from Peggy, but since she had
never catered for such a large number before, she quickly lost
confidence in her ability to calculate fractions of cucumbers
multiplied by people, and instead reached for the phone to talk
to Chris Pope and Gary Strange to elicit their help. On
informing the former that she was ordering the cutlery and
plates on Sonia's behalf, Chris Pope went into instant melt-
down on price just as John Connor had predicted, and offered
her a discount of ninety per cent. When he heard no response
(due to Kate having lost the power of speech in her surprise)
he caved in completely, and waived his fee altogether. 'Make
sure you tell Sonia that I'm making her a present of it,' he said
anxiously. 'I've got two dogs to think of, and I've fallen foul of
her appointments system before.'

If Kate found that remarkable, it was because she had yet to
make her second phone call, for it led to the immediate,
breathless offer of a meeting with Gary, doyen of the Green
Lake Amateur Dramatic Society, which was strange indeed.
Not, as it turned out, because he was old enough still to
remember the pancake make-up of his New Romantic prime.
Not because he could still, after all these years, procure it. Not
was it because he had the pizzazz and the daring still to wear it.
It was because on laying kohl-rimmed eyes on Kate, he
clapped his hands in delight, sank to one knee clutching his
heart, and declaimed, 'My God – it *is* you!' before going into
full prostration at her feet.

Sensing, through this display, a fellow thesp of a theatrical
bent who clearly enjoyed impro, she extended a hand to help
him back up and said, 'Arise, Sir Knight, my good and faithful
servant. Your Queen commands it.'

'Darling-lovie-angel-heart,' he said, climbing up her arm
hand over hand to arise as instructed, and clasping her to
him as if she were a much treasured and long-lost friend, 'I

will always be faithful, but I can't promise to be good.' Holding her then at arm's length the better to gaze at her features with undisguised adulation, he continued, 'I can't believe you're here! They said it was you, but I didn't dare hope! I thought I recognised your voice on the phone when you called me, but then I said to myself, "Gareen, do not get beside yourself, kid yourself not, it could all yet be miasma." I'm a devil for wishing something to be true, but mostly, I fear, this foolish, tender heart is doomed to disappointment. But, oh! Kate Thornton, on my very own doorstep! Sally Black here, in the very very flesh, as I live and hyperventilate! Welcome, welcome, you are a thousand times welcome to my little corner of the world!' and so saying, he drew her into it and shut the door.

'How on earth do you—' Kate started to ask, but stopped, open-jawed, to gaze in amazement at her surroundings. She had been in dozens of fellow actors' flats and houses during her time in the business and was therefore used to seeing production photos and award certificates hanging on their walls – indeed, one wall in her own home was a veritable rogue's gallery of parts she had played – but this whole environment, from skirting board to cornice, was a three-hundred-and-sixty-degree panoramic homage to her new-found fan. There he was as a child, peering out of the dirty face of the Artful Dodger in a stage production of *Oliver!* Here he was spruced up and gentrified for his eponymous role in *The Winslow Boy*, on through black and white TV stills from *Doctor Who* and various other children's shows, some long forgotten, until suddenly he was pictured with three other good-looking young men in a series of glamorous photos of air-brushed perfection which made both Kate's jaw, and the penny which was teetering in her teeming mind, drop.

'My God!' she exclaimed, echoing Gary's first words to her. 'I had this up in my bedroom! You're Gary of Gary and The Strangers!'

'Pictured here in the country now known as One-hit Wonderland, in the hey of my day,' he smiled, joining her to admire his younger self.

'You turned my life around!' Kate enthused, and together they burst into harmonised song, ' "Since you ca-a-a-ame, you have turned my life around, baby, O-oh bay-yay-yaby, Turned my life around." '

'I worshipped the very ground that you walked upon!' Kate told him.

'Not as literally as I just worshipped the ground that brought you here,' said Gary in a wounded tone, 'since I notice that you're still on your feet. But gratifying to know, nonetheless, that I had some influence on your early adolescent years. How old were you when you dreamt of our future together, you poor deluded female creature – twelve, thirteen?'

'Thereabouts,' Kate admitted.

'And now fate has brought us together at last, due, I understand from the local gossip, from you chasing after one of our very own cowboys.'

'One of *our* cowboys?' Kate asked. 'I thought you were English?'

'I'm an immigrant of love, like your good self,' he informed her. 'But unlike you and your quest for the rugged country hunk, I fell for a computer nerd. Imagine! Canadian *and* a nerd! It's almost tautological!'

Kate laughed, but felt she had to clear up a point. 'Local gossip has run away with the story of why I am here,' she said. 'I didn't chase after Andy because I fancied him, I came because the person I thought was Andy had been a good friend to me over the internet, he sounded as if he could do with some help at the time, and I was in hiding because of the wretched Sally—'

'The *divine* Sally Black,' Gary corrected her. 'The personification of all that is evil, an arch-villainess to rival Cruella de

Vil, Scarlett de Hara, Joan de No-Wire-Hangers – an icon, in short, of her age. Long may she be remembered, reviled and revered!'

'Anything but that,' said Kate, but she found she was hugely cheered to have such a different spin put on her misfortune. 'She's made me unemployable and the subject of death threats,' she told him, trying to whip herself back into dolorous mode, but even this was beginning to seem absurd and funny to her now.

'I know!' said Gary gleefully. 'At least, I know about the death threats. I tap into the websites occasionally – oh, all right then, if we must be literal! – a couple of times a week, to see what the weirdos are saying about you. Have you caught Mad Mel's blog yet?' Kate shook her head. 'No? Oh, my dear, I must show you before you go! That woman is so twisted it's anybody's guess how she gets her tights on of a morning! The things she would do to you if she met you in a dark alley would turn Hannibal Lector quite pale. But don't worry, darling. If you ever go missing, at least we'll know to start looking for a woman from Wigan wearing a coat made of your skin.'

Kate shuddered, but despite the fact that he was giving her such chilling news, Gary's enjoyment of her situation was infectious. She hadn't realised how much she'd missed having the company of someone who could banter back and help put things into perspective, and *this* particular somebody had clearly learnt to take life rather less seriously than she'd been doing of late.

'So, Gary, what are you doing running the local Am Drams?' she asked. 'Why aren't you acting professionally? Or still singing?'

'Because of living out here in the sticks and being a married woman,' he told her. 'Entré nous, I've become a bit of a hausfrau in my middle years, and the thought of touring now, or even having to stay in Vancouver for any length of time, away from my Cherubchops, just makes me come over all under-motivated and nesty. Besides, we've put in for adoption, so with a bit of luck I'll soon be a full-time Mum.'

'Congratulations,' said Kate. 'When's the happy event?'

'Not long, we hope. We've been meeting with a brother and sister of six and four who we've completely fallen in love with, and they seem to have fallen in love with us, so we're really hoping it all works out soon. You, of course, will be catering the celebration party, after all that I've heard about your skill in the cucina.'

'God, this place and its news network!' said Kate. 'I've never known anything like it.'

'Really?' said Gary archly. 'I thought you'd worked in theatre?'

Kate laughed, conceding the point.

'Small communities feed on fresh flesh,' he instructed her. 'Everybody already knows everybody else's business here, so we're utterly dependent on newbies coming in, like you. I was a newbie once and – do I need to say? – I caused quite a stir, but now I've become a fixture and fitting like everybody else. They have woven me into the rich tapestry of their lives as Strange Gary, I believe, which I have to say I rather like. I have always comforted myself with the notion that I was born to glitter in dark places, and I like to think that I add a dash of much needed local colour. I mean, somebody has to provide a contrast to all that denim blue.'

'So if you're a fixture and fitting now and have been taken into the fold of the gossip circle, what do you hear about who Robyn's father is?' asked Kate.

'Robyn being . . .?'

'Robyn Barrett, the little girl at the Blue Yonder.'

'Oh! The tomboy with the charming scowl who lets her pony pee on my front lawn as she passes by on her way to school,' said Gary, 'of course. In a town this small, how *could* I have forgotten her name?' He put a finger to his chin in a theatrical display of thinking. 'Perhaps it's because I've come to know her as The Horse Weesperer. But isn't Andy her father?' he asked in surprise. 'I'd always supposed that he was.'

'Apparently not. Or so he told me last night.'

'Then we shall have to try to do some digging,' said Gary. 'Although I have to tell you it will be hard. I'm still regarded as a foreigner, having been here only five years, and they like to keep their older gossip in the family.'

'What about Cherubim?' asked Kate. 'Isn't he local?'

'Cherub-bum has returned to his three-generations-old roots, and so although his ancestry is local, he is not in the fold on account of his forebears having been flighty enough to relocate to Vancouver and become City Folk. Besides, in order to get answers you have to know how to ask questions, and the only questions my better half knows how to ask are of an acronymic nature and mostly to do with computing,' Gary informed her. 'Well, shall we and go and look over your barn? I'm a computer widow today – he's upstairs in his office working to a tight deadline and must not be disturbed for anything less than impending death.'

'Sure,' said Kate. 'I'll be really glad to have your help.'

Grabbing his jacket, he called up the stairs, 'I'm going out, sweetheart. BRB. TTFN.'

'OK,' came the reply.

'C?' he said, turning to Kate.

'Plus plus,' was her witty reply, which earned her a screech of delight from her new best friend.

Once in her rented Butchmobile, as he admiringly called it, Kate remembered the question she had been about to ask when she'd first entered his house. 'How do you know about Sally Black?' she said. 'Is Canada that up to date with the episodes?'

'Is Canada up to date?' mused Gary. 'Only on the gay marriage laws, darling, and in that they are leaders of the field. No, your secret is safe with this great unwashed public for another nine months, but some of us can't wait that long. For immigrants the world over, there are some home-grown things that one misses dreadfully. For many Brits, I believe, it is now the takeaway curry, it having supplanted fish and chips as the national dish. For me it is all things soap, but in particular *Paradise Street*. I've tried to live without feeding my addiction, but it simply can't be done, so I've trained my mother to work the DVD, and she sends me parcels from home twice-weekly. We're both huge fans of yours. Things had been getting a little dull in paradise before you arrived to shake the Heywoods out of their cloying complacency, we felt. Let's face it, it had been a long time since either of them had been set on fire or run over by a dust cart, and the life-and-death difficult birth of their last baby didn't really cut the mustard in the high drama stakes, despite the fact that they were at the zenith of the Pepsi Max rollercoaster at the time. Oh, my dear! The ups and downs of Sara Heywood's life were never so vivid as then, but even then she was dull! But *your* plot line was inspired, I thought. Viewing figures practically doubled, didn't they, for the car-chase episode when you fled down the M1 with baby Leigh strapped to your chest? I have to say, incidentally, that I'm relieved to discover you don't drive that recklessly in this life they call real. My heart was in my mouth when you hit the central barrier and skidded across three lanes. I feared we'd lost you under that juggernaut.'

'I think your heart was supposed to be in your mouth for baby Leigh's safety, not mine,' Kate laughed, having received endless letters to that effect.

'Oh, baby Leigh is indestructible. He's a Heywood, for goodness sake, for which there is no known antidote,' Gary said dismissively. 'No fire burns hot enough, no public services vehicle is heavy enough to wipe them from the face of the earth. Like the cockroach, they are probably even resistant to irradiation. And lest we forget, the little chap was born two hundred feet above Blackpool Pleasure Beach, travelling at seventy-four miles an hour with a G-force of three point five. After that kind of an entrance, life will be all downhill for him from here on in.'

They were passing by Peggy Davies' place, and on impulse Kate slowed down to pull in. 'Hope you don't mind a brief stop,' she said. 'I need to warn Peggy about our large order this week.'

'You think she doesn't already know?' said Gary, unbuckling his seat belt. 'You doubt the efficiency of our local ladies' phone network? By now, she'll have had a dozen calls to inform her that not only are you catering Sonia's wedding, but also that you are on your way over right now. She'll probably have your order all bagged up and ready to go.'

'I also want to try to see if I can get her to tell me about Robyn's dad,' Kate admitted 'Although I know she doesn't go in for gossip much.'

'Blood from a stone,' Gary concurred. 'If you can get so much as a drop of information out of her, by the livin' Gawd that made you, you're a better man than I am, Gunga Din. Then again, love, as we know, that's not so very hard to accomplish. Especially in those boots.'

Kate gazed down at what was left of the turquoise snakeskin trim on her nearly new but almost ruined cowboy boots. 'They were very pretty when they left the shop,' she said, 'but I think they're looking more authentic now.'

'Darling, I'm all for the distressed look, but they are practically suicidal,' said Gary. 'However, it does make you appear almost as if you were born here.'

'Let's hope that qualifies me to join the gossip circle then.'

Gary gave her a pitying look. 'Far be it from me to come

between a desperate woman and her hopes. Let's put it to the
test right now.'

They found Peggy squatting in a bed of squash, and
fortunately for Kate, in time to avoid trampling her on this
occasion. 'Hi, Peggy,' she greeted her. 'How are things?'

'Better now,' said Peggy. 'Thought I had gummy stem
blight there, but must've just been spots before my eyes.'
She nodded a succinct greeting to Kate's companion. 'Gary
Strange.'

'Peggy Potato,' he rejoined. 'How does your garden grow?'

'Pretty well,' she said, getting up to dust down her knees.
'What can I help you folks with today?'

'Oh, come now, Potato Peggy,' said Gary, 'don't tell me you
don't already know that Kate is catering John and Sonia's
wedding, for which she will need the help of your fruit and veg
in large number. I can't believe you've been left out of the loop.
After all, the news is at least twelve hours old.'

'Might've heard something to that effect,' Peggy acknowledged. 'But me, I like to be informed of stuff by the person
involved in the issue. Till then, in my experience, anything you
hear usually tends to have been bent and twisted clear out of
shape.'

'So beautiful *and* so wise,' Gary marvelled. 'How is it
possible?'

An eyebrow lifted in his direction pointed the way, but a
slight twist at the corner of her mouth also signalled her
amusement. 'Could be that the only bullshit I go in for is
to make my vegetables grow bigger, not my stories,' she
said.

'And you're so right to do that,' Kate complimented her,
trying the soft-soap approach. 'For instance, when I was first
here I was asking you about Robyn's mum, but since then I've
found out that the information I'd been given about her wasn't
true at all.'

'That a fact,' said Peggy, in a manner which encouraged no further discussion.

'Yes,' Kate persisted. 'I'd been told by whoever it was who was pretending to be Andy that she was a hippy called Rainbow, who'd abandoned Robyn as a baby to go and make bead necklaces with the Red Indians.'

'We don't call 'em that these days, on account of them not being red,' said Peggy, taking up the wrong part of the story as far as Kate was concerned.

'Oh right, yes, sorry. But I mean, what do you think about that, Peggy, that whoever it was decided to call Laura "Rainbow"?'

Peggy shrugged. Clearly she didn't think much of it at all.

'Excusez-moi,' Gary interjected, 'but I fear I am under-gossiped in this respect. What do you mean, "whoever it was"? The way I heard it, you seduced Andy on the net. Are you saying now that it was somebody else altogether?'

'Well, if you take the "seduced" part out of the equation, yes,' Kate told him. 'When I got here it quickly became apparent that Andy knew absolutely nothing at all about our supposed games of backgammon, and besides, the real Andy isn't anything like the person I'd been getting to know.'

'You don't say!' said Gary. 'Heavens, we're in Miss Marple territory. Small community. Notes sent by a false hand. Mistaken identity. All we need now is a murder.'

'We'll have that in a minute if you don't leave off trampling my beets,' Peggy told him.

'Oops! Sorry, Peggy Pots.'

'The other thing I've found out since, about which I was also wrongly informed,' said Kate, trying to wrest focus away from Gary's feet and Peggy's vegetables and back to her chosen subject, 'is that Andy isn't Robyn's father.'

'No news to me,' said Peggy, in response to Kate's questioning look. 'Well now, dear, you haven't come here to talk, I know that much. You'll be real busy trying to get the wedding fixed up in time. So what is it you'll be wanting from me, and when d'you want it delivered?'

Discomfitted both by being outwitted by the wily horticulturalist and by Gary's look of 'I told you so', Kate stammered, 'I'm not exactly sure on quantities yet, Peggy, I still have to fine-tune my calculations. I just came to give you a bit of forewarning, in person, as I was passing, that I would be placing a large order soon.'

Peggy nodded. 'That makes me forearmed and you singing flat I guess,' she said. 'Give me a call when your pitch is perfect and we'll see what deal we can strike.' She licked her lips in anticipation. 'That'll be a mighty amount of beef I'll be needing to store in my deep freeze. I'll need to make some room.'

'Yes indeed,' Kate said, but Peggy having already disappeared into her potting shed, she was forced to conclude that, for the present at least, she had been dismissed.

'Nary a drop,' said Gary gleefully as they continued on towards the Blue Yonder in Kate's SUV. 'That's my Mrs Spud. I swear, if you put that woman on the rack, the only information you'd get out of her would be about carrot fly, and then only if the carrot had consented. But hey, woman of mystery, what is all this about your internet amour being an imposter, and why is it so important for you to know who the Horse Weesperer's daddy is?'

'Again,' said Kate severely, 'I must ask you to rid yourself of any notions of love interest I have had at any time towards Andy. It was a purely platonic friendship and continues to be so, even if the Andy I was being platonic with at the time isn't the Andy I'm being platonic with now.'

Gary turned in his seat to look at her and gasped in horror. 'Oh, Pinocchio!' he said. 'Does your nose always do that?'

'If it has grown in any way it will have more to do with

inhaling fertiliser at Peggy's place than because I am telling porkies,' she told him. 'As for the second half of your question, about why I want to know about Robyn's father, well, it's just curiosity on my part. How does Andy come to be bringing her up if she isn't his?'

'Maybe he put in for adoption like me and the Cherub,' Gary suggested. 'The local fishwives have it that the dish they would all like to feed on prefers to be the one who got away. Maybe he wanted a child without the inconvenience of having to have anything as messy as a relationship.'

Kate considered this possibility for less than a microsecond. 'You'll know more about the ins and outs of adoption than me,' she said, 'but how likely do you think it would have been, twelve or thirteen years ago, for the authorities to have given a baby girl to a single, male, working cowboy?'

'Put that way,' Gary replied, cocking his head on one side the better to contemplate the possibility, 'I think we are short of a working hypothesis. So, moving swiftly on, what's your theory?'

'I just don't know,' Kate admitted.

'Tell me all the clues so far.'

'Where to begin?' she said, but find a beginning she eventually did, and by the time she was finished they were inside the barn, and Gary's attention was split between solving the mystery and making a temple of Hera to beat all temples of Hera, bar none. In this respect, muslin was mentioned by the mile, and appended to its name with great enthusiasm from both were other words like draped, billowing, ruched, swagged, knotted, cascade, frothy, bedouin, romantic, and best of all, cheap. This having been decided, then, together with the layout of tables and the procurement by Gary of same, he returned to their previous theme with, 'I suppose you know that you go all gaga when you mention his name?'

'Don't be silly,' said Kate, looking about as gaga as it is

permissible for a person to be while still living in the community, and which Gary was quick to point out.

'Look, love, kid yourself if you want to, but it's no use trying to pull the wool over these gorgeous pools of adamantine brilliance. I can spot over-excited hormones blindfold, and yours are doing the tango. Admit it. He's lush.'

'Oh, he's lush all right,' she admitted. 'But—'

'And muscularly economical of flesh in the buns department.'

'Agreeably lean,' she conceded. 'However—'

'With Michaelangelically carved features.'

'Handsome,' she allowed. 'Nevertheless—'

'Nevertheless?'

Invited now to expand upon her negative theme, her mind was caught napping and she could persuade no argument to come to the fore. 'Tricky,' she offered eventually.

'Not so tricky that it can't be mastered,' said Gary. 'Birds do it, bees do it, even educated fleas do it, or so I've heard it sung.'

'No, *he*'s tricky,' said Kate. 'And I've promised myself not to go after any more tortured souls with dark places where their hearts should be.'

Gary regarded her with an irritatingly knowing smirk. 'We'll see,' he said. 'But let us return for the nonce to our list of the known and the unknown in respect of the mystery of the cowboy imposter. Fact: he or she knew enough about the people here at the Blue Yonder to get their names right, and to be able to describe their personalities more or less accurately, even though he/she got some of their history wrong.'

'Ye-es,' said Kate, 'and no. The names were right, obviously, but the personalities were rather more idealised than in real life. Old Pete, for instance, came across in the telling like a sort of cheerful Father Christmas type, white beard, benevolent smile, very genial and ho-ho-ho kind of thing, whereas in fact—'

'He's a crusty old bugger with a drink problem.'

'Not any more,' Kate hastened to correct him. 'I think he *was* falling foul of the bourbon bottle when I first arrived, but since he's been released from the kitchen and allowed to go out hunting, shooting and a-fishing, he's been much better be-haved around the demon drink.'

'What you can achieve with that spoonful of sugar is nothing short of expialidocious, Mary!' Gary commended her. 'And Robyn?'

'Robyn was described as a lovable tomboy who was a bit naughty about going to school because she loved life on the ranch so much.'

'And this differs from reality how, exactly?'

'Not much at all. Except where her relationship with Andy was concerned. There was no hint of the sulkiness and the resentment she feels towards him. Felt, I should say, rather,' she amended. 'They are actually getting on much better now, since I suggested to Robyn that she should treat him as she would a difficult horse.'

'Oh! Can't you just see that medicine go down, in the most delightful way? I almost feel impelled to join you in a quick chorus of "Chim Chim Cher-ee", and I would, if we could only lay hands on your brolly, Miss P.'

'Do you think helping people is naff?' Kate challenged him, cut to the quick that she was reminding everybody else of Mary Poppins these days, as well as herself.

'If I did, would I be here now discussing the imminent frou-frou-age of this cow shed?' he said. 'I think it's a perfectly delightful quality. Rare, the gift of giving without seeking reward, but marvellous. I wonder if I've yet mentioned the fee for my services here?'

'No,' said Kate, somewhat taken aback. 'Fee, of course. Quite right. Why should you do all this for nothing? I just hope it's not going to come too expensive,' she warned. 'We're trying to clear a debt rather than add to it.'

'No more expensive than yours I suspect,' Gary told her. 'To be able to bask in the warm light of praise when it's done. Isn't that what we're both after? The chance to shine in the spotlight, and to lap up the audience's applause?'

'Are we that shallow?'

'We are that extravert. It's in our chemistry. We are forever doomed to prove ourselves lovable to others. But enough of gazing at our own navels, Cagney. Let's get back to playing lady detectives and gazing at the navels of others. Pray continue. How does the flesh-and-blood Andy differ from his internet self?'

'That's easy. Chalk and cheese. The Andy I thought I'd be meeting was wise, funny, kind—' She paused to reflect a moment. 'But then again, he is starting to be more like that in real life, of late.'

'Since you changed his brimstone and treacle diet, I've no doubt.'

'Well, naturally I'd like to flatter myself that I've made a slight difference for the better in his life,' she said tersely, 'just by trying to take some of the weight off his financial worries. But in all honesty I get the feeling that he's been doing quite a lot of thinking on his own account.' She smiled at the re-membered image of Robyn curled up on his knee. 'And of course, he's responded beautifully to Robyn being more affectionate and forgiving.'

'So the bogus Andy the Cowboy did in fact describe every-body accurately?'

'They described the potential in them, I suppose,' Kate conceded. 'But then there's Andy's prickliness that doesn't seem to get any better at all. Having a conversation with him is like walking through a minefield most of the time. You've just no idea when you're going to put a foot wrong and get blown up. The best way I can pin it down is that he has some really bad secret thing deep inside that plagues him, makes him hate himself almost. But don't ask me what. He can't bear to give anything away about himself. You should have seen him bolt from the room last night, after he'd told me he wasn't Robyn's father.'

'But at least he did tell you,' said Gary.

'True, true.' True, she thought, heartened.

'So back to our list,' Gary instructed. 'Fact one: Bogus Andy described the *potential* of the people here at the Blue Yonder, if not the reality that you experienced when you first encountered them. Agreed?'

'Agreed.'

'So in bringing you here, Bogus Andy has changed their lives for the better?'

'Well, yes, I hope so, but I mean, he or she can't have banked on that happening, can they?'

'Not unless it's God, working in his mysterious way, no. But what if it was a well-wisher, who hoped that by you arriving to take them in hand, things would be bound to improve?'

'Like who?' said Kate, puzzled.

'Like Peggy Potato, for instance, or another of the matrons of the community? They are all agreed, you see, the female elders, that what Andy needs is a good woman beside him. And since all the maids of the community, for their part, have exhausted themselves trying to be that good woman and all been rejected, perhaps this beneficent spirit decided that a new kid was required on this tired, inbred old block?'

'But I could have been lying too,' Kate protested. 'I could have lied about who I was, about my age, my—'

'Don't you?' asked Gary archly.

'Well, I – I rarely mention it actually,' Kate blustered.

'Still admitting to twenty-nine?'

'Thirty-one actually,' she admitted stiffly.

'Whereas in fact you are . .?'

'A little older,' she conceded.

'You see, it's irrelevant, because it is a given,' Gary explained. 'Just as doctors double the amount of what you tell them you drink, so everybody knows enough to add seven or eight years onto the age of women of, shall we say, *un certain?*'

'Steady,' Kate warned. 'It's not a day more than six in my case.'

'A child,' said Gary warmly. 'Practically an infant. But to return to our theme. Fact: Bogus Andy claimed to be Robyn's father, when the real Andy says that he is not. Why?'

'And which is true?' said Kate. 'Is Bogus Andy lying, or Real Andy?'

'Let's start with motive,' said Gary. 'What's in it for Real Andy to lie to you about whether Robyn's his?'

'I honestly can't think of any advantage it might be to him,' she said after drawing blanks in every corner of her mind. 'Can you?'

'Nada,' he admitted. 'So what about Bogus Andy? There are two possible lines of enquiry here, Watson. One: they didn't know that Robyn wasn't Andy's child, just as I didn't – they just assumed she was. Maybe it isn't common knowledge.'

'Peggy knew,' Kate reminded him.

'Peggy knows much but reveals little, which makes her a perfect confidante. Andy could have confided in her. Or Laura/Rainbow might have.'

'Yes, but she didn't treat it like a secret, did she? She admitted that she knew Robyn wasn't his. If she'd been confided in, wouldn't she have been more likely to have been noncommittal?'

'Yes, you're probably right. Okay, second like of enquiry: what advantage was there for Bogus Andy to lie to you about being the Horse Weesperer's pater?'

Kate gave up quickly. 'No idea. But you seem like you've got an inkling – you're looking unbearably smug, Holmes. Give it up.'

'When you were chatting with him on the net, how did you feel when he told you he was bringing up his daughter single-handed, after her flaky mother had run off to play cowgirl and Indians?'

'Impressed,' said Kate at once, her face softening in a smile. 'Approving.'

'A-ha!' said Gary. 'Exactly as I thought. Chick-magnet territory. *Heteropater responsibilis*, a species constantly on the verge of extinction, and the most sought after, I believe, by the hunting *Heteromater potentialis*. He or she upped Andy's desirability by it.'

'The desirability would still have been there if they'd told the truth,' Kate protested. 'Maybe even more so. To bring up your own child would, one would hope, be taken as a given, but to bring up somebody else's child – well, that shows a certain philanthropic bent, wouldn't you say?'

'Speaking for myself, who is just about to do so, no. For me it's because I love children, but Cherub and I lack the necessary equipment for their manufacture. But yes, in Andy's case, or indeed in Bogus Andy's case, it is as you say. It would simply make him twice as fanciable.'

'Not that I did say that exactly,' Kate corrected him firmly. 'And anyway, we were speaking in the general rather than in the particular.'

'Whatever,' said Gary with an airy wave, his brain having fused with too many facts not nailed down. 'Okay, we're getting nowhere fast with the father issue. Let us turn to the known and unknown facts about Rainbow/Laura. Fact: you were told that the young Andy had impregnated a hippy type called Rainbow at a rodeo, who had no maternal leanings but a big yen to make jewellery. Correct?'

'Correct.'

'And the first you knew of this not being true was yester-day, when you mentioned it to Sonia and she told you that

Rainbow was really called Laura and was not a bit hippy? Also correct?'

'Mm,' said Kate thoughtfully. 'Actually, no. It wasn't the first I knew that something didn't add up about her. I'd already tried to pump Peggy about it, but she—' Her voice trailed off as she searched her memory.

'—she is unpumpable,' Gary prompted her.

'Normally yes, but without me pumping her, she actually volunteered that Rainbow – no, she didn't call her Rainbow, I remember now, she said "Robyn's mother". We were talking about me making a vegetable garden here, and she said that Robyn's mother had made one years ago, and that when I cleared the jungle of weeds back, I'd probably find the raised beds she'd made.'

'And did you?'

'What? Oh, yes, I did. But then I said something about how weird that was, because it showed some commitment to staying around, and then I criticised her for abandoning her baby, and then Peggy got really put out. She said something like, "Do you think she planned it that way?" And yes, of course I did, because that's what I'd been told. Rainbow was always going to leave the baby with Andy from Day One. So then I tried to pump Peggy for more, and asked her, you know, was it a spur of the moment thing then? And then she clammed up, but not before freezing my blood with one of her looks.'

'This is very interesting,' said Gary, pacing the breadth of the barn. 'So, in effect, Peggy was saying that Rainbow/Laura didn't jump ship exactly, more that she was pushed?'

'Sounded like it,' said Kate, 'but I can't really make any sense out of that, can you?'

'Aren't we coming back round to my initial suggestion, that Andy wanted a baby but not a wife?' Gary posited. 'If, that is, he was the one who did the pushing.'

'Well, now we come to the photograph I found at the back of his desk drawer,' said Kate.

'You've been looking in his drawers? You hussy!'

'I know, it was a bad thing to do,' Kate admitted, guilt colouring her cheeks. 'I was actually looking for bills at the time, which isn't right either, I know, but I was just trying to help.'

'And what made you think you'd find Bill's in Andy's drawers? Wouldn't you be more likely to find Andy's? Or is there something else I should know about our cowboy?' Gary asked eagerly.

'Very funny. Paperwork, then. I wanted to find out how much Andy owed.'

'Oh, that kind of bill,' he said. 'Okay, so, coming back to the photograph?'

'It was of Andy when he was much younger, with a woman I took to be Laura, although I still thought she was called Rainbow at that time, since she was holding a baby who I assumed to be Robyn. And there was another man there too, who looked a lot like Andy, so I wondered if they could be related. Anyway, they all looked really happy together.'

'So putting two and two,' said Gary, following the trail with the zeal of a bloodhound, 'if Peggy Potato confirms that Andy is not Robyn's father, and also tells you that Laura didn't plan on leaving, did Andy ride her and her lover out of town once he'd somehow discovered that they were bonking behind his back?'

'And he says, "I'll keep the child," and they say, "Okay then, it's a fair cop, she's yours," and trot off together into the sunset. Oh yes, that sounds eminently plausible, I don't think,' said Kate, with withering irony.

'Ooh, back in the knife box with you, Miss Sharp,' said Gary. 'What's your theory then?'

'It was the same as yours, actually,' she admitted, 'but it just doesn't hold up, does it?'

'Can we see the photograph?'

Kate glanced at her watch. 'I don't know. I've no idea what time they'll get back. What if he caught us?'

'Caught two practising thespians like our good selves in the act? We would improvise our way out of it with wit and with verve,' Gary said dismissively. 'Come on, don't hog all the evidence to yourself, I must see it! I might pick up on a vibration, sense something from it that passed you by.'

'All right then,' Kate allowed. 'But we'd better be quick about it. Come on.'

23

It should have been a better day even than the day before, Old Pete having elected to go out hunting coney, leaving Andy and Robyn all to themselves to go ride around the herd, but Andy's admission to Kate the evening before kept tugging at his mind, pulling his spirits down low. She'd know the rest of it now, soon enough. She'd go asking more questions and somebody would tell her what he'd done.

Well, it would be a relief in a way, he decided, trying to make the best of it. Nothing could be worse than not knowing if she knew, always half expecting to see blame show up in her eyes, and never knowing when that might come. Annoyed with having the same circular thoughts eating into his day, he demanded of himself why he even cared whether she knew or not, but that was easy enough to answer: he cared about anybody knowing. Kate wasn't special in that respect.

For Robyn's sake he tried to pull himself out of it, but Robyn wasn't exactly helping him to do that, what with her throwing our little hints the size of British Columbia that Kate was a great gal, wasn't she, that Kate had come to their rescue like nobody else could've, that Kate was a great cook, and wasn't it great having supper to look forward to after they'd eaten their great lunch, cooked by great Kate; that Kate was a great looker, had a great figure and a great smile; that she was a great big bundle of laughs, always ready to play, and wasn't that great? He had started out finding the kid's lack of subtlety amusing, but as the greats mounted up, they'd started to grate on his nerves, and his answers had become increasingly snappy.

Here came that sense of claustrophobia again. When anybody tried to get too up close and personal, even Robyn, it just made him feel hemmed in and fighting for air. It didn't do to feel like that about the kid. It was crazy and just plain wrong. She meant no harm by it, he knew that. She just wanted what she wanted, and what she wanted, she wanted real bad. If he could have, he'd have given it to her but as that would involve him having something that he absolutely didn't want and never had wanted – at least, not since his life had changed in oh, so many bad ways – he was left in the graceless position of withholding from Robyn the one thing that she clearly felt would have made her life complete: a mother for her, and a wife for him – preferably the same person, and the preferred person this time was Kate.

Another worry was on his mind too, another corner that he had backed himself into without thinking when he'd been talking to great Kate in the kitchen last night. He'd said something stupid about her being welcome to stay on at the Blue Yonder gratis for as long as she wanted, meaning it as a way of finding out when she was planning on leaving. But what if she took him at his word and stayed on for weeks, or worse, for months? Robyn would get more and more attached to her the longer she was here, and then it'd be even harder on the kid when Kate finally went back to England. And Robyn would blame him for letting her go, of course, there was no question about it. They'd be squaring up to each other again within minutes of Kate driving away to the airport, all this getting on well together forgotten. Leave aside the fact that their money problems were far from over. Sure, this wedding thing would get them out of the bad situation with John Connor – a factor he was duly grateful for, of course – but it wouldn't keep the flapping old roof from flying off one windy day, wouldn't pay for feed for the livestock, or wages to hire in more hands. Short of winning the lottery, which was pretty unlikely since he had never bought a ticket in his life, the Blue Yonder was doomed as a going concern. The best they could hope for was a slow descent into insolvency, rather than a quick one.

So he was feeling bad enough about himself already before Robyn, having come to the end, thank God, of her eulogy to Kate, started in on her stud idea again and backed him into yet another corner where he was forced, being older and wiser, to be the death of her dreams.

'See, I been thinking about things since I went ape about Jed Gray buying that bit of land,' she enthused, 'and I see now that you was right. No skin off our noses to sell it, if it'll raise us some cash, specially if we downsize on the cattle side of the operation. Then we use that money to buy us some bloodstock and bang, we're in business!'

'Yeah,' he said, trying to speak at her level and not down to her, as he had in the past. 'Only thing is, even if Jed Gray might still want it, it wouldn't begin to raise the kind of money we'd need to buy in good breeding stock. You know as well as I do that the last stallion you had your eye on fetched over ten thousand dollars. That land isn't worth a half of that even.'

'So we use the mares I've bred up and take 'em to stud at first, hire in a stallion's services. We could get that for less than a thousand, then we could breed our own damn stallion.'

'Less than a thousand per. How many mares were you thinking of trying to breed with?'

'Couple maybe?' she said, with touching optimism. 'Jed'd give us more'n two thousand, wouldn't he, for that parcel of land?'

'Well now, I don't know about that,' he told her. 'Things are only worth what somebody else is willing to pay, and in that respect he's got us over a barrel. We'd be wanting to sell more than he's wanting to buy, that's for sure. He made it pretty plain to me that if he did buy it, he'd be doing it as a favour to help us out. He doesn't need it. And he also knows that if he waits long enough, he could have it real cheap. All he has to do is sit back and wait for us to go under.'

'We won't go under now we've got Kate working for us!' was her instant and joyous reply. 'She'll be doing weddings and stuff, and bringing in more business through the guest side of things with her cooking. You said yourself she's brought us luck. We got people coming this weekend on recommendation from other guests who have been here. When did that ever happen before? Never in a million years, that's when.'

'Two guests aren't going to save our bacon,' he said, kicking himself for having opened his stupid mouth to say anything positive about Kate in Robyn's hearing. Yet again he had been hoist by his own petard of politeness.

'That's just the start of it,' said Robyn, undeterred. 'This two'll go back to the city and tell their friends, and then they'll come here and go back and they'll tell their friends, and before you know it, Katie will have us fully booked out and going at full stretch!'

'Kate has her own life back in England,' he warned her. 'It would be wrong of us to keep her from what she loves best. I was talking to her last night, after you went to bed. She loves the theatre, it's in her blood. How would you feel if she asked you to give up horses and take up cooking?'

'She can be in Strange Gary's plays,' said Robyn. 'She wouldn't have to give anything up that way. She could have the best of both worlds.'

'Those plays are amateur, she's a professional,' he said. 'And don't call him that, it isn't polite.'

'Everybody else does,' she countered.

'Which doesn't make them right, just ignorant.'

'Anyway, he should think himself lucky,' she said hotly, 'Hell, I get called a lot worse than that!'

Now this was news. 'You do?' he said carefully. 'Like what?'

'Stuff that isn't polite,' she responded, unwilling to expand.

'Kids at school?'

She nodded reluctantly, wishing she hadn't given away as much as she had. 'Don't you go doing nothing about it though!' she told him with a scowl. 'I've got it covered my own self.'

'Is that why you don't like going?' he asked, committing himself neither one way or the other to this instruction.

'That, and math,' she said, which raised a smile in him that had to be quashed.

'At your age, you guys are at a difficult time in your lives,' he told her. 'Everybody's growing up fast, and they're scared because they don't know what they'll grow into. It's all uncharted territory, and that can be frightening as much as it's exciting. And when people are scared they lash out sometimes. Call other people names, for instance, to take the heat off themselves.'

Robyn, who had been scowling, now broke into a broad grin. 'See, this is where you and Katie have so much in common,' she told him. 'She gave me almost the exact same lecture!'

A pang of jealousy shot through Andy's heart. 'You talked about this with Kate?' he asked.

'Some,' she admitted.

'Well now, I wish you'd felt you could have come and talked to me.'

'You and me weren't getting on so good back then,' she reminded him. 'And anyways, I've told you now, so what's the big deal?'

'No big deal,' he hastily conceded, for indeed, whose fault had it been that she'd chosen to confide in somebody who wouldn't bite her head off? 'I'm glad you felt there was somebody you could talk to, I guess. I'm just sorry that wasn't me at the time. We're getting on better now though, aren't we?'

Robyn laughed out loud. 'Sure are. Ever since I started treating you like a bad behaved bronco like Kate told me!'

'She did *what*?'

'She said if I wanted you to change I had to start treating you gentle, so that's what I done, and it worked, didn't it?' she challenged him.

In all conscience he couldn't deny that, damn her. 'What else did she say then?' he asked, curious despite himself.

'Said I was being too hard on you, because you were already busy blaming yourself for the mess we're in with money, but it wasn't your fault 'cos times had been bad.'

Couldn't criticise that line of reasoning either, blast it. 'Kind of her to guess at how I was feeling,' he said, with a return to his curmudgeonly ways.

'Was she right though?' Robyn asked him, looking at him with an almost maternal concern.

'I guess,' he admitted.

'Well don't,' she instructed him, pushing her pony up close to Rusty's side so she could grab hold of his arm. 'We're partners, partner. We're in this together, and we'll get out of it together, sure as eggs.'

Unaccountably for such a windless day, some dust found its way into his eye and he was forced to wipe it away and to clear his throat most forcefully.

'You're right,' he said, when he'd recovered full use of his sinuses. 'United we stand. Let's never forget that again, hey?'

'No way, José,' she assured him, and added with a cheeky grin, 'you'll always be my bad little bronco from now on.'

After that, the ride became much more pleasurable, the weight on his heart eased, and his good humour returned.

'Reckon you can beat your little bronco back home?' he asked her when it came time to call it a day.

'Blindfold and hobbled,' was her answer, and without waiting for starter's orders, she urged her pony to race on ahead and didn't stop galloping until they pulled up together in the Blue Yonder yard, arguably neck and neck, to find Old Pete staggering in too, under the weight of four unlucky conies.

'It's feast time!' he told them gleefully. 'Now, where's that little chef of ours?'

24

The little chef in question having turned sleuth (or some might say nosy parker, or trespasser, or indeed, sneak thief, since she and her fellow self-appointed lady detective were engaged in making and stealing a copy of the only photographic evidence at their disposal) went into a flat spin when she heard voices next door in the kitchen, causing her to scream into the phone and thus render Minnie McAlpine momentarily deaf in her right ear, despite standing in her granddaughter's executive-housing-estate kitchen at the time, at what might have been regarded as the safe distance of some sixty miles away.

There is a phrase which is usually applied to semi-professionals of small talent in the business known as Show, which offers the warning, 'Don't give up the day job', but it was at least equally applicable in this instance to the two talented showbiz professionals (albeit, perforce, both at that time in semi-retirement) who were currently making a complete pig's ear out of investigating a person whose only known crime was to have been photographed at a distance and in long-shot, thus leading us to the conclusion that the names Thornton and Strange should never, ever grace the frosted glass of a door which also bears the legend, 'Private Eyes'. Eyes could be mentioned in this connection, of course: had Gary Strange not been too vain to wear the prescription glasses he evidently needed for close work, there would have been no necessity to have scanned the small snapshot into the computer in the first place, and therefore its larger, A4-sized copy would not have been grinding out of the printer at exactly the moment when Robyn Barrett bounced through the office door accompanied by the man who was not her father, who was followed in turn by a grizzled man carrying a quartet of dead bunnies, the last of which caused Mr Strange to part with a scream which surpassed that of his partner in both decibels, and in the molto of his vibrato.

There was much to tell on all sides, and little time to tell it, for the colour copy currently squeezing itself out of its hiding place had at all costs to be kept from the view of the incomers, Minnie McAlpine's demand of 'What the bugger's going on there?' had somehow to be addressed, Gary's palpitating heart had to be slapped back into place with his shock-driven hand, his retching subdued, his explanatory statement, 'Vegetarian', understood and acknowledged, the offending leporid corpses hidden behind Old Pete's back, so it was small wonder that the rest of the party marvelled at the timing of Kate Thornton's sudden, implacable desire to express herself in dance, to abandon the telephone and her place behind the desk, to spring across the room with extravagant hand gestures and fancy footwork, and to come to rest at last in front of the laser printer in a dazzlingly showy finish which concluded with the vocal emission, 'Ta-da!' In these circumstances, then, there is no need to say that for several moments she was the only one smiling, the mouths of the others being fully employed in the wordless expression of 'O'.

Who spoke first is anybody's guess, and without audio equipment and men in white coats to analyse and argue over the recorded results we must, alas, remain in perpetual ignorance on that point, for the resulting shocked silence quickly transformed itself into a towering babble of exclamatory remarks from those who had witnessed this astonishing homage to Terpsichore, all of which centred on the mental and emotional health of the woman who would be Isadora. Suffice it to say that to pick one at random, *viz*, 'Are you *feeling* all right, Mata?' (the asking of which, by its young interlocutor, being uttered through lips surmounted and dwarfed by eyes the size of dinner plates), would be to sum up the concerns of all parties; barring of course Mr Strange, who knew exactly how she was feeling and why, and who could not fault her commission of his earlier command to 'improvise with wit and verve', should they be discovered. For as he was to remark later, in his retelling of the tale to the nerd known as Cherubchops, she had taken the bounds of 'vervaciousness' to a previously unassayed height.

In contrast to the clamorous outpourings of her audience, the prima ballerina herself took rather longer to formulate a response, and when it came it baffled them afresh, for it took the form of, 'I'm just happy to see you!' followed by 'Minnie!' and while the three of them checked the room for a newcomer of that name, Kate was dancing her way back whence she'd come, this time with a piece of A4 paper balled in her hand, scooping up the abandoned telephone receiver into which she said, 'Hi! Can I call you back?' before returning her attention to them to enquire, with feverish interest, how their day had been.

'Pretty uneventful up till now, I guess,' Old Pete said drily, dangling the conies for her inspection while interposing his body between them and Mr Strange. 'Brought you a present, girlie, but there's no need to dance me any thanks. Just cooking 'em will be reward enough for me.'

'Righty-ho!' she said brightly. 'Be with you in a minute.'

'I'll go help 'em off with their coats,' said Old Pete, departing. 'Make 'em feel at home here.'

Remembering his manners, Andy said, 'How are you, Gary? Hear you're helping with the preparations for the wedding. Thanks for that.'

'You're more than welcome,' said Gary, remembering his

manners too. 'Sorry to be taking up space in your office. We just needed the computer to . . . work out the menu and . . . things.'

'Be my guest,' said Andy. 'Leave you to it then. I'm going to take a shower before supper. Come on, Robyn. You'd better do the same.'

'Right behind you,' she said, but hung back in the doorway until he and Old Pete had gone. 'Hi there, Stra— Mr Strange,' she quickly amended. 'You asked Mata to be in your next play yet? She's a *pro*-fessional actress from London, you know.'

'No I haven't,' said Gary, his eyes widening at the prospect. 'But what a wonderful idea! I've been burning to do *Hedda*, darling, but I couldn't face the prospect of seeing Eileen Townsend or, God help us all, Sonia Driesen, murder the play instead of themselves, by the end of Act Four. Would you consider it?'

What actress wouldn't, thought Kate? 'God, I'd love to, I love that part. I haven't given my Hedda since I was at drama school, and I didn't know quite enough about life then to do her justice.'

'No, I don't suppose you did,' Gary mused, adding archly. 'Thirty-one is a much better age to attempt her than nineteen. So can I assume I am cast?'

'It would very much depend when you do it and if I'm still here,' Kate answered, deciding to let the age issue drop.

'She'll still be here,' Robyn assured Gary confidently, and left the room with a satisfied grin, muttering something about a rabbit and a briar patch.

Alone at last, the two would-be gumshoes breathed sighs of relief as one, their pulse rates slowly returning to normal. 'Close shave,' said Kate.

'To the bone, love,' returned Gary. 'A millimetre from a scalping, in fact. Thank heavens for those dancing feet!'

Tension escaped both of them in a snort of giggles. 'God, if they thought I was bonkers before,' said Kate, 'they must think I'm certifiable now.'

'Would that be a photocopy wadded up in your sleeve, or are you developing a canker?' asked Gary.

'Bloody hell, take it,' Kate instructed him, retrieving it from the arm of her sweatshirt and bundling it into his hand. 'Get it out of here. Destroy it. Eat it, if you must.'

Declining to make a meal of it, however, Gary smoothed it out on the desk and peered at the young faces of the happy trio. 'I see what you mean about Andy and the other hunk looking alike,' he said. 'They could be brothers. Or cousins. Or just victims of the same barber and gentleman's outfitter, of course. It's rather hard to tell. Making it bigger has just made it fuzzier. I wonder if Cherubim can enhance it at all? I could j-peg it and send it as an e-mail.' So saying, he sat at the computer and proceeded to do exactly that.

'What if he should come back in?' Kate protested hotly. 'For goodness sake, at least put the copy in your pocket.'

Absent-mindedly, Gary did as he was told while saving and attaching the picture and committing it to the ether. 'Done,' he said and, remembering an earlier promise, he got on the web and keyed in MadMelsBlog. 'Almost forgot to show you my favourite website,' he said, shifting over in his seat to make room for her to join him. 'What's the rabid old bag saying about you today? Oh, the slow torture of being hung up by your toes, covered in honey and abandoned in an apiary is the death du jour! Really, her imagination knows no bounds! Doesn't it make you proud to be the Muse of such fervid creativity?'

'Not really,' said Kate hollowly, as she peered at the screen to read Mad Mel's fulminations. 'I've been so happy here, I'd almost started to forget how much I'm hated back home. Just look at all the links she's got to other people's sites!'

'Yes, but none of them are as good as hers,' said Gary,

clicking on one to demonstrate his point. 'They're really quite tame by comparison. You see? Derek of Great Yarmouth thinks you should be merely tarred and feathered.' He eyed her critically. 'Not a look I'd recommend for you, darling. We'd lose your lovely smile.'

Kate thought that she might never smile again. 'Well, thank you so much for showing me these sites,' she said. 'You've really cheered me up.'

'You don't find it funny?' Gary queried. 'They're just saddos, love, who can't tell fantasy from reality. We should feel sorry for them.'

'Then you'll have to excuse my empathy gap,' she told him. Another anxiety suddenly floated into her mind, and grabbing the mouse from him, she exclaimed, 'Oh my God! Delete, delete, and delete deleted!'

'Are we playing Name That Tune?' Gary asked, listening to the rhythm for want of words which made sense. 'Because if so, I think you have me beaten.'

'We've got to get rid of all trace of the e-mail attachment you sent,' she said feverishly, going into Outlook Express. 'What if Andy found out we'd been messing about with his photo?'

'Covering our tracks,' he said admiringly. 'I'm going to have to rethink my role in this detective duo. I had thought that I was the brains, but it appears I'll have to take the position of brawn.' He flexed his arm in a vain attempt to raise a bicep. 'Heavens, if it comes to fisticuffs, I'm afraid we'll be sunk.'

'There,' said Kate, as they watched the offending mail disappear from the screen in the blink of an eye. 'If only I could do the same thing with the wretched blogs.'

Noticing the time on the toolbar, Gary got up to go. 'Got to go and feed my hungry boy,' he told her. 'And I suppose it's time you went and boiled those poor bunnies.'

'Yes,' Kate acknowledged. 'But I'd better call Minnie back first.'

'Oh yes,' Gary remembered. 'With the posse arriving un-announced I quite forgot. Who is she, by the way, and why did you go into agony-aunt mode when you were talking?'

'She's a woman I met on the plane,' Kate said, already dialling Minnie's number, 'and she's not having a great time visiting her relatives.'

'Such a helpful girl,' Gary opined affectionately, kissing her on both cheeks. 'We'll speak on the morrow, my love. In the meantime, I shall get busy busy busy buying muslin, and finding tables and chairs.'

Kate waved an acknowledgement, and before he was out of the door she was already talking Minnie down from high-tailing it back to Yorkshire, and into a mercy mission to the Blue Yonder to help cook for the wedding. 'You said you wanted adventure, Minnie,' she told her. 'And we've got a hundred mini-Yorkie puds to make and fill by Saturday!'

Having transformed Old Pete's catch into something more edible than it had hitherto looked, and aiding the others in its despatch, Kate squared it with Andy for Minnie's impending visit. 'I took your point last night about it being a lot of work,' she told him, 'and I came to the conclusion that it was probably too much for me to do on my own. I hope you don't mind one extra staying here?'

'Not at all,' Andy replied. 'Good of her to offer to help. And no accommodation fee necessary, of course.' Having eaten another of great Kate's great dinners, and having been cleared by Robyn of his sense of guilt about his lack of business success, he was in a mood to be generous and expansive.

'Is she an actress like you, Mata?' Robyn wanted to know.

'No, she's a retired school teacher,' she said.

'Good,' said Andy. 'She might be able to help you with your math homework better than I've been able to. I was doing okay with the algebra, but that new thing they're teaching you – what's it called? – Standard Form? Totally got me beat.'

'Never even heard of that,' said Kate, whose grasp of mathematics had ended with her failure to master the notion of long division many years before.

'It's got something to do with scientific notation,' said Andy. 'Just remind us, Robyn?'

Kate could see Robyn going practically cross-eyed at the thought of trying to do any such thing, and her own eyes were giving every indication of following suit in anticipation. 'Don't worry,' she said hastily. 'It would be wasted on me. But Minnie McAlpine will probably be a whizz at teaching it to you.'

'I'd sooner pay her to do it for me,' said Robyn. 'I could do with raising my grades.'

'Speaking of school,' Andy said, glancing at the clock, 'you'd better get some shut-eye before it's time to go back there. You can leave the washing-up to me and Old Pete.'

'Already on it,' Old Pete announced, getting up on stiff muscles to take the plates to the sink. 'See these off, and then I'm for my bed myself. Forgotten how tiring the outdoor life can be.'

'Can't we play just one game of backgammon?' Robyn moaned.

'Nope,' said Andy firmly. 'But I'll play you three games tomorrow night, if you're up for being beaten.'

'Dream on,' was the happy reply. 'By the way, Andy,' Robyn said with a smug look, as she was taking her leave. 'Did Mata tell you she's going to be starring in Gary Strange's next play, Header Gobbler?'

'No she didn't,' Andy returned levelly. 'Is that a new play about cannibals, Kate, or should Henrik Ibsen be revolving in his grave right now?'

'Doing cartwheels, I imagine,' she laughed, impressed yet again with Andy's knowledge of subjects beyond the normal realm of a cowboy. 'But I didn't say I'd definitely do it. It's more of a pipe-dream really. I doubt it will happen.'

'It'll happen,' said Robyn cheerfully. 'With or without the pipe. Goodnight one and all.'

Having washed the dishes in record time, Old Pete was soon following her out, once again leaving Andy with a tea towel in his hand and only Kate for company. 'Help yourself to a bourbon if you want one,' he told her.

'That would be lovely,' she said gratefully. 'Help me to unwind. It's been quite a day, one way and another. Can I pour one for you?'

'Just a small one,' he conceded. 'Feeling quite tired myself, but there's something I wanted to talk over with you before I go up.'

Kate's cheeks flamed scarlet with guilt, and she was glad that her back was to him as she poured the bourbon into two glasses. 'What about?' she asked fearfully, willing it not to be his suspicions about her dance around the laser printer.

'Couple of things actually,' he said, and turning to face her with a wry smile, continued, 'I hear I have you to thank for casting me in the part of an unmanageable horse.'

For a moment Kate faltered, and then reddened again, remembering. 'Did Robyn tell you about our talk?' she asked.

'She did indeed.'

'I'm sorry. I didn't mean to be insulting. She was just asking my advice, and it came up as a sort of a metaphor.'

'Good choice,' he complimented her. 'And it certainly seemed to do the trick. We've had a couple of good days together, and I'm very grateful to you for it.'

'Really?' said Kate, brightening. 'Well thank you. I'm glad it helped.'

'I believe she confided in you about something else,' he prompted her. 'Regarding bullying at school?'

'Oh, the name-calling. Yes,' said Kate. 'I don't know that I was much help there, though.'

'Did she say what the names are she's being called?' he asked, gazing at her intently.

'Well no, but I should think we can both imagine,' said Kate.

'Not me,' said Andy. 'What do you think it is?'

Kate swallowed, trying to pick words that wouldn't be inflammatory. Surely he could see what she saw? Or was he too close to see the wood from the trees? 'Well, she's not like other little girls her age, is she?' she offered. 'In her choice of clothes, let's say.'

'You mean the fact that she's a tomboy and prefers to wear jeans?' he asked.

'Mm,' said Kate. 'That kind of thing.'

Andy was quick to pick up on her hesitancy. 'What else?' he asked.

'You don't think it's possible that she might turn out to be gay?' Kate offered, biting the bullet and hoping to find that his education had been as liberal as it had been broad.

'Robyn, gay?' he checked. 'I hadn't even —' His voice tailed off as he turned it over in his mind. 'To me she's still a child,' he said.

'Of course.'

'But if she is, then—' Again his mind was too busy working overtime to vocalise his thoughts.

'If she is, then—?' Kate said gently.

'Then she is,' he concluded, for what else was there to say on the matter? 'I guess we're just going to have to wait and see.'

'I'm glad you feel that way,' said Kate, relieved both for herself for being let off the hook, and for Robyn. 'It's not a thing that she has a choice about, exactly, if it does turn out that way, despite what the religious right-wingers may have us believe.'

'No,' he said slowly, and he sat down to drink his bourbon and to reflect. 'You probably know more than I do about these things, working in the theatre, where there are a lot of gays, I imagine?'

'There are a lot of gays everywhere,' she informed him. 'It's just that in theatre they're not so afraid to reveal themselves as such.'

'Could a person's inclinations be swayed by how they were brought up?' he asked, looking suddenly vulnerable. 'If, for instance, a girl had grown up in a very male environment with no female person to guide her?'

Kate smiled, glad to be able to reassure him. 'Absolutely not on that score,' she said. 'And I believe from my gay friends that the very first thing a parent asks in these circumstances is usually along the lines of, "Where did I go wrong?" The answer is nowhere. I've mentioned before, I hope, that I think you're doing a really terrific job with her. She's a lovely girl, and an absolute credit to you.'

Andy breathed out a sigh, his features softening somewhat. 'I hope you're right,' he said, and after a long reflective pause, continued, 'I'd been thinking of going down to the school in the morning, talk to her class teacher, even though she told me not to. I don't know what to do. I don't want to cause her worse trouble, or make her mad about me interfering.'

'Whatever you do, you should talk it over with Robyn first and get her blessing,' Kate warned him. 'She might hate the intrusion, feel disempowered by it. Getting to know yourself can be an awfully private business sometimes, don't you think? And that's her job. We can't know better than her who she is.'

'You're right,' said Andy, and he nodded across the table and smiled his thanks. She had impressed him with that insight. He hadn't taken her for a person who knew much about privacy, least of all respected it. Every time he thought he'd got a handle on this woman, he ruminated, she showed him something new about herself.

'Why not ask Minnie's advice, too, when she gets here? She'll probably have dealt with this sort of thing hundreds of times during her career.'

Andy nodded. 'I might do that.'

Emboldened by his openness, Kate said, 'Would you mind me asking one of my nosy questions?'

Andy looked her straight in the eyes, deliberating, it seemed, what to say. 'She's my brother's child,' he said at last, and rose to wash his glass at the sink. 'I guess that was what was on your mind, was it?'

'Yes,' she admitted. 'So how come you—?' But he was already making his escape towards the door.

Politeness getting the better of him once more, he checked himself and forced himself to turn back to say, 'That's one of those private things that you mentioned earlier, Kate, and I don't like talking about it overmuch. Another time, maybe. But now, goodnight, and thanks again for your help.'

'Goodnight,' she said, following his egress with regretful eyes. She'd pushed him too hard and frightened him off, she thought, inwardly cursing her own stupidity, just when they'd been getting on so well. But again he surprised her by rematerialising almost at once.

'Forgot to ask,' he said. 'Did you check back on your e-mail to your agent? Any hope for you on the horizon yet?'

'No, I didn't,' she said, to her own surprise. 'I got too discouraged by Gary Strange showing me some horrible web sites about myself.'

'Sorry to hear that. Well, you're welcome, as always, to use the computer,' he told her, in a bid to ease his claustrophobia. It had been good to have someone to talk over Robyn's problems with, but you could take intimacy a step too far. Better for all concerned if Kate got a nice job offer back in

London, and left them to get on with their lives. That way, Robyn couldn't blame him either, he reasoned, for he had already laid the ground for not keeping Kate from her career, Header Gobbler notwithstanding. 'And help yourself to the bourbon if you've a fancy to stay up. You're probably used to keeping later hours than us countryfolk. Good night again.'

'Good night again,' she said. 'Sleep well.'

Sitting there alone in the cowboy's kitchen, she availed herself of his generosity with the bottle, but was too interested in mulling over his latest revelation (and what it revealed about him) to want to look at her mail at that moment.

Thus she put off knowing, yet again, what catastrophic news lay in wait for her.

25

It was three days later (and three nail-biting days closer to the wedding reception) before the cavalry was to arrive in the person of Minnie McAlpine, and in that time, whether by accident or design, there was never a moment that Kate was alone in Andy's company. It was almost like having leprosy or some other catastrophically communicable disease, she thought (not knowing, at the time, the dreadful irony of her choice of metaphor) for, if Andy did find himself in a room with her and unchaperoned for a second, he as quickly found an excuse to vacate it on some urgent pretext that an errand must be run without delay. Where, or for what, was irrelevant, it seemed. His overriding impulse was simply to put distance between himself and the person to whom he had held out the possibility of telling more about 'a private thing' than he evidently felt comfortable about imparting now.

In contrast, Kate had hardly been out of Gary Strange's company in those seventy-two hours for a moment, the cleaning and decoration of the barn bringing them together as if they were joined at the hip. There had been heated discussion between them as to whether Sonia Driesen would be as charmed as Mr Strange by the idea of festooning the horns of Milkers One and Two with garlands of flowers and to feature them as symbols of fertility, centre stage, or whether, like Kate, Mrs Connor-to-be would be happier for them to be relocated to the paddock for the day, and this point had yet to be won by either party. But on the whole they had been getting along famously, agreeing on most things and sparking off on each other's ideas. Naturally Kate had shared the news about Robyn being Andy's niece and for that, Cherubchops at least, was duly grateful. As he had wearily informed his beloved on receipt of the j-pegged photograph, his skills lay in creating software solutions for telecoms, not in forensics. But neither Gary nor Kate could come up with any satisfactory explanation as to why Andy was bringing up his niece single-handedly, nor what the child's mother or father thought about this arrangement, and both of them were far too busy setting the nuptial scene in the barn to go out gathering evidence on the matter, even if the good folk of the locality had been willing to tell them.

The cleaner the barn became, and the more swagged with muslin, the more its designer was inclined towards a bedouin theme, but here he met resistance from the entire Blue Yonder staff for, once he had explained to them that they must be themed likewise, dressed in billowing trousers caught at the ankle and going bare-chested save for small jewelled boleros, they rebelled to a man. Even Robyn, offered this choice of costume instead of the slave-girl harem pants initially put forward, refused on the grounds that Gary could shove it anyplace he liked but about her person: she'd be coming as a cowboy and that was it flat.

'What can I do with cowboys and billowing gauze drapes, love? They just don't go together,' Gary had complained to Kate, full of angst. 'How on earth can I tie in two disparate themes like that? I can't. It can't be done. I defy anybody to come up with a solution.'

'Have them dress as cowboys, but in white?' Kate suggested absent-mindedly, her thoughts on the bigger fish she had to fry. And bake. And roast. And, come to that, to quantify, since she had continued to balk at the arithmetic involved in ordering the definitive amount of vegetables from Peggy, and in the meantime, Old Pete was filling freezers beyond capacity from his hunting and fishing expeditions.

Gary's eyes had narrowed in thought while his mind's eye constructed the scene. 'Perfect!' he cried at last, clasping Kate to his chest. 'Pure genius! White satin with rhinestones! But don't say a word,' he added hastily, putting a finger to his lips and casting about anxiously to see if they'd been overheard. 'I'll have the costumes made in secret and present them as a *fait accompli* on the day.' He held her at arm's length and cocked his head on one side to give her the eye-narrowing treatment personally. 'And you, darling, are going to out-Stanwyck Queen Barbara, once I've got you cocooned in culottes. You must practise striding about in a no-nonsense, gun-totin' kind of a way.'

This Kate was happy to begin at once in the direction of her SUV, since, on checking her watch, she saw that it was high time that she drove to Eighty-three Mile House out on Route 97, this being the closest the bus would bring Minnie to their door. After the fever-pitch that was Gary she was in need of the Yorkshirewoman's phlegmatic calm, and this, she found, was available by the barrow load.

Old teachers never die, it transpired, and neither, like old soldiers, do they fade away, at least not when their name was Minnie McAlpine and they had recently escaped from the brain-death known as suburbia. Noticing a sign to a museum not far from their pre-arranged pick-up point which promised educational enlightenment on the subject of Farm Equipment, it was all Kate could do to persuade her that there was all the antique farm equipment a person might want to see in a lifetime, rusting at the Blue Yonder Guest Ranch, a willing teacher at her disposal called Old Pete, and a buttock-clenching sense of urgency to get her helper home quick sharp, to aid her in the counting of cucumbers.

'I just keep going boggle-eyed at the calculations,' she

admitted. 'It's nerves, I think. Every time I sit down at the computer to try to work it out, it seems that my brain just shuts down completely.'

'Pity your brain didn't shut down when you were on the computer getting yourself into this mess in the first place,' Minnie told her. 'Then again, I suppose it did. Nobody in their right mind would fly out to the back end of beyond to cook for cowboys unless they were either bonkers or being paid a heck of a lot of money, which, I take it, you are not?'

'No, I'm just bonkers,' Kate told her.

'No need to sound so pleased with yourself about it,' Minnie censured her with a sniff, folding her hands over her handbag on her lap. 'Any road, you never did tell me what all that screaming was about on the phone the other day. What on earth was happening – blue murder?'

So Kate filled her in on all that had been happening, sounding suitably ashamed of her digging about in other people's desks, and explaining all the complex and contradictory evidence she had discovered to date.

Having had her mind exercised by nothing more taxing than jigsaws and crosswords during her incarceration on the executive housing estate, Minnie set to work with alacrity to untangle the deepening mystery. 'You're sure it isn't the little girl?' she quizzed Kate, as she sifted through the evidence coming her way and weighed up the available options. 'Sounds to me like she sorely misses having a mum.'

'I know what you mean, but I'm almost positive it wasn't her,' said Kate. 'She's far too young and far too hot-headed to have chatted in the mature way that "Andy the Cowboy" did.'

'And you're equally positive it wasn't your man himself?'

'Whose man?' Kate protested, taking her eyes off the road to eyeball Minnie. 'Not my man, I assure you.'

'Just a figure of speech,' Minnie countered, turning in her seat to eyeball Kate back with great interest. 'But by the sound of the lady protesting too much, you'd like him to be, I'm guessing?'

'Guessing wrong,' Kate told her firmly, but without the conviction which might have persuaded her older and wiser friend, who merely sucked in her cheeks beneath eloquently raised eyebrows and kept her own counsel.

'I suppose you've tried the obvious?' she asked finally, after several minutes of quiet reflection, and several Polo mints noisily sucked.

'Probably not,' Kate sighed. 'Just remind me what the obvious is again?'

'Going online to find him, of course,' said Minnie.

'Oh, that obvious,' said Kate. 'Yes, I did once, but he wasn't playing at the time, and then I just forgot about it, I suppose. It seems a bit like looking for a needle in a haystack, though.'

'How so?' said Minnie. 'The *Yoohoo* backgammon room is a pretty small haystack, and if you know what time of day you usually played him, we can make it even smaller.'

Kate pondered the question, the answer eluding her while she did what was for her the complex conversion from English time to Canadian. 'Never before six thirty in the evening, and rarely after midnight,' she said finally.

'Five and a half hours,' Minnie mused. 'Well, that's all right. We'll just have to take it in shifts.'

Having hurried her co-caterer home to the Blue Yonder, Kate as quickly rushed her to the computer to work out what they needed to buy, and after a lightning quick lesson in the art of arithmetic, drove her away again at speed to put their order in with Peggy Davies. The two women met each other with an intense interest born of a shared passion for gardening, and which began with the complimentary ejaculation from Minnie, 'Ee, lass, you've got your work cut out here, looking after this big patch all on your lonesome. I take my hat off to you, it's a veritable Garden of Eden!' which earned her huge favour and the invitation to share Peggy's flask of tea.

'Got you to fly out from England to help at the wedding, did she?' Peggy asked her, with a nod in Kate's direction, after they had given her their order and had settled down on her verandah in comfortable wicker chairs.

'No, I was already here to see my granddaughter and meet my first great-grandchild,' Peggy explained.

'Good of you to break a family visit,' Peggy proposed.

'Not really,' Minnie informed her. 'Ever lived in a cul-de-sac? It's like a ghost town in the day, and there I was all on my own with nothing to do but twiddle my thumbs. No good for the likes of me. I like to be up and doing.'

'Well, if you plan on staying on after the heat's died down over at the Blue Yonder, feel free to come and be up and doing over here,' Peggy invited. 'I been hearing how young Kate's been helping out at their guest ranch, and I'm of a mind to make myself into a guest garden on the strength of it. Got a couple of nice spare rooms, you can take your pick. You'll find my rates competitive.'

'Very kind of you, but unlike some folk,' this said with a circling of the eyes towards Kate, 'my return flight's already booked. I'll think on, mind,' Minnie promised. 'But as I understand it, I'll be stopping over there for free.'

'Fierce competition,' Peggy conceded. 'But I reckon I might match it if you proved worth your salt. Big time of year for me right now, and this hip of mine ain't getting any younger.'

'Your hip, is it?' Minnie sympathised. 'It's my bloody knees. Tried extract of green-lipped mussels?'

'Till I was green in the face,' said Peggy dismissively. 'Same goes for all the other so-called remedies. Only one I found beneficial is the power of denial.'

'Mind over matter,' Minnie rejoined approvingly. 'That, and a couple of glasses of scotch and water before bed.'

'I don't know whether you'd be interested in trying a bit of massage, Peggy,' Kate volunteered, 'but I helped Old Pete's shoulder by it, so it might be worth a go.'

'So I hear,' she responded. 'He's about emptied the rivers round here of salmon since you got your hands on him, way it got told to me, and the conies are all taking cover.'

'I thought you didn't listen to gossip,' Kate teased.

'People tell me things sometimes before I can stop 'em,' said Peggy, easing herself out of her chair and walking them to the gate. 'Well, ladies, it's been fun, but there's work for me to get back to here, and plenty of it waiting for you back at the ranch, I've no doubt. Come visit again soon, Minnie, you'll be welcome any time, particularly with a hoe in your hands. And Kate, I'm going to break the habit of a lifetime here and pass on something that's come my way, seeing as you're so hell-bent on helping Andy Barrett out of his hole.'

Intrigued, Kate stopped in her tracks to listen to what came next.

'Got roof problems over there is what I heard,' Peggy told her, which was no news to Kate.

'That's right,' she concurred. 'But I don't know what I can do to help there. I'm not big on heights, I'm afraid.'

Peggy shook her head impatiently. 'That's the trouble with the young,' she remarked to Minnie. 'Never got the time to wait for you to finish up.'

Minnie nodded sagely, but couldn't resist saying, 'From where I'm standing, you're a bit of a nipper yoursen, young Peggy.'

The nipper grinned sheepishly. 'I'll take that as a compliment.'

'Me too,' said Kate, happy to jump on any bandwagon on offer.

'Fair enough,' said Minnie disparagingly, 'if you think not

having lived as long somebody else is an achievement worth congratulating.'

Suitably chastened now on two counts, Kate said, 'Sorry for butting in, Peggy. You were saying, before I rudely interrupted?'

'I was saying that they've got a problem with their roof and with their pockets, and I know a builder who's got a problem with a pony. You and me have talked before about the barter system – a system you've put to good use in John Connor's direction, I believe.'

'You believe right,' Kate smiled. 'So what's the builder's problem with the pony, and how might it be of mutual benefit?'

'His problem is that he don't have no pony, and his daughter is driving him to an early grave with her hinting and huffing on the matter,' Peggy explained. 'Young Robyn Barrett's got an eye for horseflesh, and plenty of horseflesh to choose from, it seems to me. Could find yourself doing a straight trade, if maybe she threw in a couple of lessons for the kid.'

'Fantastic, Peggy!' Kate enthused, and gave her an impromptu hug. 'What's his name and where do I find him?'

'Wrote it down for you next time you showed up,' said Peggy, fishing a scrap of paper out of her pocket and handing it over before ducking back to safety. 'No need to go squeezing the life out of me again on the strength of it. I'll be pleased enough if it comes off. Good day to you, girls. I'll get that order of yours ready, and bring it on over tomorrow.'

26

There was much to-ing and fro-ing through the kitchen while Kate prepared supper and Minnie, once she'd settled into her room, sat at the kitchen table and watched the permanent residents of the Blue Yonder come and go. First she met Robyn, who, arriving home from school, had hardly said hello before sitting beside her and trying to sell her the idea of doing her homework in exchange for the hard cash of one Canadian dollar.

'I'd prefer to sit here and watch you do it for nowt,' Minnie told her, but nevertheless she was unobtrusively helpful and supportive when Robyn, sighing, started to tackle it, Kate noted.

Next up was Andy, striding in through his own back door and stopping in his tracks to find that two women had now taken root in his kitchen. Polite as always, though, he removed his hat and shook Minnie's hand, and thanked her for coming to help them before scurrying away for his shower and a change of his dusty clothes.

As Robyn was packing up her school books, homework accomplished, Old Pete made his bloody entrance, a brace of wild ducks in his hand, and did a double-take to rival Andy's reaction when he laid eyes on Minnie, but for rather a different reason, it transpired. For when it came time for them to eat, he reappeared spruced up almost beyond recognition, a clean shirt buttoned tidily to the neck, his normally intractable hair licked down to his scalp and forced into a straight parting, and displaying the kind of nice table manners during dinner which, hitherto, Kate hadn't realised were within his gift. It was, 'Potatoes, my dear?' and, 'A drop more of this good gravy? Want me to pour it?' and never once did he eat with his hands, nor lick his plate, as had been his habit to date.

Tickled pink as Kate was to see the unexpected sight of Old Pete flirting, she also felt rather envious at the ease of Minnie's passage. She'd hardly arrived, and already she'd been offered a room in Peggy Davies' home and, if Old Pete kept going on the track he seemed set on, his hand in marriage, it seemed. What was her magic? Kate wondered, but as the evening progressed and she watched her, the answer became quite clear. She was who she was, and was totally comfortable with being that way. She didn't go out of her way to please, she didn't flatter, didn't go out of her way to entertain, or to get any attention at all, though she got it in bushels for just being herself. It was an object lesson in self possession, and Kate acknowledged to herself that she could learn much from that, and certainly would, at some later date. But for now, she was bursting to tell everyone her good news and to feel the warmth of their approval.

'News, news!' she cried. 'You'll never guess what we found out we can barter for next!'

'Go on,' said Andy, with sinking heart, for this kind of Kate-outburst, as he'd come to think of it, usually signalled some kind of huge change to his way of life, like one hundred people tramping all over his property, or having Gary Strange tell him that he's to wear pantaloons, and have his chest rubbed down with oil. But even he was impressed when he heard Peggy Davies' idea about the roof and the pony, because it had the potential of releasing him from one of his least favourite chores and one of his biggest all-time failures, his numerous, fruitless attempts to keep it dryer on the inside of the house than it was on the outside, whatever the weather.

Naturally Robyn was delighted too, for it was her horse-breeding skills which were being used for the barter. 'Look at this, Andy,' she crowed, 'I'm bringing money in while I'm still in school! Just think how much I'll be able to make for us when I get out of that damn place!'

'Language,' Andy chided, with an apologetic glance towards their new visitor, but he followed it up with, 'you've always brought money in, partner, every time you do a chore.'

There followed excited talk about which of the ponies would be suitable for the swap, one that would be equal to the worth of the work on the roof, but one she could bear to part with. 'I guess it comes down to the weight and height and experience of the girl,' she said, after putting forward several equine possibilities. 'Who is it?'

Consulting Peggy's handwritten note, Kate said, 'Sam Taylor's little girl, Frances.'

The effect on Robyn was explosive. 'Cissie Taylor? No way! She's one of the worst—' She stopped in her tracks, realising that she'd revealed more of her private life than she'd meant to. 'Cissie Taylor is a brat,' she continued sulkily. 'No way am I giving her one of my horses. I'd sooner eat shit and die.'

The revelation about the identity of one of his niece's biggest tormentors was not lost on Andy, and he eschewed chewing her ear off about the choice of language concerned with her wished-for demise. 'Would you sooner be rained on indoors, is more the point of the matter?' he said gently.

'Sure, why not?' came the combative reply, said with eyes lowered to her lap and her bottom lip thrust out in an expression of obdurate inflexibility.

'Well, we all have to do business sometimes with people we don't care for,' Andy offered, beginning to sound just as obdurate. 'Jed Gray isn't my favourite person in the whole world as it happens, but I was willing to—'

'—but you didn't!' Robyn cried. 'And neither will I!'

This was certainly not going in the happy congratulatory way she had planned it, thought Kate, but before she could add her twopenn'orth to the heated discussion, Minnie McAlpine added a couple of pennies of her own.

'There's an English saying,' she offered reflectively, 'about cutting off your nose to spite your face. Funny expression, isn't it? Just imagine, taking a knife and cutting your nose right off and leaving a hole there. What it means, of course, is that sometimes you hurt yourself more in the doling out of punishment than it might be worth. I've found it's a handy saying to keep in mind, when you're faced with these tricky decisions that life throws your way.'

Robyn 'humphed', but studied the teacher intently before returning her attention to her plate, to eat with dulled appetite.

Light conversation filled the silence from the adults while they left her to consider this, Old Pete wanting jocular reassurance that Gary Strange would now permit them to go fully dressed amongst the guests on Saturday.

'Have them damned hay-reem pants been kicked off the menu?' he wanted to know.

'They are dead as a dodo,' Kate assured him. 'We'll all be going as cowboys, and that's flat.' She sneaked a cheeky smile over at Robyn and received a grudging one back.

'Something to be grateful for,' said the child.

Watching her struggle with the kind of complexities and grey areas that tormented him daily, Andy felt pained to witness how she was being forced to grow up. As everybody had to grow up eventually, of course, he knew that. But he had been so enjoying her childhood, he felt a pang of preemptive grief that it would soon be over. However, his pride could hardly be contained when she lifted her head again to reluctantly admit, 'Okay then. I guess I'd sooner Cissie Taylor had a pony than I had a damn hole in my face.' The resulting applause this earned her bringing a return of the sunshine which had been lost from her smile, he thought his heart might swell beyond the confines of his chest.

Kate's sense of relief was hardly less great, and she decided that this was not the time to come clean about the six riding lessons she had negotiated away on the phone to Sam Taylor, but that it might be appropriate to reveal Minnie's plan about how to catch 'Andy the Cowboy' red-handed, and this was indeed seized upon with great interest from all parties, although Old Pete's contribution was confined more to the negative.

'Can't understand that game no more now than when it was first explained to me,' he said, 'Counters coming and going every which way. I'd like to help catch the fella, but more likely he'd catch me.'

'You don't have to play, actually,' Kate explained. 'Just watch to see if the name "Andy the Cowboy" comes up on the players list.'

'Me first, me first!' claimed Robyn, once the shift work at the computer had been explained to them. 'I'll play him and mash him!'

'Well, don't get too excited, we might have missed him tonight, we've already lost three and a half hours of his potential playing time,' Kate warned.

Alerted to the lateness of the hour, Andy decided to relax the rules a little regarding weekday bed-time on this occasion, and granted Robyn the first watch of thirty minutes and not a second more.

'Robyn!' Kate called after her fast-disappearing form. 'If you get him, just call me, don't say anything about us knowing he's an imposter. Getting himself to reveal his true identity is going to be tricky, and we don't want to frighten him off.'

The meal being over, the two men set about the business of tackling the dirty dishes while Kate and Minnie took their ease as a reward for all their endeavours.

'Would you care for a glass of bourbon, Mrs McAlpine?' Andy enquired.

'Aah, a man after my own heart,' she rejoined warmly. 'I will at that. But call me Minnie.'

Now why the dangnation he hadn't thought of that his own self irked Old Pete something grievous when he observed the warmth of her smile for his young boss, but he seized his advantage back by insisting on being the one who got the bottle and poured.

'I'll take a little water with it, Pete, if you please,' she said as he handed her a glass with due ceremony, and while he obeyed her instruction and surreptitiously licked down his hair over at the sink in its commission, Kate was interested to see that Minnie was also adjusting her plumage, tidying a stray wave behind her ear and revolving her necklace so that the biggest of the small cultivated pearls she was sporting was positioned exactly front centre. Even Andy noticed the nascent courtship rituals beginning to evolve under his nose, and being torn between embarrassment and wonder at the change being wrought in Old Pete, he excused himself after the last pot was dried, to join Robyn in the office.

'I'll come with you,' said Kate, excusing herself from the table where Old Pete and Minnie were exchanging their histories thus far.

But if she'd thought that by doing so, somebody else might take it into their head to follow their employee's example, she was doomed to disappointment. Nor was there any satisfaction to be had during the ensuing two hours that she sat and watched the computer screen (the last hour on her own), of ensnaring the bogus cowboy, for it was not until the next night, during Old Pete's watch between seven and eight, that the air was electrified with the sound of his whooping 'Yee-ha!' and his youthful sprinting into the kitchen.

'Got him!' he cried. 'He's there, large as life, on Table

Seventy-three, playing against some fancy woman called Satin-n-lace!'

'Is he now?' said Kate, grim-faced, as she marched into the office to face the person who had had such an influence on her recent life.

'Damn, I can catch any damn critter alive!' Old Pete couldn't resist crowing for Minnie's benefit, in case she hadn't quite got the point yet about what an excellent provider he could be. 'Duck, salmon, conies, you name it! Now I got me a big old cheating cowboy!'

'You're a marvel,' she told him, getting up to guide him across the room with a hand on his arm. 'But come on, let's follow the others. We don't want to miss out on all the fun.'

27

The Blue Yonder posse now swollen to five, there was crowded standing room only for four of them round the computer, while Mata Hari took the hot-seat behind the desk. And there, as Old Pete had said, was 'Andy the Cowboy', chatting and playing with Satin-n-lace. With the real Andy standing close beside her, peering down at the screen, it was quite a surreal moment for Kate, for here in the flesh was the real cowboy, and there in cyberspace was the man she had flown out to meet.

'You see what I mean about him being gentlemanly and a good sport?' she asked the assembled company, as A-the-C neatly side-stepped Satin's double entendre about his 'big roll', demurred that getting two sixes twice in a row had just been plain lucky, and assured her that she was playing frighteningly well. But suddenly, to the spooked amazement of the Blue Yonder gang, there appeared the words:

AndytheCowboy: Hey there, Mata Hari! Long time no see. How you doing?

Satin-n-lace: Oh boy. Is somebody watching us? Git gone. This is a game for two only, and he's taken.

'How does he know you're here?' asked Minnie, intrigued, as Kate deliberated how to respond.

Robyn leant forward and pointed at the screen. 'See here, where it says the players' names at the table? And just here, there's Mata Hari's, "Observing". They could click on this privacy button if they wanted, then other people couldn't see what they're talking about.'

The same thing, apparently, was on Satin's mind, but Kate was of a mind to be polite – at least in the beginning.

MataHari: Hi, Andy. Yes, long time. How've you been?

AndytheCowboy: Pretty good. Missed our chats though.

MataHari: I need to talk to you now, actually, about something really important. Satin, would you mind?

Satin-n-lace: Yup. Shove it. I told you, this table's taken, and this cowboy's mine.

'Persistent little beggar, isn't she?' remarked Minnie, who wasn't used to the rudeness that passed for conversation of this kind.

'Tell her to shove it back!' Robyn counselled hotly. 'Coming on all hot with my Andy. What a nerve!'

But Mata had now made the other 'Andy' anxious.

AndytheCowboy: What is it, Kate? Another death threat?

Kate's fingers hovered indecisively over the keyboard, before typing:

MataHari: It is kind of life and death, yes.

Satin-n-lace: She's getting death threats. And she's surprised?

'What a minx!' said Minnie, indignant on Kate's behalf, if less confrontational than Robyn. 'She's no better than she ought to be, I'll be bound.'

'Wait! Look! I'm getting rid of her,' said the real Andy. 'I mean – goddammit! He, she, it's getting rid of her.'

And indeed, 'Andy' had resigned the game, excused himself in a most gentlemanly fashion and, since Satin-n-Lace refused to cede her place at the table, said he'd meet Kate at their usual.

'What does he mean by that?' Andy said with a frown. He didn't like the idea at all that he had a 'usual' he didn't even know about.

'We used to meet up on Table Forty in a different Games Room to this when we wanted to chat and shake off the likes of Arsenic-n-Lace,' Kate explained, as she navigated her way there. 'We just agreed on a place for future use, after a similar situation as this, because otherwise if you tell them exactly where you're going, they try to get in first and keep you out.'

'Oh,' said Andy uncomfortably, as he watched Mata Hari and Andy the Cowboy sit down together and saw himself say, 'Now, Kate, tell me all about it. I'm so sorry to hear there's been more trouble. Are you okay?'

He felt no more comfortable when he saw Kate's face soften into a mushy smile in response, and was glad when Minnie poked her in the back and said, 'Aren't you going to answer him?', because the way he was feeling, if she hadn't, he would've. Embarrassed out of her reverie, Kate typed:

MataHari: I'm okay. How are you? How's the broken arm, Andy?

AndytheCowboy: Healing pretty good now thanks. Bit stiff is all.

MataHari: And Robyn? How's she? Back at school yet, or still bunking off?

AndytheCowboy: Oh, you know Robyn! Caught her hiding in the hay loft this morning when I thought she'd got off to school an hour ago. Said it's just'cos she loves me and can't bear to let me out of her sight!

It hardly needs to be said that these remarks provoked remarks in return of a shocked and abusive nature from the parties concerned, and calls for Kate to, 'Get on with it and call the two-faced liar out!' But Kate was enjoying herself too much to bring her quarry to a quick kill, on the one hand because it was too delicious to have whoever-it-was at her mercy like this, but also – and weirdly, under the circumstances, even to her – it made her feel really good to be talking to him again. She'd missed his gallantry and his sympathetic concern, missed confiding her troubles to him. It made her come over all unnecessarily girlie to meet him again after their time apart, a state of being which Robyn was quick to criticise, with her candid demand, 'Why are you grinning like that, Mata? Do you *like* being lied to?', which did the trick in bringing her back to earth with a bump, and gave Andy some satisfaction, for his niece had taken the words right out of his mouth.

'Of course not,' Kate said guiltily. 'I'm just thinking how to go about this.' She flexed her fingers like a concert pianist before striking the keys. 'Okay,' she said. 'Got it.'

MataHari: What would you say if I told you I'm going to see you really soon?

Cheers of approval from the assembled company, and a very long typing break for 'Andy'.

MataHari: Are you still there?
AndytheCowboy: Excuse me. Yes. I'd say, how so? Are you planning a visit to Canada?
MataHari: More than planning. I'm here already.

Another pause before:

AndytheCowboy: You're where exactly?
MataHari: Can't you see me? I'm sitting right in front of you.
AndytheCowboy: Oh, I see. Funny. Well, Kate, I wish you really were here at the Blue Yonder, instead of just your words on this old computer screen. But tell me about your life and death matter. What's wrong?
MataHari: What's wrong, Andy, is that you can't see me, when you're standing right behind me in your office.

Whoops of victory in said office and yet another thinking break, it seemed, for 'Andy'.

'Has he got scared and run?' Old Pete asked anxiously. 'Before you had chance to tell him what a low-down, conniving, son of a – beg pardon, Minnie.'

'I have heard the expression,' she told him with typical northern phlegm. 'It's just that I never understand why they always blame the mother for the son being a prat.'

'Wait, I'm back,' said the confused, but real, Andy, whose eyes had never left the screen.

AndytheCowboy: Kate, are you telling me you're at the Blue Yonder now, in person?

MataHari: That's what I'm telling you. And what I'm asking you is who are you and why have you been lying to me like this?

'That's got him thinking!' said Old Pete with a wheezy chuckle, slapping his thigh in approval.

'Yeah, thinking what lie he's going to come up with next,' said Robyn.

'Oh no!' said Kate. 'No, no, no!'

For Andy the Cowboy had suddenly left the table with no word of farewell, and was gone without trace in less than the blink of an eye.

There was a sense of anticlimax, and a frustrated feeling of unfinished business from the group when they finally acknowledged that he was definitely not coming back to take his punishment like a man, and the office computer was switched off for the night.

'Well, at least now you know it wasn't me,' Robyn told Andy, and Andy said, 'Same goes both ways.'

'And now you all know I wasn't making it up,' said Kate.

'We're just none the wiser about who the bugger is, bugger

it,' said Minnie, summing up everybody's disappointment precisely. 'Well, I'm for my bed. Tiring work, this detecting. Good night.'

'Me too,' said Old Pete, leaving the room on her heels.

'Good night then, Mata. Sorry we didn't get to kick his ass some more,' said Robyn, and dropped an unexpected and awkward kiss on the top of Kate's head before leaving the room.

'Me too,' Kate smiled sadly.

Andy was out of the door before you could say, 'My goodness, there's just the two of us left in the room,' but Kate was growing used to that now. 'You okay?' he asked, turning to look back at her from the safety of the corridor.

'Fine,' she said, with forced cheerfulness. 'Good night.'

In fact, she was anything but, being the victim of a tumult of conflicting feelings after spending time with both Andys at once. Her response to the cyber-Andy had taken her quite by surprise, and she was forced to acknowledge to herself, as she sat there alone in the small pool of light from the desk lamp, that she had been in love with him, in a strange and spooky way. Although her London life had seemed so far away only minutes ago in the companionable cosiness of the Blue Yonder kitchen, she could remember now how intensely she'd looked forward to their chats during her lonely imprisonment in her flat, how 'Andy' always seemed able to make her feel better about her situation, however grim, and how she'd felt so special with his chivalrous attentiveness. Searching through her lexicon of emotions and trying to be ruthlessly honest, she was forced eventually to conclude that 'romantic' came closest to describing how she'd felt about him, and 'fantasy' seemed to sum up the relationship which had so engaged her interest that she had flown out here, all this way, to meet him. To have him abandon her so abruptly as he had done just now, felt almost like a betrayal, however absurd that might seem.

Since she was in the mood for some scrupulous introspection, her thoughts strayed to the real Andy, whose presence beside her had felt almost as palpable as a touch on her skin while she'd talked to the imposter. What was it she felt about him, she asked herself, besides frustration at his lack of communicativeness, and rejection at his lack of trust in her with whatever 'private matter' he was keeping secret, when she'd been so open with him about her own life. Why had she felt such a frisson when she had been sandwiched, almost, between the two Andys in the same room at the same time? Was it that old Butch and Sundance fantasy again, being the focus of attention of two cowboys at once? Because of course she found the real Andy Barrett attractive. No sentient woman could fail to respond to his good looks and his lean muscles and the lines at the corners of his eyes in his sunburned skin, and the smell of him when he came in after a hard day's riding, part horse, part man, and the no-nonsense soapy smell of him when he reappeared for his supper, showered and changed, and the heart-tugging warmth and vulnerability of him when he looked at Robyn, and the economic competence of his movements and strength when she caught sight of him through the kitchen window, doing some cowboy thing or other, like toting hay bales across the yard, or swinging his long leg over Rusty's back . . .

Yes, well, speaking of romantic fantasy, she thought, whipping herself back to a rather harsher reality, you are on an absolute hiding to nothing in that direction, Kate Thornton. Catching and keeping cyber-Andy would be easier than lassoing his real-life twin.

Having come to this rigorous conclusion, there seemed nothing left to do but go up to her bed to sleep, but she was aware, as she reached across his desk to turn out the lamp, of a slight heaviness in the area of her chest where her heart lived, a small pang of pain. 'Oh no you bloody well don't,' she admonished herself severely. 'Fancying him from afar is one thing. Don't you dare tell me you're starting to fall in love with the wretched man!'

Her temper was not improved, once she'd mounted the stairs, by the sight of Old Pete and Minnie 'canoodling' – the only way of describing it – outside Minnie's door, and wearing the kind of mirrored grins which are the sole preserve of people who are exploring that most enviable of states, mutual attraction.

'Good night!' she said loudly, and had the satisfaction, at least, of seeing them spring apart like scalded cats. The effect of this *schadenfreude* was short-lived, however, for on gaining her room and closing her door on the day, she distinctly heard Old Pete murmuring, 'Okay, we can take it slow as you like, Minnie, my dear. Hell, it's been thirty long, slow years since I had a feeling like this for a girl. I figure I can wait a while longer.'

'Bloody hell,' Kate thought crossly, as she made her way to her lonely narrow bed. 'Now why can't somebody say that kind of thing to me?'

She would undoubtedly have been cheered, though, had she had access to Andy's thoughts at that moment, as he turned over and slammed his head on the pillow in a vain attempt to change the direction in which those thoughts had led him. For he had been similarly engaged in an audit of the complex emotions which had arisen during his encounter with the backgammon fraud, and he'd been forced to the unwelcome conclusion that, although he still couldn't bring himself to put a name to the overriding feeling he had experienced in the office, he couldn't fail to acknowledge that it began with a 'j' and ended in a 'y'. And what made it even harder for him to bear was that the only honest answer to that 'Why?' was the intimacy, and the ease of communion there had been, between the man who was his imposter and the woman who was known as Mata Hari.

28

By nine o'clock on the eve of the wedding, even Kate felt that her passion for cooking was sated, at least in this lifetime, and Minnie, who had been her indefatigable (if rather bossy) helper all day, was 'just plain tatered' in her own words, and was threatening to sit down and stay down for the rest of the night. But still the troops needed to be fed and watered, and to this end, weary foot soldiers had started to gather around the kitchen table like iron filings to a magnet.

'Hungry,' Kate observed, as she whisked by two expectant faces on a mission to the fridge. Old Pete and Robyn nodded with as much vigour as they could muster, having both been worked to the bone by Gary Strange in the barn, all day, in Old Pete's case, and ever since coming home from school in Robyn's.

'Would you mind eating party food?' Kate asked them. 'There's plenty of quiche – I've probably made a few too many.' No yelps of enthusiastic assent came her way. 'What?' she had time to ask, as she whisked back the way she'd come, carrying eggs, and witnessed the gloom which had dragged down their features.

'Don't mind eating party food as such,' said Old Pete, 'but I seen a joint of beef go in that oven, and so far as I've noticed it ain't come out yet.'

'It's to fill the mini-Yorkies we're making,' Kate told them possessively. 'And unlike the quiches, I might have under-calculated on the meat.'

'Oh Katie,' crooned Robyn, as one might sing to the severely cranially challenged to soothe their savage breast. 'You're living on a ranch full of steer. You want more beef to cook? We got plenty, hanging up in the cold store.'

Kate sighed. 'I'd thought I'd stop cooking after this,' she said. 'I'm getting really tired myself.'

'Aw, come on, Kate, how much energy does it take to slam a piece of meat in the oven?' Robyn asked. 'Andy!' she said, as he'd just stepped in the back door looking as if he was at the end of his rope. 'Roast beef or quiche for your supper. Which do you choose?'

'Beef thanks,' he said, innocent of what had gone before, as he washed his hands at the sink. 'Boy, I tell you, decorating a barn is a lot more exhausting than roping steer all day long. And Gary is such a damn perfectionist! I been up and down that ladder a hundred times today, "tweaking" muslin. Last time he ordered me up again I felt more like tearing it down than doing any tweaking of it.'

'How's it looking?' asked Kate, who was coming back in from the cold store carrying another joint of sirloin with a long-suffering air.

'Like the bedouin tent it's meant to be, I guess,' Andy replied with a smile. 'Not having ever seen the real thing, I'll have to take Gary's word for it. But I think he's "almost pleased" with it. That's what he said, anyway, as I was leaving. But you can ask him yourself. He's coming across.'

'We don't have to wait for that one to cook, do we, Katie?' Robyn whined, as Kate put the joint in the oven and pushed back her damp fringe wearily with her forearm. 'We can have some of that one you've prepared earlier, can't we?'

'Yes, Robyn,' said Kate, about as humourlessly as any of them had ever heard her sound.

'You okay there, Kate?' Andy asked, glancing at her with

some concern. 'Can't you stop now, and take a break? Looks to me like you could use one.'

'I could use sitting down for a week with my feet up, and a limitless supply of wine at my elbow,' she said. 'But just now, I'd better keep going or I'll never get up again.'

'What's left to do can be done in the morning. There'll be plenty of time, they're not coming till six,' Minnie said firmly, sliding onto the bench with an 'ooph' of relief and a look of expectation about her. 'Now, who mentioned wine?'

'I'll go fetch a bottle from the guest stock,' said Andy. 'We all deserve it after the last few days. Sit down, Kate, for pity's sake, before you fall down,' he admonished, and taking her by the shoulders, guided her across to the most comfortable seat.

'What's this – slacking?' Gary cried, as he came through the door.

'Just for a minute,' Kate assured him. 'How are we fixed over there?'

'Perfectomundo,' he told her. 'Tables laid, places set by our young redbreast—'

'He had me measure between the knives and forks with a ruler!' Robyn informed them.

'But it was so worth the labour, sweetness and light,' Gary said airily. 'It looks fabulous. Mr Andrew has been an absolute treasure and a trouper with his manly mounting of ladders and fine-tuning of drapes. And Mr Peter the Elder has simply transformed the entrance doors with two coats of Eau de Nil. You ladies, I see, have been busy with the food, and I poor, worn-out wretch, have come to take my leave until the morrow.'

'You'll take a glass of wine before you go, Gary?' Andy asked, being useful with the corkscrew.

'Do you know, I won't,' Gary demurred. 'I'm a dreadful driver even when I'm stone-cold sober, dear. Well lookee here, you got company,' he said from the door. 'Two city folk have pulled up in your yard and are getting out of their nice saloon.'

'Who can that be?' asked Kate. 'And what makes you say they're city folk?'

'They're wearing designer outdoor wear, love,' he informed her, with an arm swept round the room. 'Look around you at how the locals dress for weather. Tartan twill does for them in the main. Well, toodle pip. I'll leave you to your visitors. See you in the morning, early if not bright.'

'Oh oh!' Andy remarked, slapping himself on the forehead, as he at last remembered the guests who had booked some time ago in the forgotten past, and who were presently walking their way. 'It's those two friends of Nancy's come to stay for the weekend.'

Panic replaced exhaustion in the room as Andy went outside to meet the couple and delay them, Robyn dashed upstairs to prepare their room, Old Pete went to set up the dining room, and Kate, with a practised eye, swept the room of food, concocted a four-course menu of what was available, and started to peel potatoes like a woman possessed.

'Don't worry about me,' Minnie commented, luxuriously putting her feet up and stretching her legs now there was more room on the bench. 'I'll hold the fort here with the wine till you all get back.'

Jessica and Paul had been warned by their friend Nancy not to expect too much in the way of creature comforts in their room at the Blue Yonder, indeed, that they'd have to ignore the stains on the walls. 'Not from recently committed murders,' she'd assured them. 'Just from the rain coming in.' But she had urged them that in high summer like this they were probably safe, and anyway, getting slightly damp in bed was a small price to pay for the pleasure of sampling Kate's cooking. 'Make sure she gives you some of those Yorkshire gravy suckers with your meat,' she'd advised them, and in this they were not disappointed. Nor had they cause for complaint in anything she had described. The stains on the wall were present and correct, there was a slightly damp feeling to their room, their shower did indeed, as she had promised, alterantely poach them and freeze them, Kate Thornton's cooking was out of this world, and the gravy suckers – for they were there in force – were nothing short of a scientific marvel. Hence, after they had finished their third course they sent word to the kitchen that they'd like to meet the cook, who was slumped, half asleep, over the kitchen table, when she received it.

'Want to talk to you, Katie,' Robyn announced as she shook her awake.

'What! What?' asked the happy sleeper, starting unhappily awake. 'Is it time for the milking already?'

'No, it's time to go get your praise next door,' Robyn reassured her. 'Go! Git!'

Blearily, Kate made her way across the room. 'Do I look a sight?' she asked them, turning for her co-workers' inspection.

Gazing fondly across at her, 'For sore eyes', was out of Andy's mouth before he had any warning it had formed itself inside his head, and now everybody's eyes were upon him. He cleared his throat in a businesslike way and looked back down at the notebook he and Robyn had been sweating over while Kate had been snoozing. In his experience, ignoring things was often the best policy. 'I think we've nearly got this advertising leaflet idea of yours taped down,' he said gruffly. 'Come and see if you're happy with it and we'll go type it up on the computer.'

'Of mine?' Kate asked, now doubly confused, for surely, unless her ears had deceived her, hadn't he just paid her a compliment?

'No, mine,' Robyn told her, suppressing a grin of pleasure, sure as she was that her young ears had heard right. 'We got one hundred future customers trapped in our barn tomorrow. Figured we should tell them what's on offer.'

'What a brilliant idea,' Kate said, and went into the dining room to take her bow from the guests, to deliver their dessert, and to apologise in advance for the disruption to service that they would experience the next day. Having been previously briefed by Nancy and Louise what a tough taskmaster led the horse-trekking, they were glad to be able to reassure her that they were in no way disappointed about not being able to go out riding on account of the wedding, and invited her warmly to sit down with them and to partake of their wine. This Kate was pleased to do, and she was even more pleased with the volley of compliments which was fired at her across the table for the next hour, which was just as well, since it was to be the last time she was to feel happy and at ease before she was forced to pack her bags and leave the Blue Yonder.

This was not the case for Minnie McAlpine, however, for when Robyn and Andy retired to the office to type up their advertising copy, it left her and Old Pete with the privacy to discover whether they had arrived at the hand-holding stage of their relationship yet, and, on finding they had, the leisure time in which to pursue it. Indeed, it was during this halcyon hour that all members of the guest ranch staff were perhaps at their most content, never suspecting for a moment that this state of being was so fragile, nor so contingent on such a flimsy, tiny thing, as a six by four piece of paper remaining hidden from view.

Being the computer whizz of the family, Robyn was typing up the copy and playing with the format of her advertising leaflet while she set Andy the task of searching through drawers and shelves in the office to find a suitable photograph for its decoration. He had found, and she had rejected, several possible candidates before she was satisfied, and the one they both finally agreed on was of the ranch house, taken on a sunny day, which featured them both looking good on horse-back in the foreground.

'Hell, we look handsome and happy, don't we?' she told him approvingly, and then gave the fateful instruction which was to shake their lives to the core. 'Well, don't just stand there admiring yourself, scan it in,' is what she said. And that is what he did. And the rest, as they say, is history.

Given the lateness of the hour when Jessica and Paul finally left the table and headed upstairs to bed, Kate was unsurprised, on her return to the kitchen, to find that Minnie and Old Pete must already have done likewise. She was more surprised, however, when she pottered into the office, to find Robyn still up and – shall we say astonished? – at what was in the girl's hand, and what that hand pushed under her nose for her inspection. Should we say rather that she was shocked? Or would guilt-stricken perhaps describe her state best? For, on raising her eyes to meet Andy's, she saw plainly in his that her previous trespass with Gary had been rumbled. Though Robyn was chirruping ten to the dozen, nothing she was saying could match the eloquence or intensity of the expression on Andy's face, which was a mask of barely controlled anger.

'See what Andy just found?' Robyn was telling her. 'I never seen this photo before! See here, that's me when I was a tiny little baby! And here, that's my mom and dad. Now you can see where I get my good looks from. But look here at Andy! Doesn't he look cute with that haircut? Isn't that the funniest thing you ever seen?'

'Where did you find it?' Kate asked tremulously, but she knew the answer before Andy had even begun to give it.

'In the scanner,' he said in a hard-edged tone, his eyes glittering with barely suppressed rage and betrayal. 'I'd thought it was lost. Who would have imagined that's where I'd left it?'

'I—' said Kate, as he strode past her.

'Bed time for us, Robyn Barrett. Big day tomorrow,' he said, before adding coldly, 'the office is all yours, Kate. I know how you like to make yourself at home in here. Good night.'

Left alone with only her sense of guilt and shame for company, Kate couldn't bear the silence or the solitude. It was too late to disturb Gary by calling him up on the phone, and anyway, what could he say to make her feel better? Not a lot. Her thoughts in turmoil, she wandered blindly into the kitchen in search of more wine to steady her nerves, found the bourbon bottle, sat with it at the kitchen table until it was half empty, and then, seeking greater oblivion than mere alcohol could offer, wandered back into the office, now blind drunk, to turn on the computer, and revisit her old addiction, the distraction of playing backgammon on the *Yoohoo* site. And it was then, when she was three sheets to the wind and out of her mind with worry, that she found Andy the Cowboy waiting patiently for her at their old rendezvous place, Table 40.

Having nothing to lose except her reputation for good manners, she joined him at once and typed, 'You bastard,' and watched the screen in wonder as his reply came back:

AndytheCowboy: I know, Kate. I'm so sorry. Really. I never thought it'd come to this. I've been waiting and hoping you'd come back and I could explain.

MataHari: And?

AndytheCowboy: And I find that I can't. Not like this anyhow. You deserve to hear the story face to face.

MataHari: How do you propose we do that?

AndytheCowboy: Would you consider coming to meet me in Vancouver?

MataHari: Why Vancouver?

AndytheCowboy: It's where I really live. Not, as you know by now, at the Blue Yonder Guest Ranch.

MataHari: When?

AndytheCowboy: Sooner the better. Tomorrow?

MataHari: Can't.

AndytheCowboy: Sunday then?

MataHari: OK. Where?

AndytheCowboy: Press your privacy button. I'll do the same, and I'll type the address.

MataHari: Done.

AndytheCowboy: 214 Greek Street, Kitsilano.

No sooner was it on the screen than it was off again, and AndytheCowboy had gone with it.

'Two-one-four what? Shit!' Kate said feverishly, her previous worry about the real cowboy in her life now replaced with the anxiety that she was too drunk to remember the address. 'Greek Street, that's right, like in Soho. Kit-si-lan-o.' She scored the office notepad with a Biro to that effect. Tearing the top sheet of paper off the pad, she rose unsteadily to her feet and swayed upstairs, grabbing banisters and walls all the way to Minnie's door, on which she knocked.

'Minnie,' she whispered loudly. 'Minnie! Are you awake? I need to tell you something!'

There was a hurried rustling from within, and some shushing and muttering, before Minnie's voice returned, 'Not just now, Kate. I'm – asleep. I'll see you in the morning, love.'

Staggering back to her own room, Kate couldn't help but wonder under what lucky star Minnie McAlpine had been born, and to demand of the gods what had stopped them from making a similarly propitious celestial arrangement at her own nativity. But alas, no answer came before she fell into bed and lost what little there was left of her consciousness.

29

As to whether it had been the wedding of the century there was some contention among the departing guests, but everybody was happy to agree that it had, at least, been the reception to beat all others in their lifetime. From the red-carpet welcome which had awaited their eager footsteps, to the quintet of glittering rhinestone cowboys and cowgirls who were at their service in the wonderland of white muslin found beyond the richly painted doors of the Blue Yonder barn, everything that could have been done to wow them had been done, and wowed is what they'd been. No adjective of approbation had been grudgingly withheld by even the most exacting member of the wedding party, and as that title was in the undisputed possession of the bride herself, it can safely be assumed that complete satisfaction had been given and received. All this was before even a morsel of Kate's feast had so much as touched their lips, but once her dishes had begun not only to brush against those oral sentinels, but also to be admitted through them, the search for new superlatives had been abandoned by mouths too happily occupied to utter more than 'Mmmm!'

John Connor's choice of wine similarly met with general approval, and after its consumption, those assembled to celebrate this popular vet's new union, found it easier also to join him, at the end of his speech, to toast his choice of bride. Further remarked upon with approbation, and no small measure of titillation, by the gossips amongst the connubial throng, was Old Pete's unusual state of beatitude, and the apparent cause of this utter contentment, the little lady with the twinkling eyes who rarely left his side. Andy Barrett had been, as always, gorgeous to look at but hard to make smile, according to the as yet unmatched ladies present who cared to attempt such foolhardy endeavour; Robyn Barrett had been both characteristically upbeat and uncharacteristically polite; and, due to the popularity of his flair for design, Mr Strange was paid the compliment of being alluded to as Mr Strange, or as Gary, but never again from that day forth as Strange Gary. Yes, everything had been perfect – or almost everything, for it was heard being muttered behind several hands, as their owners made their way back to their cars at the end of a heavenly evening, that the soap-star actress hadn't been quite the looker that they'd heard tell, her beauty being marred, it was generally accepted, by the dark circles beneath her eyes and the puffiness of the lids which all but kept those orbs from view.

The happy couple were the last to take their leave, John Connor clasping each of the rhinestone posse to his breast, either in expression of gratitude or perhaps in rehearsal for where his duty lay next, and with his usual unfailing generosity, pointed out the few remaining bottles of unopened wine, of which he made a present to those whose office it was to stay and clear up behind him. As quickly as the barn had filled with people, so had it emptied, and all that was left to those who had, by their waiting, also served, was to ferry dirty plates and glasses to the kitchen, to wash and to dry them, to deconstruct the bedouin tent, to roll up the red carpet . . .

'Aw hell,' Old Pete ventured with a grin, whose hand-holding stage with Minnie in private had been superceded by the public display of wearing the whole happy woman inside his arm, 'let's do it in the morning.'

The excellence of this suggestion being seized upon with

enthusiasm by the person under his wing, by Gary Strange, and by young Robyn, followed by their rapid egress from the scene, it went unremarked by those who hurried to their longed-for beds that they had left behind them a man and a woman who could not meet the other's eyes, the taller of whom held himself rigid with anger, the posture of the shorter being softened by exhaustion and remorse. A turning on the heel of the male of the party, followed by his quick strides away to the door elicited the anguished plea, 'Please stay and talk to me about it,' from the chastened female who remained.

'What's there to talk about? Nothing!' Andy asserted, although the alacrity of his aggressive return belied there being any doubt in the matter of plenitude in this respect. 'Oh, except maybe about somebody nosing into other people's business. Was that what you had in mind? The small business of some hypocrite who once mentioned that she valued privacy, but who likes to look through people's possessions secretly, uninvited, and even to make copies of them? Is that what you wanted me to talk about, Mata Hari? That you picked that damn fool name because what you like doing best is to spy?'

'Yes,' Kate conceded, shame-faced. 'That's about the size of it.'

'Well, that's done that then,' said Andy. 'And all that remains is for me to say goodbye and have a good flight. When are you leaving? Tomorrow? Can't come quick enough for me!' So saying, his heel was put to the employ of another sharp turn, and his legs to the mission of carrying him out with all possible speed.

'For God's sake!' Kate shouted after him, with an anger, finally, to match his. 'Must you always try to solve every single bloody problem you encounter by storming out and never facing it? Is that the kind of example you want to set Robyn?'

'Just leave Robyn out of this,' he growled dangerously. 'In

fact, leave all of us out of it. Go back to England where you belong.'

'I did a dreadful thing and there's no excuse for it,' Kate admitted, projecting her voice across the twenty yards which separated them. 'I found a photograph and I tried to blow it up so I could see it in more detail because I wanted to know more than I knew. Yes, you're right, it was a sneaky thing to do, and I'm ashamed and I'm sorry.'

'And it never occurred to you just to ask?' Andy said, his voice full of contempt.

'To ask! Who? You? The king of non-communication? That's a laugh!' Kate told him, and demonstrated her assertion with a forced sounding bray. 'But okay, I'll give it a shot. Let's see, what was it I wanted to know about you? Oh yes, how come you're bringing up your brother's child? I'm sure you'll want to help me out solving that little conundrum.'

The muscles in Andy's jaw were hard at work flexing their strength, she could see, as she crossed the distance between them, but more for the purpose of holding his anger in rather than for uttering any words of elucidation. 'You see? Look at yourself!' she invited him. 'You'd sooner break your teeth than let anything out of your mouth!'

'What business is it of yours who I bring up or why?' he managed to challenge her coldly.

Kate's anger evaporated as she recognised the truth of this. 'You're right,' she told him. 'It isn't my business now. But at the time, I thought maybe it was.'

Unable to trust himself to form the words, 'How come?' Andy lifted his head in an attitude of at least being ready to listen.

'I was trying to solve the mystery of who had brought me here,' she volunteered. 'And a lot of what I'd been told on the internet turned out to be true, but a lot of it seemed to conflict with what I was finding.'

Despite himself, Andy was interested to know. 'Like what?' he ventured icily, involuntarily taking a step back as she neared him.

'Like that Robyn's mother had been a hippy called Rainbow who you'd made pregnant after a rodeo, and who ran off and left you to bring her up on your own.'

'Bull shit,' he drawled with venom. 'I told you she was my brother's child.'

'Yes you did,' Kate protested, 'but only the other day, and since then nothing. But I found that photograph ages before.'

'When did you find it, and where?' he demanded. 'I haven't seen it in years.'

'At the back of your desk drawer,' she admitted, her head hung in shame.

'Nice,' was his response, which sounded anything but.

'I know! I've told you what I did was inexcusable! And it's no excuse when I tell you that in fact I was looking for John Connor's bill at the time, to see how much it was and if there was anything I could do to help,' she said, tears springing to her eyes. 'And I know that even that was none of my business, that I'm a nosy bloody cow who meddles in other people's affairs without being asked, and that it was an underhand and sneaky thing to do.'

His mind fused, taking in the debris of the occasion which had saved his bacon. 'No,' he found himself forced into saying.

'No?' she asked querulously.

'Well, yes. But—' Some of his tension was released with the tiniest of dry laughs. 'I don't approve of your methods, but thanks, I guess.'

Kate dared a faint smile in return. 'You wouldn't sit with me for a while, and have a farewell drink, I suppose?' she asked, having already resolved that she would leave the next day, as he had demanded.

He sighed deeply, a picture of Robyn struggling against her hatred of Cissie Taylor coming unbidden into his mind. 'Hell, I guess,' he said at length. 'But not this wine. I'll go get my bourbon.'

'Ah,' said Kate. 'You'll find I did some serious damage to that bottle last night, I'm afraid.'

'Anything else you might want to confess to?' he challenged her, but with more humour in his voice at last.

'I'll give that some thought while you fetch what's left of your bourbon,' she told him.

He was almost out of the Eau de Nil doors when, without turning back, he said, 'Oh, and that other thing you were curious about? How I come to be bringing up Robyn?'

'Yes?' she said, with an expectant smile.

'It's kind of on account of me having killed her mom and dad.'

30

If ever a nosy parker had cause to regret her curiosity, it was Kate Thornton that night, as she waited in a Canadian barn tricked out as a bedouin tent for a self-confessed killer. She found herself shaking from head to foot after he'd left, but told herself it was tiredness rather than fear, persuading herself that the Andy that she knew could never have killed anybody in any other way than by accident, and advised herself to sit down and begin the journey to the bottom of a bottle of wine.

'Well, you always thought he had a dark and guilty secret,' she remarked to her reflection in the glass. 'And – bingo! Got it in one.'

It was to no great surprise on her part that when he did reappear and sat down beside her, he poured his bourbon in silence, showing no inclination to reopen the subject he had left her with. She was only surprised, and duly grateful, that he'd had the courage to return at all.

'Cheers,' she said, daring to touch her glass to his. 'Your health and happiness, and once again, my heartfelt, abject apologies.'

'Received,' he responded, before emptying his glass and recharging it to gaze into its depths. 'Hell, and debt cancelled, just like you got us with all this,' he added impulsively, sweeping his arm round the room.

'Thank you,' she said sincerely. 'That's more than I deserve.'

The silence in which they sat for several minutes couldn't be described so much as comfortable, as having the quality of an exhausted cease-fire on Christmas Day in the trenches.

'Old Pete and Minnie were a bit of a surprise, weren't they?' she prompted him, deciding to re-open lines of communication on a neutral subject.

'Can say that again,' he concurred, dispatching the bourbon the way of the last.

'Oh! And I didn't have time to tell anybody yet that I found "Andy the Cowboy" again last night,' she informed him.

His face came alive with interest. 'Who is it?' he asked.

'I don't know, but he lives in Vancouver, apparently.'

'Vancouver! Can't say I know anybody over that way.'

'No? Well, maybe he just got the details which he *did* get right, from the web site that Robyn constructed – and when I think about it, you know, there wasn't really much more than the names of the ranch and those of you who live here that turned out to be true,' she suggested, having had almost twenty-four hours to reflect on the matter.

He shook his head in amazement. 'I'll be damned.'

'But anyway,' she ventured, carrying on despite the warning look that was fired towards her from under beetled brows, 'you were saying, before you went to fetch the bourbon?'

'Yes, he said, gazing at the bottle, 'you were right about the damage you did. It was almost lethal.'

'Oh, Andy,' she sighed in exasperation. 'If it's not storming out of rooms, it's using distraction methods with you, isn't it?'

'Oh, Kate,' he said in harsh mimicry, 'can't you ever leave things be? Can't you just make your apology, get forgiven, and share a simple goddam drink?'

'Not something like that, no,' she told him. 'What? Solve one unanswered mystery, and then be presented with another? No way. Not when I'm leaving tomorrow.'

'You're leaving tomorrow?' he asked her, sounding surprised.

'Yes, you've no need to worry,' she assured him. 'I take your point, I've taken over your life for more than long enough. I'm going to Vancouver tomorrow to meet our friend, and from there I'll fly back to London and try to resurrect my ailing career.' She raised her glass to him. 'So this is your last chance to get your guilty secret off your chest, to somebody you won't ever have to see again.'

Andy said nothing but sat gazing into the distance, where he blinked from time to time as he digested this information and computed it with a conversation he'd had with Robyn, about how cruel it would be to keep Kate from her work. That's right, he thought. And so it would.

'So, I'm guessing it was a tragic accident,' she said, 'since you're not in gaol.'

The blinking rate increased in intensity as he summoned himself back from the distance and into the here and now. 'You can call it that if you want to,' he said abruptly. 'At the end of the day I made an orphan out of Robyn and killed my own brother and his wife – a woman who was more like a sister to me. A mother even, at times.'

'But I'm safe in assuming that you didn't shoot them, let's say?' she posited.

His shoulders sagged with the effort of having to talk about it after all these years. 'No, but I took their lives just the same as if I did.'

'Can you tell me?' she asked gently, well aware what she was putting him through.

'We were driving back from Hope,' he began, and gave a humourless laugh. 'And hope's been behind me ever since. Anyway, correction, *I* was driving us all back from Hope – and the weather came down like a grip of ice. Could hardly see for snow and sleet.' He stopped to empty first the bottle, then his glass, twirling it forlornly in his hand. When he continued, it was in short sharp sentences, as though parting with each word brought unimaginable pain. 'Lorry appeared out of nowhere, my side of the road. Driver had fallen asleep, turned out. Couldn't miss him.' A hand rubbed vigorously across his forehead said more than he was able to tell about the memory of the car rolling over and over, of finding Steve killed outright at his side, of Laura's dying moments, her terror on discovering that her baby was no longer in her arms and his panic when he realised she wasn't even in the car. 'Was a miracle Robyn survived it,' he said merely, neglecting to say how he had frantically searched the snow outside for her tiny form, how he'd run wailing and sobbing from drift to drift until, by that same miracle, he'd spotted a corner of her shawl and lifted her out of what might have been her frozen grave. The tears coursing down his cheeks were given the short shrift of a swiped sleeve as he excused himself with a half-turned face and, 'See now why I don't talk about this overmuch.'

She nodded, and didn't even bother to hide her own tears. 'Andy,' she said, covering his hand with her own. 'Andy, how dreadful, I'm so sorry.'

He nodded curtly and, sniffing loudly, poured himself a glass of wine with his free hand. 'Damn hole in my bottle,' he complained. 'And I know who put it there.'

Kate laughed obligingly. 'Sorry,' she said, and seeing a returning smile, continued, 'so there was no way at all that you could have avoided crashing?'

'I don't know,' he said hoarsely. 'I've asked myself that every day for twelve years.'

'But Robyn, at least, doesn't seem to blame you?' Kate pursued, squeezing his hand not only to reassure him, but to focus his increasingly drunken attention.

'No, she doesn't,' he admitted, his face softening as he called her up. 'She's a good kid.'

'And neither does anybody else around here – everybody

who's ever mentioned you to me speaks only with admiration and respect.'

A dismissive humph. 'Mighty nice of them.'

'So it seems to me that the only person who blames you is you?' Kate pushed him, together with her luck.

Her reward was his hand roughly removed from under hers on the pretext of refilling his wine glass. 'Who better?' he said.

'So who better to forgive you?'

He shook his head stoically. 'Not going to happen.'

A tough nut to crack, thought Kate, and she sat back in her chair and sipped her wine in silence. If only he'd talked all this out after it had happened, years ago, and resolved it then. Now, it seemed, he had a habit of intransigence that was deeply ingrained. Every day must be a living hell for him. Well, if talking was what was needed, she was the woman for the job.

'You said the other day that I'd been told wrong by "Andy" about your great-grandfather building this ranch,' she reminded him. 'What's the real story then?'

Released from the subject he feared most, Andy looked almost relaxed as he answered, 'Steve and me, our dad died, and left us some cash. Our mom had died when I was seven.'

'My God!' she exclaimed, not expecting that. 'You've been so unlucky!'

An ironic twitch of the eyebrows acknowledged the truth of it. 'It had always been Steve's dream to live and work on the land, and he and Laura found this old place. It was in bad repair, and we got it cheap – took all the cash from the sale of Dad's house. I was in college, but I was pretty happy to leave and come here with the two of them. Year or two later it was the three of them, of course. It was hard work. We never had enough money. But those were great days. We used to sit around the table in the kitchen and make our plans.'

'Plans you've felt you had to stick to,' Kate said, understanding now why his ideas on running the ranch seemed so inflexible to Robyn. 'You all look so happy in the photo. You must have loved them both very much.'

He nodded. 'I did. Steve was kind of my hero, you know? I looked up to him, always had. And Laura, well,' his eyes misted over again as he endured the pain of remembering her. 'Laura was just wonderful. Always happy, a hard, hard worker. Knew her since I was fourteen, and she practically adopted me. Loved them? There isn't a word big enough to describe how I felt about them.'

Looking at him, his bereavement still so wounding to him after all this time, so lacking in self forgiveness and so full of undeserved guilt, her heart went out to him, and she checked herself with an inward groan. Damaged soul alert! She warned herself. Do not go there! But who could fail to be moved by his story, she asked herself. Who, on God's earth, wouldn't want to hold him now and give him comfort? What terrible things he'd had to endure, and at such a young age! It made her feel pretty stupid that here she was, the wrong side of thirty-five, getting all angsty about a stupid soap opera.

'Would you believe it,' she said, shaking the few remaining drops of wine into her glass. 'Yet another defective bottle. I'll get us another.'

She was glad of the small corridor of thinking time which crossing the barn to the makeshift bar afforded her. What comfort could she offer him that he could accept, she wondered? If he'd been a fellow actor it would have been easy, she'd know exactly what to do. She'd have hugged him, encouraged him to cry, calmed him with touch, rubbed his shoulders, tried to help him connect back to his body and get out of his guilt-ridden head. Her massage course had taught her the effectiveness of that, if her years in the theatre hadn't. But Andy? He wouldn't be quite so at ease with all the touchy-feely stuff, would he? Probably think she was coming on to him and run a mile. What would the lovely Laura have done in my shoes? she asked herself. Wouldn't she have done the same? Unaccountably, an image came into her head of Robyn handling nervous horses, firmly, gently, and unflappable. Worth a shot, she thought. Here goes nothing.

On her return to the table, she put the wine down in front of him and standing behind him, she laid her hands on his rigid shoulder muscles with a light but firm pressure. Though his whole posture stiffened, she just kept them there, not moving, until he got used to it, while she talked in a conversational tone.

'I used to make the mistake of thinking that people could be loved better,' she told him. 'Show me the man with the difficult childhood, and I'd be falling in love like a shot. If I could just show them how lovable they were, I used to think, then they'd be okay, they'd be happy.' Still talking, she applied pressure with her thumbs into his tense flesh, and worked them with a circular motion. Well, at least he was putting up with it, she thought, though he was far from being putty in her hands. In fact, if anything he'd grown more tense, if that were possible. 'Finally I learned that nobody can love anybody better,' she continued, 'only the person concerned can do that. It seems to me that you are loved by everybody who knows you, except yourself.' She worked the top of his shoulders in a businesslike way, squeezing them firmly, and running her thumbs up his neck. Against his will, it seemed, his head fell forward slightly. 'A dreadful, tragic accident happened which wasn't your fault, and you were left to pick up the pieces, which you did and have been doing ever since. What a shame that you still feel guilty. Doesn't help Steve and Laura, does it? And it can't be helpful to Robyn, having the person she loves most in all the world hating himself, surely? Not exactly the most relaxing way to grow up.'

'I do the best I know how,' he said, his voice thickening with unshed tears, his head snapping back upright.

'Of course you do,' she soothed him.

'Stop it!' he said, putting his hand over hers to hold it still.

'You're a good man, Andy Barrett,' she told him, with a small shake of his shoulders. 'Even if you don't think so. And I think it's time that you did.'

The shaking beneath her hands told her that he was weeping, and her arms encircled him from behind to rock him gently and hold him safely in her embrace.

He'd come apart. He knew it. He'd always known that this would happen if he talked about it. There was a dreadful, helpless pain in his guts, a feeling that everything had spun out of his control, an overflowing sensation of spilling, of splitting fortifications, like a river busting out over its banks. He wanted to be held so much, so much, but it was that holding that had sent him over the edge like this. He felt the flesh of her cheek against his cheek, could feel her tears mingle with his, heard soft crooning like a soothing chant, 'There, there, I know, poor you, it's all right, everything's going to be all right,' and before he knew it he had turned in his seat and grabbed her like a drowning man might grab at a rock or a tree, holding on for dear life. Pathetic! He felt her warm hand stroke his hair, his back. It was all too much. His heart was breaking. He had to get free.

Throwing her hand off him, he stood up abruptly, knocking over his chair in his haste, and meaning to leave the room with all possible speed, to put distance between himself and this interfering, dangerous woman, he was as surprised as she to find himself grabbing her again and kissing her with more passion and hunger than he had ever felt before for any of her sex. She fitted so well in his arms, it felt like the natural place for her to be. It would be the simplest thing in the world just to keep holding her for ever, to kiss her neck like this, to push his hands up inside her shirt to feel the soft skin, to luxuriate in the heady scent of her, the flesh of her, to provoke more of these eager responses from her, to let her love him, to love her back—

'No!' he said, and pushed her away. 'This is wrong, all wrong. You make it seem so easy, but it isn't. You should go back to England, back to your life. What do you think you're doing, going after another broken reed like me? Didn't you tell me you'd learned that lesson?'

Letting her go, he strode over to the door and said, 'Go back home, Kate, where you belong,' and left her, breathless, with her own thoughts.

Well, that told you, is what her thoughts told her. And quite right too.

Nevertheless, it was with dragging feet that she finally left the scene of Sonia Driesen's connubial celebration, and returned to Andy's office to book her flight before retiring to her Blue Yonder room for the last night ever.

31

Something was either very, very wrong, or very, very right, and Robyn didn't know which it was after she'd bounced on Mata's bed and found nobody in it. Pulling open the curtains revealed information on the very, very wrong side of things, and a dash to Andy's room to find him sleeping alone backed that up.

'She's gone!' she shouted, as she grabbed his senseless body to shake him awake. 'Mata's gone, her suitcase has gone, her clothes are gone, her car's gone. Mata's gone, god dammit, wake up!'

The pounding of her fists against his chest was as nothing to the pounding he felt in his head, and he grabbed her hands to keep them still, which reminded him of another occasion that he'd had cause to do that, quite recently. His head sank back against the pillow, trying to collect his thoughts, but Robyn wasn't in a thinking mood. 'Get up!' she demanded, pulling at his T shirt, dragging the covers off him. 'Get up and help me find her!'

'Robyn!' he protested, sounding more angry than he'd meant. 'Okay, I'll get up,' he relented, in a gentler tone. 'But if she's gone, she's gone. I told you we couldn't keep her for ever. She stayed to do the wedding, and maybe she, you know, maybe she woke up and decided her work here was done.'

'But not to say goodbye?' Robyn asked him in a broken voice, her head turned away while he got out of bed, to hide her tears rather than for modesty's sake. 'I thought she liked us.'

'She did, she did like us, of course she did,' he soothed her, pulling her to him as he sat back down on the side of the bed, and rocking her, just as he'd been rocked. 'But we talked about this before, didn't we? About Kate's life being back in London, not stuck out here on a ranch. It would be like keeping a wild bird in a cage, just so we could look at her. She'd die like that. The spirit would go out of her. She needs to do the job she loves, not wash dishes here.'

'We wash the dishes!' Robyn protested through her tears. 'All she has to do is cook something to put on 'em. And if she didn't like even doing that, I can learn, can't be that hard! She's going to star in Gary's Header Gobbler, what in hell does she need to go to London for?'

'Shh, shh, there, there, it'll all be all right, we'll be okay,' Andy crooned, imparting more comfort to Robyn, he hoped, than he felt for himself by repeating Kate's words to him.

Robyn pushed him away, her eyes glittering with anger. 'How can everything be okay without Mata?' she demanded. 'It wasn't okay before she come, how can it be any better now? All you had to do was what any man'd want to do! I heard some of 'em at the wedding last night, saying how they'd like to date her! What is wrong with you, that you can't even do a simple little thing like that?'

Andy stood to put on his clothes. 'You can't just force these things for other people, Robyn,' he told her firmly, his anger now rivalling hers as he struggled to match buttons with holes. 'Just because *you* like somebody doesn't mean that everybody has to, or can.'

'Ha ha,' she said, with venomous sarcasm.

'And what's that supposed to mean?'

'You didn't hear what else they were saying last night either?' she asked incredulously.

'Nothing anybody might have said could have any meaning for me,' he countered dismissively. 'I make up my own mind about things.'

'They said your mind was already made up!' she told him. 'But Peggy Davies, she said that the only person left in the room who didn't know that was you!'

'Nonsense,' he said, and strode from the room with her hot on his heels.

'Even Eileen Townsend said you never took your eyes off Kate all night, and she should know! She was spitting when she said it!' she shouted, as she pursued him down the hall.

'Will you stop that yelling?' he demanded in a loud whisper. 'You'll wake up the guests!'

Ignoring him, Robyn yelled after his now-retreating back, 'It's true! After I heard that I watched you! Your eyes followed her everywhere that she went!'

'That was because I was angry with her,' he said, pausing momentarily before going down the stairs, 'for sticking her nose in where it didn't belong. Just like you're doing now. And look at the time, how late we are getting started! Have you done your chores?'

'No,' she said sulkily.

'Well do them!' he called back from the flight below, not caring now if everybody was awake it seemed. 'Get and see to the milking. You know the rule. Animals first, people second!'

'Ain't that the truth,' the girl muttered. She stood irreso-lutely for a moment, before raining blows on Minnie's door. 'You'd better both come on out!' she shouted. 'Katie's gone and somebody's going to have to help me go after her, I can't drive myself!'

Downstairs there was plenty of evidence that Kate hadn't slept, but had used her time to tidy up behind her. Not the barn, of course, which would take all of them the rest of the day to put back to rights. But the tables in the dining room and in the kitchen had been laid up for breakfast, and instructions on how to cook it from start to finish had been left out on the side, addressed to Old Pete, together with advice to feed the guests leftover party food for their lunch, and to give them her apologies. There were envelopes containing notes too for Minnie, for Andy, and for Robyn, which she tore open in the desperate hope of finding a clue. No such luck. Just sorry for not saying goodbye, about how she thanked her for being such a good friend, how she'd miss her, but how they could stay in touch through e-mail, maybe even play backgammon together on the net. And three kisses and one heart and much love and fond memories. As if that was any use to anybody now.

'What's in yours, Minnie?' she wanted to know of the woman in the comfy dressing-gown who was reading her letter. 'She wishes me happiness,' said Minnie. 'Says nice things about Old Pete, and wishes us well.'

'Andy?' Robyn demanded, but seeing his tears fall on the sheet of paper he was holding, she touched his arm, and said, 'What's wrong?'

'Nothing,' he said, brusquely swiping at his eyes. 'Hangover. Headache. Drank too much last night. Damn fool.'

'What's she say to upset you?' Robyn persisted, pulling the letter out of his hand and dodging out of his way to read it. ' "Dear Andy, I'm so sorry I upset you. As usual, I was just trying to help, but as usual I got it wrong. You're right. I should learn my lesson. But about sticking my oar in where it's not wanted or asked for, not about what we were talking about last night. You are no broken reed, Andy Barrett. You're a lovely and wonderful man. Take care of yourself. Forgive yourself. Be happy, Kate." '

Robyn's voice failed her and she burst into grief-stricken

tears. 'Don't know why you'd want to go crying at a letter like that!' she sobbed. 'There's nothing wrong with that letter that you running after her can't put right!'

But Andy had sunk to a sitting position at the table to cover his eyes with his hand, and was not about to run anywhere.

'Coffee, I think, young Pete,' said Minnie to her toyboy lover. 'Will you do the honours?'

'I'd die trying for you,' he assured her, as he consulted Kate's notes and counted the precise amount of spoonfuls into the pot which she'd prescribed.

Coming up behind him, Minnie laid her hands on Andy's shoulders in an unknowing echo of Kate, and sat down at his side to take his hand in a motherly way. 'I suppose you know she's mad for you?' she asked him.

He shook his head. 'Doesn't matter. I'm not mad for her.'

'Of course you're not,' Minnie agreed softly. 'Quite right too. Ugly creature, wasn't she? And so meddlesome. Better off without her.'

'Fact of the matter is, she's better off without us,' he said. 'She's got her own life to go to.'

'Mm,' said Minnie. 'I suppose she's gone off to the airport in Vancouver then, has she? Did she say as much when you were talking last night?'

'Vancouver' rang an ominous bell in Andy's mind, and a quick return of lost memory. 'She told me she'd found "Andy the Cowboy" back on the web,' he said, propelled to his feet with a sudden rush of anxiety. 'Said she was going to meet him, then go on to the airport.'

'Where was she going to meet him?' asked Minnie, his anxiety spreading to her voice. 'She wasn't daft enough to agree to go to his home, was she?'

'I don't know,' he said slowly. 'She didn't say.'

The thought of what danger Kate might have put herself in produced a stampede to the office to turn on the computer and to try to raise 'Andy' on the *Yoohoo* site, but nobody by that name was on any of the players lists.

'She must have made a note of where she'd meet him,' Minnie asserted, riffling amongst the papers on the desk. 'She would have jotted it down, surely?' Her hand found the notepad on which Kate had done exactly that, the top sheet of which had been untidily torn off.

'And took it with her,' said Robyn in a doom-laden voice.

Taking it to the window, Minnie squinted across its surface. 'Good job I like crime novels,' she said, while selecting a soft pencil with a satisfied smile.

32

It didn't even occur to Kate that she might be in any danger, until she had parked her hired SUV outside 214 Greek Street in Kitsilano. Her thoughts had been elsewhere on the long drive back to Vancouver, but now, as she looked across the street at the house which she knew to contain the man who'd only ever lied to her, who'd turned her life upside-down with his dirty low-down tricks, she suddenly felt anxious and her hand reached for the key to turn the engine back on to make her escape.

'No,' she said finally. 'No. I can't bear it. I'll regret not knowing for the rest of my life.' She would just knock on the door and refuse to go in when he answered it. They could have their brief conversation in full view of the street, and if he tried any sudden lunges, she'd scream and run away. He wouldn't want any unpleasantness or awkward questions asked by his neighbours, would he? It stood to reason that he wouldn't want to foul his own patch.

Getting out of the car, she glanced up and down the road and was comforted to see a couple walking a dog, a skateboarder, a kid on a bike, and a pizza delivery man going to a house a few doors down. 'There you are,' she told herself, as she launched herself across the street. 'Safety in numbers.'

Ringing the front-door bell, she stepped back out of reach of any arm that might shoot out to grab her, and her pulse quickened as she heard the tap tap tap of feet crossing the wooden floor within.

Being smacked across the face by a wet fish couldn't have elicited more of a change in her expression, as she gazed at the woman who came to the door.

'I—' she said. Quickly she consulted the note in her pocket. '— must have got the wrong—'

'Mata Hari?' the woman asked, with an embarrassed smile. 'Y-yes?'

A hand came towards her for the purpose of shaking. 'Andy the Cowboy, ma'am,' said the woman. 'I believe I owe you an apology.'

Angry words had been spoken about Andy's adherence to stupid speed limits, but after the first hour, Robyn had given up on trying to get him to understand the urgency of their mission, and had used her energy instead to bite her nails and wring her hands. When, finally, they saw Kate's familiar hired car parked in the street, it was only Andy's quick reflexes which prevented her from flinging open her door and dashing out into the path of an oncoming car.

'Will you calm down!' he told her severely, his hand now on the handle of his own door. 'Just sit there and wait for me, don't move a muscle! Don't follow me, we don't know what this guy might do. You promise?'

'Just hurry the hell up then!' she told him, but as he turned to get out, they both saw Kate coming out of a house and hugging a woman goodbye. The same quick reflexes which had just saved Robyn's life were now employed to duck for safety under the dash.

'What's she doing?' he hissed.

'Getting into her car and waving,' Robyn told him, and made another bid for escape.

'No!' he said, again beating her to it, this time locking her door. 'Leave her. We came to make sure she wasn't in danger, and now we know she isn't, we can go home.'

'I've seen that woman before,' said Robyn. 'She stayed at the Blue Yonder last year. The sad one. Don't you remember?'

Peeking over the steering wheel, Andy also dimly recognised the woman who was returning indoors. 'That doesn't make any sense,' he said, and then as an afterthought added, 'what makes you say she was sad?'

'Caught her crying in her cornflakes one morning,' Robyn told him. 'Said she'd just finished with a man and that all men were bastards.'

'Language!'

'Wasn't my language, was hers, that's what she said!'

'Doesn't make any sense at all,' Andy repeated with a shake of his hung-over head.

'Yeah? Well make sense of this, we're losing Kate, she's driving away!' Robyn cried. 'And if you don't goddam follow her, I'll goddam get out of this vee-heecle and run after her, soon as I get the chance!'

'Don't do anything stupid,' he warned her.

'Don't you do anything goddam stupid either!' she countered. 'Are you going after her, or am I leaving home?'

'Don't be so dramatic,' he said, his mind scrambling to catch up with his thoughts.

'What if she knew that woman and just wanted to say goodbye?' Robyn demanded. 'What if she's on her way to meet "Andy the Cowboy" now?'

'Too much of a coincidence for her to know her too,' he said.

'Goddam it, do you want to bet Kate's life on it?' Robyn asked, reasonably enough, it seemed.

'We'll follow her and make sure she's going to the airport,' he said, turning on the engine and gunning his truck down the street.

'At last, some speed,' Robyn congratulated him.

'Nothing to be proud of,' he said through gritted teeth as they approached a T junction. 'See which way she turned here?'

'Left, left, goddam it!' Robyn cried.

'Language!' they both shouted together, as their truck roared down the street.

Of all the ways that Kate had ever imagined Andy the Cowboy might look, it had never been anything remotely like Maggie Hawkins. She was still processing the information she'd just been given after she'd returned her car to the hire firm, and was checking in at the airline desk.

'Sorry?' she said, realising she'd just been spoken to by the clerk.

'I said you're too early for check-in,' he told her, handing back her ticket and her passport. 'You have another couple of hours yet. Sorry.'

'Oh. Right,' she said, as she put her suitcase back on the trolley and wandered aimlessly away. Well, fine, she told herself, looking about her for internet access and gratefully following a sign. I can check in at last for my e-mail, see what's cooking with Richard, and warn him I'm on my way home.

Settling down behind a console, she accessed her e-mail account and trawled through a few messages from friends, and an awful lot of spam before finding Richard's name in her inbox.

'Aha!' she said, and then, 'Oh no!' as her eyes swept down his message to read:

'Hi, Kate, No, sorry to report no work of any description on offer, so I decided to beard the lion in its den and call up the *Paradise Street* production office. I know, I know, but my thinking was that if they're making so much capital out of you, why not try to cash in on it? Tried to persuade them to have you back, but – Kate, I assume you're sitting down if you're reading this? If not, do so at once, darling. Do NOT on ANY ACCOUNT come home, certainly not now, and possibly not ever! The news is just about to break that Sally Black had a history of heroin abuse and she has died of AIDs, after infecting Steve. If you're still with me and conscious after reading that, then I know you'll also be strong enough to hear that Steve has in turn infected Sara, and Sara has probably infected the wretched baby Leigh through her milk. So sorry, love. Richard.'

So punch drunk was she after reading this, she exited her mail on autopilot, and wandered blindly across the concourse in a blur. Of course! Of course she'd infected the whole of Paradise Street with her deadly disease. It made just as much sense as Andy the Cowboy turning out to be a woman. Why on earth should she be surprised? And why should she find it equally surprising to see Robyn Barrett running towards her with her arms outstretched?

'What are you doing here?' she asked her, from inside the hug she was receiving.

Robyn released her at last, but kept hold of her hand, as if she were afraid Kate might bolt. 'Andy's got something he forgot to tell you,' she said, as he approached them slowly from a distance, a distance which Robyn urged her to close.

'Go ahead, Andy, tell her,' his young charge instructed, her gaze going between the two adults in frustration as they stood silently facing each other.

'I—' he said.

'Don't,' Robyn prompted.

'I don't—' said Andy.

'Jeez! He doesn't want you to go, Mata,' expostulated Robyn, before turning to Andy and commanding, 'now tell her why, god dammit!' A fractional pause on his part was all it took to tip her over the edge. 'Because he loves you!'

Flying wet fish seemed to be raining down to slap Kate's face by the barrelful that day, so it was fairly remarkable that she found the presence of mind to question, as she looked deeply into his eyes, 'But does he love himself?'

Words were beyond him. 'I—' managed to squeeze its way out of his tongue-tied mouth, but it could find no fellows on the outside.

'He's learning fast,' Robyn provided. 'Too quick for his brain to catch up is all.'

'Is that how it is, Andy?' Kate queried.

Looking at the faces of the two most precious females still living, he made a helpless gesture which turned into a hug of himself. 'Come here, you gorgeous hunk,' he told himself, in one of the few jokes Kate had ever heard from him. 'Ooh, I love you! You're my kind of guy!'

Delighted by this, Robyn turned to the laughing Kate. 'And he's your kind of guy too, Mata, isn't he?'

The smile fading from her face, Kate nodded her dumb assent.

'Well hell, don't you think you'd both better kiss and stuff?' Robyn instructed them, smiling enough for all three. 'Don't mind me, just go right on ahead!'

One step took Kate Thornton into her future husband's arms, and miles away, for ever after, from the hell that she'd known in *Paradise*.

'So who was that woman?' Andy remembered to ask as they drove back towards Hope. 'And what did she have to do with Andy the Cowboy?'

'She *was* Andy the Cowboy,' Kate explained. 'She'd stayed with you once after a horrible break-up with a bloke.'

'We know that,' said Robyn. 'We saw you come out, just before Andy was going to go in there and raise hell to rescue you.'

'Really?' said Kate, sending an affectionate glance at him. 'I wish I'd seen that.'

'So, and?' Robyn demanded. 'You can carry on the mushy stuff once we get back home, for Pete's sake.'

'So, and,' Kate continued. 'She met you, Andy, and thought how attractive you were, and thought how horrible the men in her life had been, and decided to invent a nice one, based on you.'

'A nice one like me?' he said disbelievingly. 'Can't remember exchanging more than two words with the woman.'

'Based loosely on you,' Kate amended. 'On your name and good looks.'

'Yeah, yeah, don't make his head any bigger than it is,' Robyn complained, as the two people in the front of the truck smiled lingeringly at each other. 'And you might want to watch the traffic,' she added, which didn't, of course, fail to get Andy's attention back on the road.

'She was just having a fantasy to comfort herself at first,' Kate continued. 'A sort of, "what if" kind of thing. Actually, it turns out she'd like to be a writer, and so she started making up a story about you. Hence "Rainbow" and all the other silly stuff. But at the same time, she'd been playing backgammon, as herself, on *Yoohoo*, and had been getting really miffed at how rampant the male players can be to women who play, so she logged on calling herself "Andy the Cowboy". At first she told herself that she was just doing research for her book, but she got so addicted to internet backgammon, she never wrote it!'

'I hope she isn't thinking of writing it now,' Andy said disapprovingly.

'I don't think so,' said Kate. 'I assured her I'd sue.'

The miles rolled by, and even when they were way past Hope, hope was still ahead of them, waiting where it had always been, at the guest ranch called the Blue Yonder.

THE BLUE YONDER GUEST RANCH OFFICIAL WEBSITE

Designed and built by R. Barrett
Spelling and grammar checked by M. McAlpine, teacher (ret'd)

First off, apologies to all you city folk who've been trying to get to stay with us and found we're full, but my advice is, don't wait till the last minute. We're taking bookings now for next year, so get in quick.

Those of you who know us, click on this link to check out the double wedding photos. Who d'you think looks the coolest dude in his tux, Andy or Young Pete? Me, I could be biassed (that means partial, by the way, not that I got two behinds) but I think we can all agree that Kate and Minnie both make beautiful brides. (Dresses designed by G. Strange. Follow this link to see photos of Kate as Hedda Gabler in his latest production, and you can take it from me, I never knew before how that was spelt. Makes it much less of an interesting play than it might have been, in my opinion, but Katie took her part well, and at least there was some shooting at the end.)

Check out this link to British Columbia's Best Eating, and read the brilliant but true review there left by the famous food critic Jessica Shaffer, who stayed here in disguise. Thanks, Jess, particularly as we weren't running quite as smooth that weekend as we are doing now.

NEWS FRESH IN!

We have now added home-grown organic vegetables to our menu, so don't delay, book right away!

Come visit us soon at the home of good food,
good horses, good riding, good hunting, and good fishing.
A good ol' Blue Yonder Welcome awaits you!